Behind German Lines

ALSO BY RONN MUNSTERMAN

FICTION

Operation Devil's Fire – A Sgt. Dunn Novel

NONFICTION

Chess Handbook for Parents and Coaches

Available on Amazon.com

Behind German Lines

A Sgt. Dunn Novel

Ronn Munsterman

Behind German Lines is a work of fiction. Names, characters, places, and incidents are the product of the author's imagination or are used fictitiously. Any resemblance to actual events, locales, or persons, living or dead is coincidental.

BEHIND GERMAN LINES – A SGT. DUNN NOVEL

Copyright © 2013 by Ronn Munsterman
www.ronnmunsterman.com

Cover Design by David M. Jones
www.beloeil-jones.com

Printed in the United States of America
1 3 5 7 9 10 8 6 4 2

ISBN: 1-490-96619-6
BISAC: Fiction / War & Military

Acknowledgments

To my readers, a big thank you! Your enthusiastic support for *Operation Devil's Fire* sparked the writing of this second Sgt. Dunn novel. I always believed that this would develop into a series, and your interest proved the point to me.

Thanks to my fantastic group of FIRST READERS for your encouragement, support and hours of slogging through a messy first draft. Each of you provided such marvelous help in making the book a better story. I found it very interesting that you have such diverse perspectives. Some of you pointed out grammatical errors and others gave me ideas that expanded and deepened the story. Each of you helped me make terrific changes to the book. Nathan Munsterman (my son, who I love dearly), David M. Jones (my true first FIRST READER way back in 2006, and the cover designer), Derek Williams (my thoughtful and insightful friend), John Skelton (who keeps my story honest and makes me laugh at myself for my weird writing errors), Steven White (who uncovered a glaring disconnect in the book), Steven E. Barltrop, (who I see most every day, and who politely suffers through my running commentary on the book's status that day, as well as his World War II knowledge), Dave J. Cross (who helps me make the book as good as it can be), Robert (Bob) A. Schneider II (a positive influence on everyone he meets and a terrific editor), and Dan Schiefen (a smile every day). Also thanks to Dave Cross, Steve Barltrop, Dave Jones, and Bob Schneider for letting me use your names for characters.

Every book on World War II should contain a thank you to the generation of men and women who lived and served during that time. Today, sixty-eight years after the end of the war, it's easy to forget just how terrible the world had become. Our present time owes a debt to those folks that can never be repaid, only paid forward.

To our modern day warriors, thank you for your service and dedication.

To my oldest granddaughter, Alexandria, I love you and am proud of you. Thank you for *your* service and dedication.

To my youngest granddaughter, Julia, you're a bright light in everyone's life.

To Stefanie, my daughter, your spirit and passion for civil rights and civic duty is nothing short of extraordinary.

1943

July						
Su	Mo	Tu	We	Th	Fr	Sa
				1	2	3
4	5	6	7	8	9	10
11	12	13	14	15	16	17
18	19	20	21	22	23	24
25	26	27	28	29	30	31

1944

June						
Su	Mo	Tu	We	Th	Fr	Sa
				1	2	3
4	5	6	7	8	9	10
11	12	13	14	15	16	17
18	19	20	21	22	23	24
25	26	27	28	29	30	

July						
Su	Mo	Tu	We	Th	Fr	Sa
						1
2	3	4	5	6	7	8
9	10	11	12	13	14	15
16	17	18	19	20	21	22
23	24	25	26	27	28	29
30	31					

August						
Su	Mo	Tu	We	Th	Fr	Sa
		1	2	3	4	5
6	7	8	9	10	11	12
13	14	15	16	17	18	19
20	21	22	23	24	25	26
27	28	29	30	31		

Prologue

Tank battles are mankind's reply to God's thunder and lightning.

Broken, burning German and Russian tanks lay scattered across the Russian steppe, smoldering crematoriums for their crews. Some were victims of opposing tanks or anti-tank cannon, many others to the onslaught of aerial attack from both the *Luftwaffe* Stukas and the Soviet Air Force Ilyushin Il-2s. Fire had raced over the landscape burning grass and trees, and catching survivors in the open, roaring over them, leaving charred remains behind. Smoke still swept across the battlefield, carrying the stench of death so strong it made the men nauseous even inside their iron monsters.

Tiger tank commander *Oberscharführer* Gustaf Boehm scanned the field directly in front of him. He spotted a Russian T-34 coming out of the swirling smoke just fifty meters away, headed right at him. Before he could say a word, the Russian fired. Almost instantaneously, a tremendous clang sounded on the front of the Tiger. The Russian round had simply glanced off the angled 100mm-thick frontal armor and skipped skyward. The rushing T-34 passed by Boehm's tank on his right only a few meters away.

"Right turn. Right turret. Target to the rear," he shouted into his mouthpiece. The tank swayed to its left, heeling over like a battleship making a fast turn. The turret spun on its axis.

The gunner peered through his Leitz Turmzielfernrohr TZF9b sight and the ass-end of the T-34 filled the view. "Target acquired."

"Fire!"

The Tiger rocked as the 88mm high-explosive round exited the gun. The rear of the T-34 erupted in a ball of flame. The entire turret blew ten meters straight up before falling back to earth and tumbling across the flaming ground like a child's discarded toy.

With no time to celebrate, Boehm was already looking for a new target. His wait was short. The damn Russians were everywhere. A scream pierced the air, coming from behind them. Boehm recognized it immediately as an anti-tank round which, being much larger, had a deeper tone than that of the T-34 shells. The sound passed just over the turret and Boehm's knees went weak at the close call. The Red Army's anti-tank weapons were true tank killers.

"Left turn!" ordered Boehm, hoping to ruin a second shot by the Russian cannon, and the tank swayed again. No shot came.

The Germans' Operation *Citadel* had started on July 5th, one week ago, and nothing had gone to plan. This was because the Russians knew it was coming, had known for months, having captured a German intelligence officer who broke quickly under horrific torture. Russian defensive positions were built up for almost three months with the help of nearly three hundred thousand civilians. Carefully laid anti-tank minefields, which forced the advancing Germans into predetermined fields of fire, had seriously hampered and slowed the German advance.

The battle that day had begun at first light with Field Marshal Erich von Manstein's armored forces moving northward. Their goal was Kursk, fifty kilometers to the north where they were to meet Army Group Center under the command of Field Marshal

Kluge. This pincer action would cut off at least eight Soviet Divisions, encircling a half-million Red Army soldiers completely. It would also flatten the front line, squeezing back the bulge created by the Russians just weeks earlier, giving the Germans a unified front, and protecting the previously exposed flanks.

Today, as the 3rd SS *Panzers* moved northward, the Red Army's Fifth Tank Guard roared toward them from the east, near Prokhorovka. The Germans had to wheel to the right to meet the surprise attack head on. The opening of the battle had found Boehm as the lead tank in the infamous *Panzerkeil Panzer* formation, which loaded the center of an arrow-shaped phalanx with the sixty ton, powerful Tigers and the rear and outer edges with lighter, less formidable, but yet dangerous *Panzer* IVs and *Sturmgeshütz* III turretless tracked vehicles. A total of fourteen to twenty tanks in all. Boehm and his gunner, Rupert Varner, had scored seventeen kills since their arrival mid-morning. At twenty-four, Boehm was the old man of the crew of five, and Varner, at eighteen, the youngest.

Firing on the German side had started the moment the charging Russian T-34s were spotted. The Russians had continued their charge, even as their leading tanks exploded, shooting flames skyward. They closed on the Germans at over fifty kilometers per hour, well over the Tiger's thirty-three. Within minutes, the Russian tanks were inside the German formation rushing past the Tigers and *Panzers* alike, firing madly, trying to hit the Tigers in their side armor, which was far less effective against the T-34's 76mm cannon than the frontal armor.

Since that moment, the battle had been a melee with tanks firing on each other from point blank range, sometimes as close as ten meters.

Over the sounds of screaming shells, Boehm had been hearing sounds from the two air forces: the unmistakable siren of the Stukas in their dive, and the roar of the Russian heavy bombers overhead. Many times he'd been looking through his viewfinder and watched as a Tiger burst into flames and crumpled in on itself from a Russian bomb. Listening intently, he realized the Stukas had ceased flying over. What did that mean?

Were they rearming? Or giving up?

Blue sky dotted with large, puffy white clouds. Maximum visibility. Excellent, smooth air. A pilot's dream. Except for the rising clouds of smoke from the battlefield ahead and below. The target.

The Heinkel was flying straight and true at 500 kilometers per hour. Although she was escorted by five Messerschmitt 109s in formation, pilot *Oberleutnant* Konrad Sauder fretted. He had started worrying when the mission was first assigned, just two days ago. His crew had been restricted to barracks right after the assignment, something everyone, Sauder included, and been furious about. Meals were even brought to their quarters. Attempts to leave the barracks were greeted with armed Waffen SS. Finally, one hour before takeoff, they'd been released, so to speak, when the same Waffen SS soldiers escorted them to the Heinkel.

As he walked, Sauder had a moment to think that, fortunately, their plane was of the latest design, and was not prone to bursting into a fireball due to problems with the engines as had been the earlier versions, aptly named "flying coffins." So many needless deaths.

Sauder and the other five members of his crew had watched as the bomb had been loaded into the bomb bay. It reminded Sauder of a torpedo, but a misshapen one. It was three meters long and a meter across at its fattest point, which was one third the way back from the bulbous nose. In addition to what appeared to be normal tail fins, it had extra ten-centimeter-tall fins at four points on the thickest portion, at three, six, nine and twelve o'clock. Obviously designed for better than usual stability during flight. Why a bomb would need that was not explained during the briefing. The closing words of warning given by the *Oberst* in charge haunted Sauder:

"The moment you release the weapon, turn immediately to a

heading of 350 degrees and make all best speed. You have less than sixty seconds to clear the danger zone."

Sauder had known not to ask why. He wished he had anyway. What was the weapon? He suddenly realized he was sweating, no easy feat at this altitude. Wiping his brow with a brown-gloved hand, he peeked at his copilot, *Leutnant* Manfred Hasse. Sauder imagined his and Hasse's expressions were identical. Faces frozen in concentration. Eyes darting from the sky around them to the instrument panel.

Out of sight and five kilometers ahead, two Focke-Wulf 190s flew at a much lower level, five hundred meters, at exactly the same speed as the Heinkel. The spotter planes. Two, just in case.

The radio crackled in Sauder's ears, and a voice said, "Passing enemy line."

Sauder knew from previous calculations that they would fly over the same position in two minutes.

Speaking to the bombardier, Sauder said, "Two minutes."

"Understood."

A moment passed, then Sauder felt the bomb bay doors open. He knew the bombardier was now looking at a stop watch.

Time slowed. Sauder glanced out the port window and was certain he could see the individual blades of the propeller like a slow-turning ceiling fan in the lobby of the elegant Hotel Excelsior in Berlin.

The battlefield smoke was upon them, seemingly at their feet. Seconds passed.

"Bomb away!"

The plane bucked and rose several meters. Sauder turned the wheel hard left, pushing in to lose some altitude and gain more speed. Hasse pushed the throttles to full. The Heinkel responded. The 109s turned in perfect synchronization, as if in an aerial ballet.

Far behind and below, the weapon screamed earthward.

The weapon hit the predetermined altitude of 750 meters.

Boehm's tiger roared across the scarred battlefield at full speed. The commander spotted another T-34 and gave the order to target it to the driver and the gunner. Working in concert, the two crewmen aligned the Tiger and the 88mm cannon with the enemy tank.

Then the Tiger's engine stopped. The monster rolled to a stop.

The interior of the tank went dark. All sound disappeared. Boehm's body tingled everywhere, the hair on his neck and arms stood up. He was sure his chest would explode at any moment. The pressure was unbearable and he cried out in pain. He shouted through the intercom, "What is happening?" but heard nothing in reply, nor could he hear his own voice.

Inside Boehm's head, something rang and buzzed. Blackness surged and he collapsed against the side of the commander's hatch.

Ten minutes passed. Boehm stirred, eyes opening slightly. Blinking rapidly, full consciousness returned quickly. None of the turret's interior lights were on. Dim light filtered in through the two-centimeter-tall vision slits around the commander's hatch. He could barely make out his gunner's shape below him. Leaning down to peer into the darkness of the lower turret, he looked around expecting to see a hole where a Russian round had entered. He found nothing. Puzzled, he grabbed Varner's shoulder and shook it vigorously. The gunner groaned as he woke up.

"Rupert, are you all right?"

Varner put his hands to his head as if to hold it together. He twisted around and stared at Boehm for a moment, trying to work out what the *Oberscharführer* had said. Finally, he replied, "I think so. What happened?"

Boehm was shocked to see blood pouring from the man's nose and ears. Touching his own lip, Boehm drew back fingers sticky with blood. He wiped his hand on his uniform shirt and said, "I don't know. I thought we got hit, but I don't see a hole anywhere." Speaking into his microphone, Boehm said, "Anyone there? You men all right? Kurt, are you there?"

No answer.

Boehm pointed toward the motionless forms of the loader and the radio operator. "Rupert, check on them, then on Kurt." Boehm yanked off the useless headset and tossed it aside

Varner nodded.

Boehm leaned into the scope's eyepiece. He slowly rotated the scope, not believing what he saw. Tanks of both armies were stopped, some on fire, others not. The entire battlefield was motionless. The stillness seemed to have crept into the tank interior.

"*Was ist das?*" he muttered to himself. He peeked through the slits and saw the same in all directions.

Boehm was relieved to see the radio operator, Erhad Hertzog, stir awake and sit up.

"Erhad, get on the radio! See if anyone knows what happened."

"Yes, *Oberscharführer.*"

Hertzog rotated a dial to tune to the intertank frequency. Hearing nothing, he flipped the power switch off, then on again. Nothing. Frowning, he put his hand on the top of the radio and jerked it back. "Ow! Hot!" Staring at the set as though it had just bitten him, he said, "*Oberscharführer*, the radio is out."

"Well, fix it!"

"Of course." He twisted in his seat and found his toolkit. Unrolling the leather wrap holding the tools, he selected a small flashlight and switched it on, but it was dead. He shook it and tried again. He rapped it against the hull and tried once more. Sighing deeply, he tossed it to the floor. He reached into his shirt pocket and removed a small cigarette lighter. He thumbed it and a little flame leapt into life providing a surprising amount of light. He put a glove on his left hand to protect against the heat, selected a screwdriver, and set about loosening the radio's casing.

The tank driver, Kurt Glotzback, turned around in his seat and looked up through the tiny opening between his compartment and the turret. Like everyone else, his face was blood-caked. "*Oberscharführer*, the engine will not start. There is no power."

"Can you tell what happened?" asked Boehm.

"No. It's as if the engine and electricity have been killed."

Boehm considered what he should do, and realized he had no choice but to pop the hatch and get out of the tank with Glotzback, who also served as the primary mechanic. As he raised his hand to unlock the hatch, Hertzog shouted, "*Oberscharführer*! All of the wiring has burned to a crisp. It looks like there was an electrical fire in the radio. I cannot fix this."

"Rupert, hand me the MP40."

The gunner snatched the tank's only portable machinegun from its storage rack in the hull and lifted it to Boehm.

Boehm worked the bolt and flipped the safety off. Holding the weapon in his right hand, he unlocked, then threw the hatch open with his left. The sunlight blinded him, and he waited a moment for his eyes to adjust. Rising slowly, he lifted himself until he could peer over the hatch's lip. With unbelieving eyes, he took in the sight all around him. As it was through the scope, the battlefield was completely still. Good German infantrymen lay scattered across the field, unmoving heaps. Turning around to look behind, Boehm was startled to see a T-34 not fifty meters to his rear. Clearly it had been following him and lining up for an ass shot. Fortunately, the gun barrel wasn't quite lined up, and pointed just enough to Boehm's left that the round would miss completely.

The T-34's presence behind them complicated matters. Glotzback and he couldn't even consider working on the engine. That left only one choice. Lowering himself back into his seat, he reached into a little cubbyhole and grasped an object.

A moment later, he clambered out of the hatch as fast as possible. After getting to the rear deck of the Tiger, he jumped off and ran toward the Russian tank, staying to his right to, hopefully, avoid getting shot by the machinegun on his left.

Covering the distance quickly, he vaulted up onto the tank over the left track. Although he doubted it would be unlocked, he grasped the hatch handle and pulled. No good. He tried looking in the vision slit, but it was too dark to see anything clearly. He waited a little longer and as his eyes dilated enough, he realized he could see the motionless form of the tank commander sitting there.

Stepping back slightly, he jammed the barrel of the MP40 into the slit and shouted the few words of Russian he knew, "Come out! Surrender!"

For a few seconds nothing happened. About to squeeze the trigger, he heard the wheel turning to unlock the hatch. He took another step back, careful not to pitch over the side of the tank.

Then he grasped the stick grenade he'd snatched up, and unscrewed the base closing cap, which let a porcelain ball drop out. That, in turn, was attached to the detonator pull cord. He prepared to pull the ball if anything except empty hands came out of the hatch.

The hatch rose slowly, then reached its apex and fell back to its full open position with a clang. Empty hands followed, then the tank commander, whose nose and ears were dripping blood. Boehm noted the vacant stare of a man with at least a mild concussion. Motioning the man out of the hatch with the barrel of the MP40, Boehm said, "Crew." He raised the grenade high indicating what would happen if any funny business took place.

The Russian gazed at Boehm, uncomprehending at first, then nodded once in acceptance, and slowly leaned over the edge of the hatch. He then called out instructions to the crew that Boehm couldn't understand. Soon, the other three men climbed out of the tank. Boehm motioned toward the burnt ground with his weapon and watched carefully as the men climbed down. Boehm got down and gestured with his weapon for the Russians to march ahead of him toward the Tiger. When they reached the rear of the tank, he motioned for them to sit. Keeping his weapon trained on the enemy soldiers, Boehm called for his crew.

His men made their way out of the tank and greeted the presence of the Russian tankers with surprise. The T-34's position was noted, too, with a high degree of shock. They had been moments from death and hadn't even known it. Whatever had happened to their tank had happened to the Russian and saved their lives.

Boehm quickly gave orders to bind the Russians' hands and feet with rope and lean them against the massive left track wheels, keeping them separated. Once that was accomplished, Boehm gave the MP40 to Hertzog to stand watch, then said to Glotzback, "Kurt, let's get the lid up and see what's going on with the engine." Then he turned to Varner, "Rupert, go see what you can salvage from their tank." Varner loped off.

Boehm and Glotzback were staring at a complete mess in the engine compartment. Gloztzback's expression was one of disbelief at the sight of his beloved engine. Gingerly, he grasped one of the thick sparkplug wires. It disintegrated in his fingers. In a panic, he touched several others with the same result.

"What could have caused this, Kurt?" Boehm asked.

"I have only seen this on wiring that has been overloaded. It's like if you tried to plug an ordinary toaster into an industrial-strength power source of over four hundred volts. Then, whoosh!" He put his hands together and then mimicked an explosion. He shook his head, then said, "This cannot be repaired here. All the wiring would have to be pulled and replaced. A day's work at a fully supplied maintenance depot."

Boehm raised an arm and swept it indicating for Glotzback to look around the battlefield. "What could possibly have done this to everything we can see?"

"I have no idea."

Boehm continued eyeing the terrain strewn with dead tanks and spotted other tankers, German and Russian, milling about around their vehicles. Suddenly, sounds of sporadic gunfire drifted to him. It seemed that the tankers had turned into infantrymen and were trying to kill each other with the meager supply of weapons typically carried in a tank. He watched as a group of Germans was gunned down only two hundred meters away. Boehm turned to look at the four Russians. He had hoped to be able to take them back to the German line, but they would be a liability. Feeling unexpected compassion for men who could have been in his position if they'd recovered more quickly from whatever had happened to everyone in sight, he considered releasing them, but quashed it, knowing he could not allow them to someday return to the battlefield and kill Germans.

He dropped his right hand to the flap of his 9mm Luger's holster and undid it, then drew the weapon. Carrying it pointed at the earth, he walked quickly over to the Russians and, one by one, shot them in the head.

Returning the pistol to the holster and snapping it shut, he ordered his men to fall in and they walked abreast toward the T-34. Varner suddenly came out of the tank carrying two Russian PPSh-41 submachineguns. These were fine weapons that were very similar to the Germans' own MP40, the primary difference was the round drum magazine on the Russian gun.

Varner hopped down to the ground and waited for his crewmates to join him. He looked at Boehm, but didn't bother asking where the Russians were, having heard the shots. He kept one of the Russian weapons and handed the other to Boehm.

Boehm gave the order to march west, toward the presumed safety of the German rear line. As they were passing another dead Tiger, they came upon a dozen German infantrymen lying in crumpled heaps behind the Tiger. Clearly they had been in attack formation, and were following in the great beast's tracks.

Boehm knelt by the first body and grasped the man's shoulder, then rolled him over onto his back. The tank commander, a veteran of the Russian campaign since the first day of *Operation Barbarossa* on 22 June 1941, jerked back as if shot. He jumped to his feet, stumbling away from the grisly sight in front of him.

"Mein Gott!"

The other men gathered around their leader and stared down at what surely had once been a man. The face and hands were burned as though he'd been roasted over a fire, or caught in a burning vehicle, except he and the others had not been in a vehicle. His clothing, helmet, and weapon were all untouched, looking completely normal.

As one, the men stepped back, wanting absolutely no part of the gruesome mess before them.

Boehm turned in a full circle, taking in the battlefield, and thinking, what could have laid waste to an entire battlefield? What could roast a man and not his clothes? And kill the tanks? He could think of nothing.

He looked at his men and, as they stared back with haunted eyes, he understood it was unnecessary for him to give the order.

All five men, battle-hardened men, turned west and ran.

And ran.

Chapter 1

Firing Range – Camp Barton Stacey
2 miles northeast of Andover, England
27 June 1944, 0718 Hours, nearly 1 year later

As far as firing ranges went, the one at Camp Barton Stacey was huge. Most were about fifty yards wide by a little over a hundred long. This one was seventy-five wide and extended off in the distance toward a steep hill that peaked almost seven hundred yards away. It made the perfect backstop with rounds expending the last of their kinetic energy deep into the soft soil of England. The day was perfect for target practice; a bright blue sky, what baseball players called a 'high sky,' and just a whisper of a breeze crossing right to left, north to south. The sun would be behind the shooters.

Staff Sergeant Tom Dunn led his squad of ten men, counting himself, down the dirt road to the range. Each man carried a rifle slung over his shoulder and a Thompson .45 caliber machinegun in his hands. Even though the men were not marching at the standard one hundred twenty steps per minute, they moved as one, with the graceful and fluid movements associated with athletes.

They were all lethal, dangerous U.S. Army Rangers, an elite squad whose primary role was to solve problems and do the impossible. Except for the four replacements, the squad had flown into Germany and eliminated the Nazi's atomic bomb program and laboratory just nine days ago. Awarded a week's leave, most had gone to London for some partying and relaxation, and had returned just the day before. The replacements had arrived at Barton Stacey while they were gone and introductions took place last night after mess.

Instead of going on leave, Dunn had worked out his squad's organizational structure which included the newbies. Although these weren't your typical green recruits. They had all survived and graduated from the same Commando / Rangers school run by the British in Achnacarry House, Scotland, that every man in Dunn's squad had. Three held the rank of corporal and one was a sergeant, and they had all proven their abilities. However, a forty percent replacement figure was high and could cause problems at first. Which is why Dunn chose to split the squad up so that his Assistant Squad Leader, the recently promoted Sergeant Dave Cross, and Dunn himself would each have two veterans and two newbies under their wings.

The men walked in two columns, with Dunn leading the four men on the right and Cross the other four. Behind Dunn were his two replacements, Sergeant David Jones, a quiet, lean, six-footer from south Chicago, and Corporal Bob Schneider, a funny man with a hearty laugh and the talent of being fluent in German and French. Dunn had discovered on the last mission that having someone conversant in other languages was needed. Bringing up the rear of the column were the veterans Corporal Stanley Wickham, a Texan whose southern accent and word choice had mysteriously blended with a British one, and Corporal Patrick Ward, a Yale graduate and a stellar mathematician, who at twenty-four was the same age as Dunn.

Cross's men were all corporals. Replacements Eddie Fairbanks, Eugene Lindstrom, and veterans Jack Hanson and Daniel Morris. Fairbanks resembled the actor Douglas Fairbanks, Jr. down to the moustache. Eugene Lindstrom's parents had a sense of humor naming their son after the Oregon city in which he was born. Hanson was cursed with a high-pitched voice that earned him the nickname "Squeaky." Morris grew up a farmer's son in northeast Kansas and hoped to have his own farm someday.

Dunn had signed up for the range several days ago and was able to secure the first time slot of the day. When they arrived at the range, Dunn told his men to halt and stand easy, then he found the range sergeant and checked in. After all was set, and he'd verified that the men manning the targets were in place, he moved back to his men. The firing range sergeant, a brawny redhead named Keyes, followed.

Dunn said, "Thompsons first, men. Two clips each standing, then kneeling, fifty yards." The Thompson was the Rangers' preferred weapon, being extremely deadly at close range and firing 700 rounds per minute from a 20-round clip.

Each man stacked his rifle in a small olive drab metal weapons rack, big enough for four weapons, next to the firing slot, then stepped up to the line, weapon ready.

Dunn turned to Sergeant Keyes and said, "All yours, Sergeant." Dunn took a spot in between replacements Jones and Schneider.

Keyes nodded, then lifted a shiny silver whistle to his lips and gave a long blast. He watched ten man-shaped targets rise from underground as the men at the dangerous end pulled them into place with a rack and pulley system.

Ensuring all were in place, Keyes said, "Safeties on." Then, "Load weapons."

There were the clicking sounds of the magazines being slapped into place.

"Safeties off. Fire when ready."

The deep-throated sounds of the Thompsons shattered the peace of the English countryside as the men all fired controlled bursts of two or three rounds at a time. When the last shot was fired, Keyes blew the whistle and the targets were pulled down and replaced with fresh ones.

Time passed and targets were replaced after each clip. Eventually the men completed their work with the Thompson and Sergeant Keyes blew the all clear.

RONN MUNSTERMAN

The range men brought up the targets and gave them to their respective owners. Each had a number written in chalk telling what the score was, and the total score for all four targets was on the first one.

Dunn's men were competitive by nature and started comparing scores.

"Ha! Seven fifty-seven," hollered Ward, proud of his results out of a possible 800. This was followed by a chorus of scores that surrounded Ward's number, until the next to last man gave his, Cross, who claimed 773, the high.

Then David Jones lifted his targets like a shield, and said quietly, "Eight hundred."

This was greeted by complete silence as the good-natured ribbing fell away at this news. No one scored that high with a Thompson. It was impossible. There were too many variables including the natural kick and rise of the weapon's barrel after each shot. Correcting for it was always difficult. The men, curious now, gathered around Jones, some grabbing a target out of the marksman's hands to see for themselves. After a few moments, someone whistled in admiration. The men handed back the targets to an unsmiling Jones.

Dunn stepped close and asked, "How does a Chicago boy know how to shoot like that?" He was shaking his head incredulously.

Jones shrugged. "I don't know, Sergeant. It just comes naturally is all." He looked like he was embarrassed by the sudden attention.

Dunn, still surprised, finally turned to his squad, "Who's low score today?"

"Uh, that'd be me, Sarge. Blimey, I don't know what happened. Must 'a' been that there bug flew up muh nose," said Wickham in his Brit-Tex accent. He lowered his head in false shame.

The squad erupted in laughter at the tall tale.

"Uh huh. Right. Well, you know the rules. You buy beers for Sergeant Jones tonight. All of them." Dunn looked at Jones. "Make sure he doesn't try to shortchange you."

Jones gave a little smile. "Will do, Sarge."

"Time for rifles. Prone first. One hundred yards."

The men switched out their weapons and lined up, awaiting Sergeant Keyes' order to load. It came quickly, but not until he was satisfied as to the safety of each man's position, and that all ten targets were in place and clear of men.

Dunn lay on the ground in the textbook prone position for a right-hander, left leg straight, right leg bent at the knee, left elbow on the ground, left hand on the fore stock, right hand on the grip, finger along the trigger guard, but not on the trigger. He sighted down the barrel of his M1 Garand.

This weapon had become the Army's new standard in 1936. Weighing in at 9.5 pounds, it held an eight-round clip, which ejected after firing the last round. The near sight aperture was a round disc with a hole in it, like a tiny washer. This was used to correct for distance and windage, as well as the small variations in the rifle itself. Everyone's rifle was sighted in for one hundred yards. The front sight was a blade bracketed by two other blades that curved away from the middle one, like a blooming flower.

Sergeant Keyes gave the fire-when-ready command. Dunn slid the pad of his forefinger onto the trigger and squeezed rapidly until the metallic twang of the ejected clip sounded. He was about to slap another clip into place when the sounds of the rifle next to him being worked made their way into his awareness. Something was amiss with Jones' weapon. Dunn continued listening. What was wrong? After a few more seconds he had it. After every shot, there was a split second delay before the next bullet flew away toward the target. Then Dunn recognized the faint sound of a bolt being pulled back, then slammed forward.

Frowning, Dunn safed his M1, ejected the clip, and stood up, raising his hand. He looked for Keyes and found him behind the men in the center, his head swiveling like radar. As soon as the piercing eyes saw Dunn, Keyes blew the whistle. All firing ceased. Then each man cleared his weapon as Dunn as done.

Dunn racked his M1 and stepped over behind Jones.

"Jones, on your feet."

Jones stood and faced Dunn, his rifle across his body at port arms, as if in line for inspection.

Dunn glanced down and anger rose in his chest. Dunn's brown eyes had taken on an almost black appearance making it impossible to discern where the iris and pupil met, a warning sign for those who knew him.

"What are you doing with an oh-three Springfield?"

"I, er, Sarge, I have an explanation."

"Yes, I'm waiting for one." Dunn snatched the weapon from Jones and examined it quickly. He had to admit it was a beautiful rifle. Jones had clearly taken great care of it.

While Dunn was looking at the rifle, the squad had wandered over and stood around to see what was going on, something that caused Jones' cheeks to flame red. Sergeant Keyes also came over and pushed his way in to stand next to Dunn.

"Wow, I haven't seen one of these babies in a long time."

"Me either," replied Dunn. He handed the weapon back to Jones. He looked at the man and raised his eyebrows. "I'm still waiting. What are you doing with an unauthorized M1903 A1 Springfield?"

Jones' eyebrows went up in surprise. Not many people knew the difference between a model A1 and the A4, which was the one the army used. The Marine Corps had selected the A1 Springfield over the model A4 due to accuracy problems with the A4. Weighing in at about eight and a half pounds, it was a pound lighter than the M1, and fired .30-03 or .30-06 152 grain bullets from a five-round clip.

Jones decided truth would be his best shot.

"It belonged to my uncle in the Pacific. He was a Marine sniper. He got killed last year on Guadalcanal. One of his buddies arranged to have it shipped home. I started working with it, and well, it just felt right, so I use it instead of the M1."

Dunn's expression softened at the mention of a man killed in action on Guadalcanal, a horrible place from all accounts. A six-month campaign, the battle of Guadalcanal killed over seven thousand Allied troops.

"I see. Where's the scope?"

"I have it here." He pointed to a small cylindrical bag about two feet long resting next to the weapons rack, his shooter's bag. He bent down and picked it up. Unzipping it, he lovingly removed the scope, then attached it to the rifle quickly.

"Is that a Unertl scope?"

"Yes. John Unertl's eight-by power."

The Unertl sight was far better than the Weaver scopes found on the A4, which tended to fog up because they weren't waterproofed. Simple high humidity could render the weapon useless as it had no open front and rear sights.

"What's the scope sighted in for?"

"Six hundred yards."

"When was the last time you fired at that range?" Dunn was becoming interested and his anger had completely dissipated.

The men all took an involuntary step forward, their interest earned as well.

"A month, maybe. Didn't really get much opportunity at Achnacarry House."

Dunn had already decided he wanted to see just what Jones could do. Turning to Keyes, he asked, "Can you set up some targets at six hundred yards?"

"It's going to take a little time, we aren't set up for that distance. The target will have to be propped up and freestanding, and my men will have to return to the safety slot at one hundred yards. Maybe fifteen minutes."

Dunn nodded.

"Okay, we'll wait." To Jones, he said, "I'm going off the books for you, Jones. Don't make me sorry."

Jones grinned for the first time, showing his eagerness to please, and what he could do. "I wouldn't think of it, Sarge."

Keyes went about getting things ready. Dunn told his men to find a comfortable spot on the small hill rising behind the firing line, so they could have bleacher-like seats to the show.

The men clumped together in their respective new teams. Most pulled out their Lucky Strikes, white packages with a big red dot on the front, and lit up using their flip-top Zippo lighters.

Sooner than promised, Keyes told Dunn all was ready. He handed a large pair of binoculars to Dunn. "I think these are strong enough."

Dunn nodded as he took the field glasses. Six hundred yards was indeed a long way, a hair over a third of a mile.

To Jones, Dunn said, "You're up. Show us what you've got. Two clips."

Jones nodded solemnly. No time for smiles now. He glanced at Keyes, who said, "Fire when ready."

Jones loaded the Springfield quickly, seating the first round with a gentle closing of the bolt. While the range men had been setting things up, Jones was busy himself. From his shooter's bag, he'd pulled a smaller bag packed with fine sand. He dropped it on the firing line then got into a prone position, propping the fore stock on the sack. He wiggled the rifle, burrowing an improvised custom-fit groove into the sack.

Putting his right cheek against the dark wood of the stock, he could smell the oil he'd carefully applied to the gun metal just an hour ago. The smell of the cordite from the previously fired rounds also wafted into his nose. He loved the combination of the smells.

Jones flipped off the safety with his right thumb. He closed his left eye and sighted through the scope. He quickly found the man-sized target, which filled the preset scope's field of view. Slowing his breathing by taking deeper breaths, Jones could also feel his heartbeat slowing.

The men were frozen in anticipation.

Dunn raised the binoculars to his eyes.

Jones took one more breath, held it, then let it escape slowly. In the moment when he was not breathing, he waited for the gap in his heartbeat. Then he squeezed the trigger. The rifle roared and kicked straight back into Jones' shoulder.

Six-tenths of a second later, Dunn saw a puff of debris as the bullet tore through the ten ring of the target, center mass, right over the heart of the poor target.

Jones worked the bolt action, repeated the process four more times, then inserted a new clip and continued through five more rounds. When he was done, less than a minute had passed.

He got up, took a deep breath and turned to Dunn, who was still staring through the binoculars.

Dunn lowered the field glasses. He looked at Keyes and handed over the glasses without a word.

Keyes took a look and muttered, "Son of a bitch. That can't be."

"I think the grouping is less than ten inches," Dunn said.

Jones cleared his throat. "I believe you'll find it to be about eight inches, Sarge."

Keyes stared at the marksman for a moment, then blew his whistle for the all clear. A man climbed out of the safety ditch and ran out to get the target. A few minutes passed and he made it back to the firing line where the men were gathered around Jones.

Keyes took the target, eyed it, pulled a folding ruler from his pocket and measured the size of the ten-round grouping. "Seven and one-half." He turned the target so everyone else could see it.

As one, the men began clapping and whistling in admiration.

"Way to go, Jonesy!" hollered Hanson.

Dunn had been watching Keyes measure the grouping, thinking all the while, *You don't see this every day.* He glanced over at Jones, who was withstanding the new attention with an aw-shucks look on his face. He felt Dunn looking and returned the gaze calmly.

Then in his South Chicago accent said, "So, Sarge. Can I keep it?"

Chapter 2

The sleek, silvery form of a P-51D Mustang roared over the air base at one hundred fifty feet, banked gracefully to the right, then left in a large curve heading back to line up on the runway. Lower and lower she floated. Landing gear appeared below. At the exact spot selected by the pilot, the wheels touched down with a crisp chirp. As her speed bled off, the tail wheel settled smoothly to the ground. When her speed was low enough, the pilot guided her carefully into a right turn, then spun her around to face the runway. The engine complained as it was turned off, as if disappointed the flight was over. The bubble canopy slid back. A slender shape climbed out of the snug cockpit. It took two steps toward the back of the wing and hopped down.

Captain Norman Miller walked around the port wing toward the engine cowling. He looked up at the picture of a beautiful young woman, modestly dressed, unlike the risqué pictures the

B-17 pukes loved. Below the woman were painted the words *Sweet Mabel II*, Miller's wife. *Sweet Mabel*, the first, had been destroyed, not by enemy fighters or anti-aircraft fire, but by Miller himself.

Recently, he and a squad of British Commandos had flown to the Horten brothers' hanger south of Götha to blow up the Nazi's jet bomber. Instead, Miller had strayed from his mission orders and convinced a disbelieving Sergeant Saunders, the squad leader, that he could fly the bird home. A few minutes of discussion ensued, but Miller got his way and he had stolen the jet right from underneath the Germans' noses. It had broken his heart when he'd been forced to drop the satchel charges meant for the Horten 18 into *Sweet Mabel's* cockpit, but he could hardly leave her behind intact.

He'd been right, though, he'd gotten the Horten 18 home, although an engine fire marred the event, and the landing had been fraught with danger. He'd also nearly been court-martialed when he'd said the wrong thing to Colonel Mark Kenton, the mission commander, "Sir, I believe it's always better to ask forgiveness rather than permission." But things worked out and Kenton got a measure of revenge when the reluctant Miller had been assigned to help some Northrop engineers who were coming over from the states to examine the jet bomber. Miller's first meeting with them was coming up in a few minutes.

Miller had discovered at the age of ten that he was born to fly. He'd won a free ride in a barnstormer's bright yellow biplane and instantly knew he was in love with flying. He grew up in a large German family in central Indiana, speaking German at home, church and school. His grandfather had changed the family name from Mueller to Miller to sound more American during the Great War.

When Miller entered the Army in 1939, right after high school, they'd sent him off to flight school after he had proudly showed them his pilot's license. Miller finished first in his class. Years and thousands of flight hours later, he had become a talented pilot and a smart aerial tactician, which led to his ace status.

Three mechanics ran across the grass infield and saluted Miller when they got close. He snapped off a return salute.

"Morning Captain," said the sergeant, Hampstead's crew chief. "She's looking good this morning." This was Miller's second trip from his home base, Leiston, and the chief had made sure the brand new *Sweet Mabel II* got his personal attention. Anything for the man who'd brought back the beauty inside the hanger behind him.

The other two men were already under the wings placing the wooden wheel chocks.

"Morning, yourself, Sergeant. Hope you guys didn't mind the little flyover." Miller smiled.

The chief looked aghast that Miller had apologized, of a kind. "No, sir. Never."

Miller clapped the chief on the shoulder as he walked away toward the hanger. He glanced up at the blue British sky and unhappy thoughts charged into his head. Just a few weeks ago, Miller had written letters to the parents of two of his men killed on a special mission to locate the jet bomber's base in Germany. It had conveyed his deepest regret that their young sons had been killed in the line of duty. It said that their sons had contributed to the war effort and had been doing their duty with courage and devotion. It didn't say that he'd loved them like brothers, nor would the parents ever know of the tears in his eyes as he wrote. The letters and the box of meager belongings left behind by Bill Murphy and Chuck Thompson were the only things their parents would ever receive.

Miller stepped through the hanger's wide open door. He stopped and eyed the Horten 18, as he always did. She was a breathtaking beauty. With roughly the same wingspan as a B-17, she filled the hanger, with little room to spare. Still painted the mottled grey the Germans liked, her lines were sleek and with a tricycle landing gear setup, her nearly-pointed nose sat poised for flight. A bubble cockpit was visible just aft of the nose. The swept-back wings gave her a predatory look, like an eagle about to strike. Each wing had three jet engines, now known to be the Junkers 004B. As Miller's eyes scanned the plane, he marveled again at the complete absence of vertical surfaces, recalling her fantastic response to his control.

With a satisfied sigh, he turned to his right and marched into an office built into the corner of the hanger. Four men in suits sat at a work table, thick red binders were open in front of three of them. An empty chair was next to the fourth man, Howard Lawson, the right-hand man of Wild Bill Donovan, the Director of the Office of Strategic Services. Lawson was facing Miller, and when he saw the captain, his face broke into a wide grin. Standing quickly, he rushed around the table to greet Miller.

"Captain Miller. Good morning. It's great to see you again." Lawson stuck out his hand.

Miller shook hands and said, "You too, sir. I didn't realize you would be coming back over."

Lawson had made two trips in the span of one week from the States for events leading up to and during Operation Devil's Fire. The last time Miller had seen Lawson, the man had been so exhausted he'd barely been able to stay on his feet,. It was also Lawson who'd "suggested" in the strongest terms, that Miller be the man to work with the Northrop men sitting around the table.

Lawson shrugged. "Mr. Donovan thought it prudent for me to be here for some time. We all got in around five last night." He half turned toward the table and said, "Gentlemen, let me introduce someone to you."

Up to this point, the men had been seemingly oblivious to Miller's presence, and the conversation. They all looked up, surprised to see an army captain in their midst. Remembering their manners, they rose and approached Lawson and Miller.

Lawson said, "This is Captain Norman Miller. He's the man who's responsible for bringing the Horten airplane here."

As one, the three men turned to Miller with wide-eyed admiration. One by one, they extended their hands.

The tallest man, with light brown hair and a broad friendly face, said, "Mechanical engineer, propulsion. Greg Gillespie, Captain, a real pleasure."

Next was a short, round fellow with soft features, and blue eyes. "Cockpit and instrument equipment design, Fred Laughlin. Nice to meet THE MAN." His eyes twinkled.

"Aeronautical engineer, designer, and team lead. Gary Babcock. I agree with Fred. You did something quite extraordinary. We can't express just how wonderful this is. We have a million questions for you." Babcock was completely bald, even though he only seemed to be around thirty, and wore gold spectacles.

Miller thought it was odd that each man had introduced himself by what he did first, then realized that airmen did the same. Pilot. Bombardier. Radio man. It made Miller smile.

"It's nice to meet you guys. What's the plan for today?"

Babcock replied, "Let's sit down and we'll fill you in. Would you like some coffee?"

"I would."

Babcock gestured toward the table then went over to a coffee stand, in front of the large window facing the runway, to fill a cup. Everyone got seated and Babcock handed Miller his cup before sitting down on the pilot's right. Tapping the red binder in front of himself, Babcock asked, "So, how was it you got these?"

Miller smiled and pointed to his right, "Well, I saw the file cabinet just sitting there in the Horten's office. Didn't have time to go through it, just decided to take the whole thing. Thank goodness for all the commandos I was with. They muscled it on board the C-47." Miller paused before continuing, "I wanted to translate it, but just didn't have time."

Miller glanced at the OSS man, "I take it you found someone to do that, sir?"

Lawson nodded. "I did. They finished it yesterday. The originals, the blue binders, are stored someplace secure."

"Good. What's your goal, Mr. Babcock?"

"It looks like everything the Hortens needed to build the aircraft, and everything we need to duplicate it, is in that cabinet. It's just going to take us a long while to work through everything. We need to prioritize things."

"You'll be wanting to repair the damaged engine first, I'd guess, sir."

Gillespie answered the question, "Oh, we sure do. Followed by getting her airborne again."

Babcock leaned forward, hands folded on the table, his eyes dancing. "What was she like in the air?"

Miller grinned like a school boy. "Look, I love my Mustang because she's the best damn fighter in the world. She's fast, super responsive, and tough. But the Horten is much the same. For a plane her size, she feels smaller, more compact than she really is.

On the trip home, I had to stay with our little formation of three P-51s and a C-47 to make sure I wouldn't get shot down coming here, otherwise I would have goosed her more than I did." He shook his head in wonder. "When she got in trouble with the engine fire on number three, she did everything I asked her to and came through smelling like a rose. A charred rose, maybe, but still a rose."

"So you enjoyed flying her?"

"I did." Too late, Miller noticed Lawson shift in his seat, looking more than a little guilty. Miller frowned at Lawson and said in a tone like a father scolding a son, "What did you do, Mr. Lawson?"

Lawson glanced at Miller, then at Babcock, before looking back at Miller, his expression fully guilty now. Before he could reply, Miller stood up abruptly.

"You promised me! We had a deal. I get to go to Leiston once or twice weekly to join my squadron for escort duty. You know I need to be there."

Lawson held up his hands, palms out in surrender. "I know, I know. I'm sorry. I did what I could, but the order came down last night from General Doolittle. He overrode your boss, Colonel Nelson."

Miller sat down at the mention of the Eighth Air Force's Commanding General's name. He was deflated, and stared at his hands for a long moment.

"General Doolittle said that since you were the one who flew her back, you would be the one to fly her here, and the one who would teach other crews," Lawson said quietly. "If it's any consolation, Chuck Yeager has agreed to take command of your squadron."

In spite of his anger and disappointment, Miller smiled. Yeager was an outstanding pilot with many kills under his belt and, more importantly, a strong leader. If he was going to lose his command, as long as it wasn't to someone still wet behind the ears, he could live with it. He looked at Lawson. "I see. I suppose I'll be staying here for some time now?"

Lawson nodded.

"I also suppose I'll be reporting to you? Since you're so familiar with the Army way?"

Lawson had never seen a day of active duty in the military. He gave a wry smile at Miller's right-up-to-the-insubordination-line sarcasm. "I trust I can count on you to be courteous and professional?"

Miller laughed, then said, "Whatever makes you think I'd be anything but?"

Lawson laughed in return, then said, "Oh, let's see, how about every single time you ever talked to me since we met a month ago?"

"Okay, you got me."

All during this exchange, the Northrop engineers' heads were swiveling back and forth like a tied up dog watching a prowling cat just out of reach.

Miller noticed their expressions and said, "Don't worry, guys. I'm only tough on bureaucrats." He paused, eyes sparkling, "You aren't bureaucrats, are you?"

They replied, "No!"

"Well then, we're off to a good start, aren't we?"

Nods all around the table.

"Where would you fellows like to start?" Miller asked, as he took off his hat and flight jacket. The other men in the room thought he was going to roll up his sleeves. After a moment, the only Allied Horten pilot in existence did just that.

Chapter 3

"What would you like to have, young Miss?" asked the slender waiter, who was wearing, as usual, a perfectly pressed black suit. Just because there was a war on didn't mean the customers would get less than his best.

Pamela Hardwicke smiled and said, "The chicken, please."

"And you, sir?"

"The same, thank you."

The waiter replied, "Very good," and left.

Dunn grinned at his fiancée. They had ordered chicken every time they had dined at the Star & Garter Restaurant over the past month, and always the waiter asked the same way.

A blonde with blue eyes, Pamela was twenty two, and had grown up on a farm a few miles south of Andover. She wore a pale pink dress that accented her fair skin. She worked as a nurse at the Camp Barton Stacey hospital, which was where she had first met Dunn. He was recuperating from surgery for a bullet wound received at Achnacarry House, the training facility for Rangers and Commandos, when he saved the life of a recruit during a live-round exercise.

Something about him had attracted her. It wasn't his good looks, which he had plenty of, but his quick laugh and smile, and his uncomplaining attitude even when she knew he was in pain. A few days after his arrival, she had noticed that she was becoming happy at the prospect of going to work every day because she knew she'd see him. She'd tried unsuccessfully, over the course of a week or so, to get him to ask her out by dropping hints, subtly at first then finally blatantly, that she was available. Like a none-too-bright mule who had to be whacked in the head with a two-by-four, he'd finally gotten it through his thick noggin and asked in a stupid way, 'You wouldn't want to go out with me, would you?'

She had forced herself to refrain from screaming, 'Yes! Yes! You big lunk.'

Dunn was, at six-two and 183 pounds, a lean and fit American soldier. He wore the standard uniform of the day: khaki slacks and shirt, with an olive green waist-length jacket and black tie. He had short-cropped, light brown hair and his slim nose sat between dark brown eyes capable of flashing in anger or twinkling with laughter.

They talked for a few minutes about each other's day; hers was hectic, his was busy training with his men. A comfortable pause settled in and Dunn put his hand out on the table and Pamela slid hers into it.

Dinner arrived and they set to work demolishing the chicken. About half way through, Pamela set her fork down gently and looked out the window onto High Street. There was no activity; everyone was inside for dinner. She rolled her lower lip under her teeth and began to nibble.

Dunn glanced up and laughed. "Okay, what's going on?" He'd discovered her nervous tell long ago.

Pamela immediately stopped biting her lip and focused her blue eyes on Dunn. "I've been thinking."

She paused just long enough for Dunn to jump in with, "And it always ends up with me saying, 'Yes, Dear.'"

"Well, of course, it does. I am always right, anyway." Leaning closer, as if letting Dunn in on a secret, she said, "It's time to set a date"

"Uh oh."

Smiling sweetly, she continued, "I think August would be a perfect time."

Dunn's mind was running a hundred miles an hour. How do I tell her? Theirs had been a whirlwind romance, common among American-British war couples. Intense. Passionate. While on the last mission, he'd discovered that he knew for certain she was the one. He'd thought long and hard about asking her to marry him. But he hadn't actually thought through the wedding part. He'd just sort of had this nebulous time frame in mind. He now understood he should have realized what it would be like for her. The expectations. The worry. The joy.

Pamela watched Dunn's face, which was frozen in a neutral expression, his way of thinking before speaking. His tell.

Pamela jumped in during the pause, "I know you didn't expect this tonight. But we do need to at least start talking about it."

After another moment of silence, Dunn said, "I just . . . worry. You know, with the war and everything." He turned away to scan the restaurant and the heavy dark wood bar. A few couples sat on the other side of the room and three men, locals, by their dungarees and boots, were at the bar.

Dunn was not quite sure how to say what he had to say. At last, he realized he would just have to throw it out there. He took a deep breath, as if preparing to make a shot on the firing range, then let it out slowly. His lips compressed and then he said, "You know I love you, Pamela."

Suddenly growing fearful, all Pamela could do was nod silently.

"I think maybe we should wait until after the war is over. I'm afraid of what might happen." His voice caught a bit, but he continued, "It's possible I might not return from a mission. I wouldn't want you to be a war bride turned war widow. I can't hurt you like that."

Pamela sat back in her chair, relieved. She had thought he was going to back out, maybe even break up with her. She wiped her brow with the back of her hand and laughed. "Is that all?"

This caused Dunn to blink in surprise, then he said, "What do you mean, 'Is that all?'"

"I swear, sometimes you think I'm some porcelain doll that will break at the first sign of trouble. Don't you forget, I'm a farm girl. I'm tough and I refuse to live my life waiting for something bad to happen. We have happiness together, and we'll always be happy. I told you a month ago that you were going to survive, that you had to. So you just be smart and careful and that's final."

"It's not that simple. Things can always go wrong. Men don't come back. Some of them had girl friends and fiancées, too. This is war, not some game where everyone shakes hands at the end and runs down to the pub for a beer afterwards. Men get killed, men just like me. Men like your brother, Percy." As soon as he said it, he regretted it.

Pamela's cheeks flamed pink, a sure sign of anger. Percy had been killed at Dunkirk in 1940, a member of the Royal Norfolk Regiment, 2nd Battalion, who fought a rear guard action allowing 330,000 British and French soldiers to escape on an armada of eight hundred boats. She opened her mouth to speak, but Dunn beat her to it.

"I'm sorry. I'm sorry. I'm sorry. I had no right to say that. I don't want to hurt you. Ever. And I just did." His own face turned a bright red. "Maybe we should talk about this another time."

"No, that won't do. We need to do this now, or we'll never get around to it."

"But we disagree. How can we talk about it, if that's the case?"

"We only disagree because you're so stubborn." Pamela's eyes danced with delight. This wasn't the first time she'd mentioned this particular point.

Dunn sighed the sigh of the defeated. "So you're fine with the possibility of being a war widow?"

She shook her head. "No, I am not 'fine' with it. I accept it, but like I just said, I won't live my life in fear of it."

Dunn stared at his nurse-farm girl-fiancée with wonder in his eyes. She *was* tough. His heart did a tumble and he felt a charge of deep emotion welling up. He gently grasped her hand and rubbed the soft skin with his thumb absently. Maybe she was the one who was right. If they got married, then even if something bad did happen, they would at least have had some time together as man and wife. What had his dad told him? Dunn's father had developed the habit of delivering seemingly arcane advice at innocuous times, especially during Dunn's teen years. Like his explanation of what it meant to be a family man: "*It means you will do anything and everything for your family. That you will forego personal needs and desires in favor of your family's. That nothing is more important than your family.*" On marriage: "*Your wife, whomever she turns out to be, is not just a promoted girlfriend. She is your partner in everything. She helps decide what's best for both of you. Contrary to common thought, she is not your property.*" Thanks, dad, thought Dunn.

A feeling of contentment washed over Dunn. Smart enough to recognize it for what it was, he smiled at Pamela.

"If you're sure?"

"Yes."

"Okay, then. I'll have to speak to Colonel Kenton. Army regs require that I get my commander's approval."

Pamela's eyes grew wide. "You're having me on!"

Dunn gave a mischievous grin, then said, "No. It's true. All marriages to a local girl, a *foreign* girl, must be approved. Most commanders want to interview the girl before making the decision."

"Interview? Interview me like for a job?"

Dunn nodded vigorously, enjoying the moment immensely. "Yes, I'd say just exactly like that."

"That is so demeaning."

"The army is just protecting its soldiers. It doesn't want some poor unsuspecting schmuck to get taken advantage of. The army is worried the girls might be after the money and benefits."

It was Pamela's turn to grin mischievously, "There's money?"

"Oh, yes. Loads of it, I'm sure."

"Well, now, let's get this going. It's suddenly sounding even better than before!"

Dunn laughed and so did Pamela. The other couples turned and smiled at the sound of laughter.

"I'll go talk to the colonel first thing tomorrow. Just so you know, this request has to be submitted sixty days before the wedding date, so we can't get married earlier than August twenty-eighth, sixty days from tomorrow."

"Sixty days, hm?"

"Yes."

"Do you think you can really last that long without," she paused and looked down demurely, then back at Dunn, "you know, it?"

Dunn's mouth dropped open. "You wouldn't . . ." His eyes widened, "Would you?"

Pamela giggled.

Dunn sighed at having been had again.

Pamela batted her eyelashes. "Take me home, Tom." This was what Pamela had said the first time, and it had become their code for an afternoon or evening of combined pleasure.

"I thought you'd never ask."

Chapter 4

The weapon rested on what looked to be an overgrown torpedo rack supported by four large rubber tires. Its skin was an unpainted, brushed aluminum, which gave off shiny swirls of reflected light from the overhead fixtures. It was just over four meters in length and had a diameter of one meter at its thickest point. Its new design was longer than the first one and the extra fins had been removed and replaced with an airfoil.

Fritz Rademacher, a mechanical engineer from Munich, stood at the nose of the weapon. Next to him was his rolling workbench on which he kept the tools of his profession. He ran his hand over the weapon's snout. Right at the tip he felt something he didn't like and grabbed a tiny Phillips screwdriver from his workbench. He found the offending screw and tightened it with only a one-quarter turn of the tool. No one else would have been able to detect such a minute difference in the weapon's surface.

Johann Pachter noticed what Rademacher had done and smiled. "If you have such sensitive fingers, Fritz, why aren't you a surgeon? Think of the money you could earn!"

Rademacher glanced at his electrical counterpart, his lip almost twitching into a smile. "*Ja*, except then I'd have to work on people!"

Pachter laughed and turned to check his instrument panel.

Max Mayerhofer, the project's lead engineer got up from a desk that had been shoved into a corner of the twenty-by-twenty meter room. He walked over to a worktable in the center of the room and leaned over to examine some schematic drawings that were spread out carefully.

"Fritz, Johann, come here."

Both men stopped what they were doing and joined Mayerhofer.

Mayerhofer rubbed his face with his hands, then swept them through his ruffled brown hair. He, like the other two, had been up all night, and the crappy French coffee was definitely not helping in the least. Scanning the drawings, he selected the one he wanted and slid it on top. This was a map of the battlefield around 1943 Kursk.

"I know we've looked at this damn thing at least a million times, men, but one more time cannot hurt. We have to stay motivated."

Rademacher snorted in disbelief.

The three men in the room were among the very few on the project who knew the full story of what the weapon could do. The German Minister of Armaments, Albert Speer, had been quite clear from the beginning on that. Then on the 20th of June last, Speer had unexpectedly arrived at the facility with a dozen Gestapo agents and another dozen Waffen SS soldiers. Speer and two Gestapo agents had pulled everyone working on the project, nearly one hundred men and women, one at a time into a small room and grilled them for hours, threatening and cajoling them into revealing who they were working for. Accusing each of being a spy. In the end, nothing had come of it. Everyone survived the near-torture sessions and went back to work, more fearful for their lives than ever before. Security had been increased and put on high alert immediately. No reason had been given. Only Speer knew that the German atomic bomb program, Project Dante, had been destroyed the day before, presumably in a cataclysmic accident. However, Speer was a careful man. In case it had not been accident, he was taking no chances with the last-hope project of *Geheimwaffe Projekts Abteilung*, his Secret Weapons Projects Division.

The three lead men had not been excused from, nor were they immune to, the questioning, but they did not talk of it. Ever. Trust had been destroyed. It was only safe to speak of the project or non-consequential things, and never to anyone in the outside world.

Following the colossal disaster at Prokhorovka, Russia, all members of that team had been rounded up and shot, then dumped into a mass grave; there would be no grave markers for failures of men in the Third Reich. Of course, details of the deaths had not been passed on to the new team members. They'd all been working on the project together since August of '43 . . .

"Lights, please," said Speer. A slender, handsome man with brown hair, Speer stood at the front of the small meeting room. Less than a dozen men were present. All were engineers, except for the three dressed-in-black Gestapo agents, sitting in the back, watching the men in front of them. They had been seated prior to the engineers' arrival to make a more powerful statement. Gestapo presence was exceedingly effective.

When the room darkened, Speer turned on the slide projector. The first image was a picture of a map showing the terrain around Prokhorovka. It was the first time anyone in the room had seen it, except for Speer.

He picked up a rubber-tipped wooden pointer and tapped the most remarkable item on the map, an hourglass-shaped outline following an east-west line.

"This is the zone of destruction following the detonation of the weapon. It covers an area one point five kilometers long and one wide at the top and bottom with the waist narrowing to about one hundred meters."

Inside the outline were dots and Xs made with different colored pencils. They had been painstakingly drawn on the map from aerial photos taken after the calamity and from reports from the ground in the aftermath.

"Red Xs and dots represent Russian tanks and men respectively and black indicates our troops' positions. The dispersal of the markers is indicative of the fact that the battle line was blurred due to the Russians charging headlong into our formations, as was reported by survivors."

Speer held up an index finger, "One massive error led to the failure. One. And that is why each of you, our top engineers, have been assigned to this project. The error was that when the weapon discharged, it affected everything in both directions, forward and backward. It's tragically obvious that the original designers failed completely on directional focus of the discharge, which should have presented itself like this."

He triggered the next slide. The same map appeared, however, instead of the previous slide's hourglass, an outline of a cone shape ran west to east, with the pointed tip at the western end. "Note that the expected kill zone is a kilometer farther east, in essence directly over the Russian rear lines, and nowhere near our own men."

Another slide appeared. It showed the gruesome burned remains of a German soldier lying on his back on the ground. A few audience members coughed to cover up the sound of their gagging and looked away.

"We know that the men exposed in the open were likely killed instantly. The cause of death was complex; their skin, whether covered by their uniform or not, was burned to the third degree point, and much of the skin sloughed off when the bodies were handled, even gently. Bodies selected for study from differing points within the target area revealed the exact same injuries regardless of location relative to the discharge point."

The fourth slide appeared with the splayed open body of a man on a steel table and more gagging sounds came from the engineers. The Gestapo agents were silent.

"Autopsies performed on a select few showed extensive damage to the internal organs, muscle and other soft tissue. Dr. Bader, who performed the autopsies, said the organs all appeared to have been cooked, as if in an oven. And if you will pardon the detail, he said if they had been a cut of beef they would have been well-done." Speer paused for a moment. "Again, the effect was uniform throughout the bodies."

Sounds of vomiting came, and Speer waited.

"None of the injuries to men were expected. The tank crews were all spared, although every single one of them reported losing consciousness and having a subsequent disorientation for several minutes after regaining consciousness.

"The one piece of good news we have is that there was also one hundred percent failure of all electrical components on the ground. Radios and engines failed, and flashlights were useless. Wristwatches continued to work. One Stuka pilot who mistakenly flew too close to the kill zone reported complete failure of his engine and his instrument panel dials stopped working. He was barely able to get the canopy open and jump to safety.

"However, weapons of all types were still in working order. Anything with a mechanical component, such as a tank gun or a rifle or pistol, could function properly. Although, of course, with no power, the tank gun could not be moved."

Speer said, "Lights."

Everyone blinked in the bright light.

Speer's eyes scanned the audience, making eye contact with many of the men.

"Your job is to correct the failure of your predecessors. The Allies have taken North Africa from us. They have taken Sicily. They are trying to take Italy from us. And let there be no doubt, they will attempt to take western Europe from us. We must have the *Elektromagnetischen Impuls Waffe* ready when they invade France. We must have many of these weapons to stop the advancing red tide from the east. They will forever change the battlefield's landscape and alter the balance of power. The Third Reich will remain as the master of Europe, where she belongs."

He snapped off a stiff-armed salute and said, "*Heil Hitler!*"

The men jumped to their feet and responded with their own salute and shouted, "*Heil Hitler!*"

Mayerhofer looked up from the map at his two men. "The test is in just five days."

Speaking to Pachter, he asked, "How did the tests of the electrical components go?"

"Everything checked out. Circuitry for the deployment is good. We still believe the seven hundred fifty meter detonation altitude is correct to give us maximum ground coverage with zero loss of effect, and the altimeters have been tested dozens of time. The throughput at the detonation switch was as expected. Redundant wiring checked out perfectly."

"You have everything documented, of course?"

Pachter looked offended and said, "Certainly, I have."

"Don't get upset. Part of my job is making sure we not only achieve the expected results, but that we are also able to replicate the weapon exactly, and in numerous quantities. It is as Minister Speer said a nearly a year ago, that the fate of the Fatherland is in our hands." Mayerhofer looked at Pachter, then Rademacher. "You both have families. Our work ensures their safety. Don't ever forget that!"

Neither man replied. There was no need. They knew how important this upcoming test was to Germany.

And to their future.

Chapter 5

"Sergeant Dunn reporting, as ordered, sir."

Colonel Mark Kenton returned Dunn's salute. "Be seated, Tom."

Kenton almost always called Dunn by his given name when in private. Their relationship, while still officially following the protocol and bureaucracy of the United States Army, had evolved over time into a deep, trusting friendship. It allowed them to work together in concert with each other's ideas in a more give-and-take style than simply "I order, you follow." However, when necessary, both men understood perfectly that sometimes it had to be an order-follow decision. When the two disagreed, it was most often a misunderstanding, as had been the case when Dunn had learned that he and his squad weren't participating in D-Day. He'd mistakenly thought Kenton was punishing him for a seemingly failed mission in Calais, France. It turned out that

Kenton had a higher priority mission in mind for Dunn. A mission called Operation Devil's Fire, the destruction of the Nazi atomic bomb program and their jet bomber intended to carry the atomic bomb to the United States.

Kenton was slight of build and barely five-nine, with black hair graying at the temples. Contrary to his size, he had a deep voice.

Dunn sat down and crossed his legs. He glanced around the office, then asked, "Where's Lieutenant Adams, sir?" Adams was Kenton's aide and was typically present during discussions of mission orders.

"On leave in London. Be back in a couple of days."

Dunn nodded.

Like many men, Dunn had signed up the day after Pearl Harbor. He was just a semester short of graduating from the University of Iowa. His path to England went by way of North Africa, where he'd earned the Bronze Star for leading his squad in taking out a German machinegun nest. After training at the Rangers school run by the British in Achnacarry House, he went ashore at Anzio, which is where he first came under the command of Kenton.

Kenton shoved a stack of papers on his desk toward Dunn. "I have orders for your next mission."

Dunn picked up the papers. He unfolded a map of Normandy and spread it out over his crossed legs.

Kenton continued, "Now that Cherbourg has been taken, you can see that the Seventh Division is advancing across southern Normandy. Montgomery's Brits are moving toward Caen. The strategic plan is for the two forces to meet near Falaise and surround the remaining Germans in the Normandy Cotentin Peninsula.

"You're going into La Haye-du-Puits, which is centered at an important crossroads. French Resistance tells us there is a high level German headquarters there. We believe it's the Eighty-fourth Division."

Dunn examined the map and found the village of La Haye. He immediately saw that including La Haye, four towns formed a rough square with sides about fifteen miles in length. La Haye was in the northwest corner, Carentan northeast, Coutances southwest and St. Lo southeast. In the approximate center of the square, like the middle dot on a die's five, sat Peiers. Roads connected all the towns and would provide the Germans with ease of movement if they had to shift vehicles and troops from one spot to another along the front.

Blue pencil marks indicated the Allied deployment and red for German. The front line was a few miles north of La Haye, going east for a stretch then southeast to Carentan. Finished with getting the layout, Dunn looked at Kenton expectantly.

"You'll be after all papers at the German headquarters. Any collateral high level kills would be acceptable, but absolutely secondary to obtaining the papers."

"Transport?"

"Goonie Bird from Hampstead. Path is going just north of Cherbourg, around the horn, then south along the coast, crossing the Gulf of St. Malo, then inland east about seven or eight miles. Should get you within two to three miles from La Haye."

Dunn returned his attention to the map, found the relevant points and studied it for a time. He set the map on the desk and picked up the top sheet of paper, the official order signed by the colonel. He noted the date of departure: 2 July, just four days away. Not a lot of preparation time for a squad, especially one with four new members. As he got to the end of the order, it was clear one piece of information was missing.

He looked up at Kenton, "After action plans?"

"The Seventh Division is going to be launching an all-out attack along the line, crossing the Douve river. They should make it to La-Haye on the fourth or fifth. You'll travel the other way to Cherbourg. Hand off everything you find to General Collins and only him.

"Once you've accomplished that, you hightail it back here for the next assignment."

"Yes, sir."

A new opportunity to kill the enemy. His men and he himself enjoyed their elite status as Rangers and were proud of their accomplishments, including the daring destruction of the Nazi atomic bomb lab near Stuttgart. They'd landed in a C-47, not jumping from it, right into the laps of the Germans. After destroying the barracks of an entire German platoon, they'd gone in to the lab. With the help of the lead physicist, Dr. Herbert, Dunn had come up with the idea of triggering the Uranium-235 into a chain reaction and atomic explosion. When the men later learned that the bomb had been destined for America, New York, perhaps, or even Washington D.C., they'd realized just how important their mission had been. It had been a sobering moment to fully understand that they'd saved the lives of possibly hundreds of thousands of American men, women, and children.

They'd only been back in England nine days from that adventure when Dunn had overheard his men talking in near whispers about how much they wanted to get right back over to the continent and face and defeat the Germans. He'd felt the same way.

Dunn gathered the orders together and folded them over, then slipped them into his jacket's breast pocket. Instead of rising, he said, "Colonel, I'd best ask this while I'm here, since I might be away for a time."

Kenton raised his eyebrows. "Go ahead."

Dunn had already thought this through and had no hesitation. "I'd like to officially request permission to marry Pamela Hardwicke, sir."

Kenton grinned broadly. This wasn't exactly a surprise. Dunn had already told him about her. "Congratulations. Have a date in mind?"

"I know there's a sixty day waiting period, so it'll be in late August or early September."

"Well then, permission granted, Sergeant."

Dunn was surprised. "Begging your pardon, sir, but aren't you supposed to, uh, interview Pamela?"

Kenton grinned and waved his hand. "Yes. Army regs do require an 'interview' so why don't you ask Pamela to call me and we'll get together sometime. I'll be sure to ask her some really tough questions."

Dunn tilted his head and gave Kenton a lopsided grin. "Sir, excuse me again, but you act like you aren't really concerned."

Kenton's expression turned somber. "Look. When I called Pamela to tell her your plane had gone down, I heard the pain and fear in her voice. I know love when I see it or, in this case, hear it. I know she's not out to get your money. You do make so much, after all." He pointed a forefinger at Dunn. "And don't you ever forget how much I trust you and that means I trust your judgment. You're not a kid, you're twenty-four, and you've seen and done more things in your life than most men even dream of.

"Come back tomorrow morning. I'll have the official letter you'll need to get the marriage license."

Dunn smiled broadly and got up. "Wow. Okay, thank you, sir."

"You're welcome, and congratulations!"

Dunn saluted and left the office feeling like a high school kid. A thrilled and excited kid. A kid getting a 'yes' from a girl to go to the prom and better yet, approval from her dad. As Dunn walked back to his men's barracks, he pondered this next personal step. While he was now convinced he should get married soon, he didn't really understand how it would work. Since he was a non-commissioned officer and not an officer, he doubted he would be permitted to live off base whenever he was home. What that looked like was hard to envision, and eventually he gave up and turned his attention, not to the new mission, but to the world around him.

Instead of taking the direct route to the barracks, he turned right at the next cross road. This was to give him more time to think about an attack plan. It seemed his brain worked on two levels, or maybe to be more accurate, in two different ways, depending on what it was doing. Dunn had learned this about himself while preparing for various high school tests early in his freshman year. He would spend a hour or so reading the material, then work on something else that didn't require recalling the new information, like mowing the lawn, or even fishing. This low demand on the brain seemed to relax it and allowed it to store the information in an easily accessed place during the test the next day. This helped raise his GPA from 3.5 to 4.0 on a four-point scale, and the eventual and inevitable valedictorian award.

The other part of his mind was what did the problem solving. It also worked in tandem with his body. This was where his battlefield tactical skills came from. He was able to, almost at impossible speed, concoct a perfect plan based on few known facts, while extrapolating others.

By focusing on what he saw as he walked, a squad of soldiers double-timing down the road ahead of him; a jeep with two men in it, a sergeant and a corporal; on the trees, his mind was working out solutions to the coming attack at La-Haye. The makeup of his current squad complicated things somewhat, but that, too, was kept under consideration.

After a fifteen minute walk, he arrived with a working solution at the wooden barracks where his men were quartered and pushed open the door. About half had returned from the mess hall where they'd had an early lunch, and were on their bunks reading letters. Dunn figured the others might be dawdling or maybe stopped at the PX for personal items; letter writing paper, pencils, envelopes, and stamps. One of the biggest pastimes was reading and replying to letters from home, whether from mom and dad or girlfriends. It was a common sight to see ten men hunched over a letter, scribbling something down, raising the pencil tip to their tongues to wet it down to make the writing darker. All of this took place in total silence. Possibly the only time Dunn could count on the men being quiet. Except in combat, that is.

The men glanced up when the door opened, saw it was Dunn, and started to get up, but he quickly said, "As you were."

The men relaxed and resumed reading.

Dunn scanned the wide-open room. It was big enough for about a dozen men, with metal beds evenly spaced out, each one with a footlocker at the end of the bed. On the far side was the armory, such as it was. It was just wooden frames for the various weapons these tough men carried: Thompson machineguns, 1911 Colt .45s, and M1s. Dunn noticed Jones' 1903 Springfield in with the M1s, its bolt handle jutting out slightly, making it stand out amongst the other long weapons. Also at the far end was Dunn's private room.

All of the windows were open, and a relatively cool British breeze blew through giving some comfort to the day's heat.

"Sergeant Cross? A word?" Dunn tilted his head toward the door.

Cross sat up, neatly refolded the letter from home and put it away in his locker. Then he grabbed his hat and slipped it on.

The two men stepped outside. The front of the barracks faced north and, in the shade, a few wooden chairs were scattered about. Dunn grabbed one and set it side-by-side to another and gestured for Cross to sit, and sat down himself, legs sprawled out. He pulled the papers from his jacket pocket, peeled off the top one and handed it to Cross.

Cross read through the order and looked up at Dunn. "I suppose you went for a long walk and figured out a plan?"

"I did," Dunn replied, then he told him.

"Give me the map."

Dunn handed over the map and Cross examined it for a several minutes. He found the various points Dunn had mentioned and using the tip of his forefinger as a measuring stick determined all the salient distances. Using an old trick, he turned the map so he was viewing it from the north, typically considered to be upside down. He checked line of sight and distances again. Finally, he finished. He knew that if Dunn had figured out the plan while walking, he'd done it without the map, relying on his memory which was particularly sharp when it involved maps and tactics. A sudden thought made Cross smile.

"What are you grinning about, you big goof?"

"Just picturing you so busy working out this solution that you walked right on by some sorry assed lieutenant without saluting." Cross performed a mock left-handed salute. "Oh, sir, I'm ever so sorry . . ."

"Don't quit your day job, buddy."

"What? And give this all up?" Cross spread his arms wide.

"Remind me to revoke your next two-day pass, will ya?"

"Will do." Cross handed the map back to Dunn, then said, "Your plan looks okay to me, but I think it's got some risk to it. We'd better work out some contingency plans."

"That's fine." Dunn checked his watch and said, "Let's do that around fourteen hundred hours, I have to head into town to talk to Pamela. Have some good news to give her."

Cross's face lit up at the mention of Pamela's name. Like everyone in the squad who'd met Dunn's lady, he liked her. "What good news?"

"Asked the colonel for permission to marry her."

"Well, that is good news. Congratulations." Cross stuck out his hand and Dunn shook it, grinning. "Does he want to interview her?"

"Not really. Seemed ready to accept her on my say so."

Cross's blue eyes sparkled as he laughed. "At least that's a good sign, huh?"

"Yep." Dunn got up.

"You going to tell the rest of the men today?"

"This afternoon, yes. Then we have to get the men ready for Sunday's departure."

"See you later, then, Sarge." Cross stuck his hand out and when Dunn grasped it, pulled him in for a hug and pounded his back.

Dunn clapped his second in command on the shoulder and turned away.

Five minutes later, Dunn entered another barracks, although this one was full of British soldiers, Commandos. As in his own barracks, the men rose and he waved them back. He knew them well, having been on a mission with them in Calais, France.

One of them called out, "Hey, Sarge, Dunn's here."

A door swung open in the back and Sergeant Malcolm Saunders marched through. Saunders was a big man with wide shoulders that filled the doorway. His red hair and trademark handlebar moustache gave him a distinctly Viking appearance, although he was actually from London's East End. He had grown up within earshot of the Saint Mary-le-Bow church bells, which made him a true cockney. A graduate of the same school as Dunn, Achnacarry House, Saunders had fought his way across North Africa with General Montgomery.

"Dunn, my boy." Saunders hollered as he strode forward. He crossed the long room, seemingly in just a few strides, then shook hands with Dunn.

"Hello, Malcolm. Up for a little chat?"

"Sure."

Once outside, the men found a couple of chairs and pulled them close to each other, then sat down. Dunn offered a cigarette, which Saunders took with a nod. Both men lit up and puffed away contentedly.

"To what do I owe the pleasure of your stopping by, laddie?"

"Just wanted to see how you guys are doing."

"We're fine. Training our arses off. Heading out soon."

"Us, too. Back to France. Where are you headed?"

The Commando shrugged. "Colonel Jenkins is holding that until the last moment, you know the old arse hole."

"Yep."

Jenkins had been the no nonsense, and unpleasant, commander while both men were undergoing commando or ranger training. They'd been there at the same time and Saunders had taken delight in pulling numerous pranks on Dunn and his men.

Colonels Jenkins and Kenton both commanded several elite units like Dunn's and Saunders', and on occasion were forced to work together, in spite of an intense mutual dislike.

"Maybe tonight he'll deign to tell us. Be nice to do some fookin' advance training."

"I'm taking the plunge, Malcolm."

"Going swimming, huh?"

Dunn laughed, then said, "You're just a riot, aren't you?"

"Aye."

"I'm getting married. Pamela said 'yes.'"

Saunders pretended to gag and cough. "Another British lass stolen out from underneath our noses. Why don't you Yanks just go home and take care of the American girls?"

Dunn ignored Saunders jab, "We'd like you to come, if you're available. We don't know the date yet."

"I'll be there."

"Good."

"Congratulations."

"Thanks."

The men then looked off in the distance, tending to their thoughts of the upcoming missions and how they were going to bring everyone back alive.

Chapter 6

30 June, 1412 Hours

A lone figure walked slowly down the street, his fedora pulled down, shading his eyes. Tall, maybe six-one, and lithe of build, his steps were long. He passed a men's clothing store, a drugstore, and finally reached the end of the block. The street signs said he was at the intersection of Broadway and Fifth Avenue. He crossed Broadway and turned right.

The sun was bright, the sky a beautiful blue, and his shadow followed him faithfully. A few stores down, he found the one he wanted and went in. The shop was small, but the heavenly smell of tobacco hit his nose and he drew a deep breath savoring it with pleasure. Dark wood cabinets lined both sides, one filled with cigars, the other with pipes, everything from corn cob to the outlandishly expensive meerschaum.

An older man, wearing a brown suit, stood behind the pipe counter. He greeted the customer with a smile and said, "Good morning, sir. What may I get for you today?"

The man stepped toward the pipes and carefully eyed the

meerschaums. He pointed at one and said, "Might I see that one, once?"

A flicker of disapproval crossed the older man's face, but the tall man didn't see it. Removing the pipe, carved with a three mast sailing ship, the shop owner held it out.

The tall man took it, hefting it to get a feel for its comfortable weight. "I like this. I will take it. What is the cost?"

The owner sighed and shook his head. Still the man didn't see.

"It's fifteen bucks."

The tall man placed the pipe on the glass counter and pulled his black leather billfold from his back pocket. Opening it, he thumbed through the bills, selected one, and held it out for the owner. "Here is a twenty."

In exasperation, the owner couldn't hold back any longer. "Oh, for God's sake, Joe."

Joe, whose real name was Reinhard Vogel, looked up in surprise.

"What did I do wrong, sir?"

Oberst Kalb handed back the twenty dollar bill. "You sound like an Englishman trying to sound like an American with German thrown in for icing. 'Might I see that one, once?' Don't put 'once' at the end of the sentence. That's German for sure. You should have said, 'Can I see that one?' 'Can I,' or 'could I.' Americans don't use 'might' like that.

"You must use contractions. Americans use them like toilet paper, every day. 'I like this. *I'll* take it. What's it cost?'

"When you hand over the money, you don't need to tell anyone what it is unless they really are blind. Say, 'here you go,' or just 'here' or say nothing. And look at them. And smile. Not just a smile, grin like you're having fun. Like your day has been wonderful all day.

"Now, get back to the classroom. I'll be there in a little bit."

Joe's demeanor changed as he slumped, deflated by his performance. He went through to the back of the store, found a stairwell and stomped down them, angry with himself. He'd worked so hard these past four weeks. One of two dozen carefully selected soldiers with a gift for language, he'd arrived at the unusual facility in northwest Germany, just a few miles northwest of Wilhelmshaven. Everything above ground at the training site was American, a few square blocks of replica buildings, while below the tobacco shop sat a warren of training rooms, a firing range, and an infirmary.

On a bleak, wet day in May four weeks ago, *Oberst* Kalb swept through the door of the lecture room and strode to the lectern at the front. There were no windows, but the room was brightly lit. Behind Kalb was a blank chalkboard. Looking at the recruits, Kalb took his time making eye contact with each one. He already knew their names, their backgrounds, strengths and weaknesses. He had helped select them. It had been an arduous task and the men in front of him had been given no indication they were even being considered for a top secret mission. Neither had any of the almost two hundred others who had been weeded out for different reasons, everything from temperament concerns to just having one year less of English language classes than the others. Kalb had hoped to find some who had spent time in the United States, but most of those who had returned to the Fatherland out of duty had already been killed or captured.

Kalb picked up a wooden pointer that had been stationed on top of the lectern. Stepping out to the right side of the lectern, he grasped the pointer with one hand at each end. In a fluid movement, he raised his left knee and slammed the middle of the pointer against his leg. It snapped, sounding like a gunshot. Not one of the students flinched, so thorough was their previous training and combat experience.

Kalb held up the two pieces of wood, then turned and threw one piece toward the door. It sailed through and clattered against the concrete floor of the hallway. Holding up the surviving piece, he finally spoke. His voice was soft, barely carrying to the back of the room, but it carried a unspoken menace. "In two weeks, half of you will be gone. You will go back to your unit. My name is *Oberst* Kalb. Everything you will do here has been planned and approved by me. I decide your fate. My word is final."

He moved back behind the lectern, setting the broken pointer on the top.

"You are an elite group of men. You have been selected for this mission by me, and approved by the *Führer* himself." He paused to the let that sink in.

"In nineteen forty-two, a previous iteration of this mission was launched and because of one man's lack of courage and loyalty, became a complete failure. This mission will not be a failure. Do I have everyone's full attention?"

"Jahowhl, Oberst!"

"Ten minutes past midnight on thirteen June of nineteen forty-two, submarine U-622 landed six good German soldiers, much like you. Their disembarkation point was a beach on the southern shore of Long Island, New York, U.S.A."

A ripple of approval went around the room, as did a few smiles. This was exciting news, after all. German soldiers on American soil.

The colonel held up his hand and the men grew silent. He turned and picked up a fresh piece of chalk. He wrote four names on the board, then turned back to the class. "Remember these names: George John Dasch, Ernest Peter Burger, Heinrich Harm Heinck, and Richard Quirin. These men failed the Fatherland. Dasch, in particular.

"When they landed in New York, it was a foggy night, but instead of good fortune, the fog brought bad luck. While the men gathered their gear, explosives, primers, and detonators, and then buried the empty boxes, Dasch scouted ahead by climbing over a sand dune."

Kalb paused for effect. "To his shock, not one hundred meters from him was an armed sailor, walking toward them. We don't know exactly what happened, but Dasch successfully talked themselves out of the trouble, perhaps saying they had shipwrecked, and the sailor left. The men made their way to the nearest train station with no further problems. From there they went into New York City."

A few appreciative whistles sounded.

"Each man had a specific assignment and they dispersed to those locations. Unfortunately, the sailor passed on the sighting of these men and a manhunt was started by the Federal Bureau of Investigation.

"On the fourteenth, Dasch was arrested and underwent

interrogation. He gave up the names of his men and they were all arrested only six days later. On the eighth of August, all but Dasch were executed. Dasch received a life sentence, we assume because he 'informed' on the others.

"All of these men had spent time in America when they were younger and returned to the Fatherland out of loyalty. However, the weakness of one man collapsed the entire operation."

Kalb put his hands along sides of the lectern's top and leaned forward. "Understand this: we have sympathizers all over America. If any of you try doing what Dasch did to save your own skin, it won't be a life sentence you'll get. You'll be killed while in custody, I promise you!"

Joe entered the classroom, surprised to find it empty. He sat down in his chair in the front row, and leaned onto the table, putting his head in his hands. His thoughts were racing. What if he was the last one cut from the operation? To be sent back to his unit after bragging that he had been picked for an elite operation? The dishonor would be unbearable. He lowered his hand to his hip where usually he would find a Luger in its fine leather glove-like holster. Perhaps that would be better.

He lost track of time and was jolted by the sounds of the door closing and footsteps. Looking up he saw the colonel standing in front of him. Joe jumped to attention.

"Sit," said Colonel Kalb.

Joe sat down, a fearful expression crossing his face. *Here it comes,* he thought.

The colonel took off his officer's hat and laid it down on the table, upside down. He ran his hands through his hair, smoothing the fly-aways. Grabbing a chair sitting next to the lectern, he put it in front of Joe's table, then sat down.

"Do you realize you are the only Waffen SS man here?"

Joe mentally ran through the men's backgrounds and saw that the colonel was indeed correct. The majority had come from the Wehrmacht, three or four from the Luftwaffe, and two from the German navy. Nodding, he said, "I do, sir."

"Why do you suppose we have only one from the Waffen

SS?"

Thinking for a few moments, Joe examined the question. He tossed aside a few thoughts, and finally said, "From what I've experienced, they can be too rigid in their thinking. Too fanatical to consider alternatives."

Kalb smiled. "Yes. At their core, they do adapt well to changing battlefield conditions, but tend to revert to what has been proven to work. They rarely go outside the current doctrine of battlefield tactics. And yes, their fanaticism causes them to be blind to choices that might include retreating to gain time and a better position. Once an inviting solution has been advanced, they stop looking for alternatives.

"You recall the tests you took before you were told to report here?"

"Yes, sir. I was told they were to see if I might qualify for officer's training."

"Correct, although each of you was told a story that meshed with your personal story."

"A lie."

The colonel grinned, then crossed his legs. "A suitable subterfuge."

"Of course, sir."

"All of you were given the exact same tests. There were problems on the test that you solved that no other Waffen SS men did. That put you at the top of the list." He paused to let that sink in.

"You've been here for a month. You have shown uninhibited thinking when presented with a problem. Who do you think is first in the class?"

"I am."

"Such confidence. Are you sure?"

"Yes, sir. Permission to speak candidly?"

"Granted."

"You ride me the hardest. You hold me to a higher standard than the others. Even when I make smaller mistakes, you pounce. Just like a few minutes ago. Others have used the same terminology as I did, yet you say nothing. Therefore, I must be first."

"Perhaps you are last, eh? Instead?"

"Very unlikely, sir."

"You are indeed first. You are the most gifted of the entire group, not only in language, but in all other skills, including demolition. But do you know where it is you truly excel?"

"I await your comments, sir."

The colonel laughed, and shook his head slightly. "You are a smart one. You excel in dissecting a problem. Looking at it from many directions and not making potentially fatal assumptions. You typically arrive at a sound solution before anyone else, and I have noticed that you routinely develop a secondary and tertiary solution.

"Frankly, I'm amazed you haven't already been sent for officer's training." Kalb turned his head to look at a large map of the United States hanging on the wall. Next to it were smaller, but finely detailed, maps of New York, Washington, D.C., and Pittsburgh.

He pointed at the maps and said, "Those people are not evil any more than we are. But their government means to destroy us. To take us back to the twenties when most Germans faced hunger and unemployment. The only thing that stands between that and the Fatherland is us. Dedicated soldiers."

"I understand the responsibility, sir."

"Yes, I know you do. I am making the final cuts today and that's why you are remaining here."

Joe swallowed the lump in his throat as relief swept over him. After a moment he was able to speak. "Thank you, sir."

"Don't thank me. I am also appointing you leader. I do have high expectations of you. You will have to lead these men. You will have to organize not only the sabotage efforts of the team across that vast space, but to recruit sympathetic Americans who will be willing to, at the very least, support us financially. We have only days to finish training and mission planning. Are you ready?"

"Yes, Colonel."

"Go get your men. Assemble them in the gymnasium." Kalb pulled a piece of paper from his shirt pocket and handed it to Joe. "Tell these three men to meet me in my office."

Joe took the list, read the names and nodded, more to himself, agreeing with the colonel's assessment. He rose, clicked his heels and saluted the colonel. "Right away, sir."

Kalb returned the salute and watched Joe leave. He rose and walked over to the map of the United States. He examined it briefly, then bent over slightly to peer closely at Texas. Using his hand as a measuring stick, he calculated that the expansive state was a thousand kilometers wide. It was wider than Germany was tall.

Stepping back, he had one thought, not for the first time. *My God, what have we done?*

Chapter 7

The long, low form left the port at Edinburgh, Scotland, its bow slicing smoothly through the water. She was making two knots, and as she pulled away, gliding eastward into the Harbor Edinburgh, she accelerated to ten knots. Smoke poured from the submarine's exhaust. Her twin diesel engines, each rated at 1,550 horsepower, were powerful enough to push her along at almost fifteen knots on the surface. She carried twelve torpedoes, all in the bow. The men below numbered forty-two crewmen and six officers, plus an additional ten men, guests along for a ride. By the time she cleared the bay and entered the wide-open waters of the North Sea, she had hit full speed, her bow rising and falling five feet on the sea swells.

The captain of the *HMS Sea Scout*, Lieutenant Commander James William Kelly, was seated at the mess table, which was a whopping four feet square. Kelly, a slight man of only five-eight and one hundred forty pounds, nevertheless garnered the respect of his crew. An officer in the Royal Navy since 1939, he'd previously served on board the destroyer *HMS Sardonyx*, rising to the job of executive officer quickly. During the many missions of convoy escort duty, Kelly had overseen the sinking of several U-boats, and the shooting down of quite a few German Stuka dive bombers trying to punch holes in the transport ships. The *Sardonyx* had also ferried British soldiers off Dunkirk in May 1940.

In June 1943, Kelly had asked to switch from surface ships to submarines because, as he told it, that was what he'd always wanted. Not unheard of, but rather rare, he'd had to endure almost a dozen interviews with various officers, each one in turn questioning his choice, some even chastising him. Eventually, he persevered and his request was approved. Two months later, after completing submarine school, he was assigned as executive officer of the *HMS Seawolf*. Here he learned many things from the captain, Commander Adamson, who'd been a member of the submarine service since May 1940. In February 1944, Adamson had called Kelly to his quarters and had given him the news that he would be getting his own command, a brand new boat, the *HMS Sea Scout*, due to launch the very next month. When Kelly had suggested Adamson take the newer boat, the captain had just shaken his head and told Kelly he'd rather stay aboard the *Seawolf;* she was like an old friend and parting ways just wouldn't be possible.

Kelly had reported for duty the next week and then spent a month getting to know her as she went through the final stages of finishing. Launched on 24 March, Kelly and his new, but partially experienced crew took her through her paces. On 19 June, just a few weeks ago, she was commissioned. This mission was the first for the *Sea Scout* and her crew.

Lying on the top of the small table was a map showing Great Britain, the North Sea, and the continent's northwest countries, Holland, Denmark, and Germany. Penciled lines had been drawn on it showing their planned route.

Seated on the captain's right was Sergeant Malcolm Saunders, squad leader of the British Commandos on board for a ride. Across from Saunders was his second in command,

Sergeant Steve Barltrop, who had been with Saunders since North Africa, and had then followed his sergeant to Achnacarry House almost a year ago. A true landlubber, he had been none too thrilled at the prospect of getting on a thing that moved around on the water due to previous miserable bouts of sea sickness. To his relief, he'd been told that once the sub went underneath, the sea sickness would go away in the smooth, dark world below.

When they'd left Edinburgh, the other eight members of Saunders' squad immediately racked out, getting some extra shut eye while Saunders and Barltrop met with the captain. Before heading off to sleep, a squad mate, Tim Chadwick, had ribbed Barltrop about sea sickness; he just didn't understand, having grown up in a fishing village on the west coast of England.

Kelly slid his finger across the map. "There are a series of islands, like barriers against the North Sea. Wangerooge is the easternmost of the large named islands. Three others are southeast of it. We can drop you in the water just east of this one, in between it and Mellum Island." The captain pointed to the one farthest from Wangerooge, then slid his finger a little left. "Right here, puts you about a half mile out. That's as close as we can get according to the depth charts. When you make landfall, you'll be about twelve miles northwest of Wilhelmshaven."

Before leaving Barton Stacey, Saunders had studied all available reconnaissance photos. One thing that bothered him was the landscape, which appeared to be as flat as a billiard table and nearly as naked in terms of trees and shrubs. Crossing twelve miles in the open would require nighttime passage and could take four to six hours depending on what they ran into, or had to avoid.

Saunders examined the captain's map. The German sub pens, the target, were located two miles north of Wilhelmshaven. He ran his eyes up the coast a little ways and noticed a breakwater, a jab of land extending half a mile out into the main channel leading to the port. It looked to be only one and a half miles from the pens.

Pointing at it, he asked, "Can you drop us near here instead? It would cut the travel risk considerably."

The captain leaned forward. After a quick look, he sat back, shaking his head. "No. We can't set you off there. That's probably inside the submarine nets they have set up. Even if we got lucky and got inside, we might never get back out. I cannot risk the boat. No."

"But what if the nets are farther in than you think?"

"They could be, but we don't know exactly where they are. We can only base it on where we would place them." He pointed to a line crossing the water from one shore to the other of the channel. "Here is where it could be. We might be able to find the support floats in the daytime, but we can't be anywhere in those waters," he swept a finger indicating the area around the breakwaters. "In that shallow water, any plane flying over would be able to see us the same way you can see a trout in the shallows of a stream."

"Wouldn't they just think we were one of theirs?"

"No. The silhouettes are different. Even if they weren't, they would radio in to find out whether any of their subs were going out or coming in. Once they got the answer, they'd kill us all."

Saunders shook his head, then asked, "Okay, how about a compromise? Land us halfway closer. That'd be outside their nets, but would shave several hours off our travel time."

Kelly leaned forward again and picked up a pencil and dividers. Measuring from the initial location of the drop, he marked off six miles and checked it against the line representing the submarine net. Just outside. He pondered this briefly, then said, "All right, Sergeant, I'll agree to half way, but no more."

Saunders smiled. "Thank you, sir. I do appreciate this."

"You're welcome. Any other questions?"

Saunders glanced at Barltop, who gave a slight shake of his head. "No, sir. Not at the moment."

"Fine. You can find your way to your quarters?"

"Aye, we can, sir." Saunders hesitated.

Kelly raised his eyebrows. "Something else after all?"

"Well, sir, I was just a wondering. After I stow my gear, might I come along for a looky-see?"

Kelly's lips curled into a smile. "Curious?"

Saunders nodded. "I like to learn things."

Kelly stood and clapped Saunders on the shoulder. "You come on up. I'll answer all your questions."

"Thank you, sir."

Kelly turned to Barltrop and said, "You're welcome, too, Sergeant."

Barltrop gave a sickly smile and said, "Ah, no thanks just the same, Captain. I do have one question, though."

"Please."

"This boat, er, when it goes under the water, it always come back up, right?"

Kelly laughed. "Most of the time, Sergeant, most of the time." And with that, he turned and left the two commandos.

Saunders laughed, then said, "Worried are you now, laddie?"

Barltrop frowned and said, "Bugger off, why don't you?"

The tips of Saunders' red moustache twitched as he laughed again.

Barltrop laughed, too, then lowered his voice to a whisper and said, "You didn't really expect him to give you those ten miles did you?"

"No, of course not, laddie. I got the six I wanted!"

Chapter 8

Dunn knelt and pulled a poncho over himself so he was completely covered. Next came the map, which he unfolded inside the makeshift darkroom, followed by a switching on and placing of a penlight between his teeth. He kept his dominate eye closed to preserve night vision.

He found the intersection they'd just passed, walking carefully and quietly by it from a distance of ten yards. He'd sent Patrick Ward scurrying over to get close enough to read the road signs in the moonlight. As he examined the detailed map, he saw that they had indeed landed within the target area, about three miles east-southeast of La Haye-du-Puits. The intersection was just over a mile away.

To mask Dunn's C-47 Goonie Bird's arrival, he had orchestrated a dozen B-26 Martin Marauders, a twin-engine bomber, attacking the northwest corner of La Haye, each dropping four thousand pounds of bombs just as Dunn and his men were stepping into the black, cool French night over their target zone.

Dunn examined the map for another few minutes, then when he was satisfied, he clicked off the penlight and began putting everything away. After pulling off the poncho, he looked around at his men, all with blackened faces. Each and every one of them had given his full attention for the nearly two-day practice and planning sessions, memorizing the map, including the location of the target building, the German headquarters which, predictably, occupied the largest private home in the town.

In a low voice, he said, "We're where we're supposed to be." Pointing toward the rising glow of bomb-induced fires, he said, "About a mile to go. We're sticking to the plan. Anyone have any questions?" He waited a moment, but no one said anything. "Okay. We shouldn't really run into anything between here and the town, since we're far behind the front line, but remember, no contact whatsoever. We bypass everything we find. Make mental notes on any big gun emplacements you see."

Dunn rose, as did the men. Dunn eyed each man in turn, liked what he saw, tough, prepared men, then nodded once. Tonight, the men were carrying, not the Rangers' favored weapon, the Thompson .45 caliber submachinegun, but the British 9mm Sten submachinegun with a sound suppressor. Named for its chief designers Major Reginald Shepherd and Harold Turpin, and for Enfield, the manufacturing location in northern London, the weapon first saw service in 1941.

"Wickham, take point."

Stanley Wickham slid past a couple of men and Dunn, and led the way. The men kept their interval, about three yards, and followed. Dunn's previously established path was to follow the main road that ran first through the hamlet of Les Lisieres, sticking to south side of the road, walking in the fields that lay next to it.

The land rose gently and trees lined both sides of the road. In places, they were dense enough to block sight of the road completely. Sounds of the night wafted to their ears: a few birds and insects, but no barking dogs, thankfully. From off in the distance came the sounds of vehicles moving, probably Germans trying to escape the blazing fire.

Soon, they skirted the hamlet, which only amounted to a dozen buildings stretched out along the road for less than a quarter-mile. No lights were on in the few houses.

Making good time, even in the darkness, the squad reached the jumping off point after about thirty minutes, having passed no enemy soldiers. This was not unexpected, but because they were approaching the town itself, things could change.

A low stone wall, likely a hundred years old, ran perpendicular to the road across the field to their left. It spanned a distance of over a hundred yards before disappearing into a small grove of trees. Wickham knelt behind it and held up a fist. Everyone else knelt and waited while Dunn slid up to join him.

Dunn slowly raised his head until he could see over the top of the wall. Fifty yards ahead was a two-story stone house. It was adjacent to the road, which was on its right, and a smaller one-story house stood a mere two yards to its left. This would be the entry point to the next street, on which the headquarters home was situated. Lowering himself, Dunn then turned and waved to his men. They quickly moved up and spread out to Dunn's right and left along the wall.

Dunn made the first move, slithering up onto the top of the wall and down the other side. Knowing his men were right behind him, Dunn took off in a crouching run, heading for the dark gap between the houses. He darted into the slot and stopped about halfway down. The only evidence of nine other men moving in behind him was the whisper of their boots on the grass. Dunn glanced back at the men, who were lined up half on each side, with Cross directly across from himself. With a nod, Dunn moved toward the end of the gap. Once at the corner, he knelt and peeked out onto the street, checking both directions. Good, nothing moving.

The house the Germans had appropriated for their headquarters was a three-story stone and wood structure set back from the street only a few feet. In the center was a wide set of stairs rising only three steps to a large front door. The symmetrical design of the house put the front door dead center, flanked evenly on each side by multiple-pane casement windows all the way to the top floor. All were dark, as was to be expected.

Dunn watched the outside of the house, waiting for any tell-tale moving shadows, but saw none. It appeared that, as he had hoped, the Marauders' bombing attack had driven everyone into the air raid shelters, leaving the house temporarily unguarded.

Deciding quickly, he rose and simply stepped out onto the street as if he was just going for a walk. The four men behind him followed, walking in the same manner. Cross's men provided cover from the darkness.

They marched up the steps to the front door. Dunn put his hand on the door knob and turned. The door opened silently as he pushed gently. It opened onto a long hallway, which ran the length of the house, and on the left was the staircase going to the upper floors. Dunn gave the stairs a once over, then turned to the door on his right. Although the hallway was dark, a sliver of light escaped under the door. Jones pulled the front door closed quietly and the men fanned out around Dunn.

Dunn took a deep breath and released it. Everything depended on the next few seconds. Any loud sound would mean setting off the alarm in a town full of effective enemy soldiers.

The door opened by swinging left, so using his left hand, Dunn turned the knob and opened the door, praying it wouldn't squeak. It didn't. Leaning forward, he pushed gently again until he could see into the room. An officer sat at a desk reading papers, facing Dunn's left. No one else. Not unusual for the early hours of the morning. Lifting his Sten, Dunn slid it through the small opening and fired twice, striking the German in the ear. His head exploded and he slumped at an awkward angle.

A suppressed weapon is not totally silenced, but the suppressors on the Sten worked remarkably well. The sound of the discharge was no louder than a man's cough, although the action of the bolt sliding back and forth produced a slightly louder metallic sound, like someone lightly tapping a steel handrail with a wrench.

Dunn ran into the room and pulled the man from the chair, settling him to the floor to make sure he didn't accidentally fall out and make unwelcome noise. He searched through the man's pockets until he found his identity papers. Dunn briefly examined the papers. They were nothing out of the ordinary, a *hauptmann*, captain, in the *Wehrmacht*, serving since 1938. He folded them and shoved them into his shirt pocket.

Schneider was first in behind Dunn and he started examining the papers on the desk. Most were orders of the day, but there was a stack of maps with details of not only the German locations, but the American. Schneider pulled one of three empty satchels from his shoulder and began putting papers into it. He filled all three.

Jones and Ward rushed in and began placing charges, setting the timers for five minutes. Some of the charges were high explosive and others were incendiary. Wickham had been left to stand guard in the hallway.

At the last moment, Schneider spotted a small leather messenger pouch on the desk and grabbed it without bothering to open it, stuffing it inside his uniform shirt.

Working quickly, the men finished their tasks and ran back into the hallway. Wickham was at the front door already, peering out through the lone window, which was at eye level. Seeing nothing dangerous, he pulled the door open, and as before, stepped out walking like a man with a purpose. The other four men followed, Dunn bringing up the rear. They made it safely across the street and into the alleyway, joining Cross and his men. Silently, they moved quickly down the alley, across the backyard, then back up and over the stone wall.

Morris had point and led the men along the path they'd taken earlier, escaping the way they came in. After traveling nearly four hundred yards, the unmistakable sound of the charges going off slammed toward them. Dunn looked over his shoulder and a bright flare of light silhouetted the large house they'd crept past. Dunn was slightly surprised that they'd gotten in and out without being seen, but having the Marauders' bombs as a diversion had worked perfectly. Part one of the mission was accomplished. Part two, getting home through the German lines, still lay ahead.

When the squad was almost back at the hamlet, Morris took a left. There were a few trees and some undergrowth and he pushed his way through, stopping when he reached the road. He checked both directions, saw that it was clear and ran across the road, then through the trees and undergrowth on the opposite side. Soon, the remainder of the squad was across. With Morris still leading, the men resumed their early morning march.

Dunn picked up his pace and as he passed each man, he

patted him on the shoulder, getting a nod in return. Good job, he'd said silently. Shortly, he caught up with Morris, tapped him, then moved into the point position. Morris dropped back. Dunn drew up the map of the world around him in his head. Rotating it mentally to orient it with what he saw. He already knew it was a little over five miles from the village to the American lines near St. Sauveur-le-Vicomte. It was to their advantage that they were traveling the "wrong" direction, coming in behind the Germans, but he also knew sunrise was less than an hour away and daylight was definitely not a stealthy fighter's friend.

Chapter 9

Though generally flat, the countryside Dunn and his men were stealthily moving through was part of the difficult bocage country. Hedgerows. Some twice as tall as a man and at least six feet thick. These had been built centuries ago to separate one piece of farmland from the next. There was no rhyme nor reason to their location or the shape of the land they protected on all sides. Some were rectangular, some were rounded off triangles. They were a defender's dream, an attacker's nightmare. They were the reason the Allied advance, once they were off the beaches, had ground nearly to a halt. You could poke your head through one side of a hedge and come literally face-to-face with the enemy.

Stories of lucky heroism abounded. The most famous was private—now corporal—Bill Johnson. Known for his prowess with his M1 rifle, he was walking on point down a lane with his squad one afternoon when he heard low voices speaking German on the other side of a ten-foot-tall hedgerow. Waving at the men behind to stop, Johnson got down on his hands and knees and started working his way through the scratchy, tough, unforgiving hedgerow. After a few minutes labor, he made it far enough to see who was talking. To his left were six officers from the look of things. Already thinking about capturing them single handedly, he burst out of the bocage and shouted, "*Hände hoch*. Hands Up!" The officers had all turned and ran off in different directions, like rats scurrying away from a barn cat. Johnson simply picked them off one-by-one.

Some of the hedgerows were so tough that tanks even had trouble breaking through. Until a farm boy from Nebraska rigged up a shrub-clearing mechanism, nicknamed the Rhino that, when fitted to the front of a Sherman tank, made quick work of the gigantic wall of dirt and vegetation. Finally, real progress was possible, difficult, but possible.

As Dunn and his men crouched behind a hedgerow, he checked his map and the recon photos in the dim morning light. They needed to get under cover and quick. He spotted what appeared to be a large, dense wooded area about a mile to the north of their present location. There were maybe four or five more hedgerows to burrow through. The ones in this area seemed to be smaller and required less effort, which was a relief.

He called Cross over and outlined his plan. Cross nodded in agreement, then said, "We have to cross a road there." He pointed at the map.

"Yep, we're going to have to stretch out along the road in a line and then run across at the same time. Five seconds is all we need."

"Okay."

Cross took point and his half of the squad fell in behind him. Dunn and his group tagged on. Advance was slow and silent. They moved along staying close to a hedgerow on their left. When they came to the corner of the field and another hedge, one man would crawl through, taking field glasses with him. He would spend several minutes examining the field they were about to enter, searching for German locations. Once he gave the all clear, he would complete his path through the hedge, sometimes practically popping out like a cork from a bottle and landing sprawled on the ground. Then the squad would find itself running fast in a crouch to the next barrier to burrow through.

Soon, they arrived at the last hedgerow, the one adjacent to the road. Dunn made his way to the front and joined Cross.

"I'm going through and checking out the road. Get them lined up for crossing."

"Okay. We'll be ready."

Dunn dove into the hedgerow. A few moments later, he was able to poke his head out. He turned to the right, east, and could clearly see the road as it went downhill about a mile and a half, then curved left toward the north and out of view. Looking the other way, at about one hundred fifty yards, the road turned sharply left, then out of sight behind other hedgerows. The road was clear in both directions. Dunn closed his eyes for a moment, listening. Satisfied that he could detect no noise associated with the movement of German men or vehicles, he turned back to the hedgerow and called out softly, "Cross. Send them."

In less than a minute, the entire squad had made it through and were kneeling at the road side. Dunn listened again, heard nothing, eyed the road to the north and south, saw nothing, then gave the order to go.

Ten men double-timed across the road, down and through the ditch, which was mercifully dry, and up the other side. Then into the dense French woods and safety.

Ten yards in, Dunn put up a hand to halt the squad. Everyone crouched, waiting.

Dunn went over to Jones and Ward and said, "Scout ahead ten yards at a time. Stay ten yards apart. Go a half mile, then come back."

Both men nodded and took off, moving carefully.

Dunn rejoined the rest of the men and told them to lie down for a rest.

Sunrise had fully bloomed off to the northeast. Dunn had noticed it as he'd run across the road, although, here in the dense forest, only part of the light was breaking through.

The men pulled off their jackets, balled them up and put them under their heads for a pillow, and closed their eyes.

Dunn sat up watching and listening as his men rested. He was tired, having been up close to twenty-four hours. However, his mind was racing. They'd have to spend the day here in the forest, then cover the remaining four miles to the American lines at St. Sauveur at sundown. If all went well, they might make it by around twenty-two hundred hours. He expected no pursuit. With the Marauders dropping their bombs, the Germans would likely assume that the headquarters building had been hit, or that a bomb that had failed to detonate at first, but finally did, minutes later.

Thirty minutes passed and Jones and Ward returned, weaving their way through the sleeping forms to get to Dunn, where they sat down. Each man removed his helmet and set it on the ground next to himself. Jones gave Ward a "you go ahead" look. Ward nodded.

"Good news, Sarge. We found nothing of the enemy, not even evidence that they'd ever been in here. The walking's good."

"Good job, men. Find yourselves a spot and get a few minutes shuteye."

"Yes, Sarge."

Both men moved off and settled to the ground, asleep in less than a minute.

About a half hour later, Dunn heard planes approaching. As they flew overhead, he couldn't see them, but the unmistakable scream of the Merlin engine inside the P-51 Mustang greeted him. They flew over and Dunn guessed their altitude at less than five thousand feet; *must be on ground attack assignment*, he thought. The beautiful sounds of friendly aircraft diminished quickly and silence resumed. Checking his watch, Dunn decided it was time to move deeper into the forest and set up for a more comfortable and lengthy stay. Then he could, with Schneider's help, decipher the papers they had stolen from the headquarters.

He roused each of his men, who all came awake instantly. He gathered them around himself and was about to give orders to move out when a low humming sound caught his attention. It was coming from his left, the east. He was pretty sure of what it was and told his men to follow him.

He took off at a run, dodging trees and low-hanging branches. They quickly reached the edge of the forest and Dunn, staying behind a large oak for cover, peeked out with his binoculars. He was right! A convoy of four trucks had just made the curve a mile and a half away and was heading this way. Dunn gave his orders and the men took their assigned spots.

The trucks approached, the men inside completely unaware of their fate. They were moving at about thirty miles an hour, and were spaced about ten yards apart. Steadily, they came closer. The lead truck's engine suddenly changed pitch as the driver downshifted for the upcoming sharp left-hand turn. The truck slowed.

Dunn and his half of the squad opened fire, targeting the first truck's gas tank just behind the cab. The explosion shot flames straight up into the cab and cargo area, turning the truck into an inferno. The right front tire and wheel blew off from the force and it flipped end over end, like a tossed silver dollar, as it sailed through the air. It caromed off the big oak Dunn was hiding behind with a whack and bounced back toward the road where it landed ablaze.

"Whoa," said Dunn to himself.

Cross's group had started firing when Dunn had, and the last truck in the convoy suffered the same fate. Next, the men turned their firepower onto the remaining two trucks. The ambush lasted less than thirty seconds. No one escaped.

Dunn waved his men back into the forest as he stepped out from the trees to keep an eye on the road in both directions. Suddenly, above the roar of the flames engulfing the trucks, Dunn heard a Merlin screaming toward him. He watched a silver P-51 Mustang fly over at low altitude, the pilot's wingman to his right and behind. Dunn raised a hand. As the planes streaked away, both waggled their wings, acknowledging the mysterious, lone American soldier standing where there weren't supposed to be any.

Dunn checked the road once more, and seeing it was clear, he turned and disappeared into the relative safety of the dark forest. After about ten minutes, Dunn found his men much deeper in the woods than before and in various stages of getting comfortable on the ground, a couple of them already out, sound asleep, Cross among them.

Dunn sat down cross-legged and shucked off his backpack, then lay back using the pack as a pillow. Not very comfortable, he thought, but better than a stone. He closed his eyes, intending to sleep, but his mind kept spinning. Ever the curious man, he couldn't help but want to know what was in the papers they'd stolen right from underneath the Germans' noses. He was pretty sure they would contain information like battalion, company, and platoon deployment. Probably logistics plans as well. That's what you'd find in an American divisional headquarters, anyway.

He rolled over, thinking that would help him fall asleep, but all it did was painfully shove a strap buckle into his ear. Sitting up and rubbing his ear, he yawned. Looking around at the men, he saw Fairbanks and Hanson busy setting themselves up as sentries about twenty yards farther out in the woods, one to the north and one to the south. Then he spotted Schneider, who was sitting up, leaning against the beautiful white bark of a Birch tree, eyes wide open.

Dunn got up and ambled over to sit down next to the big kid born in Austin, Texas in 1925. Bob Schneider's dad was Army, so he'd grown up in a lot of places. Last was Junction City, Kansas, which was only a few miles from Fort Riley.

"You doing okay, kid?"

Schneider turned his brown eyes toward Dunn and nodded. "Yes, I'm okay."

"Have any questions for me?"

"Not really. I'd say we all know what we're doing and that we're quite good at it."

Dunn grinned. "That's right. Don't you ever forget that, kid."

"I won't."

Dunn pointed at the three satchels of papers that Schneider had his arm draped over protectively. "What do you say we take a look at that stuff?"

Schneider grinned. "Yes. I've been chomping at the bit." He picked one up and opened it. He pulled a few papers out and scanned them quickly, then put them back in the satchel behind the ones yet to be read. "Those are all supply orders, food and medical."

He repeated the process as he read through the remaining papers. When he was done, he looked at Dunn with disappointment in his eyes. "These are the same things. Nothing earth shattering in there."

"That's all right. Just move on to the next."

Schneider nodded. The second satchel was better; it contained orders and maps for movement and fire direction for the German artillery along the front.

Dunn smiled. "This is good."

The third was even more valuable. It contained maps and orders showing the deployment of the infantry units along the front and the positions of the units being held in reserve, the reinforcements.

At the bottom of the stack were several innocuous messages mostly covering promotions, and transfers in and out of the division. Schneider laughed lightly at one in particular, which had a list of a dozen or so names. "These guys all got transferred to the Eastern Front. Must have been bad boys."

"Too bad for them."

"Yeah, I'd say so." Schneider undid a few buttons on his shirt and removed the black leather messenger pouch he'd grabbed at the last moment. "Maybe this will have something interesting."

Both men stared at the pouch. Schneider said, "Oh my."

Engraved into the leather was a swastika two inches wide. Under that was one word. He glanced at Dunn. "It says 'secret.'"

Dunn's felt his heart begin to race.

Schneider unwound the leather string that was connected to the top flap and was looped around a thin disc attached to the bottom of the pouch. Opening the pouch he removed a handful of papers. All had a red swastika and the same word 'secret' stamped at the top.

Schneider leaned forward reading. When he finished the first one, he said, "This one talks about Rommel's orders to redirect the Seventh Panzers toward Caen. It's meant as an FYI for this divisional commander." He put that message at the bottom of the stack and read the next.

"Huh."

"What?"

"Well, this one is quite odd. It's a direct order to ensure no German men or vehicles are within five kilometers of certain coordinates."

"Does it say why?"

"No. Hm. Well, wait a minute. At the bottom it says any one

who disregards this order will be killed."

"'Will be killed?' Not 'will be shot' or 'will be executed?'"

"No, it's definitely 'will be killed.' Why?"

Dunn was thinking fast. Germans were always, always, precise even when they were using disinformation. What did this mean? What were they up to?

"Sarge?"

"Let me think."

"Okay."

Why would anyone want an area clear? The only thing that came to mind was weapons testing. *Can't be. We destroyed their atomic bomb program. What the hell were they up to now?*

"Where are the coordinates?"

"Forty-six degrees, forty-two minutes north, two degrees, thirty-five minutes east."

Dunn got out his map of France and opened it. "La Haye is about forty-nine, fourteen north and one, twenty-six east." He scanned the map as far east as it went, which wasn't far enough. "It's got to be southeast of us, but I can't see where. Anything else in the pouch?"

"No. Nothing."

"All right. Put it all back together. Keep it safe. We'll pass it on to Colonel Kenton." Dunn got up. "Try to get some shut eye."

"Will do."

Chapter 10

Aboard the *Sea Scout*
North Sea − 5 miles from the outer islands
2 July, 2123 Hours

Saunders and his nine men gathered in the *Sea Scout's* galley, seated around the tables. All wore black outfits and watch caps. Under the black streaks of nighttime war paint, their faces showed the strain of waiting.

Most of these men had worked together for nearly a year and they were accustomed to each other's movements and style. They anticipated things well, and most importantly, they trusted each other. The men on Barltrop's half of the squad were Neville Owens, William Endicott, George Mills, and Edward Redington. Endicott and Redington were recent replacements following the promotions and transfers of Graham Brisdon and Varner Bishop. Both led their own commando squads now.

Barltrop had turned down having his own squad, preferring to stay with his friend, even though Saunders had tried his hardest to get the man to go. He deserved it so much. In the end, Saunders was grateful for the loyalty.

Saunders' group was made up of Casey Padgett, Wesley Merriweather, Tim Chadwick, and Christopher Dickinson.

Saunders finished going over the plan of attack for what seemed to be the millionth time.

"Any questions?" Saunders asked. After waiting a moment, he placed his hands flat on the table and leaned forward. "Men, it's our responsibility to inflict as much damage as possible. We have our primary targets, but be prepared, as always, for the opportunity to inflict more harm on the Germans."

The men just nodded their understanding.

"Okay, let's get our gear and make our way forward."

At that moment, Captain Kelly stepped into the galley.

Barltrop spotted him and said quickly, "Ten-hut."

The men rose to attention.

"As you were," said Kelly. "I just stopped by to wish you good luck." He extended his hand to Saunders and they shook.

"Thank you, Captain."

"I'll see you all in a few minutes."

"Yes, sir."

After the captain left, Saunders said, "Move it, gentlemen."

Five minutes later, the British Commandos were standing in the control room. They were formed in a line starting with Saunders and ending with Barltrop. The submarine's interior lights were all red to preserve night vision.

"All stop," ordered the captain.

"All stop," replied the executive officer. He waited a moment, then said, "Engine room reports 'all stop,' Captain."

"Bring the boat to periscope depth."

The crew worked efficiently and quickly, and the boat began to rise.

The executive officer flipped a switch on the hull and the periscope rose. Captain Kelly grasped the handles as they went by and pulled them outward, forming a cross on the tube. He leaned on the handles and pressed his forehead against the view finder's rubber face guard. Taking small steps, he began walking in a sideways circle, rotating the periscope. When he completed a full three-sixty, he flipped a switch on one of the handles to magnify his view. Turning the periscope a little left and then right he examined the coast of Germany directly ahead. Satisfied that there was no movement on shore, he stepped back and slapped the handles into an upright position.

"Down scope. Surface the boat."

A few minutes later, the boat broke the surface and a sailor scrambled up the ladder to the hatch in the conning tower. He unlocked and rotated the wheel, then flung the hatch open. Cold sea water splashed over him, then onto the flooring below. Cool, refreshing sea air flowed down into the control room.

"Landing party to the deck," said Kelly. Turning to Saunders he said, "Up you go, Sergeant."

Saunders nodded and climbed up the ladder.

Once all of his men were on the deck, Saunders oversaw the handling of the two black dinghies. The sailors lowered them carefully over the port side. The submarine rocked gently in the small swells and the little dinghies bobbed up and down with her.

It took nearly ten minutes to get the men and their heavy gear into the boats. Each man carried fifty pounds of plastic explosives. It didn't seem like much to go up against the submarine pens, but would do the trick if used the way Saunders planned.

"Cast off," ordered Saunders and the sailors top side pulled up the ropes that had been released from the boats. Using their oars, the men pushed away from the sub, then began paddling.

Saunders stared at the coast a half mile away. It was a clear sky with a three-quarter moon and brilliant starlight illuminating the beach clearly. As the boats made their slow progress toward the beach, the *Sea Scout* slid beneath the waves silently, leaving only a small ripple behind.

Saunders' boat hit bottom and he jumped out along with Wesley Merriweather. They grabbed the tow rope and together pulled the boat farther up onto the sand. The other three men jumped out and helped manhandle the boat twenty yards up to the rising point where the beach gave way to the grasses and soil of the outlying terrain. Behind them, the other boat made landfall and the men dragged their boat up next to the first one. As each man arrived, he knelt to reduce his silhouette.

What to do with two fifteen-foot-long boats could have been a problem, but while still kneeling, the men set to work scooping sand out to make a shallow depression. When they were done digging, they unloaded the satchels of explosives, then flipped the boats over and covered them with a tarp made to look like sand. Next, they tossed sand loosely over the tarp and worked the edges so it blended in with the rest of the beach. It wouldn't stand up to close examination, but anyone driving by on the road, just the other side of the rise, would see what they expected to see: sand.

That task completed, the next was to get everyone's fifty pound satchels into place. They couldn't put them on while in the boats in case the boat sank, or someone went overboard. Getting back to the surface would have been difficult even without the extra weight. Two-man pairs helped each other wriggle the packs into place, more or less comfortably, and gave a thumbs-up sign to Saunders when done.

Saunders gave a sign to line up facing the road. Then they advanced using a combat crawl, their Sten submachineguns resting in the crook of their elbows. Just before reaching the one-lane dirt road they stopped and waited.

Saunders raised his head, lifting a powerful set of field glasses to his eyes. He swept the terrain, moving the glasses slowly, going from north to south, right to left. The land was dishearteningly flat, which would make finding decent cover a challenge. He stopped momentarily and focused on one spot. At a distance of about three hundred yards and in the southwest direction, he could just make out a large farm house. Next to it were several outbuildings, a barn for sure, and perhaps a chicken coop, and a work shed.

Continuing his arc with the binoculars to the left he found the road. It ran alongside the water and was the only raised area in sight, sitting atop a slight rise intended to act as a levy. He followed it out of sight where it disappeared into a dark shape that rose from the ground and spread across their path. Saunders smiled. Trees. Lots of them.

Lowering the binoculars, Saunders tapped the shoulder of the man next to him, Chadwick, who rose to a crouch and ran across the road, then down the shallow ditch on the other side.

As soon as Chadwick made it across, the rest of the men followed quickly.

Saunders moved to the front of the line, preferring to take point at the moment. Moving in front of Dickinson, Saunders then moved out, taking the first steps of a six-mile journey.

An hour later, Saunders estimated they'd covered two miles, one-third the way. They'd skirted, by a wide margin, perhaps half a dozen farm houses scattered across the forlorn landscape. Using what little cover there was in the way of tree lines and small but helpful groves of trees, movement had been painstakingly slow, having to stop every couple of hundred yards or so to survey their surroundings. When they arrived at the trees Saunders had seen earlier, it turned out to be a small forest, much to Saunders' relief. The road atop the levy ran alongside the trees for a couple of miles. Saunders waved his men closer to the tree line and they had continued only a few paces when they came across a clearing in the trees. It was perhaps a quarter-mile square and appeared to have . . . buildings? It looked like a small town or village, but Saunders knew it wasn't on his map.

Saunders lifted his binoculars and studied the town for several minutes trying to make sure of what he saw. It appeared to be a facility of some sort, with a high fence running around it. It was perhaps three hundred yards on a side, nearly fully occupying the clearing. Saunders now realized the clearing had been made just for the facility. In the middle stood a number of one and two story buildings. He could make out what seemed to be a street between some of the buildings. No lights were visible.

Turning around, Saunders said to Merriweather, "Barltrop."

Merriweather passed the word and soon Barltrop was standing beside his squad leader. Saunders handed over the field glasses and pointed. "What do you think?"

Barltrop took a good long look, then lowered the glasses and said, "It looks like a small town, but there isn't one on the map, right? And what's with the fencing around it?"

"Aye, that's right, and hell if I know about the fence. Something about it doesn't quite look right. Here, gimme those back." Saunders took the proffered glasses and examined the facility again. "I can't make out enough to figure this out." He lowered the field glasses and checked his luminous watch. Maybe they could spare a few minutes.

"I want to get closer. Something's odd about that place."

"Okay, Sarge."

Saunders led the way and it only took a short while to make it to a point near the closest fence. Close up, the facility definitely resolved itself into a small town. Saunders focused on a street sign. He could make out the names of both streets. He snorted. "Bloody hell. You won't believe this, but one street sign says 'Broadway' and the other says 'Fifth Avenue.'"

He lowered the glasses and looked at Barltop. "That's a famous intersection in New York, right?"

Barltop shook his head in wonder. "Yes. I've seen it in the movies."

"Yeah, me, too. In fact, it looks like a movie set."

Saunders took another long look through the glasses. "I can only make out one of the signs on the buildings. 'Johnson and Sons Tobacco.'" As he tried making out other details, he realized something was bothering him. What was it? Finally, it hit him. "There aren't any cars on those streets. I think you hit on it. It does look just like a movie set. I don't get it. Why would the Germans have an American movie set out in the middle of nowhere."

Saunders pondered this for a moment longer, then said, "We have to go."

Saunders and Barltrop rejoined their men and set off for their primary target, only two miles away, but Saunders couldn't let go of what he'd just seen and his mind kept poking at it while they walked. To his great annoyance, no answers came.

Chapter 11

2 miles north of La Haye
2 July, 2230 Hours

Ward poked Dunn, who stirred and opened one eye.

"It's time Sarge."

"Okay. I'm up." Dunn stretched, then sat up. The forest had been kind to them by providing a dense covering of dead leaves and soft grass that made sleeping not only tolerable, but downright comfortable, a rarity these days.

They had settled down about a half mile into the forest, and were also comforted by the fact that for as far as the eye could see, there was nothing *but* forest. Off in the distance they could hear the whumps of explosions, which sounded like artillery, whether the German eighty-eights or the American one-oh-fives, they couldn't quite tell. In spite of the sounds, they'd all fallen asleep easily. Dunn had assigned Fairbanks and Hanson to take the first two hour watch.

Now that it was full on dark, it was time to move. Dunn put Cross's men in front, with Morris on point. Moving through a forest at night was a challenge, but the light from the moon filtered through the tree cover well enough.

The going was tough, but they had unknowingly stopped for the day on the top of a hill, and now were traveling downhill. After half an hour, Morris stopped and held up his hand. They had arrived at the northern edge of the forest. It turned out to be a mile across.

Morris slithered out beyond the tree line and tilted his head, listening carefully. He swiveled his head, taking in all he could see. Directly ahead, not ten yards away, was another hedgerow that ran east and west as far as he could see, curving slightly to the south on the right. Morris returned to the forest and filled in Dunn.

"We have a hard night ahead of us," said Dunn. "Let's go."

An hour later, and perhaps another half mile found Morris scratching his way through another hedgerow, cursing under his breath. If not for the long sleeves, his and everyone else's arms would be shredded, as if by a demented cat. At last, he was at the other side and peered out, and listened. Suddenly, the muffled sound of conversation drifted to his ears. Turning his head slightly left and right, like a radar operator trying to focus in on a blip, he narrowed down the location. Peering into the moonlit spaces in front of him he finally made out two shapes standing close together between his hedgerow and the next. At about fifty yards away, and to his left, the shapes had the unmistakable German helmet on their heads.

The enemy soldiers talked for few moments more, then waved at each other, turned and walked in opposite directions, one going north and one south. They disappeared from Morris's view and he realized there must be an opening in the hedgerow on each side of the field. Probably for the farmer's access. They had come across several of those and they had made the transit through the hedge a blessing instead of a curse.

About to go get Dunn and the squad, Morris heard an engine start and, judging by the sound of the roaring exhaust, it was a large truck. The truck drove away to the north and its sound faded.

Slipping back into the hedge, Morris weaved his way back to Dunn and said, softly, "Sarge, did you hear the truck?"

"I did."

"I saw two sentries walking along the west hedgerow. Then they disappeared through it at each end."

Naturally curious, Dunn wanted to go see what was being guarded so far behind the line. On the other hand, the intelligence they had lifted from the German headquarters was invaluable. Risking its loss was not his priority. Taking out the trucks on the road had been one thing, had actually been an easy attack, with low risk to the men and the mission. Attacking an unknown target with unknown numbers of Germans protecting it could place his men and the mission in serious jeopardy. Even as he argued with himself, Dunn new what the decision would be. They were *Rangers* after all. And they had one primary directive: inflict damage on the enemy.

Whispering instructions to Cross, he then grabbed Morris and pushed him toward the hedge. Morris stooped and began leading the way back through the unforgiving branches. After Morris checked the field to make sure it was still clear of the enemy, he stepped through into the open. He led the way toward the southwest corner where he'd seen one of the sentries vanish.

Reaching that same corner, they found the opening. It was just wide enough for a farm vehicle, maybe eight or nine feet. Edging down the path, Dunn was on the left and Morris opposite him on the right. When they got to the other side, they squatted and glanced at each other in the darkness. Right in front of them was a road; Dunn knew it went straight north on to St. Sauveurs, their destination. Just off the road was a German truck. Beyond it, parked in a neat row were a half-dozen more, all silent and unoccupied. A little farther to the right, opposite the six trucks, were several large tents over which was draped a gigantic camouflage net, propped up by poles set in the ground at ten foot intervals.

Dunn examined what he saw. It was obvious they had stumbled into a supply depot. The question was, what kind of supplies? He estimated they were still three miles from the American lines. He knew intelligence had learned that the Germans tended to keep food, medical supplies, and ammunition close to their lines. Americans and the British kept supplies father away, allowing for a rapidly changing and fluid front line. It made it easier to redirect the flow of supplies as needed, and reduced the likelihood that the depots would be in the wrong place.

Dunn had an unobstructed view of the road to his right and it was clear. He signaled for Morris to check the other way. Morris soon replied with an OK sign. Dunn then pointed back to where the rest of the squad was and motioned for Morris to get them and come back.

Morris departed.

Dunn mulled over a plan of attack and kept an eye out for the sentries. A few minutes passed, and he saw the red glow of a cigarette off to the north. It was amazing how bright it was. The German's face was completely illuminated, although he was too far away to make out any features. Suddenly, he veered to his left and Dunn lost sight of him. Dunn knew immediately where he was going. Back into the field. That meant . . .

A boot scraped on dirt not ten feet from Dunn. He softly laid his Sten gun on the ground beside him. Even though it was suppressed, the sound of the bolt action moving after firing a round would make a little noise, and as still as the night air was, he couldn't risk that the other sentry might hear it. He drew his knife from its scabbard on his right hip. Rising and stepping back slightly, he waited. He switched the knife from his right hand to his left.

The soldier walked into the farmer's path, his rifle slung over his right shoulder. He passed right by a perfectly still Dunn.

Dunn jumped toward the hapless German. He shot his right hand over the man's right shoulder. His hand clamped over the man's mouth and he yanked back with all his strength. His left hand drove the knife into the man's back at an upward angle, piercing the heart. The man went slack and Dunn let him slide to the ground.

Pulling off his own helmet, Dunn retrieved the dead soldier's, which had rolled off onto the ground, and put it on. He jerked the knife free, wiped it on the man's uniform, and removed the Mauser rifle. He rose and slipped the rifle's sling over his left shoulder, and switched the knife to his right hand.

Calmly, he walked through the opening of the field and turned left. At the far end, the other sentry raised his hand. Dunn did the same and continued walking. When they were about ten yards away, the sentry said, "*Zigarette?*" and held out a pack.

Knowing he couldn't exactly say anything, Dunn shook his head and waved a hand dismissively. As they got closer, Dunn tilted his head down slightly to obscure his face. He'd gotten closer than he'd expected, what with a considerable difference between the uniforms.

At three steps away, the sentry stopped and said hesitantly, "Ralf? *Was zum Hölle?*" Then he tried to get the rifle off his shoulder.

Dunn leapt, twisting to his right as he flew through the air. The knife flashed. The German's life sprayed out of his sliced throat and he fell in a heap. Dunn landed on his right foot and pivoted away, just missing getting drenched.

Pulling off the ill-fitting helmet, he dropped it on the ground and knelt beside the dead man, careful to avoid the blood, which glistened in the moonlight. He went through the pockets quickly, looking for papers. He found the man's identification booklet in the uniform top, but nothing else, so he slipped it back in the pocket and rejoined his squad.

"Both of them, huh?" asked Cross in a whisper. He handed over Dunn's helmet and Sten.

"Yep," replied Dunn, taking the equipment. "Thanks."

Dunn gathered his men and gave them his plan. They only had four satchel bombs left, but each man had four grenades attached to his shirt. Dunn knew the sentries' routes seemed to take about ten minutes. What he didn't know was whether they met other sentries on the far end of the route. If that was the case, then the way Dunn saw it, they only had that ten minutes to get in, set the charges and get out. If the sentries didn't meet anyone, then they might have a little longer.

Dunn gave the order to move out. Cross and his men ran down the right side of the road, under the hedgerow's shadow. Dunn and his men ran across the road to the trucks, where they quickly checked the cargo areas. All the trucks were empty.

After Dunn finished checking the last truck, the one farthest from the road, he spied another camouflaged tent about thirty yards away. Kneeling, he examined this new find carefully. His men fell in behind him and waited.

Dunn spotted some turned-over wooden crates formed in a semicircle around what had to be a fire pit. That would be where the rest of the depot's soldiers would be. He stared at the tent and the area around it for another minute, waiting to see if anyone was standing guard outside. Seeing no one, Dunn directed his men back the way they came.

Once back on the road, Dunn took the lead and they ran toward the larger tents and entered the first one. Cross and his men entered the second tent.

It was completely black inside.

"Pull that flap over," said Dunn.

Ward grabbed the tent flap they'd just come through and pulled it tight.

Dunn pulled his small flashlight from his pocket.

"Close an eye, gentlemen." Everyone closed their dominant eye.

Dunn also closed one eye and turned the light on. There were stacks of wooden crates, some neatly arranged, others were simply leaning against a stack. To Dunn, the size and shape of one of the crates seemed all wrong; it was about four feet wide by six tall. He stepped closer and directed the light onto its surface. The swastika and eagle symbol was there, as was "*Deutschland.*"

"Wickham, Jones, open this one. And keep it quiet."

The two men set down their weapons and drew their knives. Using them as pry bars, they made quick work of the lid. They pulled it off, revealing straw used as packing. Then they pulled the straw away and there presenting itself was a painting of the Nativity scene. Dunn knelt to read the signature on it, but didn't recognize it. Turning, he shone his light on the inside portion of the lid. Stenciled there was "*Musée Thomas-Henry–Cherbourg.*"

Dunn's mind took off. Art work. What was artwork doing in a Nazi supply depot? Artwork that was worth, well, he didn't know what it was worth, but it must be a lot.

No one said anything for moment, then Wickham drawled in his Brit-Tex accent, "Well, that ain't ammunition."

Chapter 12

1/2 mile north of Wilhelmshaven
2 July, 2305 Hours

Saunders peered through his field glasses at the submarine pens off in the distance. Standing next to a small tree, he was afforded at least a little visual protection. The solid concrete form of the sub pens stuck out perpendicular into the bay at least four hundred yards. As he studied them, as he had done before the mission using aerial recon photos, it was clear why just bombing the hell out of them wouldn't work. You may as well bomb a mountain, so sturdy was the fifteen-foot-thick concrete roof. Thus the need for this commando raid. Get in and do damage underneath. Although getting *out* might be the tricky part. But Saunders put that out of his mind. Can't think like that, old chum.

His mission preparation also showed him the probable locations of German machinegun nests, set up to protect the sub pens from the landward side. The intelligence officer's opinion was that the defense around the pens would be able to muster close to a hundred men. When the officer first broached the subject he was wary of Saunders' reaction. Saunders had simply said, "Aye, ten to one. Sounds about right," and had moved on to other details.

The submarine pen's layout was like any standard seaside dock: a long, wide strip of concrete running about four hundred yards parallel to the water's edge. Built along the dock were several large buildings, some presumably for storage and others for mechanical and electrical equipment. He believed the barracks for the off duty men was at the far end of the dock.

The entrance to the dock was surrounded by two standard German wood and wire fencing with rolls of razor wire strung across the tops. There was about a thirty yard space between the fences. As far as Saunders was concerned the number of fences mattered not at all. This was because, regardless of the fencing, there still had to be gates that lined up with each other for the trucks to come and go. Gates had been throughout history, and still were, a defensive fortification's weak point.

However, next to each gate stood a watch tower, where it was likely the dreaded German MG42 machinegun, called the "buzz saw" for its distinctive and terrifying sound, would be stationed. It was capable of firing 1,200 rounds a minute. These were the weapons that had sent a hailstorm of death raining down on the Allied soldiers as they stormed the Normandy beaches. From Saunders' point of view, though, those machinegun nests in the towers were simply exposed targets with no real protection.

In addition to this, Saunders saw that the Germans had made what could prove to be a fatal mistake: when they'd built the dock, they'd had to first build the access road to it. To do that, they cut down a bunch of trees for the road, but had left many, many others standing. It made for the perfect, natural cover for an advancing enemy. Saunders smiled to himself. He'd thought this was what he would find after looking at the photos, and was gratified to be proven right. As usual. He put away the binoculars, ducked and rejoined his men.

The squad moved forward, advancing smoothly and silently toward the trees lining the access road. When they reached the edge of the tree line at a point fifty yards from the first gate, they stopped.

Saunders used his field glasses to peer up into the nearest

guard tower. The wood of the tower sides was rough planking, probably two-by-fours that had gaps of well over a foot between them. The MG42's ugly cone-shaped muzzle stuck out about two feet. Crouched behind the machinegun was the gunner, and to his left, the ammunition loader. Saunders peered at both men for a long moment. They were definitely awake as he could see small movements of their head and shoulders as they talked to each other. Suddenly, one of them threw back his head, clearly laughing at what the other had said.

Saunders grinned. *Better enjoy that, you bastard, it'll be your last laugh.*

Saunders turned his attention to the other tower. He could also make out the two men sitting behind what they erroneously thought was protection. The second tower was at a range of about eighty yards, a distance at the far end of the effective range of the sound suppressed Sten submachineguns his men carried. To counteract any accuracy problem on both towers, Saunders had assigned teams of three to attack the towers; two shooters and a spotter who was to give corrections as he watched through field glasses. While this was a technique used primarily by snipers, Saunders saw no reason for it not to work for his squad.

While two soldiers stood to the right of the first gate, none were at the second gate.

Saunders backed into the tree stand and signaled to his men. At the moment, he was also saying a prayer of thanks for all the hours of rehearsals. As they would say in Hollywood, everyone was hitting their marks. On Saunders' right were Owens, Endicott, and Mills. They would target the farthest tower. On his left were Chadwick, Merriweather, and Padgett, who would take out the other tower. That left Barltrop, Saunders, Redington, and Dickinson, who would be positioned in the middle and would kill the guards standing at the gate. There were about two yards between the attacking groups.

Each shooter pulled a leather strap from a pocket, looped it around the trunk of one of the small trees at about waist height, and tied it off leaving a space of several inches between the strap and the tree. Into this space they slipped the Sten's muzzle and suppressor until the strap rested against the front of the magazine. Then they twirled the Sten, tightening the strap like a tourniquet until the Sten was snug against the tree, but with enough play to traverse in all directions.

Saunders watched carefully as his men prepped their weapons. When the men took their firing stance by kneeling next to the tree, he raised his field glasses, and said softly, "Fire."

As Saunders watched, the rounds found their targets, first chewing through the two-by-fours then tearing apart human flesh and bone. The laughing solider collapsed and his gunner fell right on top of the MG42, causing its barrel to snap upward, as if in a dreadful salute. Saunders checked the farthest tower and saw the same result. The two men at the gate lay crumpled on the ground. Not one German round had been triggered. The whole affair had lasted four or five seconds.

"Cease fire," called Saunders and complete silence fell over them. The shooters quickly safed their weapons and undid the straps. Saunders led the way toward the gate at a full run.

He examined the gate briefly and saw a heavy metal latch on the opposite side. He simply shoved his right arm though, lifted the latch, and pushed the gate open. The men rushed through, and Redington, who was last, closed and re-latched the gate. The same thing transpired at the next gate and now they were in the open with the four-hundred-yard-long dock stretching out before them like a highway.

They ran toward the first building and Saunders gave more signals. At his command, Padgett and Merriweather took off down the dock, staying close to the buildings. The moon had moved so far west that the buildings threw shadows along their east side, providing a nice dark corridor for the men to run along. Chadwick and Dickinson burst open the door on the first building, Saunders had thought it would be the office, and he was right. Mills and Redington followed the first pair down the side of the dock. Saunders took the remainder of the squad and ran at a diagonal toward the dock's far edge, where the entrance to the submarine pens' pier jutted out into the water.

Inside the office, Chadwick and Dickinson found a couple of gray metal desks and a wall filled with metal filing cabinets. Stepping quickly over to the cabinets, Dickinson spun Chadwick around and opened the backpack his partner was carrying. He pulled out a small rectangular block of plastic explosive. He handed that to Chadwick who stuck it on top of one of the cabinets, while Dickinson pulled a detonator and a timer from a pouch on his chest. He set the timer, a simple, round-faced clock, for ten minutes.

Chadwick stepped aside and Dickinson slid the detonator into the explosive block. Then he attached the two wires from the detonator to two connectors on the timer and tightened the screws.

Dickinson looked at Chadwick and grinned. "I love my job!"

Chadwick laughed, then replied, "So I see."

They bolted from the office and headed to their next target.

Mills and Redington found their target and went inside. It was the electrical building, with a ceiling twenty feet over their heads. About fifty feet on a side, it was jam-packed with generators and wiring conduits going every which direction. They selected a generator that was close to the center of the building. It was running, giving off a smell of ozone and a deep, throbbing hum. They set about their business quickly and, after checking their watches, set their timer to coincide with the ten minutes set by Chadwick and Dickinson.

Padgett and Merriweather, who had the farthest to run, finally neared their target, stopping at the building next door. Crouching at the corner of that building, they paused to check for sentries. Seeing none, they started working on preparing three charges. Padgett, holding two of them, stood up and was about to move toward the target when its door opened. Padgett froze. Two German soldiers stepped through the door, their Mausers slung over their shoulders. The first one took a puff on a cigarette, then dropped it on the ground. He smashed it with his boot, then looked up. And saw Padgett.

Merriweather, who was still kneeling, leaned out around Padgett and fired, mowing down both of the enemy soldiers. That was when things went bad.

Another German leaned out the door and fired his Mauser. The round struck Padgett square in the heart. He died as he fell to the ground. Merriweather fired a burst and killed the German, who collapsed in the doorway, blocking it.

Merriweather fired another burst into the doorway to discourage anyone else from sticking their head out. He bent over and saw that Padgett was gone. Grabbing the explosives, he changed the timers to thirty seconds. He ran over to the door and set two bombs there, then reversed course and placed the last one in the space between the two buildings, along with Padgett's and his own satchel.

Wasting no time, he picked up Padgett and threw him over his shoulder, turned and ran back north along the side of the buildings. He'd only covered twenty feet when the first pair blew. The concussion knocked Merriweather off his feet. The front of the barracks disappeared in a sheet of flame and fireball. Merriweather tried to stand, but his legs wouldn't work. When he tried to take a deep breath, it hurt terribly. He looked down at his chest. A piece of wood was sticking out just below his heart. Merriweather's last thought was one of amazement. The piece of wood that had killed him looked an awful lot like part of a window frame.

Chapter 13

German supply depot
3 miles south of St. Sauveur
2 July, 2330 Hours

"Wickham, give me your knife," said Dunn, not wanting to use his own bloody one.

Wickham drew his knife and deftly flipped it around, extending the grip to Dunn.

"Set some charges over there in the middle of the tent. Ten minutes."

Wickham turned away to get started on his task.

"Jones, go find Cross and tell him to set charges in that other tent, *twelve* minutes, then meet us by the road. Well away from the trucks, which I'm going to blow. Repeat it."

Jones replied, "Find Cross, twelve minutes on charges, meet on road away from trucks."

"Go."

Jones took off.

Dunn faced the painting. Grasping the knife in his right hand

and the penlight between his teeth, he put the tip of the razor-sharp knife in the upper right-hand corner, right next to the gold colored wood frame, and pushed gently. The knife sliced through the canvas with a little brrr sound. Dunn carefully slid it straight down. He finished by cutting the other three sides. He gripped the upper left corner of the painting in his left hand while he tossed the knife straight into the ground. Then he took the painting in both hands and rolled it up on itself, with the painted surface on the inside for protection.

Digging into a trouser pocket he found what he was after and pulled it out: a bootlace, an extra he always carried. Sometimes he thought it was more superstition than practicality that made him do it. He quickly tied the bootlace around the painting, tight enough to keep it from unrolling, but not so tight that it crinkled the canvas.

"Check the outside, Ward," said Dunn.

Ward drew back the tent flap and peeked out. "All clear, Sarge."

"Here, take this. Be careful with it. It's probably priceless." Ward took the painting gingerly.

"Give me two of your grenades."

Ward unclipped two and handed them over.

Dunn stepped through the opening and pointed toward the tent with the makeshift seats.

"Run like hell for that tree. Stay away from the trucks," Dunn pointed at a tree behind and to his left, near the road.

"Got it, Sarge."

Dunn ran toward the trucks. He stopped right in front of them and realized his mistake. He couldn't just toss a grenade into each cab because the windows were all rolled up. Only one way to make sure the gas tanks would blow.

He ran between the two trucks farthest from the road and turned around facing the front of the trucks. He pulled the pins on two grenades and placed each one on the running board next to the gas tank. When he let go, the handles twanged away into the darkness. He took off, around the front of the truck, ran to his right between the next pair of trucks, where he yanked the pins and placed the grenades.

He had just placed the last two when the first two blew,

nearly knocking him off his feet. He put a hand on a truck's fender to right himself. Then he scrambled out from between the trucks and ran for cover. As the time counted down to zero in his head, he dove for the small ditch next to the road, near the tree he'd pointed out to Ward.

In quick succession, the remaining trucks blew, fireballs shooting thirty feet into the night sky, then the tent with the sleeping enemy went up, the fabric shredded and caught fire. Pieces of the trucks began to fall not far from Dunn, so he got to his feet and ran north along the road about twenty yards, Ward right behind him. He found his men gathered at the rally point.

Dunn turned and took the painting from Ward, then did a quick people count. Satisfied all were okay, he took a look down the road wondering whether it would be worth the risk.

He turned to Cross to ask his opinion, but noticed that Cross was eyeing him carefully.

"Whatcha got there, Sarge?"

"It's a valuable painting. Stolen from the museum in Cherbourg."

"Ayuh. You rescued artwork?"

"Well, it looked old. It must be very valuable and important."

"Ayuh."

"Your nor'easter accent is coming out, Cross."

"Ayuh."

Dunn grinned, then turned serious. "I'm considering a short run down the road to gain some time. What do you think?"

"Worth a try."

"Take point, let's go down the opposite side. We can dive under the hedgerow if needed."

"Will do."

Cross grabbed his men and took off, crossing the road. Dunn and his men followed. They ran down what passed for the road's shoulder, a cleared path about two feet wide. After about two hundred yards, Cross slowed the group to a walk as he listened. When he was certain, he turned, signaling everyone to take cover.

None too soon, the men got themselves down and close to the hedgerow's wild vegetation as a German truck rumbled by, presumably heading for the blaze to the south.

Once the Germans were gone and Cross was satisfied a

second truck wasn't coming, he jumped to his feet. At that moment, back-to-back explosions rocked the night as the supply tents vaporized in a fireballs. Dunn and Cross exchanged grins. The squad took off, this time running uninterrupted an entire mile. At that point, Cross held up his hand and everyone ground to a halt.

Dunn jogged up to join Cross and said, "Time to go back to cross country, huh?"

"Yup, we've got to be getting close to the rear of the German front line. Maybe a mile."

The sounds of dreaded German eighty-eights suddenly shattered the eerie night silence. Cross had stopped everyone just in time, for there, just one hundred yards northwest, the night was full of blinding flashes as four guns roared and sent their deadly shells toward the American line.

Cross looked at Dunn, who's face was alternately bright and dark according to the flashes. An unspoken message passed.

Dunn took the lead and the men crossed over to the other side of the road, moving slowly, cautiously.

About fifty yards from the guns, which were still firing madly, Dunn broke through a patch of undergrowth and trees that separated the road from the field in which the guns were stationed. Dunn pulled his field glasses out and spent a full two minutes examining the layout. The guns were about five yards apart. The crew was made up of the gunner, who yanked the firing lanyard after the loader slid the shell in and closed the breach, two loaders to ensure a rate of fire of fifteen to twenty rounds a minute, and a spotter with a radio. He found two machinegun nests placed at each end of the line to guard against enemy infantry. He swiveled his view slowly left, and checked for support vehicles and tents. There were none. Probably got their support from the smoldering depot.

Cross joined Dunn, who had to yell right next to Cross's ear due to the thunder of the eighty-eights.

Cross nodded and returned to his men and passed on Dunn's plan. After getting nods acknowledging what'd he said, Cross grabbed his men and moved north along the tree line.

Dunn got his men and they turned south. They ran twenty yards to the southern edge of the field, then west along that hedgerow, and turned north, toward the guns.

Cross and his men had reached their jumping off point and had to wait until Dunn and his men reached theirs at the opposite end. Since he knew where to look and what to look for, he was able to spot Dunn just as he reached *his* jumping off point.

Dunn knew that the first rule of attacking gun emplacements was to kill the defenders, and so that's what his men would do. As Dunn led the silent—due to the guns' roaring—charge, he couldn't help thinking about how handy a bunch of horses would be just about now. Nothing quite like a cavalry charge.

When Dunn was twenty yards from the machinegun nest, he opened fire as did his men. They shredded those three men and continued running toward the center, firing at the gun crews, who collapsed right where they were.

Cross and his men fired into the other machinegun nest, then moved on to the first gun crew, the bright twinkling of their muzzles the only evidence something was happening.

The last eighty-eight fell silent.

Dunn grabbed Ward and Wickham and gave a quick order. He tapped Jones and nodded toward the road where Cross and most of his men were kneeling. They took off at a run.

Ward went to the muzzle end of the first gun while Wickham went to the second. Next down the line, Hanson and Morris stood at the ends of the other guns. The weapons were set to a lower elevation, which put the muzzle about seven feet off the ground.

"Now!" shouted Dunn.

Ward went first, pulling the pin on a pineapple grenade and slipping it down the gun barrel. The grenade was an inch smaller in diameter, so it only slid a couple of wobbly feet down the barrel, then wedged itself. Ward took off at a run toward the road. As he passed each man, that man would drop his grenade down the barrel and run. By the time Ward passed the fourth gun, his grenade exploded with a whumping and shrieking sound as the barrel flanged apart, looking like a peeled banana.

The rest went off one-by-one, destroying the gun barrels.

The men gathered around each other smiling and started patting each other on the back.

Dunn put a stop to it. "Not now," he said through clenched teeth. "That's for later with a pint. Keep your eye on the mission.

We've still got another mile to go and it's going to be the hardest. We have to time this so we get through the German line in the dark, but don't approach our side until first light. We'll have to show a white flag to keep from getting our heads blown off by some replacement with an itchy desire to kill a German."

Chapter 14

German submarine pens
Wilhelmshaven
3 July, 0102 Hours

Saunders led his five men down the submarine pier and came to a halt when he spotted the expected defensive positions in the dim, reflected light of the moon. On both sides of the pier, which was twenty yards wide, were two machineguns manned, as usual, by two men. Saunders and his men were behind one of the massive concrete pillars supporting the monster roof that protected all beneath from Allied bombs.

Suddenly, behind them, explosions at the far end of the dock, where Padgett and Merrriweather were, went off. The rumbling sound echoed eerily off the concrete around them. As Saunders wondered why they had gone off prematurely, he could see the machinegun crews grow alert. *Bloody hell. What happened?* he wondered.

Saunders pulled back slowly from the pillar, which was on the left side of the pier. It was ten feet wide and flush with the side of the pier. Saunders moved to the edge of the pier and looked down, hoping. Yes! There was a three-foot-wide walkway about eight feet down. Looking off down the side of the pier, he saw that it ran as far as he could see. In his mind's eye, he calculated how far they'd have to move to come up right next to the machinegun on the left and how long it would take.

He tapped Owens and Endicott on the shoulder and whispered, "We're going down there." He pointed to the ledge. "Then we're going to go blow the bloody hell out of the machinegun on this side."

Turning to Barltrop, he said, "Stay here. Wait two minutes after we hit that walkway, then stick your gun out and start firing. When you hear our grenades, target the machinegun on the south side so we can climb up."

"You got it, Sergeant."

Saunders went back to the edge of the pier, handed his weapon to Owens, and sat down. Turning around and putting his hands on the cool concrete, he pushed off the edge and lowered himself to the walkway. Once there, he reached up for his weapon, and motioned for Owens to hand his down, too. Soon, Owens and Endicott had lowered themselves to the walkway. Saunders handed over their Stens, then took several careful steps toward the spot below the machinegun. He glanced down at the black water below his feet, wondering how deep it was. Tied up against a wooden dock sticking out from the pier was a German patrol boat, complete with a Nazi flag at the stern, which flapped in the northerly breeze.

Ahead, perhaps a hundred yards, lay their first target: a U-boat tied up along another smaller pier that ran perpendicular to the one Saunders was on. He looked up, and was amazed at the sheer size of the roof, as it extended outward far enough to completely cover the length of the U-boat, and then some. It was supported by massive pillars set in the water.

When Saunders got to his calculated spot, he stopped. Ten seconds later, he heard the whining and pfft sounds of rounds striking the concrete and sandbags around the machinegun. Immediately, the buzz saw MG42 set to work, spewing its 1,200 rounds a minute. He was pleased to find himself directly below it.

He yanked a grenade off his shoulder straps. Owens and

Endicott followed suit. They pulled the pins in concert, then soft tossed the grenades over the top of the wall. Ducking and covering their ears, they waited. They were rewarded with a colossal explosion as all three grenades bounded into the machinegun nest. Screams pierced the air, then died off immediately.

More sounds of Sten bullets striking concrete came.

Saunders motioned to Owens to give him a hand up. Owens interlocked his fingers and formed a foot hold for Saunders, who stepped into it and rose slowly up to the top edge of the pier. He could see the other machinegun crew firing down the pier towards Barltop. Saunders laid his weapon on the concrete floor above and, using both hands and with a boost from Owens, climbed up and over the edge. Rising to a keeling position, he picked up the Sten, aimed and fired a long burst into the German gun crew. The men toppled over and the gun grew silent.

Saunders leaned over the edge of the pier and called to his men below, "Up you go now."

Owens popped up first, then he and Saunders bent down to grasp Endicott's hands and pulled him to the top. By this time, Barltrop, Mills, and Redington had run down to join them. Saunders looked past Barltrop's shoulders and could make two out forms running low; Chadwick and Dickinson.

As soon as Chadwick and Dickinson joined the group, Saunders could see something was wrong.

Dickinson's face was ashen. "I saw Casey and Wesley go down hard. They didn't get back up. Wesley was carrying Casey when he went down."

Saunders rubbed a hand over his eyes. "Bloody hell," he said in a low voice. "You're sure?"

Dickinson nodded glumly.

Saunders turned to Chadwick for confirmation, but the man merely looked down at his boots.

Saunders expression was stoic, but inside his heart was racing and breaking. He just lost two men. It certainly wasn't the first time, but these men were all a close, tightly knit bunch. When one was hurt, they all hurt. He got hold of himself, and forced those thoughts to the back of his mind. There'd be plenty of time for recriminations on the long boat ride back to England. If they got out of here.

Taking a deep breath, the Commando sergeant asked, "You get your charges set?"

"Yes," replied Chadwick.

"See any Germans?"

"Just them," said Chadwick, pointing at the machinegun crews.

"Barltrop, take Mills and Redington. There's at least two subs docked on this side of the pier. The dry dock is on the other side. The others are with me."

Barltop nodded, then he and his men took off at a run toward the first submarine.

Saunders grabbed Chadwick by the shoulder and gave him quick instructions.

Chadwick nodded, then ran off toward his new task.

Saunders led his men to the other side of the pier. Looking east, he could see the massive topless tubes, the dry docks. There were three submarines inside a dry dock, each to its own.

Saunders ran toward the first dry dock and, searching quickly for a way in, found an up-and-over set of stairs. He climbed three steps to the top. Connected below was a ladder leading down into the dry dock where lights were strung and shone dimly, providing just enough light so a person could see well enough to move around safely. The submarine, U-622, sat on an intricate weave of iron beams. Unknown to Saunders, this was the sub that had delivered the saboteurs to Long Island, New York in 1942. Scaffolding of iron piping and wooden planks ran all over and around it. Its keel was perhaps five feet off the floor. Saunders had been expecting to find men at work, but perhaps there was a shortage of skilled workmen—he'd heard something about that in briefings of late—and there were only enough repair crews to work during the day.

Saunders had spent time talking with Captain Kelly on the trip over asking all kinds of questions about the best places for explosives to be set to put a submarine out of commission. Seeing an enemy submarine for the first time, Saunders hoped he could get the charges where they needed to be. He'd shared the information with his squad on the boat, and they had developed contingency plans.

Saunders and his men climbed down the ladder to the bottom of the dry dock. They spread out in teams of two and quickly placed charges on the main vertical beams supporting the sub's bow. The timers were set for twenty minutes. After he was done, Saunders gave more orders. While he would enter this sub, they would move on to the next and plant charges inside that one.

Saunders climbed the ladder high enough to step off onto the scaffold's floor, and the others kept on going up. Saunders crossed the scaffolding and stepped onto the sub's deck. He ran toward a small opening in the deck about ten yards from the bow. He turned on his torch and directed its light into the guts of the sub. He clicked it off and descended the ladder he'd seen there. When his boots hit the deck below, he switched on the torch again. He was standing in the middle of the forward torpedo room, just where Kelly had said it would be. He quickly checked the bunks hanging from each bulkhead. Empty. He moved forward, careful to check where his feet were landing. To his surprise, there were four torpedoes hanging in storage racks. He briefly wondered about the wisdom of that, what with the probable welding going on just outside the hull, but shrugged it off.

Working fast, he planted charges on the business end of a torpedo. After setting the timer for eighteen minutes, he ran back to the ladder and climbed out of the sub. He closed the hatch and battened it down to help contain the force of the explosion, which might just blow the bow completely off.

On the other side of the pier, Barltrop and his men had finished with the two subs there. They ran down the pier toward the last sub in dry dock in search of Saunders and the others.

Nearly two dozen German soldiers had survived the explosion at the far end of the dock simply because they had been sleeping on the west end of the barracks, on the other side of a wall of equipment lockers. The explosion had ripped the entire front of the building off shredding it into slivers of deadly shrapnel. An *Oberleutnant* managed to get to his feet. Blood seeped from his ears and his head hurt terribly.

Other men were moving in their bunks, moaning, coming awake, but the *Oberleutnant* couldn't hear them. He stumbled to the back door, found the light switch and flipped it on. Nothing. He made his way to the weapons rack against the back wall and selected an MP40 submachinegun. At the touch of the familiar weapon, his head began to clear somewhat. He turned and quickly, in his mind anyway, went to each of the still living and got them awake enough to get to their feet. Prodding and shouting through their common near-deafness he got them into their boots and helmets, then handed out weapons and clips of ammunition.

The *Oberleutnant* led the way out the back door. He looked to the west, expecting to see his own antiaircraft cannon firing into the night sky, but it was not. He'd assumed they'd been hit by an aerial bomb. His thought processes were starting to work better now, even if he still could only hear a buzzing sound. Waving his hands to get the attention of his men, he pointed at himself, then gave the universal move out sign. He led the way down the backside of the buildings and had made it about fifty meters when he felt and saw an explosion at the farthest end of the dock. He knew it was about where the office was. He put things together rapidly, an explosion in the barracks of the defenders, then destroying pertinent and important papers for the repair of damaged submarines. This could mean only one thing: a commando raid. Their next target would be the submarines themselves.

Running faster now, he found the back door he wanted. After unlocking the door, he and the men swarmed into the armory. The *Oberleutnant* handed out six MG42s. Other men grabbed as many ammo boxes as they could carry. The *Oberleutnant* consulted his mental map, and instead of going out the way they'd come in, he headed for the front door. It would come out just ten meters south of the pier's entrance. He and his men could advance down the pier, disarming whatever bombs they found.

The commandos would have no place to run.

Chapter 15

Château d'Ainay-le-Vieil
Village of Ainay-le-Vieil, 156 miles due south of
Paris
3 July, 0145 Hours

Max Mayerhofer, the project's lead engineer, woke up for no
reason that he could immediately identify. He just knew he felt
horrible. Terrified. Had he had a nightmare? He searched his
exhausted memory, and decided it had not been a nightmare. It
must just be nervousness. No, it was more than nervous. Fearful.
Doomed, perhaps. Fate. His fate depended on the test. He
checked the clock by his bedside. It told him the test would begin
in seven hours. He rubbed his eyes with the heel of his hands,
pressing hard enough to see swirling patterns. When he pulled his
hands away, he realized they were covered in sweat. His whole
body was wet. Recognizing that he'd never get back to sleep, he
got up, toweled off, and dressed.

He closed the heavy oak door to his bedroom as he stepped
into the long, dimly lit hallway. He was still amazed by the

immensity of the château that had been commandeered for all of the project engineers. Located a little more than seven kilometers northwest of the manufacturing facility, the château had been built in the fourteenth century and owned by the same family the entire time. Until the war. What had happened to the family who most recently lived there, he didn't know, and to be truthful, didn't want to know. When Max had sought help in finding a suitable place for his men to live, he'd presented to the Waffen SS colonel in charge of the region a paper bearing Speer's signature. The colonel had promptly suggested the château and Mayerhofer saw no reason to say no to such a wonderful place.

He walked up to a door and rapped on it. He leaned close to listen, then realized he wouldn't be able to hear anything through the two-inch thick door. He knocked again, harder. A few moments later, Johann Pachter opened the door and peered out through sleepy eyes.

"Max," he said in a resigned voice.

"Come on. Get dressed. You can sleep when you're dead."

Pachter closed the door muttering something under his breath, which Mayerhofer took as instructions for himself and what he could do with something.

He walked farther down the hall and knocked on Rademacher's door, which was one down and across the hall. Rademacher opened the door and stood there fully dressed.

"Took you long enough, Max."

Mayerhofer smiled. "Johann is grumpy."

"Tell me a surprise."

"He'll be along."

"I can't wait. There better be coffee when we get there."

"There's always coffee, Fritz."

The two men waited for Pachter in the marble-floored foyer. After about five minutes, they heard a door close, followed by footsteps. Finally, Pachter came down the wide staircase.

Without a word, Mayerhofer opened the front door and led the way out. They passed a guard, who nodded in return when Mayerhofer raised a hand. When they got to the car, Mayerhofer got in the left-side driver's seat. It was a shiny, burgundy and black 1937 Citroën Traction Avant Cabrio that Mayerhofer had found in the château's multi-car garage. He had immediately fallen in love. It had a six-cylinder, seventy-six horsepower engine with front wheel drive and was a delight on the road. Mayerhofer never let anyone else drive it, to the dismay of his two partners.

Mayerhofer started the engine and put the car in gear, the clutch working smoothly. He guided the car out through the castle gate, complete with a bridge over a water-filled moat, and onto the road a quarter of a mile from the house. A little over five minutes later, the manufacturing site came into view, sitting on the northeastern side of the road. In the dark, it seemed terrifying to Mayerhofer, a gigantic hulking monstrosity that previously produced French farm equipment. Now, it produced whatever Albert Speer said it would produce. In addition to housing the project, one-fourth of the main floor was devoted to making machine parts for the Tiger tank. Mayerhofer wasn't sure what the parts were, having never seen any. He had been disinclined to ask Speer about it.

The site was surrounded by a wire fence with barbed wire on top. Two soldiers guarded the gate. Mayerhofer knew there were others walking the perimeter, some with dogs, to fend off attacks by the damnable French Resistance. After showing their papers to the guards, who had shone a bright flashlight into each of their faces and carefully compared them to the pictures on the papers, he drove on through the gate. Pulling right up to the main door, he stopped the car and shut off the engine.

The men got out and checked in with the guards at the door, once again being put in the spotlight. They wound their way through the building to the weapon room, as they'd taken to calling it. Mayerhofer was first in, and flipped on the lights. Rademacher walked straight over to a large kitchen-style counter. He lifted a half-full pot of coffee and held it to his nose.

"Ah. Perfect." He poured himself a cup, then one for each of his teammates. He put them on a metal cafeteria tray and carried them over to the other men. No need for niceties such as cream and sugar, as if they could get sugar, because they all took it black.

Mayerhofer took a sip, then sat down in front of a paper-filled desk. Pachter and Rademacher grabbed chairs from a nearby table and sat down, forming a triangle with Mayerhofer.

"Is there anything we've overlooked? Anything at all?" asked Mayerhofer.

"No," said Pachter.

"We've been over everything a hundred times. The calculations are right. The weapon is ready," said Rademacher. He glanced at Pachter, the electrical engineer, then back Mayerhofer. "I swear I've ruined two slide rules."

"I agree with that. All of the electrical components are done correctly, as is the wiring and all of the connections. There's nothing more we can do now. We must go forward with the test. There's no turning back. Not now." Pachter held his hands out, palms up and shrugged, as if to say 'that's it.'

"What about the flux compression generator?"

"What about it?" asked Pachter.

"Are you positive it will generate enough power for the electromagnetic pulse?"

"Yes, it is going to be the best transient electromagnetic device Germany has ever produced. The last one I tested yielded three million gauss, Max. That's six times greater than the weapon at Kursk. When the explosives in the tube fire, in that split second, the EMP receiver will gain ninety-nine percent of the energy. That's sixty-six times more efficient than an atomic bomb." Pachter might be an electrical engineer, but he had heavily studied physics.

Mayerhofer frowned at the mention of the atomic bomb.

Both Pachter and Rademacher said at once, "What is it?"

Mayerhofer looked away. He didn't want to be untruthful with these two men he'd worked so closely with for a year. They'd formed a bond that comes rarely to engineers and actually liked each other, in addition to respecting each other. While Mayerhofer had come from Berlin, growing up the son of a math professor, Pachter and Rademacher had come from southern Germany. Pachter had been in Munich, his hometown, in 1923 when the *Führer's* Beer Hall Putsch had failed. Pachter had been nineteen at the time. Rademacher was from near Saaldorf, a small village just five miles across the Austrian border from Salzburg. His father had been a farmer who had insisted his son work hard at school.

Mayerhofer folded his hands in his lap, his expression glum.

"A few weeks ago, our atomic bomb factory was destroyed."

"What?" asked both Pachter and Rademacher.

Mayerhofer nodded.

A long moment passed as the three men considered the ramifications of that on their project.

Rademacher broke the silence. "Do you know what happened?"

Mayerhofer looked decidedly unhappy. "I shouldn't be telling you this."

Pachter crossed his arms and said, "Too late, the horse is out of the barn. Tell us."

"You can tell no one."

"We know," said Rademacher.

"Very well. On June nineteenth, the facility experienced a catastrophic accident. At least that's what Speer thinks." Mayerhofer leaned forward conspiratorially, and so did the other two men, albeit unconsciously. Mayerhofer practically whispered, "I overheard him talking on the phone one day to the *Führer*—"

"How do you know it was the *Führer*?" asked a skeptical Pachter.

Mayerhofer sat up straight in surprise. "You are kidding. Who else shouts like that on the phone to Albert Speer?"

"I take your point. Go ahead."

"Anyway," started Mayerhofer, a little miffed at the interruption, "he was telling the *Führer* that the entire hillside had collapsed in the explosion and that it looked like a crater on the moon! Then he said there were no known survivors, and that it had been fortunate that almost all of the workers were away for the night, but the two main physicists, Herbert and Winkel were missing and presumed dead."

"Did he say when the program would start back up?" asked Pachter.

"That was the part when the *Führer* really started screaming. I could hear what *he* said as if I was standing right there."

"What did he say?" Rademacher's eyebrows were raised.

"Well, it became evident that this wasn't the first time Speer had told the *Führer* about this—I have to say I was impressed with Speer's calm—because Speer finally said something like

'As I mentioned before' and then said the bad news was that there was no more heavy water, and there wouldn't be any possibility of getting any."

"What happened to the supply from Norway?" asked Pachter.

Mayerhofer shook his head. "I don't know. Speer didn't say. So then Speer said, and these are his exact words, '*Ja, Mein Führer*, I guarantee the Pulse weapon will be ready and working on time.'"

"*Ach mien Gott*," moaned Rademacher

Mayerhofer nodded glumly. "My thoughts exactly."

"When did you overhear this?" asked a white-faced Pachter.

"It was early yesterday morning. This better work today," replied Mayerhofer.

Pachter and Rademacher nodded. Now they understood Mayerhofer's incessant questions.

Chapter 16

German submarine pens
Wilhelmshaven
3 July, 0205 Hours

Saunders was busy in his second submarine. He'd leapfrogged the one Owens and Dickinson were working on. As he was tightening the screws holding the wires to the timer, he heard muffled gunfire. It was the Germans and their damn MG42s. He finished what he was doing, then bolted up the ladder remembering at the last second to close and batten down the hatch. He ran across the scaffolding and knelt on the pier's concrete surface. At the far end of the pier, now nearly a quarter mile away, he could see the flashes of the German machineguns. They were laying down suppressing fire as other German soldiers worked their way toward his men. There would be no escape in that direction.

Suddenly, Barltrop and his two men popped up over the edge of the pier. They took cover behind a stack of supply crates and began firing. Their bullets ricocheted off the pier and some of the support columns about a hundred yards away.

Across the pier, Saunders' two men began firing.

Saunders grabbed a coiled line and hoisted it over his shoulder. He gave a piercing whistle and when his men turned to check, he waved them toward the end of the pier, no more than twenty yards away.

As his men fired one more long burst, Saunders ran for the end of the pier, where there was a railing running the width of the pier. Once there, he uncoiled the line and tied off one end on one of the vertical posts supporting the railing. He glanced over the edge into the water. There was Chadwick, right on time, with the patrol boat engines idling!

As the men arrived at the end of the pier, Saunders helped them over the railing and they each slid down the line to the waiting Chadwick. As Saunders climbed over, one leg on each side, he took a quick look back down the pier. About half way he spotted movement; a dozen or more soldiers were running full speed toward him. He fired a quick burst with this Sten and the soldiers scattered behind a bunch of crates as rounds hit the concrete at their feet. Saunders brought his other leg over and half climbed, half jumped into the boat.

Chadwick's hand hit the throttles and the boat's stern sank as the propellers bit into the water. The bow raised and she roared away from the pier. Chadwick deftly turned her into a northeasterly direction.

The boat was about fifty feet long with a mast one-quarter of the way back from the bow. The emergency sail was stowed. Saunders made his way forward to the cockpit, which was an open cabin-like affair with windows on its three sides. He stepped in beside Chadwick who glanced at him, just for moment, grinning happily.

Saunders put his hand on Chadwick's shoulder and said, "Well done, matey."

"Thanks," replied Chadwick. He checked the compass and made a slight correction with the wooden wheel. "This is a nice craft. It's been over four years since I've piloted one. Feels nice."

"Just like riding a bicycle, right?"

Chadwick laughed. "That's right."

They stood there together in companionable silence. The boat cut through the water at twenty-five knots. After a couple of minutes, Chadwick changed direction to northwest. The boat rolled on her keel smoothly and when Chadwick straightened her out she settled into a rhythm.

Behind them, the blazing dock buildings threw red and yellow reflections on their wake.

As Saunders watched the water ahead, he had a sudden, unpleasant recollection of Captain Kelly's earlier comment. "What about mines?"

Chadwick patted the instrument panel and said, "Oh, not to worry. She's all wood. No problems getting past magnetic mines."

"Oh, good."

Saunders checked his watch. Almost time. Another minute passed. Then a flash of light brightened the night. A rumbling boom hit them fifteen seconds later. Over the span of the next several minutes, more flashes, and booms muted by the increasing distance, came their way. Saunders grinned in the night air, imagining the submarines' new appearance. He also imagined a German Navy admiral shaking his fist in the morning and cursing British Commandos.

"Do you know where we are?" Saunders asked.

Chadwick looked at his sergeant with disdain. "You are bloody kidding."

Saunders shrugged. "Just wondering, you know."

Chadwick pointed ahead and left at the shoreline, now a mere half mile away. "That's where we came in." He moved his hand toward a point straight ahead. "That's where we're supposed to meet the *Sea Scout.*"

Chadwick throttled back and the boat's bow settled. As the boat slowed, Chadwick made a small adjustment to starboard. Checking their position relative to the shore, he cut back the engines completely and the boat glided to a stop.

"We're here. You'll find a metal pole with a grappling hook over on the port side."

Saunders looked befuddled.

Chadwick pointed. "Left side."

"Of course. I knew that."

"Uh huh."

Saunders left the cabin, found the pole and slid the end over the side into the water. Using his knife, he tapped out the prearranged code. He repeated this over the next several minutes. He had a bad moment once, when he wondered whether he was alerting any German U-boats to their presence. Have to wait and see.

Chadwick had left the cabin to join Saunders, as had most of the men; all except Barltrop who was busy hanging over the side, barfing up his last meal. He hadn't thought he'd need a seasickness pill after leaving the submarine.

A vertical pipe appeared in the water less than twenty yards away. It rotated and the moonlight glinted off glass.

Saunders gave Chadwick a look that was part awestruck, part proud.

The pipe began to rise. Soon, the sub was floating on the surface. Men appeared on the deck. Lines were tossed and grabbed. The patrol boat edged closer and closer.

Saunders and his men clambered aboard the sub. Chadwick stayed behind for a moment, admiring the German boat one more time. Then he climbed aboard the sub. The *Sea Scout's* sailors pushed the German boat away with long poles. When it was almost twenty yards away, Chadwick pulled a grenade from his shirt, yanked the pin, and heaved it onto the boat.

A few seconds later, the grenade exploded in a flash of fire and smoke. Almost immediately the boat began to ship water through the hole in its keel. By the time Chadwick made it down the hatch, the boat had slipped under the surface, heading to its final resting place. All that was left in the bubbling water were a few shards of wood.

Chapter 17

1 mile south of St. Sauveur
3 July, 0532 Hours

Dunn stopped his men for a rest in the center of a small forest about a tenth of a mile square. They had melted into the night after leaving the gun emplacement. After they covered about a half mile, they heard several trucks roaring south, undoubtedly full of German soldiers on their way to see what had happened with the guns or the supply depot.

The first signs of sunrise appeared, light trickling through the trees. Dunn sat cross-legged on the cool, dew dampened ground and Cross sat next to him while the others were lying on their backs. Jones and Ward kept an eye out.

Sporadic gunfire sounded from the west, too distant to tell for sure which side, or if it was both sides.

It was time to decide how to break through the *rear* of the German lines, and make it safely across the *front* of the American side. Dunn had his map open in his lap. According to the last information Dunn had, the front line ran ten miles, roughly east-west, with the part on the east a little farther north, about where the Douve River went by the east side of St. Sauveur. At that point, the line broke off to the southeast toward Carentan. The main road from La Haye to St. Sauveur ran north and south three hundred yards to their west. The two armies were about four to five hundred yards from each other. The information also said the German lines were stretched thin on the eastern side. That point was about five or six hundred yards away from Dunn. They were that close to getting through.

Getting up, Dunn folded the map and put it away. Tapping Cross on the shoulder, he made his way to the north edge of the forest. When he was still a good ten yards back from the edge, he got down and crawled the rest of the way. Cross joined him.

Dunn used his field glasses to survey the land in front of him. They were on a small hill and the terrain fell away to the northeast in the direction of the Douve River. What he saw was encouraging. Several more hedgerows ran off in north-south and east-west patterns. The north-south one ran straight into a grove of trees that appeared to be about fifty yards wide. Dunn estimated it was four hundred yards away. That would put them right on top of the German line. He scanned left and then right, pausing at different spots, then moving on.

Dunn handed the glasses to Cross and nodded toward the woods ahead. "That's where we're going."

Cross took the glasses and examined the woods. Then he scanned west. He fiddled with the focus dial. "I see about five men one hundred yards on the west. They're moving north through some trees." Seeing no threat there, he scanned back eastwards, going past the grove of trees.

"Got a pair of men dug in hundred and fifty yards east of the grove." He paused a moment, then continued, "Looks like they've got an MG42. That's good. Won't be able to turn on us as quickly as they would with rifles."

"Yep, I saw them, and that's what I thought, too."

Cross continued his sweep east. "Got another pair. One hundred fifty yards farther east, close to the river. They're definitely thin there. I can see the river bend to the east there." He handed the glasses back to Dunn and said, "Want to go straight in behind the two closest to the grove? Go up along the east hedgerow?"

"Yep. Schneider and Morris can take them out. We'll follow this tree line until we hit that hedgerow. I'll meet you there." Dunn gave Cross a few more instructions.

"Okay, got it."

Cross rose to a crouch and ran back to retrieve the rest of the squad, where he passed on Dunn's instructions for Schneider and Morris. Dunn got to his feet and started walking east, staying well back from the edge of the tree line. A few minutes later, Dunn met the squad near the point he and Cross had discussed.

Dunn worked his way to the tree line and lifted his field glasses. He checked his view left to right, seeing nothing to be concerned about. He found the two German soldiers still in the same place.

The hedgerow they were about to follow took off to the northeast, running straight and true between two and three hundred yards. Then it veered to the northwest, making almost a ninety degree corner, then ended up where the two Germans were situated. The bad news was that the field the hedgerow bordered was nearly a hundred yards wide, and devoid of cover. They'd have to try to blend in with the vegetation and get a little good luck.

Dunn looked over his shoulder at his men. Their still-blackened faces stared back at him, calm, determined. Even the new boys looked okay. He checked his watch: 0540 hours.

"Let's go, men."

They stepped out of the woods and ran toward the first corner of the hedgerow. Instead of stopping periodically to check for the enemy, they just kept going. When they reached the corner, Dunn checked his watch again and thought, *Good time, less than three minutes. Not Olympic time, but pretty good for soldiers.*

Pointing at Schneider and Morris, he motioned them to the front of the line, putting himself third behind them. Cross took the last spot. Dunn tapped Morris, who in turn tapped Schneider.

Schneider started off at a slower jog, following Dunn's instructions. Just before the squad got to the point where they could see their target, Schneider stopped. He crept forward until he could see around the hedgerow. The German soldiers were still there, facing the other way. Schneider turned slightly, looked over his shoulder at Morris and nodded. Schneider turned and moved out at a slow walk, bent over, blending in, he hoped. Morris followed right behind him.

Dunn moved up to the place where Schneider had been and dropped to one knee.

As Schneider and Morris moved, they focused on their boot fall, making sure that the spot where the boot was going to come down was clear of sticks. They also used exaggerated heel-toe steps to minimize scuffling across the dirt and making a sound. They eventually covered half the distance, but it was slow going, almost brutal because of the attention it required.

Schneider could now see the two soldiers clearly, their gray uniforms blending in with their surroundings. He motioned with one hand for Morris to come up beside him. Schneider felt they needed to get within twenty yards to make the shot.

Not far now.

One of the soldiers made as if to turn and pick something up on his right side, then evidently changed his mind.

Schneider and Morris crept closer.

The soldier nudged his compatriot and pointed to their left. The men laughed and Schneider heard one say, "*Abendessen.*" Dinner.

A four-point deer broke out of the shrubbery and bounded in front of them.

The gunner lined up a shot and fired a short burst. The deer's head exploded in a cloud of red mist and it collapsed.

Knowing the men's hearing would be compromised, Schneider ran forward. Morris was right beside him.

Ten yards. Both men raised their suppressed Stens and fired three times into the backs of the enemy.

Both German soldiers dropped. Just like the deer.

Schneider ran the rest of the way and jumped in the foxhole. He quickly checked the men, and they were both quite dead. He waved a hand.

Dunn said, "Time to go gents." The squad ran toward Schneider and Morris. Dunn had no idea why the Germans had fired their weapon and had some concerns about it raising someone's curiosity, some officer who might be moving up and down the sparse line. Knowing that time was probably not on their side, he sped up.

As soon as he joined Schneider and Morris, Morris grinned and picked up the MG42, holding it on his hip ready to fire.

Dunn grinned back. "Good job, fellas." To Morris he said, "You really think you can shoot that thing?"

"Well, of course, Sarge. Never met a weapon I didn't like."

Dunn took stock of their situation. Now came the dicey part. They'd created a wider opening to slip through, but waiting at the other end were Americans with M1s and .50 caliber Browning machineguns. He lifted his faithful field glasses and examined what was in front of him. Scanning back and forth, he spotted three groups of two men each at three hundred yards out on the American line. The middle group had a .50 caliber Browning. Focusing directly to his east, he searched for and found the other pair of German soldiers he and Cross had seen down near the river. Searching to their south along the river, he found another group in the crook of the river bend.

He lowered the glasses, thinking. Getting back to the American side could be accomplished as well as disrupting the German defense and creating some havoc and confusion. He realized he now had an opportunity here to make a difference on the line. Not wasting any time on the pros and cons, he decided his squad had to act. Now.

He gathered the men around him and laid out his plan quickly and precisely. When he was finished, he asked, "Any questions?"

The men shook their heads.

"Let's go."

Dunn led the entire squad east along the tree line. When they hit about a hundred yards, they broke out of the trees on the south side. Morris and Schneider set up the MG42 in a few seconds. Schneider acted as the ammo feeder. Morris swiveled the evil looking barrel toward the Germans at the bend in the river. He had just enough elevation for the shot. Dunn and the rest of the men aimed their Stens at the enemy soldiers only fifty yards to their east.

"Fire," said Dunn, just loud enough.

The MG42 buzzed and the Stens made pfft sounds. The enemy soldiers crumpled.

Dunn ordered, "Red canisters."

Cross and Ward pulled the pins on the red smoke canisters and tossed them toward the closest dead Germans. A few seconds later, red smoke became a thick roiling cloud.

Dunn pulled a white handkerchief from his pocket. He stepped into the tree line, then broke into the open space between the lines. Holding the white flag high and waving it he advanced quickly, but not at a run. Wouldn't do to make someone think they were being attacked. He glanced over his shoulder and saw with satisfaction that his men were in line abreast right behind him. Dunn headed directly toward the American .50 caliber, hoping he wouldn't feel one of those hitting him. When he hit a hundred yards away, he could tell that he had the attention of the machinegun crew. One was raised up peering through field glasses.

The American lowered the glasses and put something to his mouth. Two crisp whistle blasts pierced the morning air. Then he stood up and started wind milling one arm, indicating to Dunn to hurry up.

Dunn broke into a run and soon he and his men arrived at the American line.

Dunn spoke to the soldier, a corporal, who had whistled, "Thanks for the assist."

"You're welcome." The corporal looked around at Dunn's men with a puzzled expression. "Where the hell did you guys come from?"

"Long story. We've busted the German line from the river to," Dunn turned and pointed, "that spot where there was an MG42. Get us to your platoon sergeant. We've got a chance to force the issue here and maybe roll up their right flank."

The corporal nodded and jumped out of the foxhole. He took off at a run and Dunn and his men followed.

After traveling less than one hundred yards, Dunn spotted a master sergeant headed their way, an M1 in his hands.

The master sergeant stopped a few feet from Dunn and gave him a once over. He noted the Rangers patch on Dunn's shoulder and lifted an eyebrow.

Dunn didn't waste any time with niceties. "I'm Tom Dunn. We're back from a mission, but I wanted to tell you we knocked out three MG42 gun emplacements along their line as far as the river. If you can get a couple of platoons going, you can take ground and start rolling up their right flank. And you have to act quickly. They'll try to fill those holes fast."

The master sergeant glanced at his corporal, who nodded vigorously. "Saw them take out two right in front of us. Laid down red smoke to alert us and then came across the open ground."

The master sergeant was a quick study and realized this was a golden opportunity. "Okay, Sergeant Dunn, follow me back to Battalion."

When they reached Battalion headquarters, nothing more than a grouping of tents with their sides rolled up, Dunn was introduced to a major, the S2 Intelligence officer. Dunn quickly related the events and the major, although skeptical, drew Dunn over to a map of the area. Dunn showed the major where the machinegun emplacements had been.

The major listened carefully and with a critical ear. At the end, he said to Dunn, "Well done, Sergeant. Some other day, you'll have to fill us in on what you were doing around here." He started to dismiss Dunn, but Dunn interrupted him.

"Sir?"

"Yes?"

"Our mission was a raid on the German Eighty-fourth Division's headquarters in La Haye. We were able to remove a few satchel's worth of documents, including maps. We need to get this material to the Seventh Corps' headquarters at Cherbourg. Forthwith."

"You broke into a divisional headquarters and got away with their papers?"

"Yes, sir."

The major frowned. "Well, aren't they going to notice they're gone?"

"No, sir. We left quite a few packages of plastic explosives. Last we saw, the entire building was engulfed. I imagine they'll assume it was a direct hit from some bombers we had flying in as a diversion."

"I'd like to see these papers, Sergeant." The major held out a hand. His expression was one of someone who saw gold and was about to get rich.

Dunn shook his head. "With apologies, sir, I have orders to get them to General Collins."

The major straightened stiffly. "Sergeant, I'm ordering you to hand those papers over to me." He jerked his hand expectantly and wiggled his fingers in a 'come on' gesture for emphasis.

Dunn was losing patience. He didn't have time to deal with a guy trying to get a leg up on the divisional ladder. Dunn shook head again. "No, sir. I cannot hand them over to you—"

"Master Sergeant, take this man into custody."

The master sergeant put a hand on the Colt .45 sidearm resting on his right hip, but hesitated. He didn't want to be known as the man who'd arrested a Ranger.

Dunn took advantage of the moment. He held up his hand in a stop gesture. With the other, he opened a shirt pocket and withdrew a piece of paper. He unfolded it and was about put it into the major's hand when the man snatched it away.

He read it quickly, it was a short note, one sentence, but when he got to the bottom and saw who had signed it, his face blanched. He knew the signature and note were real; he'd seen the letter that Eisenhower had distributed to all the men just before they left for Normandy on 6 June.

"Oh shit," he said. He glanced up at Dunn's implacable face, then back at the note again as if to confirm what he thought it said. He gathered himself and handed the note back to Dunn. Then he looked at the master sergeant and said, "Sergeant, forget the last order. Give Sergeant Dunn whatever he wants." Then he looked at Dunn, practically with awe in his eyes. "I don't know what you've done to earn this kind of note, but it must have been something extraordinary."

"Not really, sir, just doing my job."

The major nodded. "Uh huh. Right. Best of luck." He extended his hand and Dunn took it. With that, he dismissed Dunn and turned to the man operating the field telephone. He had several calls to make.

Once outside the tent, the master sergeant offered his hand and said, "Bill Woodsley. Thanks for the help today."

Dunn took the hand and replied, "Glad to do it."

"Why didn't you just wiggle your way through the line. Quiet like."

"Ah, no, we couldn't just do that."

"Thought as much when I saw your Ranger's patch. Achnacarry House, huh?"

"Yep, last year."

The two men walked away from the tent. After only a few steps, Woodsley said, "I'll get you some transportation to Cherbourg."

"Thanks."

A few steps later the master sergeant asked, "What kind of note is that?"

Dunn grinned. "That was my 'get out of jail' card." He handed it over to Woodsley, who stopped in his tracks after he read it.

"Holy shit!" He gave it back. "Did you really blow up the Germans' division headquarters?"

"Yep."

"Holy shit."

Dunn just smiled.

Chapter 18

"I'm sorry about your men, Sergeant Saunders," said Captain Kelly, his expression compassionate.

"Thank you, sir. They were good men."

The two men were in the captain's meager quarters, a room if you could call it that, with a bunk and a half desk near the head of the bunk. Kelly sat on the bunk with his back to the bulkhead, while Saunders sat on the flimsy chair by the desk. A single bare bulb stuck out from a socket in the wall, just above their heads.

"Of course. I know it's hard losing men." Kelly had seen several crewmates killed while in action on the destroyer *HMS Sardonyx*.

"That it is."

"Otherwise successful?"

"Blew up five out of six subs, their main office, an electrical generator building, and their barracks, though we didn't get all of the enemy soldiers. Had a little firefight at the end."

"That was a piece of good luck having someone on your squad who could helm your getaway boat."

Saunders smiled for the first time since boarding. "Not luck, sir. I was counting on there being a boat of some kind somewhere at the dock. I already knew Chadwick could drive it. Or whatever you call it."

Kelly smiled.

Saunders continued, "It was part of the master plan. Although we found something else along the way that's troubling me."

"What was it?"

Saunders related coming across the American-like city.

Kelly frowned as he thought about what Saunders had just told him. Finally, he said, "Well, I'm sure I don't know what to make of that. I take it you're going to send it up the chain?"

"Aye, I—" Saunders stopped his expression changing to a thoughtful one.

Kelly waited patiently.

Saunders' thoughts kept coming back to the facility. What were the Germans doing there? Why create an American city? Suddenly it hit him.

"Captain?"

Kelly had watched Saunders for a couple of minutes and was interested in the way the commando had seemed to mentally disappear into some problem. The captain looked at Saunders expectantly.

"Did you ever hear about the Germans landing a crew of saboteurs in New York?"

Kelly nodded. "Heard about it some time last year. Don't remember exactly when. Seems the landing was the year before."

"Aye. That's right. Summer of forty-two. Supposedly, the FBI tracked them all down, but the trial was never publicized. Don't really know what happened to them. Point is, they were sent on a mission to blend in and travel around the United States blowing up stuff like electric power plants and war effort factories."

"Yes, I remember that. Everyone at home was worried the Nazis would try it in England, too."

"True." Saunders paused to tap a finger on the table, as if

pointing at something there. "I think the Germans are up to it again, but with a sophisticated training facility, the site we saw. Do you know how they were caught?"

The captain shook his head.

"One of the morons decided he could become an American hero by turning in the rest of his crew. Tried to make a deal with J. Edgar Hoover himself. Evidently, it didn't quite work out the way the bloody fool thought it would and he was arrested and jailed with the others.

"Anyway, the point is, they might have succeeded if he hadn't done what he did. I'm sure the Germans have learned from that lesson. This is a training facility and is probably where only the best and brightest, and especially the most loyal Germans get sent."

Kelly, who was clearly a smart man and realized where Saunders was going, said, "Uh oh."

"Aye, 'uh oh.' We have to go back and take them out."

Kelly shook his head. "You're two men down, Sergeant."

Saunders merely stared back at the captain calmly.

"Bloody hell! No! I am not sending any of my crew on a foolhardy mission." He slammed a hand down on the desk. "You don't even have a plan. You can't just walk in there."

Saunders smiled and said, "Yes, I do have a plan. Captain, this is important. We can't wait. Now that we've done damage at the sub pens, the Germans will be thinking about getting things rolling. They'll figure we might come back in a day or so. They'll likely either move up their timetable or move the men at the training facility somewhere else."

"We could radio in and get a bombing run on it."

"You know how long it takes to get the brass off their ass on something like this. It'll be too late."

"The Germans are going to be all over the place looking for you."

"No, they know we took off in that patrol boat. When they see the wreckage floating around, they'll assume, correctly, that we got on a sub, but then assume, incorrectly, that we're long gone. They'll call off the dogs and get to work fixing what we blew up. Not to mention, strengthening the security around the pens.

"You have to trust me, Captain. I'm really good at this."

The captain sat back. The man in front of him, with his red hair and handlebar moustache, his face still blackened, had bright blue eyes that seemed to blaze with determination. His expression had turned fierce. At that moment the captain knew. The sergeant had been telling the truth. He *was* good at this. He had to be to have successfully attacked the German sub pens in the first place. And escape.

Kelly realized he'd already made the decision and he saw that Saunders knew it, too.

"Okay, Saunders. I'll commit to this."

Saunders grinned. "That's the spirit, Captain." His grin widened. "There's one more thing."

"Of course there is."

"We ran through our supply of explosives."

"Well, we don't have any plastic aboard."

"Oh, I know that, sir. But you *do* have explosives."

"Oh cor blimey." Kelly looked up at the ceiling for help. After a moment, and apparently disappointed at finding none, shook his head. "Sergeant, you can't be serious."

"I sure am. How many pounds of TNT is in one of your fish? Got to be over five hundred, right?"

A nod from the captain. "Seven hundred and fifty, actually."

"Well there you go. That's fifteen, fifty pound satchel charges."

The captain thought for a minute, calculating how long it would take to disarm, open, and extract the explosives. It wasn't that much time. Instead of answering Saunders, he got up, stepped over to the wall, then slipped the intercom microphone off its holder. Clicking the button, he spoke firmly, the way navy captains do. "This is the captain. Reverse course to a heading of one-eight-zero. One-third ahead after the turn. Chief of the boat, meet me in the forward torpedo room."

The speaker overhead answered, "Aye, Aye, Captain. Changing course to a heading of one-eight-zero. One-third ahead after the turn. The chief says he'll meet you straight away."

"Very good." Kelly turned back to Saunders and said, "Well, let's get to work."

Saunders stood up and said, "Aye, aye, sir."

Chapter 19

Pulse Weapon Factory
4 miles southeast of the Village of Ainay-le-Vieil
3 July, 0715 Hours

The three scientists had worked for five and a half hours, the only breaks were to refill either the coffee cups or the coffee maker, or to empty bursting bladders.

Papers were strewn all across the work table. To someone just walking in it would have looked like total chaos, but all three men knew where everything was and could lay their hands on anything in a few seconds.

The shiny weapon sat on the far side of the room, still on its rubber-tired, mobile support rack. Its four-plus meter length was necessary to hold the two in-serial flux compression generators, which were two meters long together. The pulse discharge tube was 1.3 meters. All in all, just the internal equipment was 3.3 meters. Add to that the bomb's shell casing for flight and the length grew to 4.4 meters, only 2.8 meters shorter than a torpedo. At the tail end were four stabilizer fins, and a tiny propeller. With a one meter diameter at it thickest point, it somehow seemed to be graceful and ugly at the same time.

Much thought had gone into the construction of the weapon. An additional ballistic problem had to be solved; this was not a drop and hope for the best bomb. It had to be dropped on a specific flight path, which was why the Heinkel 177 Greif was being used again; it had been originally designed to perform like a dive bomber, not the steep, screaming dive of the Junkers Stuka, but a much shallower dive with a twenty degree nose-down attitude. It would be like the bombardier was playing darts from five thousand meters with a one thousand kilogram dart.

Inside the *Elektromagnetischen Impuls Waffe*, Electro-magnetic Impulse Weapon, each flux generator had high explosives packed inside an aluminum tube. The tubes acted as armatures passing through a tightly wound helix of copper wiring, the stator. Attached to the stator was a capacitor. A switch, connecting this capacitor to the propeller, turned on and completed the circuit when the propeller reached fifty revolutions per minute as it flew through the air. This created the weapon's powerful magnetic field.

At the tail end of each armature was a detonator. When fired at the specified altitude, the detonator ignited the explosive, which sped forward through the helix at over eight thousand meters per second, creating a wave. The final and crucial step was as the wave raced through the helix, it short circuited the stator and created the electromagnetic pulse, which also moved at over eight thousand meters per second. Then it entered the *second* generator and repeated the process, boosting the speed and magnitude of the pulse.

Rademacher had solved the problem of the weapon's non-directional force that had been discharged over the German and Russian soldiers near Kursk. The answer came to him one night after dinner while walking around the outside of the castle, along the outer edge of the water-filled moat, thinking about his family and whether they were safe. He had built the Pulse discharge tube out of rolled lead two millimeters thick and which only weighed a little over one hundred kilograms. This acted the same way the diameter of a shotgun barrel focused the pellets and the length determined the dispersal pattern.

Mayerhofer stepped back from the table and ran his hands through his hair, then rubbed his eyes. He walked back to his desk and picked up the phone. When someone answered, he gave quick, but precise instructions, and hung up.

"The truck will be here any time. Let's open the door."

The men moved over by a double-door and Mayerhofer opened both sides, hooking them to the wall in a long hallway outside their room to prop them open. A moment later, he heard the rumble of a large truck outside the building.

Pachter jogged down to the double-doors leading to the outside of the building and opened them. The door exited onto a loading dock. The sudden bright sunlight made him wince and blink until his eyes adjusted. The truck was already backing into position. It was the standard Mercedes truck, the kind with a canvas top most often used to transport men and supplies. Except this one's canvas had been removed and the framework that would have supported it was gone. Ten men were sitting in the back of the truck, with MP40 submachineguns across their laps, armed security arranged by Speer.

The truck stopped and a man jumped down from the passenger side of the cab, and walked toward the dock. He crossed behind the truck and stepped to the side where the driver could see him in the mirror.

The man gave the 'come on back' motion with the fingers on his left hand and the truck edged closer to the dock. When the truck was about a half meter away, the man held his hands up together spaced apart to indicate the distance yet to go. He gradually closed the gap between his hands until his hands touched and the truck bumper kissed the rubber bumpers on the dock. The driver shut off the engine and climbed out.

Mayerhofer and Rademacher had joined Pachter on the dock, blinking their own reaction to the sunlight.

The driver, a sergeant, jumped up onto the dock and approached the engineers. Mayerhofer lifted a hand to signify he was in charge and the driver stepped in front of him.

"We're here to take the, ah, er, package, to the airfield."

"Very well. This way."

It took four soldiers fifteen minutes to get the Pulse weapon loaded onto the truck. They used the mobile rack with a heavy-duty block and tackle hoist connected to the roof over the dock to swing it aboard. They guided the weapon slowly and carefully onto its transport rack, which was in turn welded, not just to the floor of the cargo bay, but also through the floor to the truck's iron frame. The men secured the weapon on the rack with chains and padlocks.

Mayerhofer stepped onto the truck and double-checked each chain and lock. He gave a satisfied nod to the sergeant.

"You may cover it."

The last meter of the weapon stuck out the rear of the truck, so the men draped and secured a black tarp over the entire weapon, hiding it completely.

Mayerhofer glanced up at the sky, which was gaining its deeper blue, shifting from the pale blue of sunrise. What clouds there were appeared to be quite high and sparse enough not to interfere with today's test. He looked at the road in front of the truck. Two open-backed trucks full of armed soldiers waited about fifty meters away. One would lead. Mayerhofer and his two engineers would travel in the Citroën right behind the weapon's truck and the other truckload of soldiers would take up the rear.

A month ago, when Speer had first told Mayerhofer about the soldiers, insisting they accompany the weapon, Mayerhofer had been skeptical, after all, the distance to the airfield was only five kilometers. What could happen? Then startling rumors began surfacing about the French Resistance blowing up trucks and trains all over the area. Mayerhofer changed his mind. Now he worried about whether they had enough soldiers.

Chapter 20

Miller loved his P-51 Mustang, but he thought he could come to love the Horten 18 almost as much. He was itching to get her back in the air, to feel her enormous power—and he was fine thinking of the German plane as a she—six Junkers 004B jet engines. The one that had caught fire on the trip out of Germany had been repaired by the mechanics from Northrop, who had worked around the clock for ten days. They'd had to machine a couple of new parts, including the coupling that had broken loose and sprayed jet fuel all over the superheated engine.

She sat in the hanger sporting a new paint job to cover up the German mottled battle gray and the Nazi insignias that Miller so hated. Her underside was a light blue and her top the same green as on a B-17. The U.S. Army Air Force's star was on her wings. She'd been assigned her own serial number, 44-24485j, a tribute to the famous *Memphis Belle*, 41-24485, which had been one of the first B-17s to complete twenty-five missions with her crew intact.

Miller stood just outside the hanger's door, checking the sky. It was clear, with a few clouds. The sound of powerful engines drew his attention to the end of the runway where a flight of four P-51s was rising into the sky to the south, their Merlin inline engines screaming, sounding like no other plane in the world.

Miller sighed. *That's okay, I'm going up in the Horten today. That'll make up for it.* He was about to go inside and set things in motion to get the Horten prepped for flight, when his eye caught movement not too far away. A jeep was tearing his way carrying three men, the driver and Miller's copilot, and the navigator, who was sitting in the back seat. Miller checked his watch, glad to see that the men were right on time.

The two men hopped out of the jeep and jogged over to Miller. Both were wearing the same expression of anticipation and excitement that Miller understood perfectly well. The men all exchanged salutes.

The men, like Miller, were already in their flight gear. Captain Andy Butler, the copilot came highly recommended from another P-51 squadron by way of Miller's boss, Colonel Nelson. Butler was an ace with five air-to-air kills and a couple of ground targets destroyed as well. Like Miller, Butler had better than perfect vision at 20/10 and was always the first man in his squadron to spot enemy planes. Always. He and his wingman were said to work in such great concert that it was more like watching one man fly two Mustangs at the same time. With dark brown hair and an open, friendly face, he was often underestimated. But underneath the friendly exterior was a tough man. And that was what Miller had wanted, needed, in the first copilot for the Horten.

Miller had been forced to argue with Colonel Nelson and the engineers from Northrop because everyone except Miller wanted a bomber pilot. He'd finally lost his temper and told them that the speed difference between the Horten and a B-17 or B-24 was the same as that between a 1929 Ford Model T and the 1940 Indy 500 winning car, a Maserati. He needed someone who thought like a fighter pilot and was used to high speed maneuvers. He'd insisted that he could teach the man what he needed to know as far as understanding the complexities of the cockpit, but didn't have time to teach what he regarded as the basics of high speed flight, where to look, how to anticipate the next move, and no one could teach what had become known as a fighter pilot's sixth sense, the little burr in the head to do something *now* that saved lives. They gave in.

First Lieutenant Mike Hoffman, the navigator, who would also serve as the bombardier, did come from the Eighth Bomber Command. He had flown eighteen missions on a B-17 and had served at various times in both roles. A short, slight man at five-seven and a hundred fifty pounds, he was the antithesis to short man syndrome with a scathingly funny wit that he used often to help release the unbearable tension on the long bombing run flights. His pilot had initially tried to get the little guy to keep his mouth shut, but then soon realized two things, that Hoffman had perfectly precise timing in his use of humor, and had never used it during the moments when the entire crew had to be focused on the task at hand.

"You guys ready for this?"

"You better know it, sir," said Butler.

"Absolutely, sir," said Hoffman.

"Any questions?"

"No, sir. Just anxious to get her in the air," replied Hoffman.

"Same here," said Butler.

"Yeah, me, too. Come on, let's get this show on the road."

The three men walked into the hanger and set about getting the ground crew, already specially trained for the Horten, ready to go.

An hour later, they were.

Five jeeps pulled up outside the hanger and the occupants piled out, then walked into the hanger. The audience for the first flight had arrived. The group was made up of engineers, Colonel Nelson, a handful of photographers, one with a movie camera, a couple of other colonels that Miller didn't recognize, and a general he did, everyone did. General Jimmy Doolittle, the Eighth Air Force commander himself, had come to witness the Horten's first flight.

Nelson grabbed Miller and pulled him over to the group of officers. "General Doolittle, I'd like you to meet the man who stole this beauty from the Germans."

General Doolittle offered his hand and when Miller took it, grasped the pilot's hand with both of his own and shook vigorously. Doolittle was a little under six feet tall, with a touch of gray in his brown hair and sharp hazel eyes. He had four rows of ribbons, including the light blue one with five stars for the Medal of Honor he'd earned for his B-25 raid over Tokyo on 18 April 1942.

"Congratulations, Captain. You've done an extraordinary thing here." The general looked past Miller at the jet bomber. "Yes, an extraordinary thing." He finally let go of Miller's hand and moved closer, putting a hand on the pilot's shoulder. He deftly guided Miller toward the Horten and said, almost in a conspiratorial tone, "Tell me. What's she like?" When they reached the airplane, the general seemed to have forgotten his question. He took his hand off Miller's shoulder and ran his palm along the skin of the nose. Then he walked to the front of the port wing and, with his hands on his hips, just admired the three jet engines.

All of the photographers had broken from the pack and followed Miller and the general. Flashbulbs popped catching Doolittle's reaction, although none of the photos or moving film would make it into the public eye.

When Doolittle turned back to Miller, his face was full of delight. The sign of a man who was, and always had been, in love with airplanes, a general officer who remembered what it was like to fly. To be young again. He'd only given up flying combat missions himself the year before.

Doolittle had been caught flying missions over Europe in a B-26 Marauder even though he was risking one of the most important secrets: he was one of the select few with knowledge of the Nazi Ultra coding device and that the Allies were decoding German high command radio traffic almost instantaneously. When Eisenhower found out, he'd told Doolittle he could either fly around Europe hunting Germans or get promoted to Lieutenant General, three-stars. Doolittle grounded himself immediately and took the promotion.

The general looked at Miller expectantly, and Miller realized he hadn't forgotten the question after all.

"She's fantastic, sir. Very responsive flight control and power, too."

"I heard you weren't able to get her to top speed?"

"No, sir. I had to keep the speed down to stay with the C-47 and our Mustang escorts."

"Pity."

"Very much so."

"Is everything ready?"

"Yes, sir. Just about to take her out to the runway."

"Good luck, Captain."

"Thank you, sir."

The general returned to Colonel Nelson and the entourage left the hanger to find their front row seats.

Miller grabbed Butler and Hoffman and climbed aboard.

Once they were seated, Miller in the left chair, Butler to his right, and Hoffman in the bombardier's seat behind them, Miller gave a thumbs-up.

A small truck backed in close to the Horten's front wheel. A ground crewman jumped out and attached a tow bar to the wheel strut. He ran back to the truck cab and got in. The crew chief sat in the back of the truck, as if to keep a close eye on the bird.

The truck started moving and the Horten followed. The driver was practiced and careful, and steered through the hanger door dead center. Once clear, he turned right and followed the pavement toward the north end of the runway.

When the truck and plane arrived at the right spot, the driver stopped. The crewman got out and quickly unhooked the tow bar from the plane. After he got back in, the driver guided the truck away from the Horten toward the port side, well away from the aircraft.

Miller and Butler spent the next fifteen minutes going through the preflight checklist, a translated version of the one that Miller had used at the Horten brothers' airfield near Göttingen, Germany.

Miller glanced over at Butler. "Light 'em up, Captain."

Butler said, "Yes, sir."

Following the engine start up sequence of inboard-to-outboard, Butler flipped the buttons in pairs, carefully waiting for each pair to spin up, ignite properly, then settle into a smooth rumble.

In the back, Hoffman was changing the dials on the Norden bombsight, which Fred Laughlin, the Northrop cockpit and instrument equipment design engineer, had installed himself. Today's test flight included the dropping of one and only one practice bomb, a two-hundred-fifty pounder with no charges in it, but filled with red dyed powder. The target was on the opposite side of the runway, as far as possible from any buildings and aircraft. It was a square painted onto the grassy field using chalk similar to that found on baseball foul lines. The square was two hundred feet on a side in an attempt to match a potential German manufacturing facility. The flight path would run parallel to the runway.

Miller checked all the dials showing the engines' status. They were spot on. He looked out the window and gave the crew chief a thumbs up. The chief nodded. The truck drove off toward the hanger.

Miller got on the radio to the tower and said, "Tower, Horten 18 ready for takeoff."

"Horten 18, you are cleared for takeoff. Good flight, sir."

"Roger, and thank you. Horten 18 out."

Miller turned to Butler and grinned. He offered his hand and the two men shook. Then he lifted his hand back to Hoffman, who was also grinning.

"Okay, boys. Let's see what she can do."

Miller put his right hand on the left set of three chrome throttles and Butler put his left hand on the right set of three. Together they pushed the throttles forward part way. Then they took their feet off the brake pedals. The Horten jumped forward. The men let the bird roll straight ahead for fifty yards, then turned her left into the southerly breeze and stopped.

The Horten perched on the runway like a hawk, nose up, looking like she was already flying.

Miller and Butler pushed the throttles all the way forward and released the brakes at the same time. The Horten leapt. Within seconds she was streaking down the runway at a hundred miles an hour. The runway and the buildings flew by in a blur. The Horten accelerated, going even faster, the engines thundering.

Butler eyed the end of the runway, now just a half mile ahead.

"We do have room, right?"

"Oh yes. The last time I did this, there was a German forest at the end of the runway. We've got plenty of room, believe me!"

Butler still looked doubtful.

Miller felt the plane want to lift. "Pull her up, Butler."

Both men pulled back on the wheels. The nose gear lifted. Almost immediately, the plane shot skyward at a steep angle. Flames from her engines nearly scorched the runway. Up she went. She cleared one thousand feet quickly and continued to rocket upward, the men inside pinned to their seats, grinning.

Chapter 21

Dunn's men had fallen asleep about two minutes after the truck started moving. Dunn held off for a little longer, but finally dozed off, too. He awoke after an hour and watched the beautiful countryside slip by. The sky was partly cloudy and it was warming up.

The truck stopped frequently. There was a flood of traffic pouring out of the French port city toward the front lines and serious, unfriendly MPs were straining to direct it. Fuel trucks seemed to dominate, but there were deuce-and-a-halfs like the one Dunn and his squad were riding in, and jeeps. Some of the trucks were towing artillery pieces and, judging from their size, Dunn figured they were 105s. Then there were the Shermans. The green, sloped-front battle tank carried a 75mm gun. At times, it seemed like there were hundreds of them and the clanking sounds assailed his ears and the rumble of their powerful diesel engines seemed to come up though the ground into his chest. Dunn had to admit they were quite a sight.

Dunn spent some time going over the mission, replaying the events like a movie in his head. It seemed that every time they hit a critical point, they had done the exact right thing. However, in combat, success can turn to calamity with one small thing happening: if one of the men manning a machinegun at the artillery site had glanced their way; if the German line was more heavily manned than it was. Luck. They'd been lucky. Had he relied too much on that? He didn't know the answer.

By the time they neared their destination, the twenty-five mile trip had taken over two hours. Dunn grabbed Cross by the arm and shook it. Cross came awake immediately.

"We're there?"

"Almost."

Cross interlocked his hands, palms facing away, and pushed his hands out, stretching. He glanced at Dunn and saw something that made him ask, "What's bugging you?"

Dunn glanced around the truck to make sure everyone was still asleep. Then he said, "I probably shouldn't say this, but we were—"

"Well, don't then."

"—fucking lucky."

"Gah, I said don't say it. Now you've gone and jinxed us."

"You don't believe in that crap do you?"

Cross looked away. "Oh, ah, no course not."

"Still, so many things could have gone wrong."

"Yeah, well, they didn't. We make our own luck."

"I guess."

"We make our own luck," repeated Cross. "Don't start second guessing yourself. You're damn good at this."

Dunn shrugged and said, "Okay."

The men lapsed into silence and when the truck finally came to a stop, they moved amongst the squad waking everyone. When all were done yawning and stretching, Cross unlatched the tailgate and let it fall open. Dunn jumped down first and, while the rest hopped off, went up to the cab to give a grateful salute to the driver. "Thanks, buddy. Appreciate it."

The driver returned the salute.

Dunn looked around at the airfield. It was nearly as busy as the road had been and flights of P-47 Thunderbolts were in various stages of takeoff; some were just lifting off, others were taxiing into position, some were swarming around in the sky like angry hornets, which in a way they were. They were likely on seek and destroy missions.

As the truck drove away, Dunn looked at the building in front of him. It was a typical airfield control tower, two stories tall with a deck that wrapped all the way around the second floor for visibility in all directions. From the building's appearance, it had been built in one week and lovingly painted U.S. Army green.

While his men popped Lucky Strikes into their mouths and lit them, sending up enough smoke to worry a fire department, Dunn walked inside. The entire first floor was as he expected, as busy as the air above. About a dozen Army Air Force enlisted men and a few officers were working at desks or moving pins on a ceiling-to-floor map of Europe. Dunn knew better than to just holler for attention. Instead, he scanned the room until he found the man who was running the show, based on how many men had come up to him and asked questions in the span of a couple of minutes.

Dunn wound his way through the maze of people and desks and stopped in front of the man, another major. Dunn spoke quickly, "Major, Sergeant Dunn. I have urgent information for General Collins. Can you tell me where I can find his headquarters?"

The major gave Dunn a withering stare and asked, "Do I look I have time to give you directions?" He started to turn away, but Dunn said, "Wait, Major. I have orders. Here, read this. Please."

Dunn handed over his get out of jail card.

The major read it quickly. He glanced up at Dunn, much the same way the battalion S2 officer had, with a bit of respect and a twinge of fear, too. "Okay. Go out the door, turn right and go down the road a quarter-mile to the building marked Five Fifty-Seventh Squadron. Inside, you'll find a Sergeant Williams. I'll call him. He'll drive you out to the General's HQ."

"Excellent. Thank you, sir."

As he turned away to grab a phone, the major muttered a 'you're welcome.'

Fifteen minutes later, Dunn and his men stood outside a large command tent. Evidently, the Seventh Corps' commander didn't rate a new wooden building like the one at the airport.

The tent's flaps were folded back and, as Dunn stepped up to the two soldiers standing guard to request permission to enter, he could see inside. Major General J. Lawton Collins, the Seventh Corps Commander, was with several other officers gathered around a large table laden down with maps.

Dunn satisfactorily identified himself and was granted entry. He walked briskly up near the General, who turned expectantly to Dunn.

General Collins had been the first Seventh Corps Chief of Staff when it was formed in the western United States following the brutal Pearl Harbor attack. He'd then served at Guadalcanal from late 1942 through early 1943, where he earned the nickname "Lightning Bill." Just over forty-eight years old, he had returned from the Pacific Theater to command the Seventh Corps. An aggressive soldier, he'd been responsible for Utah Beach and then the capture of Cherbourg, and was now planning the breakout along the Cotentin Peninsula. Thus the need for the intelligence Dunn's raid had earned.

"Sergeant Dunn reporting, sir. With German papers from their La Haye commander's headquarters." He saluted, which Collins returned.

"I'll take those," said a colonel who was standing to the general's left.

Dunn handed over the three satchels, which were stacked on top of each other like books, and said, "The most important stuff is in the top one, sir."

The colonel put them on the table, opened the one Dunn had pointed out, and removed the papers. He immediately started sifting through them and found the ones with the German troop disposition.

Collins looked Dunn over for a moment. He'd been forewarned that Dunn might show up with valuable intelligence. At the time, he had thought little of it, but here he was right in front of him.

"Your operation go okay? Any losses?"

"It went well, sir. No losses."

"I take it you dropped in, stole the papers, then ran back through enemy lines?"

"Essentially, that's correct sir."

"Did you examine the papers?"

"Yes, sir. One of my men is fluent in German. They are weakest along the line that runs from St. Sauveur to Caen, with few reserves along the line running through La Haye to Lessay."

Collins glanced at the Intelligence officer, who nodded.

"Very good, Sergeant. Colonel Hendrick agrees. You look a little worn. Can we offer you some hots 'n' cots for the day?"

Dunn smiled and nodded. "That would be quite good for the men, sir."

Collins smiled in return. "I forget who your commanding officer is?"

"Colonel Mark Kenton, sir. Camp Barton Stacey."

"Yes. Very good." Collins called out, "John?"

John Baker appeared at the General's side immediately, seemingly out of nowhere. Yet another colonel. "Yes, sir?"

"Arrange for hots 'n' cots for Sergeant Dunn and his men."

"Yes, sir."

Collins extended his hand and Dunn shook it, then saluted.

Collins said, "Good job, Sergeant. Good luck."

"Thank you, sir."

Colonel Baker took Dunn by the arm and said, "Right this way, Sergeant. We'll get you and your men set up not far from here. How many men?"

"Ten of us, sir."

"Very good."

Dunn turned away to smile at himself. There had been a lot of 'very goods' in this tent.

Chapter 22

German airfield
Near Ainay-le-Vieil
3 July, 0745 Hours

The airfield was in fair shape, as far as Pachter could tell. The grass runway didn't have any bomb craters in it and both buildings were still standing. The building next to which he and Rademacher had been standing while Mayerhofer had been running around with his hands in the air, was the repair hanger. Rademacher and he had been like kids in a toy store when they discovered all the goodies inside the building, hand tools, lathes, electrical equipment. The chief mechanic who showed them around smiled as they had to touch everything in sight. After a few minutes of joyful mechanic-to-mechanic conversation with the chief they'd both sighed, then went back out to watch the goings on.

Pachter thought Mayerhofer was like a wild lioness protecting her cubs from an evil death the way he'd run around yelling instructions to the soldiers moving the Pulse weapon from the truck to the bomb dolly, which was identical to the one at the factory, then into the Heinkel's bomb bay. Only when it was clear that the weapon was properly secured in the airplane did Mayerhofer calm down.

Pachter checked his watch and realized it had taken quite awhile to get the weapon into the plane, nearly twenty minutes, due to Mayerhofer's slowing things down to achieve perfection. Pachter respected Mayerhofer. However, it was in spite of the man's incessant doubting and questioning of both Rademacher and himself, as well as all of the technicians who'd worked on the weapon. Pachter knew Mayerhofer was only ensuring the project would not fail, and was, by extension, protecting the lives of those working on it.

Mayerhofer rejoined the two engineers, his face flushed from the exertion and excitement.

"Max, for heaven's sake, take a breath before you faint."

Mayerhofer gave Pachter a look with shining eyes. Perhaps too shiny, thought Pachter.

"I'm fine, Johann."

"So you say," but then Pachter decided to drop it. Changing course he asked, "You were able to secure the vehicles?"

"Yes, we got what we asked for. Speer took care of it. There's a pair of Mark Seven tanks, a truck, a battery powered radio set, and the men."

Rademacher and Pachter both suddenly looked ill and they glanced at each other.

Pachter looked down at his shoes. He was older than Rademacher by five years and sometimes felt like the older brother. That included feeling protective over his friend and coworker. He'd stood up for him several times over the past year when Mayerhofer went off on one of his now famous rants when something Rademacher was working on hadn't been finished on time or perhaps wasn't quite what the boss expected. Each time, it had merely been a case of Mayerhofer overreacting to unexpected news. He was far more meticulous than the average, but famously detail-oriented, German and despised being surprised.

Pachter glanced at Rademacher again and knew he had to at least say what they were both thinking.

"Max? Why must we use human test subjects?"

Mayerhofer sighed, as if a child had asked a question the parent didn't want to bother answering.

"We have no choice in the matter. No more than we would in any experiment that required validation. We need those one hundred and fifty men so we can graph the results of the weapon's discharge. You know this, Johann. There's no other way to know whether our directional-force mechanism works properly. We must have enough bodies to examine afterwards."

Pachter shook his head.

"What's the matter, Johann?" asked Mayerhofer.

"I was just wondering who the men are, that's all. And why we can't use animals, cows or horses, instead."

Mayerhofer frowned his displeasure at being asked these questions. "I see. I don't know for sure. They could be communists or Jews, so what does it matter? They're enemies of the Fatherland and they will finally serve a purpose, a purpose of our choosing. As for animals, use your head, Johann! Cows are for eating and horses are for the German army to pull cannon and supplies! They are both far too valuable for us to kill in an experimental test."

Pachter averted his gaze. He was sorry he had said anything. He attempted to put those kind of questions out of his head. Looking back at his boss and friend, he said, "You're right, of course. Forget I said anything." He managed to force a smile.

Mayerhofer seemed to accept Pachter's comments as he put a hand on the man's shoulder. "That's good, Johann. Yes. All is forgotten. Come. Time to see our work take flight."

Mayerhofer led the way to the edge of the runway, putting them about forty meters from the Heinkel. They stood still and silent. They could see the pilot's head move as he went about his preflight checklist with his copilot. A few moments later, the port engine coughed to life, followed by the starboard engine. Soon, both engines were roaring. The bulbous-nosed bomber began to roll forward, picking up speed. Halfway down the airstrip, the tail lifted off the ground and then the plane soared skyward. The plane would circle the target until given instructions to release the weapon.

Two Fw-190s, that were trailing the Heinkel, took off and

caught up with the bomber.

Mayerhofer then led his men to the Citroën. The drive to the target area would take mere minutes, even on France's excuses for roads. Loaded in the trunk were several cameras, including two for moving pictures.

Mayerhofer put the car in gear and floored the gas pedal. The tires shrieked and the car leapt forward.

Near the target
3 July, 0801 Hours

Mayerhofer and his teammates had worked fast, carrying the cameras on their backs as they climbed the switchback-style stairs to the top of the observation tower, twenty meters in the air. The tower had been ordered by Mayerhofer and built a few weeks ago in a flurry of activity. No questions asked. No one dared ask where Albert Speer and Hitler's special weapons division were concerned. It didn't pay off.

As soon as the men reached the top, they set about preparing the equipment with which they would record what they hoped would be history. The top of the tower was just a simple deck surrounded by a safety railing. The whole thing was only five meters by five meters. From their vantage point they could clearly see the killing zone about two kilometers away; they were viewing it side-on. The target was a half kilometer by one and a half. The target field was a combination of several large open spaces, mostly empty pastures, and it was nearly perfectly level, with a slight, nearly imperceptible, slope toward the north. The long side of the target ran north-south.

While Pachter and Rademacher set up the movie cameras, Mayerhofer looked through a powerful, previously-mounted telescope at the target. Just as he'd requested, there were about one hundred men standing or sitting on the field at one hundred meter intervals. He focused on a captured Russian T-34 tank, whose turret had been painted red and put in the exact center of the field, the bombardier's target. The plane would fly from south to north. Several other tanks were positioned north of the center line. Mayerhofer knew each had four men inside to replicate a full crew.

Now he zoomed in on a man near the closest edge. The man wore some sort of vertically striped clothing. Mayerhofer knew it was the concentration camp garb. He was standing, but just barely. His arms hung motionless at his sides and his head drooped, chin nearly on his chest. His eyes appeared to be closed. A yellow star was stitched sloppily to his breast. Mayerhofer moved on to another one and saw the same.

He didn't know what the men had been told to ensure they would remain where they were placed, and didn't care so long as they did. Losing interest, he dialed back the zoom and scanned the entire target. All seemed in order.

Stepping back from the telescope, he looked upward. He could hear the airplanes and found them quickly. They were flying a race-track pattern around the target, the men.

Pachter said, "Max, we are ready."

"Good."

Mayerhofer knelt and opened a radio set, which he switched on. It was preset to the pilot's frequency. Speaking quickly and loudly, he gave the pilot the go-ahead code word and received the correct response. Looking up, he watched as the Focke-Wulfs peeled off and sped away to take up station several kilometers south. The Heinkel was on a northbound track and the pilot dipped her port wing to come around to a southerly heading.

Mayerhofer joined Rademacher and Pachter, who were each manning a movie camera. Rademacher's responsibility was to follow the bomber in, then once the bomb was free, to follow it all the way to its ignition point, where it should then disintegrate, then focus on the center tank. Pachter would also focus on the center tank, with the lens zoomed out to take in the entire fifteen hundred meters. Even though the men appeared as elongated dots at that range, it was hoped the film would be able to clearly show those who fell and those who were still standing, hopefully in the expected pattern. Mayerhofer would be watching through the telescope.

The Heinkel made another wide turn back to the north and bore through the air on the exact path that had been drawn for him, and that he'd practiced many times in the previous weeks. The dummy bombs had all fallen on the plywood tank practice target. Using a modified dive-bomber tactic, the pilot would bring the Heinkel in at a twenty degree down angle. Then the bombardier would use a specially modified Stuvi bombsight to deliver the weapon from a height of three thousand meters.

Rademacher located the plane in the movie camera's viewfinder. He tracked it as it began its dive. Then, still south of the target field, the silver weapon fell away. The Heinkel broke right and flew east.

The weapon flew through the blue sky at a forty-five degree down angle. Far below, one hundred fifty men plus those in the three T-34 tanks unknowingly awaited their fate. As it passed two thousand meters altitude, the stubby airfoil rotated until it was at a thirty degree angle to the weapon itself and locked into place. The nose began to rise as the aerodynamics changed. When it reached a thirty degree angle to the earth it stabilized.

The weapon fell toward the center T-34, part gliding, part falling.

The Pulse weapon hit 750 meters.

Chapter 23

Hampstead Air Base
3 miles north of Andover, England
3 July, 0705 Hours, London time

Technical Sergeant Elmer Conner stared at his radar screen in the building next door to the control tower. The radar unit had been ordered to the base just a week ago, reason not given. Yesterday, Conner had gotten his orders. At the time, he'd thought it would be a breeze. Today, he knew it wasn't.

"Well?" asked his commander, a captain, who was looking over Conner's shoulder.

Conner shook his head. "Sir, there's nothing here. Nothing at all."

"That can't be. You must have missed it."

"No, sir. Nothing showed up on the screen when the plane departed. I'm picking up aircraft fifty miles out, near London, so I know the gear is working. And I know I didn't miss anything."

The captain was about blurt out another criticism, but John Dalton, one of the Northrop engineers spoke first, "Thank you,

Sergeant. You've just confirmed that the Horten is not detectable by radar."

The captain didn't like being interrupted and his face showed it. "We'll find the blasted plane when she makes her bombing run."

Dalton gave a condescending smile to the captain that Conner saw, which made him grin.

"Captain, you're more than welcome to give it a try. In fact," Dalton nudged Conner to get up, "why don't you sit at the screen?"

The captain gave Dalton a 'fuck off' look and stomped away and out the door.

Conner laughed. "Nice one, Mr. Dalton. Not many people get one over on that guy."

Dalton frowned. "I just can't stand bullies. Good luck on the next pass."

Conner laughed easily again. "I think I'm going to need it."

"That you are."

Miller banked the Horten over on her port side and looked almost straight down at London, the River Thames a thin blue ribbon snaking through the heart of the British capital. Finishing the turn back to the southwest, he leveled out. Their flight plan had been to climb to thirty thousand feet by the time they reached London, only sixty miles from Hampstead, then fall gently to twenty for the bombing run on the return flight.

When they got to the ten mile point from Hampstead, Miller and Butler pulled back on the throttles, reducing their airspeed from five hundred miles an hour, eighty percent of maximum, to two hundred forty, the best speed for bomb accuracy according to the Hortens' flight manual.

Miller checked the instrument panel for several seconds then, satisfied with all of the readings, asked, "How we doing, Mike?"

"We're right on line. I'm ready for the ship."

"Take the ship."

Hoffman flipped the autopilot on. "I have the ship."

Miller took his hands off the wheel. He watched with some

trepidation as the wheel moved, on its own, slightly left. The plane's left wing dipped slightly, then rose again as the wheel came back to center. He glanced over at Butler and gave a 'hope this works' shrug.

Butler nodded.

Hoffman bent over the bombsight and rotated a pair of dials until he centered the crosshair on the target. He had already entered values for airspeed and altitude into the calculator. Now that the target was marked for the Norden, the internal workings of the mechanical computer determined the rest: angular velocity, and range and current angles. Finally, it determined the aim and sight points, displaying them as pips. As the aircraft moved toward the aim pip, so did the sight pip.

Hoffman continued watching through the sight, making occasional changes to reposition the crosshair as it drifted off target center due to changes to airspeed or wind. All of this led to the target remaining almost perfectly still in the crosshairs.

By feel, Hoffman flipped the switch for the bomb bay doors. "Doors open."

The picture was still rock steady. All he needed to do was make sure the crosshairs didn't drift, and let the bombsight do its job. Hoffman knew the plane was covering almost four miles per minute and they were five miles from the target. He checked his watch.

"One minute, fifteen seconds," he said.

"Roger," replied Miller.

The pips grew closer and closer to each other.

He thought the cockpit was eerily quiet compared to that of the B-17 with the bomb bay doors open. In the B-17, the bomb bay was right behind the cockpit and in order to get to the back of the plane you had to walk across a steel beam only six inches wide. Not a task for the weak of heart at twenty thousand feet. In the Horten, the bomb bay was sealed off by a hatch, which would only be opened if the ordnance didn't fall away properly and needed to be 'helped,' usually done in a B-17 with a swift kick. Hoffman hoped he wouldn't have to do that.

Time ticked down.

The pips lined up and Hoffman pressed the bomb release button.

"Bomb away."

When bombers dropped their ordnance, they usually jerked upwards, but with it only being one bomb the Horten didn't even hiccup. Hoffman closed the bomb bay doors and said, "Doors closed."

"Roger."

From twenty thousand feet the bomb would take just under thirty seconds to reach the earth. Hoffman imagined he could actually see it.

Suddenly a plume of red burst into view, well into the chalk square, not dead center, perhaps a third the way in and exactly on the vertical center line.

"Yeah! A hit! Almost dead center, maybe thirty feet off!" Hoffman clapped his pilots on the shoulders. "Great job, sirs."

Miller grinned. "You, too, Hoffman."

"Ready to take the ship back?"

"Yes." Miller grasped his wheel.

"Returning ship to you." Hoffman said and turned off the autopilot.

Miller and Butler pushed the throttle back up to eighty percent and the Horten responded. Miller kept her straight, but pushed the wheel forward and she nosed over. Soon she was breaking through ten thousand feet. Miller pulled the wheel back and leveled her out.

"Handing her to you, Butler."

Butler grasped the wheel and replied, "I have the wheel."

Butler took the Horten through a series of right and left turns, as well as changing altitude, both higher and lower, and maintained a primarily southerly heading. In only four minutes, they crossed the southern coast of Britain, flying directly over the Isle of Wight, which looked plush with greenery against the blue of the English Channel.

Butler laid the Horten over on her starboard side and they wheeled around toward the north, losing altitude due to the turn.

The pilots throttled her back to two hundred fifty.

"I'll take her now," said Miller, taking the wheel.

Butler let go.

"I have her," said Miller.

Miller got the Horten on the landing path, then called on the radio, "Hampstead Tower, Horten 18 ready for landing."

"Horten 18, Tower. You are cleared for landing. Wind speed eight knots, gusting to fifteen, direction from the south."

"Roger, Tower. Horten out."

At a thousand feet, Miller said, "Landing gear."

Butler flipped the switch and they could all feel the gear lowering. After a moment, Butler said, "Green light on all gear."

"Roger. Flaps at sixty."

Butler moved a lever to the exact point. "Flaps at sixty."

The Horten lost speed immediately.

The runway was clear and they were on a perfect line, descending smoothly.

"Drop airspeed to one fifty."

Butler pulled back on the throttles and the plane slowed even more, as if someone had stepped on the brakes.

At two hundred feet, Miller picked his spot on the runway and raised the nose. The airspeed indicator dropped to one twenty-five. Perfect, thought Miller.

The main gear hit the tarmac with a little chirp. Miller let the nose drop slowly. As soon as the front tire kissed the earth, he and Butler stamped on the brakes. The ship began to slow, still rolling at one hundred miles an hour. By the time they hit the runway's halfway point she was down to highway speed, then shortly after, down to city speed. They reached the end of the runway and Miller turned her onto the curving road that would take her back onto the flight line's tarmac.

As the Horten neared the center of the air base, close to the tower, the cockpit crew saw that a crowd of maybe two hundred men was gathered in front of the tower. The plane was still rolling at twenty miles an hours under the power of the two inboard engines, the others had been shut down. The flight line tarmac was only ten yards from the building and Miller could clearly see the faces of the crowd. All were on their feet clapping and cheering, even though the Horten crew could not hear them. Front and center, and perhaps clapping the hardest was the Eighth Air Force Commander himself, General Doolittle, an ear-to-ear grin on his boyish face. He stopped clapping for a moment and threw a quick salute. The Horten crew returned it. The plane rolled on toward the hanger.

When she arrived at the hanger, Miller and Butler went through the shutdown checklist, shutting off the last two engines.

When they were finished, Miller grinned and said, "Well done, boys."

He got happy grins in return.

Technical Sergeant Elmer Conner turned away from his radar screen and looked at his captain and Dalton, the man from Northrop.

"Nothing. There was nothing to indicate a plane of that size was right on top of us."

Dalton was all grins, but the captain seemed quite put out.

"I know you must have missed it, Conner."

Before Conner could reply, Dalton said, "Captain, stop blaming your man. I stood right behind him the whole time and there was nothing on the screen. I suggest you take pleasure in helping prove that the aircraft is what we thought it was, virtually invisible."

The captain pulled himself up and from his expression was about to give a nasty reply, but Dalton held up a hand. "Don't. I think you'd be wise to remember I'll be turning in a report to General Doolittle. Why don't we leave it at that, huh?"

The captain nodded glumly and slunk away.

Chapter 24

Pulse Weapon Test Site
Near Ainay-le-Vieil
3 July, 0810 Hours, Berlin time

Johann Pachter clutched his stomach and staggered to the railing of the watch tower. Then he threw up. He watched with some detachment as his breakfast and coffee arced earthward. After a useless, but painful dry heave, he stood up and wiped his mouth with his shirtsleeve.

Mayerhofer lowered his telescope and turned his head just in time to see Pachter's stream fly over the railing. Feeling his own stomach churn, he looked away quickly, then back. He looked at Rademacher, who returned an expression that said 'glad it wasn't me.' Mayerhofer felt disgusted and walked over to Pachter.

"Pull yourself together! We don't have time for this nonsense."

Pachter looked like he'd been slapped. Then anger took over. His eyes narrowed and his nostrils flared. His hands balled into fists and he took one step toward Mayerhofer.

Mayerhofer took an involuntary step backwards.

Pachter raised his right fist and pulled it back.

Mayerhofer hands rose to his chest, palms out in a defensive pose.

The anger disappeared from Pachter's face to be replaced by pity. He lowered his hands and said in a voice that was so calm it gave Mayerhofer chills, "You may be my boss, Max, but I'm not a child, and I am first a human being. If you can watch what just happened to those men and feel nothing, then I pray for your soul."

Pachter turned away and began taking apart the camera through which he'd witnessed, he was sure, hell on earth.

Mayerhofer glanced at Rademacher, but the mechanical engineer was studiously breaking down his own camera. Mayerhofer wanted to tell Pachter that he was just trying to get the job done, that he didn't have time to 'feel' something for the dead men. For him they were just a means to an end and that end was a weapon that could turn back the enemy that would, if not win the war, then at least keep the Allies out of Germany. Away from their families. The ones who were left.

He wondered whether it was time to get rid of Pachter. He toyed with the idea briefly before coming to the conclusion that Pachter was a genius and he needed him and his talent. He had to ensure that the production of more weapons would go smoothly and that they would stay on schedule. No, Pachter would stay, but he wasn't going to forget the engineer's behavior of late, and especially today. He didn't need anyone praying for his soul. No one could judge him. Pachter would pay for that comment.

Mayerhofer folded up his telescope and attached its carry straps. Shouldering the device, he walked over to the stairs and, just before starting down, said, "I'll be waiting for you at the car. Hurry up. I want to get over there." Then he turned and went down the stairs.

The two engineers finished what they were doing and headed to the stairs. Pachter got there first, but before he could go down, Rademacher put out his hand. The mechanical engineer took a quick peek over the railing, where he could see Mayerhofer already standing by the car, the trunk lid open.

Rademacher looked at Pachter and said softly, "Johann, it

would be wise for you to keep those thoughts to yourself. Max plays at being the friend and we all get along well, and maybe we *are* friends, but he's fully committed to this project and he has Speer's ear, who in turn has the *Führer's*. One word and you will disappear like that." He snapped his fingers.

"He had it coming, Fritz," replied Pachter, defensively.

"Maybe so, but no one is indispensable. Be smart. If you want to see your family again."

Pachter shook his head, but said, "I will."

"Good. Now let's go before he loses all patience."

After loading the car with their equipment, the drive over to the target field was done in complete silence.

Mayerhofer led a convoy of trucks along the western edge of the target area. He stopped the car when he reached a point that was roughly even with the tank in the middle. He had driven past the men who were still alive, some standing, some sitting, and all were south of the tank at the midpoint. It looked like the pilot and bombardier had done their jobs perfectly. As he scanned to his left, he saw close up what he'd seen through the telescope: prostrate, crumpled, and clearly lifeless forms. Opening the car door, he stepped out just long enough to point at the driver of the lead truck and then point at the tank. The driver nodded.

He got back in the car and, turning right, drove across the field to the tank, the truck following close behind. After stopping the car, Mayerhofer and the engineers got out. Mayerhofer waved at the driver, who knocked on the cab behind him. A moment later, two soldiers came around from the back of the truck to join Mayerhofer and the engineers.

"Open the tank," ordered Mayerhofer.

"Yes, sir," said the oldest of the two soldiers.

They climbed up on the tank and opened the commander's hatch. A hand flailed through the opening and was followed by a clearly disoriented man who was bleeding from the ears and nose. With some effort the other men inside the tank climbed out.

Mayerhofer walked over to give the men a cursory examination. He motioned to the older soldier, who rushed over to him.

"Start loading all of the dead men. Make sure you load them in the correct order." Mayerhofer had numbered each man with a patch pinned to his shirt. In this way, he'd be able to discern whether there was a diminished effect at a greater distance from the ignition point, or if it remained constant.

"Yes, sir." The man hesitated, then asked, "What of the others, sir?" indicating those still living.

Mayerhofer looked at the man coldly. "I'm done with them. I don't care what you do with them."

"Yes, sir."

Chapter 25

The Douglas C-47 Goonie Bird took off from the new airfield, rising surprisingly gracefully into the gray sky. Dunn and his men were aboard, sitting on the bench-style seats that ran alongside the curved wall of the workhorse aircraft, half on each side.

Dunn stared straight ahead and could see out the small window on the other side. The Goonie Bird had taken off into a southerly breeze and was banking right to take its heading back to Hampstead Airbase. As the window dipped lower, Dunn began to see the widespread damage the battle for Cherbourg had inflicted on the port city. It appeared that almost every building had been touched, some only slightly, while others were nothing but ragged shells from the bombs and artillery rounds. A few minutes later, the plane sped away from land and flew over the murky, rough-looking waters of the English Channel. Dunn's men were already in stages of sleep or pre-sleep. Dunn figured he'd join them soon.

Before sleep overtook him, Dunn thought about the curator for the Cherbourg *Musée Thomas-Henry* who had burst into tears when Dunn, just an hour ago, had handed him the piece of art saved from the Nazis. The curator told Dunn that the painting, entitled *Adoration of the Magi*, and was by the eighteenth century Flemish painter Jacob Jordaens. After bussing Dunn on both cheeks, the man invited Dunn to dinner at his humble home, but Dunn apologized and said he had orders to get back to England. The curator nodded, grabbed the art work and ran off with his prize.

He let his mind wander thinking about nothing of real consequence, darting from one thing to another. He realized that tomorrow would be the Fourth of July holiday and he recalled the last time he'd celebrated one. It was two years ago during training for Operation Torch, the invasion of North Africa, although no one knew at the time what the training had been for. Some knuckleheads had managed to sneak some sparklers onto the base. When it finally got dark, they lit the wands and stuck them into their helmets' camouflage netting, and then ran around the barracks a few times, trailing smoke and laughing the entire time, as were their barracks mates. The recollection made Dunn smile for a moment. Until he thought about the instigator of the whole thing. A kid from somewhere in Florida who had gotten killed on the first day of the invasion, right on the beach. A French Vichy forces cannon shell had obliterated his existence. Dunn had hated the French for a long time after that, unable to understand why they had joined forces with the Germans. Only time and a growing hatred for the Nazis had pushed the feelings against the French aside. Dunn shoved that memory away and started to drift off.

At the brink of sleep, Dunn suddenly startled himself with thoughts of Pamela. Waking fully, he realized he was going to see her soon. He thought about her touch, her smell, her blue eyes and beautiful face. He understood at some level how lucky he was that she loved him, although it was still a complete mystery to him as to why she did. After a failed first date—his fault completely—they got back together to try it again and it had taken roots. She'd forgiven him for being prickly about something she'd said that he'd taken the wrong way.

It was only after his Devil's Fire mission that he came to fully understand how important she was and would be, for the rest of his life, he hoped. She'd said 'yes' and now it was just a matter of getting to the altar.

It was while picturing her at his side saying 'I do' that Dunn finally fell asleep.

Chapter 26

Ten black forms entered the forest north of Wilhelmshaven and gathered around the leader, all kneeling. Each man carried his suppressed Sten, a commando knife and at least one fifty-pound satchel charge. Some men, the larger ones in the group, carried two. The squad had spent a couple of hours hand-making the satchels from donated or otherwise acquired duffel bags and the TNT from one, now defunct, Mark VIII torpedo.

True to his word, Captain Kelly had assigned two of his men to join Saunders' squad, Harris and Turner. Both were chiefs, who had seen action many times, although this was their first mission off the boat. Saunders had asked Barltrop to make sure the men knew how to handle the Sten, which they did. Barltrop had been tasked with ensuring that the squad carried along extra weapons and gear on the mission. That proved to be valuable foresight with the loss of Padgett and Merriweather.

About mid-morning, the sonar operator gave a warning that a

patrol boat was coming out of the sub pens. Kelly immediately set the boat nearly on the bottom of the channel and gave the order to rig for silent running. The patrol boat stopped about where the other one had been sunk by Chadwick and puttered around apparently pulling some debris from the water. Then it revved up and returned the way it had come, leaving the British submarine in peace.

At Saunders' request, the captain had brought the boat to periscope depth at various times during the day to scout for any German activity, including on land. At around three in the afternoon, they spotted a truckload of Germans running around the beach long enough to find the two black dinghies under their flimsy cover. The Germans immediately started stabbing the inflatable boats with their bayonets, then crumpled them up and put them in the truck. They spent nearly an hour trying to find the owners, then gave up and drove south, presumably back to the sub pens.

About an hour later, another truck came roaring up the road beside the beach, passing the point where the boats had been stashed and disappeared out of sight. Twenty minutes later, it came back, trundling along, then disappeared to the south. Since then, nothing had happened, which relieved Saunders. He'd told the captain what would happen and it had. The Germans had given up.

Saunders spoke in a whisper, giving last minute instructions, reminding each man of his role and area of the facility. He stood up, looked at each of his men in the moonlight, nodded, then turned away and started running. The men followed close behind, moving abreast about two yards apart.

They headed toward the northeast corner of the facility which had a convenient small grove of trees about ten yards away. The men worked their way through the grove and stopped on the side facing the facility. Saunders knelt and examined the facility through his field glasses, checking for any movement. From this angle, he couldn't see the main intersection or the so-called tobacco shop. He saw no one. Sweeping his view left, he spotted the main gate, which was actually open and unguarded. Must not think anyone would have an interest in anything here. But then again, it wouldn't be prudent to walk through that gate. Directly in front of them was a row of one-story buildings, but now that they were so close, he could see they were indeed similar to a movie set, simple frames and roofs painted to look realistic.

Lowering the glasses, he turned back to the men and pointed at Redington and Owens. The two men quickly ran to the fence, stopped short and examined it closely for ground-level tripwires on the ground and electric conduits along the top. Nothing there. They quickly snipped through the wire and pulled it back for the men to pass through.

Redington pulled the wire back into place after everyone was through.

Saunders ran across the twenty yard gap to the first building and crept close to one of the windows. Only when he was right next to it could he tell that the windows were also movie magic and were just painted on.

He wasn't positive of what he was looking for, but had a pretty strong gut feeling that whatever it was would be located at the intersection of Broadway and Fifth. Since they were "on" Fifth Avenue, it was going to be a straight run down the street, a distance of about two blocks. If this place was what he thought it was, a training facility for saboteurs, then one or more of the buildings near that intersection would be real, with real doors and windows. And that was where the men would be, too.

It took the squad a couple of minutes to carefully advance to the corner of Broadway and Fifth. Saunders knelt against the wood frame of a building purporting to be a book store and, edging up to peek around the corner, examined the Johnson and Sons Tobacco Shop without the use of the binoculars. No lights were on, but the appearance of the storefront was clearly different—it had depth and was a real space—just as Saunders suspected.

He turned his attention to the second floor and noted that it was also a façade. Scanning the rest of the nearby buildings, he was satisfied that they were all fronts only. He tapped Barltrop on the shoulder and the pair started toward the building across the street, leaving the rest of the men around the corner.

Just as the commandos hit the half way point, the door to the tobacco shop opened and two men stepped out. A moment later, to make matters worse, across the flat land, even through the buffering of the small forest surrounding the facility, Saunders heard the sounds of vehicles, probably trucks. *Bloody hell.*

The two men evidently heard the trucks, too, because they stepped around the corner to peer into the darkness toward the front gate. It was when the men turned away from the sounds that they saw the commandos. The taller of the two spoke briefly to his partner, who then bolted back into the building and out of sight.

Saunders broke into a run and Barltrop was right behind him. They stopped a couple of yards away from the man, and kept a two yard distance between themselves. The aimed their weapons at the man's chest.

To Saunders' surprise, the man seemed to be wearing an American airman's uniform.

The man raised his hands and said, with great relief on his face, "Thank God! Can you get us out of here?"

Saunders stared. The airman had spoken English. American English. From Saunders' experience, he sounded southern, a little like Dunn's man, Wickham, who was from Texas.

"Who are you?"

The man lowered his hands, even though the deadly Stens were still aimed right at him. "I'm Burnett. Joe Burnett, captain. My crew bailed out of our B-17 and we got picked up and brought here." He stepped closer, gauging the distance carefully, while smiling.

"Uh huh. Where are you from, Joe?'

"Amarillo, Texas. So can you get us out of here?" He took another step closer.

Saunders raised the Sten and pointed it between Joe's eyes. "Stand where you are, Joe. Where'd your friend go?"

"I sent him to get the rest of my crew, there's only six of us left. You're here to rescue us, right?"

"Show me your ID tags."

"Whoa, partner, we're on the same side here." Joe looked angry, but took a step back, keeping a close eye on the weapons.

"Show them to me."

"Fine. No need to get your shorts in a wad." Joe slowly slipped a hand inside his shirt, pulled out his ID tags, then lifted the chain over his head and handed them to Saunders.

Saunders held them up to get some moonlight on them. They had Joe's name and rank, captain, and his identification number stamped on them. They were worn and bent. Saunders handed them back.

Joe took them and slid the chain over his head, neatly tucking them back inside his shirt. Then he held out his hands placatingly and took a short, sliding step to his right.

His eyes shifted to look over Saunders' shoulder, but only for a split second.

Barltrop started to rotate to keep his weapon trained on him.

Saunders suddenly swung around to his right and dropped to one knee, his Sten tucked tightly into his right shoulder.

Shots rang out, and bullets whined past Saunders' head. He fired a long burst.

Four armed men, also wearing airman uniforms, fell to the ground. They'd come out of another store front farther down the street. Saunders ran over to check on them. All dead. They had all been carrying a German Mauser rifle.

Barltrop was watching the action to his right when a flash of motion to his left caught his eye.

Joe charged Barltrop, hands outstretched, reaching for the Sten. Barltrop merely pivoted left, causing Joe to slip past. On the way by, Barltrop delivered a crashing blow with his right hand to the spot right behind Joe's left ear. The ersatz American dropped like a shot deer, landing face first on the pavement where he lay in a crumpled ball.

Saunders said to Barltrop, "Let's see if we can pinch these buggers 'tween us. I'll take half the squad and we'll find the other way in, then we'll meet up inside. "

Barltrop nodded his understanding.

Saunders waved and the rest of the squad joined him.

To Owens, he said, "Tie him up. Gag him. Keep Mills with you. Be ready for the trucks that are coming."

"Sure thing, Sarge."

Owens bound Joe's wrists with the man's own web belt and stuffed a handkerchief into his mouth, held in place with some black electrician's tape; no commando worth his stripes went anywhere without that little item.

Saunders and his group ran down the street toward where

they thought the four enemy soldiers had come from.

Barltrop took point and he and his men stepped into the tobacco shop. He ran across the shop to the back, where a curtain divided the front of the store from the back. Barltrop eased through the curtain and saw a door a few yards farther back. He glided over to the door and put a hand on the knob. He turned gently and the knob turned. Unlocked. He turned it back quietly and slipped back through the curtain. He waved a hand. The rest of the squad ran up behind him.

Once back at the door, Barltrop stood to the left side. Endicott came forward and knelt just out of the door's apparent swing arc. He raised his weapon. The others were kneeling and lined up on either side of the little space.

Barltrop took a quick glance at everyone, saw they were set and put his right hand on the knob. He turned it slowly, quietly, until it was unlatched. Then he pulled gently. The door swung open an inch. There was light on the other side, but it was coming from a lower level. The door led to a basement.

He swung the door another few inches, enough to take a quick peek. The stairs went down in a straight line, no turns, but at the bottom of the stairs, a hallway took off to the right, the west. Barltrop stared at the spot where the hallway met the landing at the bottom of the stairs looking for shadows indicating a presence. Nothing.

He pulled his head back and whispered what he'd seen to Endicott, who was just behind him.

Endicott nodded.

Barltrop pulled the door open part way, and took a small step forward. He didn't see the thin silver wire strained taut at his feet where it was connected to a German potato masher grenade.

Chapter 27

German training facility
2 miles north of Wilhelmshaven
3 July, 2235 Hours

Something made Barltrop stop. Call it sixth sense or something else, but whatever it was, it saved his life as well as that of Endicott and one of the submarine chiefs who were right behind him. He looked down before taking a step and saw the glint of light off the thin strand of wire running across the doorway, six inches from the floor.

"Blimey. Tripwire," he whispered. "Bloody hell, I should have known." He got down on his knees, pulling a small torch from his shirt pocket. He turned it on and swept its beam around until he found the grenade. The Model 24 *Stielhandgranate*, known as the potato masher, had been in use by the German Army since 1915. Constructed of a metal can containing the high explosive charge atop a smooth wooden handle, the weapon was armed by unscrewing a cap at the butt end of the handle. This revealed a porcelain ball attached to a string. Pulling on the ball dragged a rough steel rod, not unlike a rasp file, through the igniter, which set fire to the five-second fuse. The tripwire was attached to the dangling porcelain ball.

This was a respected weapon, a feared weapon, and Barltrop knew he had his hands full. "Everybody get the bloody hell back," he growled without looking at his mates. He waited until he heard the shuffling of boots. Satisfied he was alone, he shone the light again, following the wire across to the other door jam. There he saw a second grenade and realized his predicament had become more serious. The tripwire wound around a dowel rod, a makeshift simple pulley. This potato masher was dangling upside down with the tripwire again attached to the ball. Even a slight movement of the wire would cause the grenade to shake and arm itself as gravity took over and pulled the weight of the high explosive downward. This was a common technique the Germans used on fences. Extraordinarily effective. If he had just cut the wire on the first grenade, the released wire would have spun around the dowel rod and caused the second grenade to slide down, igniting itself.

Looking for wires leading to the door itself, he spent a few seconds ensuring there were none. He then checked the walls to see if anything else lay in wait for him. Satisfied that the two grenades were the only problems to solve, he scooted over to his right to begin work on securing the dangling weapon. He checked closely for another booby trap and was relieved there wasn't one. He laid the torch on the floor, pointed at the nearest wall for reflected light and pulled a small wire cutter from a pocket. Sitting cross-legged, he grabbed the dangerous end of the grenade, the tin can, with his left hand and lifted it upright without moving the wire or the string attached to the porcelain ball. With his left hand, he snipped the wire near the ball. He pushed the ball and string back up into the handle, and tightened the screw cap that held everything in place. Then he laid the weapon down carefully.

He quickly cut the wire to the other grenade and put it back together. Then he clipped both grenades onto his web belt. Retrieving his torch, he put it away. He waved his hand and, as he started down the stairs, he heard his mates slide forward to catch up.

He took notice of the wall construction. It wasn't wood as he'd first thought, but concrete. If the grenades had gone off, almost everyone would have been inside a killing box due to the five second delay and the concrete would have created rebounding concussion waves that would kill even without any shrapnel. He remembered the stories of the Allies overrunning German bunkers and when they stepped inside they found the men sitting or lying on the floor with no apparent injuries. The pressure wave of five-hundred pound bombs hitting near an opening had smashed their internal organs, killing them. The close call made him shiver.

When he reached the bottom of the stairs, he leaned carefully around the corner and took a quick peek down the long hallway, which was lit by overhead bulbs running the whole length. It was also made of concrete and about two yards wide. There were two doors on each side, face-to-face, and ten yards apart. The nearest pair was ten yards down the hallway. All the doors were closed, no surprise there. Between the two on the left was an opening, clearly a branch hallway leading who knew where. At the far end, maybe forty yards away, was presumably another stairwell leading back up to the surface. Barltrop expected Saunders to come around that corner any moment and he was right. Saunders leaned around the corner as Barltrop had just done and waved.

Barltrop and Saunders led their men quietly down the hallway, stopping next to the first door on their respective right. Saunders pointed quickly indicating he, Saunders, and his men would enter the door he stood next to. Barltrop and his men would enter the door nearest himself. This put the doors kitty-corner from each other and breaching the rooms this way would prevent direct crossfire coming from the rooms.

Barltrop nodded at Saunders, who held up one hand with three fingers extended. Then Saunders started the countdown. When he reached 'one' Saunders put his hand on the doorknob and twisted and pushed. The door swung open revealing a large room. The lights were on. Student desks were the only things there.

Barltrop mirrored Saunders' actions and also found an empty room.

Withdrawing from the rooms, each group prepared for entry

into the last two rooms.

A minute later, they stood outside another set of empty rooms.

Saunders and Barltrop eyed each other, then looked as one toward the hallway entrance. Saunders motioned toward his second in command indicating Barltrop should take point.

Barltrop nodded and slid forward until he was near the opening. Without looking around the corner, it appeared that the hallway was dark, which meant anyone stepping into it from here would be perfectly silhouetted. For this problem, he opted for a bit of deception. He turned to Endicott and whispered a few words over his shoulder.

Endicott nodded and pulled something from his shirt pocket. He went prone and snaked toward the corner over Barltrop's boots. When he got to the edge he pulled the telescoping handle out to its full ten inches and pushed the two by three inch mirror out. He saw nothing but blackness. He kept it in place and waited.

With his left hand, Barltrop removed his watch cap, and pulled his commando knife from its leather scabbard with his other hand. Placing the cap on the knife's point, he edged the contraption closer to the corner. Then he tipped the knife forward and the cap moved into the hallway at head height. As he feared, the peculiar burring sound of a German MG42 pierced the air and the cap shredded, falling in pieces to the floor. Yanking the knife back, remarkably untouched, he slid it back into its scabbard.

Endicott inched backward to get out from underneath Barltrop, then got to his feet.

"Two-man team about sixty or seventy yards. They've got some sort of stone or concrete barricade to hide behind. They're firing through a slit. No chance we'd ever hit them."

"Seventy yards?" That was over twice the distance a man could throw a grenade. Even if you got lucky and it rolled another ten yards, it'd still be thirty yards short.

Barltrop looked across the opening at his boss. "No way through, Sarge."

Saunders was already nodding his agreement. He knew the machinegun's only purpose was to tie up his squad while the other Germans escaped.

As a reminder that they were waiting for them, the MG42 cut loose a burst that stitched new holes in the wall near the British soldiers, spraying fragments of concrete all around them.

Saunders shook his head. When the echo of the terrible weapon's sound faded, he said, "Go back to the street. Secure the prisoner and get out of sight. Leave the chiefs and your satchels here."

"Yes, Sarge."

Saunders waited until Barltrop and his men disappeared down the hallway and up the stairs, then pulled a grenade. He didn't want to just leave things as they were. He pulled the pin and, with his left hand, threw it as hard as he could down the dark hallway without exposing much of himself. He heard it land and skip and bounce, then it seemed to start rolling. Another second passed, and to his surprise it was still rolling. Was the hallway slightly downhill?

Stepping back from the corner, he said, "Fire in the hole."

The men covered their ears and opened their mouths just in time as the pressure wave from the enclosed space explosion crashed toward them.

Saunders stuck his Sten around the corner and fired off a long burst, keeping the barrel as lined up as possible. He stopped firing and knelt to peek around the corner. There was still a lot smoke around the machinegun. There was never a question as to whether Saunders was going to charge down the hall. The only question was if he could make his men stay put. Which he did quickly.

Grabbing Dickinson by the shirt, he pulled the man closer and said, "Cover me, but don't follow. Wait for my 'all-clear.' Got it?"

"I do."

Saunders looked around the corner again and thought he could see the barricade. Ducking down, he ran full speed toward the target expecting the MG42 to start buzz-sawing again, but it didn't. He zigzagged as he ran in the hopes it might increase his chances if the gunner started firing. As he ran, he felt the floor dropping below his feet; it was indeed on a downhill slope. He soon passed the halfway point, which in his mind was also the point of no return.

At ten yards he thought he saw movement behind the barricade.

He fired a short burst with his Sten fully aware that ricochets could be a problem.

Firing another burst, he jumped left, then fired again at five yards.

Now he could see the machinegun's ugly wide mouth. It was staring directly at him. He wondered whether he would see the flash of the bullet that killed him.

Chapter 28

Adolf Hitler was a night person. He worked until the early hours of the morning, then slept until noon or later. He was not to be disturbed for anything by anyone. Another reason he slept so late in the day was that he took all kinds of concoctions that his personal doctor, Theodor Morell, created especially for the mad leader of Germany, including his sleeping draughts.

Each day was an unknown for those around the dictator. Would he be lucid enough to follow a conversation, or would he appear wild-eyed and incoherent, shouting a rant that could last hours?

Speer was accustomed to the bad days, but he knew the man sitting next to him, Max Mayerhofer, the project leader for the new Pulse weapon, would be frightened to death in the face of a wild man. They were sitting in two of the three chairs in front of

Hitler's desk, waiting for the *Führer* to arrive.

Speer, an intelligent, dedicated man looked sideways at Mayerhofer, who seemed calm, although his gaze was darting around the gigantic office trying to take in everything.

A door opened suddenly to their right in the wall behind Hitler's desk. Speer and Mayerhofer jumped to their feet at the sight of the *Führer*. Hitler walked through, a little unsteady it seemed to Speer. He knew Hitler had been exhibiting some serious health problems recently and it included difficulties with his left arm and hand, which would sometimes just begin to shake uncontrollably, a palsy of some sort. Due to this problem, Hitler had reduced his public appearances to almost zero. The *Führer* could not be seen as weak in front of the German people.

Unexpectedly, a man strode through the door right behind Hitler. Speer was surprised, but didn't allow it to show, to see General Erwin Rommel, the Desert Rat, and the man responsible for the ill-fated and failed Atlantic Wall. Hitler sat down and pulled himself close to his huge desk, while Rommel walked around the desk toward the two men and shook each man's hand firmly. Rommel took his seat, as did Speer and Mayerhofer.

Speer examined Hitler's face quickly and concluded that the meeting might be bearable for all.

Hitler smiled graciously at Mayerhofer. "*Herr* Doctor, it's a pleasure to meet you at last." Hitler rose and extended his hand across the vast desk. Mayerhofer, not expecting this, stumbled slightly getting out of his chair, but was finally able to shake Hitler's limp hand.

Hitler sat down again and so did Mayerhofer, who was clearly suffering from hero worship. His hands fidgeted in his lap and finally he picked up a black leather briefcase containing the project's most important papers, and of course, the photographs.

Hitler looked at Speer expectantly and the Minister cleared his throat.

"*Mein Führer*, I am pleased to report an extremely successful test of the Pulse weapon earlier today and—"

"Pictures. Show me pictures. If I want a lecture, I'll be the one giving it, Speer."

Unperturbed, Speer merely replied, "Of course, *Mein*

Führer." He turned to Mayerhofer and held out his hand.

Mayerhofer opened the briefcase and rummaged around a bit, then withdrew a packet of eight-by-ten photos, which he put in the Minister's hand.

Speer rose and handed the packet to Hitler who opened it and fanned the pictures apart on his desk. He spent some time on each photo before moving on to the next. When he got to the last few depicting the dead men and their burns, he lifted his face to his visitors.

Mayerhofer was shocked by what he saw in the *Führer's* eyes. The friendliness and charm from before was gone, replaced by a wild, dangerous light, like a tiger's eyes just before making a ferocious attack. Mayerhofer knew enough not to react to what he saw, but he was certain he had just witnessed a human being devolving into madness.

"Who were these men?"

"They were Polish Jews and German communists, *Mein Führer*," replied Speer.

Hitler smiled a madman's smile. "Excellent, I like that very much. Nice and efficient."

"Yes, *Mein Führer*."

Hitler slid the photos back into the packet and handed them to Rommel.

Rommel flipped through them quickly with a tactician's eye. He noted the positions of the dead men relative to the survivors and was very interested in the pure symmetry of the weapon's attack. He had no thoughts about the dead men he was seeing. He was a pragmatist and if this weapon broke the Allies' lines apart in preparation for an all-out German attack, he was fine with it.

He gave the packet back to Speer and said, "*Herr* Minister, please tell me more about this weapon."

Speer nodded and said, "I defer to Doctor Mayerhofer."

Mayerhofer turned slightly so he could see Rommel's face, while keeping Hitler in his view.

"The Pulse Weapon is based upon the principles of . . ."

Chapter 29

German training facility
2 miles north of Wilhelmshaven
3 July, 2249 Hours

Saunders changed course expecting the barrel to follow. Instead, it suddenly tipped upward. Then he was on top of the barricade and firing down into the machinegun nest even though nothing was moving.

The Germans were both dead. The grenade had rolled right up next to the barrier and the pressure wave had done its job.

Saunders turned back toward his men and whistled. He heard a whistle in return and, in a few moments, his men joined him, including the two chiefs, who wore expressions of awe at what the commando had just done.

Saunders had a brief debate with himself over the value of expending the explosives, then decided it was better to destroy as much of the facility as possible rather than leaving it for the Germans to use in the future. He split his men into two groups, he and the two chiefs, Harris and Turner, to search for papers, and

Dickinson and Chadwick to set the charges.

Farther down the hallway, there were more doors branching off. Saunders shucked off his satchel of charges and indicated to the chiefs to do the same. Dickinson and Chadwick took the proffered explosives and ran back the way they'd come from.

Saunders grabbed the chiefs and took off down the hall. When they reached the first room on the left, he peeked in, not expecting to find anyone there, and he was right. It was the infirmary.

"You guys go on down and check the rooms on the right. See if one is an office. Whistle if you find one."

Both chiefs nodded and took off.

Saunders ran the few yards to the next room and was disappointed again. Two more to go.

The chiefs had checked everything on the right and had waved at Saunders, who waved back. He then pointed at the last door on the left. They ran down to it just as Saunders checked the third room. A whistle pierced the air and Saunders' heart jumped. *Now we're talking.* He hoped.

He made his way into the last room and it was indeed an office. There was a four-drawer file cabinet set against the right hand wall with the drawers all hanging open. To its left, was a large wooden desk, the kind found in schoolrooms the world over. While these looked inviting, there was a large pile of burned paper on the concrete floor a few feet away and Saunders' stomach dropped. *Bloody hell*, he thought. *They've burned it all.*

As he got closer and knelt down by the mess, he saw that not all was burned. One large clump of papers had stubbornly refused to ignite for reasons unknown. Perhaps the vagaries of the paper itself. Or lack of enough air around it.

Harris had started pulling open desk drawers.

Saunders said to Turner, "Chief, give me a hand here. Let's salvage what we can."

"Right-o, Sarge."

The two men set to work and quickly gathered up a packet of the partially burned papers an inch thick. Saunders handed what he had to Turner and undid a few of his shirt's buttons. Taking the papers back from Turner, he folded them carefully and slipped them inside the shirt.

In the background, Saunders heard the sound of boots coming closer. He rose quickly and ran to the office door. Peeking down the hall showed Dickinson and Chadwick coming at full tilt.

When they reached Saunders, Dickinson said, "All done back there. Timers set for ten minutes. We have plenty left for this end."

"Hop to, boys."

While the explosives were being set, Saunders and the chiefs took another look around the office. Saunders examined the file cabinet closely, pulling each of the drawers completely out and studying them inside and out, finding nothing. When the last drawer was out, something made him peer inside the cabinet. An envelope lay in the bottom of the cabinet, evidently having fallen out of one of the drawers. Saunders grunted as he squatted to reach in and grab the envelope. Knowing he didn't have time to read it, he slid it inside his shirt with the other papers.

To Harris, he asked, "Find anything, Chief?"

Harris slammed a drawer shut and replied, "Not a bloody damn thing."

"Okay, I think we're done here. Let's go."

Not waiting for a reply, Saunders headed out into the hallway and called out, "Dickinson? You guys done yet?"

From the room just down the hall came an answer, "Coming now, Sarge."

The five men wound their way together back up the hallway and to the right, then up the stairs where Barltrop had found the grenade booby traps.

Before exiting the tobacco shop, Saunders checked outside, looking up and down the street. It was clear. Just as he stepped through the door, he heard the sound of the trucks in the distance. He ran right and to the corner just in time to see faint dark shapes driving away, their engines roaring in the night air. Out of range. No way to catch them. Headed back to the submarine pens, no doubt. Saunders mulled over what this place was, then he slapped his meaty hand against his thigh in disgust at himself. He walked away from the corner chastising himself up one side and down the other. *Shouldn't have spent time searching for the office.*

A shout from across the street, out of the shadows of another fake building, brought him back to his surroundings. Soon he could make out Owens, Mills and the man purporting to be an American flyer.

A moment later, Saunders and all of his men were standing together in a clump. The 'flyer' was gagged with a cloth and his hands were bound behind him. Saunders' right eyebrow went up and he asked Owens, "What's the story?"

Owens clapped a hand on the 'flyer's' shoulder and said, "Genius here woke up and started getting antsy as the trucks got closer. He kept looking down the street like a guy about to be rescued, if you see what I mean, so we hightailed it across the way out of sight. Was just in time, too. Saw close to twenty guys come pouring out from somewhere in the back of that building. Then the trucks got here and they loaded up and took off."

Saunders patted Owens on the shoulder. "Well done, mate." He checked his watch and said, "We best be going now. A few more minutes and this place'll be going up. We can sort through things back on the boat. You take point, Owens. We'll need to double time it."

Owens nodded and, as he walked away, the men fell in line. All except the 'flyer,' who stood stock still. Saunders had been expecting this and he stepped over in front of the man and looked into his blue Germanic eyes.

"Don't want to join us for the trip back home?"

The man just looked at Saunders, his face devoid of expression.

"For a so-called American, you're displaying an odd reaction to being told you get to go home. I don't have time to argue with you or bother finding out what your real story is." Saunders stepped closer and jammed the barrel of his Sten into the man's chest. In a quiet, almost polite voice that was all the more frightening, he said, "Either come with us or die now."

The man stared at the barrel's big suppressor with wide eyes. Suddenly, he nodded and moved over to the back of the line.

Saunders lowered his weapon and took a spot a few feet behind the man.

"Good choice," said the tough British Commando. A little louder he said, "Off we go, Owens."

A moment later, the men were all double timing back toward the beach.

Chapter 30

Rommel listened carefully as Mayerhofer talked, and asked a few probing questions. When the scientist finished, the general leaned back. He pictured a map with the German and Allied forces clearly marked and the line representing the front, which meandered over the Cotentin Peninsula kilometer after kilometer. He imagined his Panzers lined up a kilometer from the line, engines idling, waiting for the attack signal.

Hitler, who still admired Rommel and was willing to permit Rommel a few moments reflection, was reaching the end of his ability to remain quiet.

"So, Rommel, this is an answer to our prayers, eh? Judicious use of this weapon will change the battlefield completely, as well as the balance of power on the front."

"Yes, *Mein Führer*. Provided the weapon is dropped accurately, it might just give us the edge on the line."

"*Ja*, of course, of course, accuracy is a necessity. I agree." Hitler turned his intense gaze on Mayerhofer, then Speer. "How long before you can begin mass-producing the weapon? What about the materials? Will you be able to gather the required materials quickly? Where will you produce the weapon? How many can you make in one week?"

Speer was calm in the face of so many rapid-fire questions. "We can begin the machine tooling tomorrow and it will take just over two weeks to complete. All the materials are relatively easy to acquire. The manufacturing facility is the same place Doctor Mayerhofer and his team have been working this past year near d'Ainay-le-Vieil, France in a former farm equipment factory. The location was selected for its lack of military importance as far as the Allies are concerned, since it's in Vichy territory. Once we begin production, we'll be able make one weapon per day."

Hitler nodded sagely, as though he already knew all this. His face wore an expression well known by the inner circle. He was about to make a pronouncement.

Speer recognized it and so did Rommel. They waited.

Hitler folded his hands on the desk and he frowned slightly to help make sure the value of his point wouldn't be missed. "Doctor Mayerhofer, you will go to General Rommel's headquarters at the Château La Roche Guyon. There you will educate his staff and commanders on this marvelous new weapon. It is of utmost importance that they all fully understand its capabilities."

Hitler smiled slightly and continued, "You'll enjoy your time at the château. It's quite beautiful there. I'm sure the general will be delighted to give you the full tour."

Mayerhofer's mind reeled at the thought of leaving the work for even an hour, let alone for several days this trip sounded like. He knew there was nothing he could do about it, so he said what everyone said, "Yes, *Mein Führer*."

With that, Hitler clapped his hands once and rose. The other visitors jumped to their feet and said, "*Heil* Hitler," while snapping off the Nazi salute.

Hitler gave his usual hand flip reply, turned and left the office leaving the three men standing there.

Mayerhofer began to wring his hands and said to Speer,

"How are we to stay on schedule if I have to travel to General Rommel's headquarters?" Then he realized Rommel was still there and looking at him with a bemused expression. "No offense, General!"

"None taken, Doctor. Don't worry, we'll have you in and out in one day." Then he gave Mayerhofer a sly grin. "Whether you take a tour is entirely up to you."

Mayerhofer sighed in relief. One day he could manage. He could lay out the day's work with Rademacher and Pachter. "Oh thank you, General. I do appreciate that."

"Not at all," said the general as he extended a hand, which Mayerhofer shook.

Chapter 31

Getting a man with his hands tied behind him on board an object that twists and turns and changes angles every second is a challenge, but Saunders, along with the help of Barltrop and Redington managed to get the man below deck. Once there, Saunders grabbed the man by the arm and squeezed, hard.

"You stand right there."

The man just stared back, but stayed put.

To Redington, Saunders said, "Take Chadwick with you and get him," he tilted his head toward the flyer, "to the sick bay."

Redington acknowledged Saunders' order and gave the man a push. Chadwick followed.

Kelly, who was standing nearby, said, "Well, Sergeant, I can't wait to hear about this little excursion. Welcome back. Again."

"Thank you, sir."

Kelly grinned. "Will you be staying this time?"

Saunders grinned back. "Aye, we will." The grin disappeared. "I expect you'd like to join us in our interrogation of this man?"

"Oh, I wouldn't miss it. I'll be along shortly, after we get underway."

"Very good, sir. Could you call the doctor to join us, too?

"Yes, I will."

"Thank you, sir."

Then Saunders wheeled on Barltrop, a frown on his face. "I heard you disarmed a couple of grenades."

"Yes, I did," Barltrop looked surprised, wondering who'd already let that little gem out.

"You daft fool. Next time be more careful. I can't afford to lose you, as terrible at this as you are."

"Yes, Sergeant. Speaking of daft fools. I wonder who charged a machine gun in a hallway?"

"Had to be done, so forget it, smart arse. Get the men to their quarters for some rest, then meet me in the sick bay." Saunders turned and headed aft.

Barltrop wasn't sure, but he thought he heard his boss and friend mutter, "Bloody hell."

Barltrop smiled to himself.

By the time Saunders got to the sick bay, Redington and Chadwick had Joe seated on one of the two chairs in the room and were standing one on either side him. Saunders closed the door and sat down across from the prisoner.

In the light, he examined the man's face and clothing. He certainly did look like an American pilot. The uniform was real as far as he could tell. But with what he'd found below street level, he was pretty sure of who the man was.

Saunders put his elbows on his knees and leaned forward, which placed him nearly into the man's lap, crowding his personal space. "Who are you, really?"

"My name's Joe Burnett. I'm with the 398th Bomber group based in Nuthampstead. Please, why won't you believe me?" His eyes pleaded. "Could you untie me, please? My hands are starting to hurt like hell."

"I'm sure they are." Saunders leaned back. "Why'd you attack my man back there when the four men took a potshot at us?'

"No, no. I wasn't attacking your man. I was trying to knock him down so he wouldn't get shot. It was a misunderstanding."

"Right."

Saunders unbuttoned his shirt and withdrew the charred papers and the envelope he'd found in the file cabinet. He turned to his left and laid the papers carefully on the metal desk bolted to the wall and the floor. Sitting down, he then opened the envelope and withdrew the single page folded and stuffed inside. He unfolded and inspected it. There were a dozen rows and four columns. Three of the columns were filled with names and a fourth with American locations. There were three different locations. He scanned the names and found Burnett on the second row, third column. He noted the location on that row was indeed Nuthampstead, the airbase.

Saunders looked up quickly to try catching Burnett's expression, but he was still looking stoic. "Where you from, flyboy?"

"Amarillo, Texas. I already told you that."

It matched. "Uh huh. Sure, you are."

Burnett looked affronted. Saunders decided the guy could be an actor. He glanced down at the paper, then back at Burnett. "Care to explain why your name is on this piece of paper?"

Just then, the captain and the doctor entered the cramped room.

Saunders rose to his feet.

The captain glanced at Burnett, then asked Saunders, "Anything?"

Saunders replied, "Not really, sir. Says he's with the 398th Bomber Group from Nuthampstead and that he's from Texas. The funny thing is, though, his name is on this piece of paper, which I found inside a file cabinet in a German facility. Odd that, don't you think, sir?"

"Indeed, I do, Sergeant."

Saunders looked at the doctor. He was a man of about forty, with Commander's insignia on his collar. About six inches shorter than Saunders' six-three, the man was slim and fit. His face was worn, as though he had seen about all there was to see as a doctor.

The captain said, "Allow me to introduce Doctor Morgan."

Morgan held out his hand and when Saunders gripped it, said in a soothing voice, "Pleased to meet you, Sergeant."

"You, too, sir." Saunders glanced at the prisoner. "Tell me, are you familiar with the dental work done in Germany?"

The doctor raised his eyebrows slightly. "Why, yes, I am. Why?"

"We're trying to ascertain where this man is from. I think we should check our friend's teeth. Let's see what we see."

"Certainly." Morgan took a step over to the desk and pulled open a drawer from which he removed a small penlight. Then he grabbed a tongue depressor from a container and turned to the prisoner.

"Open, please."

The prisoner complied.

The doctor clicked on the penlight and positioned it. Using the depressor he checked the man's teeth for fillings. After a few moments, he stepped back. "Well, there's nothing there to help us. I'm sorry."

"Hm." Saunders stared at the low ceiling briefly, then said to his men, "Okay, guys, you'll need to release his hands."

Redington drew his knife and reached behind the prisoner, slicing the belt.

The prisoner brought his hands around to his lap and began rubbing his wrists.

"Take your shirt off," said Saunders.

Burnett gave no reaction.

"Take your shirt off," repeated Saunders.

Again no reaction from the prisoner.

Saunders sighed, then nodded at Chadwick.

As soon as Chadwick touched him, the prisoner started squirming and bucking in the chair and tried to stand. Redington clouted him on the side of the head and the prisoner stopped struggling. His shoulders slumped.

Kelly asked, "What are you looking for, Sergeant?"

"Bear with me, Captain, if you would. We'll see in a minute."

Kelly nodded.

Soon the shirt was off. Saunders moved close and grasped Burnett's left wrist and pulled it straight up, extending the man's arm fully. Burnett started struggling again and Redington gripped him by the throat and pushed backwards. The struggling ceased.

Saunders peered at a mark on the inside part of the man's bicep, halfway between the elbow and armpit. The captain and the doctor both leaned forward in an effort to see.

"What is that?" asked Kelly.

Saunders gripped the man's bicep and rolled the arm over for better light. "Sir, that's a tattoo." Saunders continued to examine it. The little tattoo was about a quarter-inch tall. "It's a letter 'A.'" Saunders let go of the man's arm and it lowered slowly into Burnett's lap. He looked defeated.

"It's an SS tattoo of his blood type. Ran across these in Italy. The ones we found were all on men of the Waffen SS. So we have our proof: this man is a member of the Nazi Waffen SS."

Saunders stepped back and stared at the enemy. "Bind him back up. Captain, you have a brig or something like it, correct?"

"Yes, we have a brig. Nothing fancy, mind you."

"Oh, not to worry, I don't think our friend here will care. Where is the brig, sir?"

"It's aft. We put it next to the engine room. We like to provide a little extra comfort for our prisoners."

Saunders chuckled. "Nice, sir." He gave orders to Redington and Chadwick.

The captain looked puzzled at this apparent end to the interrogation. "Don't you want to interrogate this man further?"

"No need, sir, I know what's going on."

At this, the prisoner shouted, "You'll never win! You're weak and inferior!"

Saunders punched the Nazi in the stomach doubling the man over.

As the man gasped for breath, Saunders shouted, "That weak enough for you, you bloody bastard?"

Saunders slugged him on the side of the face with a roundhouse that nearly knocked the man out of his chair.

The commando yelled, "That's for Casey and Wesley!"

Saunders' attack had been so sudden and swift that no one had been able to move to stop him.

"Get him out of my sight."

"Wait!" said the doctor. He bent over to examine the

prisoner's face, which had a bloody cut from Saunders' knuckles.

"I need to dress this cut." The doctor gave Saunders a look of disapproval.

"Captain, I'm sorry about that," said Saunders.

The captain's eyes were wide, but he said, "Don't be."

Redington and Chadwick helped the man into the chair for the doctor. After a few minutes, the doctor stepped back and said, "You can take him to the brig now."

Redington and Chadwick helped the prisoner to his feet and dragged him out of the sick bay.

The captain looked at Saunders expectantly, waiting for him to continue his explanation.

"Take a look at these papers, sir." The burly sergeant spread the partially burned papers apart revealing that they were maps. He pulled one carefully from the group and pointed to a spot on it. "Washington D.C." He flipped it over. There was a short numbered list, one through five. Saunders read the first line, "*Ein*, 1600 Pennsylvania Street. Five hundred kilos. *Zwei*, *Das Kapitol*, one thousand kilos."

Saunders looked up to see horror in the captain's and the doctor's eyes.

Then Saunders said, "There was one sub we didn't have time to damage. When we were leaving the facility, there were two trucks filled with men from the facility where we got this guy. They were heading to the sub pen."

Realization hit the captain squarely in the face. Immediately, he grabbed the phone and got the control room. "This is the captain. Battle stations. Bring the boat about and come to full stop." He heard the acknowledgement and turned to Saunders. "Well, this is going to be a first for us: shooting another submarine."

Chapter 32

A rumpled and bleary-eyed Dunn sat in front of Colonel Kenton's desk, a cigarette dangling from his fingers. To Dunn's left was his second in command, Dave Cross, who looked as bad as Dunn. Lieutenant Samuel Adams, the colonel's aide, who had been on leave the last time Dunn had met with the colonel, sat beside the colonel's desk, on Dunn's right.

The men had already exchanged greetings and salutes. Dunn and Cross were waiting for Kenton to explain why he'd called a meeting so late in the day. Dunn and Cross had made a wager before stepping into the office: Dunn proposed ten bucks on the new assignment's jump off date being within the next seven days. Cross countered with twenty bucks and that the date would be eight days or more away and they agreed on that, shaking hands.

"Those papers you liberated from the German headquarters in La Haye have proven to be extremely valuable, gentlemen.

They've been put to good use."

"Good to hear, sir," said Dunn.

"Your attack around the river allowed General Collins to crush through the German line and he's already started rolling up the enemy's right flank."

Dunn's eyebrows went up. "Wow, that's fast work."

"It sure is. Quite an unusually speedy reaction for division headquarters staff. The general must have made his wishes known quite clearly."

"Yes, sir."

Lieutenant Adams cleared his throat and everyone looked at him.

"The mayor of Cherbourg sent a message to Eisenhower thanking him for the return of the art work. My understanding is that Eisenhower was quite pleased with that."

"Thank you, sir."

Adams grinned and said, "You're welcome. I was quite happy about that. We can use all the good PR we can get."

"Why is that, Lieutenant?"

Kenton answered, "You know I've been trying to establish us, you and your men, as an elite strike team, right?"

Dunn gave a puzzled look. He thought they already were an elite strike team. "Well, yes, sir."

"I've been getting some sideways push to move your squad back into the normal rotation, reattach you to a larger unit, and get you on the line."

Now Dunn was completely confused. And concerned. "What does 'sideways' mean, sir?"

"Pressure from my rank peers, as opposed to my chain of command."

Adams said, "I think it's jealousy. Some people in the Army don't enjoy other outfits' successes being celebrated. They think it detracts from their own."

Cross, who'd been silent so far, snorted and said, "Say it ain't so, sir!"

Everybody laughed.

Then Adams and Kenton exchanged a look, which Dunn and Cross noticed. Dunn elbowed Cross and under his breath muttered, "Uh oh."

Cross whispered, "Ayup."

"Are you two finished with your commentary?" asked Kenton, who had a little smile on his lips.

Both sergeants replied at once, "Yes, sir!"

Kenton closed his eyes, lowered his chin to his chest and shook his head, then said, "Lord, help me." Then he clasped his hands together on the desk and leaned forward. "Several things are going on right now. Normally, I wouldn't tell anyone about this, and certainly not the man whose name has been put forth, but our relationship is different from that of a 'normal' organization, wouldn't you say?"

Dunn and Cross nodded.

"I've put your name in for the Medal of Honor."

Dunn was stunned and his cheeks bloomed red. Being in the spotlight wasn't his favorite place to be.

Cross turned and clapped him on the shoulder. "Congratulations, Tom!"

Dunn was silent a moment longer, then said slowly, carefully selecting his words, an old habit learned from his dad, "Colonel, I don't quite know what to say, but I don't feel right—"

"About getting nominated for an award when you believe your squad is responsible for the outcome?" interrupted a smiling Kenton.

"Yes, sir, exactly."

"Look, here's the thing. I know you didn't do this on your own, but the enormity of what you all did has to be rewarded. Although the details of the citation are somewhat, eh, what's the phrase, Sam?"

"I think the phrase you want is 'fictionalized,' sir."

"Yes, the citation itself is a fictionlized version of the actual events due to national security. No one knows what exactly happened except for a select few because of our own atomic bomb program, which must remain secret. You'll remember signing the Secrecy Act forms after the action."

Dunn nodded. He did remember. Every man on the squad had been hauled into a room with two unsmiling, black-suited men and told to sign the papers or go to Leavenworth prison. They had also been told that if they spoke of it to anyone outside the squad, Leavenworth would still be in their future.

"I don't suppose you could reconsider, sir?"

Kenton shook his head. "Too late. When I brought this up with General Eisenhower, he was all for it, which means it's happening." Kenton stuck out his hand. "Congratulations."

Dunn shook hands. "Thank you, sir."

"Just two more things, then I can let you go get some rest. Lieutenant Adams and I have been thinking about your squad and what you've been asked to do, and who knows what we'll ask you to do in the future. We've decided we need a name for your squad. Something catchy, right Lieutenant?"

"Absolutely right, sir."

"Along the lines of Merrill's Marauders. We'd like you to think about it, maybe talk to your men and see what they might like, then let us know. I'm sure we can all come up with something."

Dunn glanced at Cross who returned the look with a dead pan expression. Dunn then turned his gaze to his usually sensible commander and just stared at him for a long quiet moment.

Adams cleared his throat, perhaps to encourage a verbal response from the Ranger sergeant.

Dunn was slow to respond because he thought this was one of the stupidest things he'd ever heard and he wanted to make his point without quite calling the colonel stupid. Kenton had always been a commander his men could count on, going all the way back to Italy earlier in the year, at the Anzio debacle. The Americans had been penned in and hadn't broken out of the beach soon enough due to the hesitation by the commander, General John P. Lucas. This led to months of digging in and suffering through daily artillery and aerial attacks. Kenton had still managed to find a way for his men to be successful.

Dunn couldn't find a graceful way out of this, so he finally said, "Sir, we appreciate your idea and your support. The truth is, though, about the only name I can think of at the moment is Dunn's Dummies."

Kenton burst out laughing and the rest joined in. After things settled back down, Kenton smiled and said, "Okay, Tom, perhaps we should shelve this idea. I appreciate your diplomacy."

Relieved, Dunn smiled back. "Whatever you say, sir."

Kenton chuckled. "You are welcome to can it now."

"Yes, sir."

Kenton opened a desk drawer and pulled out a folder and laid it on the desk. It had a big red stamp on it that read TOP SECRET.

"This is your next assignment. It's a kill order. The target's information is in there." He pushed the folder toward Dunn.

Dunn leaned forward and flipped open the folder. Cross moved closer to see for himself. On the top of the papers was an eight-by-ten glossy black and white photograph. Dunn looked from the picture to Kenton's face.

"But that's . . ."

Kenton nodded. "You have seven days to plan the operation. You're out of here on the eleventh. Give your men a couple of days leave. Take tomorrow for yourself. Then come back here and get this folder from me and start working on your plan. I want to see it by the seventh."

Dunn closed the folder and pushed it away. "Yes, sir."

Kenton put the folder away and locked the desk. "That's all, Sergeant. Go get some rest."

"Yes, sir."

Dunn and Cross stood and saluted, then left the office.

Walking in silence down the hall in step with each other, the two Rangers thought about what they'd just seen. A kill order. They'd heard of them, of course, but had never seen one.

When they got to the door, Dunn held out his hand for Cross to stop. Then Dunn dug into his pocket and pulled out two ten-dollar bills, which he handed over to Cross.

"First things, first, Dave."

"Ayup," replied the Maine native, as the money disappeared into a pocket.

Chapter 33

Aboard the *Sea Scout*
3 miles northwest of Wilhelmshaven Germany
4 July, 0803 Hours

Captain Kelly had ordered the *Sea Scout* to dive several hours ago when the sun's first light began to brighten the world. Saunders and his men had found bunks to curl up in and get some much needed sleep just before midnight. Saunders had asked the executive officer to wake him if they were going to attack the German submarine. He wanted to see for himself how that was done. The submariner's world was so foreign to him: small, cramped space, smelly air, and the only thing they seemed to have in common was the endless quiet and the waiting for something to happen.

Saunders had, of course, asked the captain for permission to be in the control room. The captain had looked at Saunders and gauged the commando's bulk against the available space and said 'yes.'

Saunders stood near the sonar operator, not out of any particular interest in the gadget's mesmerizing round display that looked like a radar screen, but out of practicality; there was more room there than anywhere else and it kept him out of the traffic way. The operator had a pair of head phones on and wore the expression of someone listening intently to a conversation that was difficult to hear.

The captain and the executive officer were standing near the periscope tube. The scope was not raised at the moment. The captain was looking at a board on the bulkhead with rows of red and green lights in pairs. All of the green ones were lit, which Saunders assumed was a good thing.

Saunders watched the other men in the room, a navigator who was leaning over a small table with several maps on it. He had a pencil and dividers in hand and seemed to be muttering calculations under his breath. Another seaman was sitting behind the biggest steering wheel Saunders had ever seen, almost a yard in diameter. This was the man who controlled the bow planes which directed the sub's vertical movement the same way the elevator on an airplane's tail did. In front of him was a big dial showing the sub's depth; it looked like they were at ninety feet. To his right, another man also had a giant wheel, the one that controlled the rudder.

Saunders turned his attention to the executive officer, a man of about twenty-five with dark brown hair. The thing that caught Saunders' attention was the silver stopwatch hanging around the man's neck. It struck him as an odd thing to have.

Time passed slowly. The men talked quietly amongst themselves.

Suddenly, the sonar operator sat up straighter. He raised a hand and everyone in the room noticed. The whispers stopped as all eyes were on the operator. Quietly, the captain moved closer. "What do you have, Ears?"

Saunders stifled a laugh. Only the navy.

"Light screw sounds, a sub, out at three-six-zero-zero yards, bearing one-eight-two. Screw sounds make it to be about five knots."

Saunders did the math: a hair over two miles and just barely west of south. Coming out of the sub pens at Wilhelmshaven.

"Submerged?"

"No, sir, riding on the surface."

Kelly grinned. Saunders thought he looked like a shark about take a chunk out of someone.

"Cheeky bastard. Thinks he's got clear sailing. XO, what do you make the time to be?"

The exec did his own quick math and replied, "Twenty-one minutes, sir."

"Very good. Let me know when fifteen minutes have passed."

"Aye, aye, sir." The exec started his stopwatch.

Saunders nodded to himself, now understanding.

"What's his heading?" asked the captain.

"He's on a reciprocal zero-zero-two."

The captain had positioned his own boat on the western edge of the deep water of the inlet, with a heading of one hundred-thirty-five degrees, southeast. He wanted to have a deflection, or angled, attack for his torpedoes. He had guessed, correctly, that the German captain would take a line down the middle of the deep water. Kelly pictured the enemy submarine's path and saw that its heading would bring it by the *Sea Scout* at a distance of only four hundred yards. Add the angled attack, and the distance of the firing solution would be just under six hundred yards.

"Take us to periscope depth," ordered the captain. He wanted to rise now while the chances of his boat's motion being detected were negligible.

"Aye, aye, sir."

Saunders heard a faint gurgling sound and felt the floor beneath him shift. It felt a little like going up a lift. He leaned over so he could see the sonar operator's screen. It was blank, which puzzled him. He'd expected to see a line sweeping around the dial like the radar screens he'd seen. What he didn't know was that the operator was using his sonar in a passive mode, picking up sounds from the water as the sound waves passed over the *Sea Scout*. To use the active sonar would require sending a signal, called pinging, and then receiving the bounced reply, which would show up as a blip on the screen. The problem with active sonar was that you might as well just take a giant hammer and whack the enemy vessel with it, because on their end, that's exactly what a ping sounded like. They could then follow the sound back to your sub like a trail of bread crumbs. And send a torpedo or three on that line.

"Open doors one through four."

The exec relayed the message to the torpedo room and after a minute said, "Doors open."

The fifteen minutes seemed to take an hour, but finally the exec called out, "Fifteen minutes, sir."

"Up scope."

The periscope tube slid upward. As the handles passed the captain's chest, he grabbed them and flipped them to a horizontal position. The exec stood on the opposite side, ready to read bearing and distance. Kelly gazed through the view finder. He sidestepped to his left to rotate the periscope to the right and the exec followed smoothly. Scanning the surface of the inlet, he spotted the German U-boat. He centered the reticules on the conning tower. He couldn't read the number from this distance. "Mark."

"Range one thousand. Bearing one-four-zero."

"We are set up perfectly." The captain rotated the scope to a position that was on line with the sub's long axis. He found a spot on the surface where he expected the U-boat to be and reset the reticules. "Mark."

"Range six hundred. Bearing one-three-five."

"Time to target?"

The exec calculated in his head again.

The *Sea Scout* carried the twenty-one inch diameter, twenty-one feet seven-inch long Mark XIII torpedoes, which had a speed of forty knots.

"Time to target: twenty-six seconds." The exec stopped his watch and reset it.

"Ears, target's speed?"

"Still five knots, sir."

Another few minutes passed and the captain watched the enemy sub closely, looking for any signs that it had detected the *Sea Scout*. The feeling he had was like the one a child has when playing hide and seek and the seeker is about to pass right by the child's hidey-hole. Except multiplied exponentially.

The U-boat was slicing smoothly through the water, leaving a small wake. Sunshine glistened off the water on the boat.

Just like leading a duck with a shotgun, thought the captain.

Come on, come on, you bastard. He had to time the fish just right.

The U-boat's snout crossed the point he'd marked mentally.

"Fire one!"

The chief hit the button for tube one. "One fired."

The exec started his watch.

"Fire two and three."

A pair of thwacks as the chief hit the buttons. "Two and three fired."

The exec checked his watch.

"Fire four."

Thwack. "Four fired."

As the captain watched, he began to see the torpedoes' wake as they rose close to the surface. He'd had them set to run at a depth of six feet.

"Ten seconds for torpedo number one." The exec began a countdown.

The captain lost sight of the torpedo trails.

"Zero," said the Exec.

A plume of water and fire ejected from U-boat's bow.

The sound of the explosion was enormous as the shock wave hit the *Sea Scout.*

Cheers went up in the control room.

"Zero," said the exec again.

Two explosions as numbers two and three struck the U-boat amidships. The conning tower separated from the boat and flew skyward fifty feet as the hull rose from the water like a breaching whale.

The exec continued a countdown and when he reached zero for number four nothing happened.

"Number four missed." said the exec.

The captain replied, "Doesn't matter. He'll be under water any moment."

Flipping a lever on the periscope, the captain changed the view angle to that of the sky. He peered closely as he maneuvered a full three-sixty circle. Satisfied there were no German aircraft in sight, he said, "Make one-quarter speed and surface the boat. We'll check for survivors."

"Aye, aye, sir," said the chief as he hit the claxon alarm.

Chapter 34

Horten Hanger office
Hampstead Air Base
3 miles north of Andover, England
4 July, 0943 Hours

Howard Lawson greeted Miller with a handshake and a smile.

Miller returned the smile, then noticed the black briefcase Lawson was carrying.

"Uh oh."

"Something the matter, Captain?"

"The last time I saw you with a briefcase, I ended up in Germany."

Lawson grinned. "Well, at least this time it's not Germany." Before Miller could say anything, Lawson continued, "And look at what you ended up with." He swept a hand in the general direction of the Horten through the office windows. "She's just a thing of beauty."

"You can stop buttering me up, Mr. Lawson."

Lawson sat down at the work table where Miller had spent

many hours going over the Horten's schematics with the engineers and gestured for the captain to join him.

Lawson opened his briefcase, with a flair, thought Miller, and removed a map. He carefully unfolded it and spread it out on the table. Miller glanced at it quickly and said, "Poland? What's in Poland?"

Lawson pointed to Warsaw, then ran his finger north. "Wolf's Lair."

"Wolf's Lair? What's that?"

"Hitler's Eastern Front headquarters. He spends a great deal of time there, as you might imagine, what with the Russian counterattack and advance. We have a source we can rely on to let us know when he's there. I measured the distance and it's about nine hundred and fifty miles. What do you think the flight time would be for your plane?"

Miller glanced at the bird again and realized he had been thinking of her as his. *Should have known*, he thought. He did the math quickly and said, "Call it an hour an half or so."

"Okay, so a little more than three hours round trip."

"Yeah." Miller shook his head. "You want me to bomb Hitler with his own airplane, huh?"

"Seems rather poetic, don't you agree?"

Nodding, Miller replied, "Yes." He looked back down at the map. From what he could tell, Wolf's Lair was deep in a heavy forest. Undoubtedly, it would be camouflaged. How would he know where it was? Knowing Lawson as he did, he must have a plan, just as he had for Operation Devil's Fire.

"How do we find it? It's got to be well hidden."

"Oh, we know exactly where it is. And yes it is. From the air it must look just like the forest around it. We have identified some landmarks, including, and especially importantly, a rail line that runs right to it."

The nickel dropped for Miller right away. "The rail line runs to it and just stops?"

"Correct." Lawson beamed as if Miller was a fine student answering a particularly difficult question in class.

"Hm, well I can see how that'd be pretty damn helpful."

"Yes."

Miller sat back in the chair and crossed his legs. Pulling a pack of cigarettes from his jacket, he offered one to Lawson, who shook his head. Miller lit up and inhaled deeply, then blew the smoke out, up and away from Lawson.

"When are you expecting us to go on this?"

"Sometime in the next two or three weeks."

Miller thought about that briefly. "Okay, we can do that. We just need a few more practice runs so we all know what the hell we're doing and what to expect from each other." He got up and went over to the desk where he picked up the black phone. He dialed a short number and when someone answered, said a few words briskly, then hung up.

Turning to Lawson, he said, "You might as well tell the crew, don't you think?"

Lawson grinned. "Yes."

Chapter 35

Aboard the *Sea Scout*
North Sea
380 miles southeast of Edinburgh
4 July, 1518 Hours

"Sonar contact. Bearing zero-three-zero, range five-zero-zero-zero yards. Course appears to be two-three-five."

Kelly asked quickly, "What do you make it out to be, Ears?"

"Screw sounds and revolutions match German destroyers at twenty knots, sir. At present speed, his and ours, he'll run about a thousand yards in front of us." Ears had been aboard with Kelly long enough to anticipate questions.

"Very good. XO, bring the boat to a stop and make depth two hundred fifty. Rig for silent running."

"Aye, aye, sir."

While everyone was thinking, *maybe the German ship would just keep on going*, no one dared say it, the level of superstition aboard a naval vessel being what it was.

Saunders felt the boat slow down from his bunk where he was

resting with his arms folded under his head like a pillow, but he wasn't sleeping. Sleep would not come this time. Although his body was nearly exhausted, his mind kept wandering. Not ordinarily an inwardly reflective man, the big, red-headed commando found his thoughts returning to Sadie Hughes, his girlfriend of two years. She was exquisitely patient and told him that she would wait for as long as it took for him to come around to the obvious conclusion; they were meant for each other.

He hadn't seen her since sometime in April, and before that it had been six months, missing Christmas with her and her funny family. Her dad was a farmer, and the wife, quite naturally, a farmer's wife, which meant she worked as hard, harder, thought Saunders, than her husband. Sadie was the eldest by eight years and her siblings were all boys ages six, nine and eleven. Whenever they got together there was always singing by the piano with the fire going full blast, even in summer, it was England after all. In between songs, each person was required to tell a joke and, like a talent show, applause determined the winner of the night, although it tended toward ties for first place. Saunders had felt at home right away, and it didn't hurt that the boys idolized their very own British Commando, and a sergeant, too.

Staring at the ceiling, which was a mere six inches above him, Saunders wondered for the first time if maybe he should follow in Dunn's footsteps and get married soon. In the midst of a mission, he was always able to compartmentalize his two lives: the soldier, the lover, and he imagined he would be able to do that if he was married. He also thought Sadie would handle the fear as well as anyone could expect.

Rolling over carefully, he decided he would ask when he got back. Request leave, take a train to her home and get down on his knees and propose. With that moment of clarity, he drifted off to sleep.

The explosion woke him seemingly hours later, but when he checked his watch he realized only ten minutes had passed. He crawled out of the bunk, nearly stepping on the sailor below, who was trying to get up, too.

"What was that?" asked Saunders. He figured it couldn't be good, whatever it was.

The sailor, a shiny-faced boy of maybe eighteen, replied in a shaky voice, "I'm not sure. It might've been a depth charge." Then he ran out the door and disappeared from sight.

As Saunders stepped through the door, another explosion hit the boat and he thought he was imagining it, but it seemed as if the passageway had changed size, as if the *Sea Scout* had been squeezed by a giant fist. He ran down the hall and looked in several rooms in succession checking on his men, calming them as best as could and telling them to stay put. Then, as he continued forward, a tinny, ringing bell sound reached his ears. It was coming at regular intervals and Saunders suddenly realized he was hearing the sonar pinging from a ship above them.

Soon, he made his way to the control room and saw it was filled with grim-faced men going about their business.

"Right full rudder," whispered the captain.

"Right full rudder, aye, aye, sir," whispered back the helmsman as he turned the wheel.

The deck below Saunders feet shifted and he grabbed onto the ladder leading to the conning tower to steady himself. He noticed that Ears had his headset off and was holding it a few inches away from his head. Another explosion sounded, but it seemed muffled. Saunders understood why Ears wasn't wearing the headset. *Good way to blow an eardrum or two.*

Saunders felt helpless and wanted to pitch in, but knew there was nothing for a ground jockey to do. He noticed that the pinging had stopped.

"XO, what's the depth here?"

The executive officer responded immediately, "Eight hundred feet, sir."

"Bloody hell." The captain had hoped he could take the boat to the bottom and blend in with it, but that was past the boat's crush point. "Make depth three hundred."

"Three hundred, aye, aye, sir."

The sub continued her turn and the angled bow planes bit into the water forcing her deeper into the cold North Sea waters.

"Destroyer is turning about, sir. He's going to port," reported Ears.

"Left full rudder."

The helmsman repeated the order and the boat rocked as she

heeled over onto her starboard side.

Saunders visualized what was happening in three dimensions and understood that the captain had ordered the left turn to go in the opposite direction of the destroyer's turn. Based on the captain's expression, Saunders also understood it might not be enough.

Moments later, the pinging sounds resumed, faint at first, then they grew louder and more frequent, which meant the destroyer was closing the distance.

"Three hundred feet, Captain."

"Sir, he's completing his turn. He's going to be right above us in less than a minute."

The pinging sounds increased in intensity and now seemed to be coming on top of each other.

Ears said, "Splashing sounds. Depth charges on the way." He pulled the headset farther from his head and looked upward.

Saunders found himself doing the same and recognized the similarities between this and being shelled. As bad as his experiences with shelling had been, he had the uncomfortable feeling that'd he'd prefer that to this.

The first one went off and rattled the boat, but just a little. It had gone off far enough above them to prevent serious damage.

Saunders decided he should be with his men through this next attack. Bolster their courage a bit by being there with them. Truth be told, it worked both ways. Taking a step, he let go of his death grip on the ladder, then in mid-step, the sound of the next explosion was so loud Saunders thought it was right there in the sub with them. The deck buckled and rose under his feet, then dropped away, he lost his footing and his hands flailed about trying to grab something, anything to keep from falling. The last thing he thought of before his head smashed against a pipe on the bulkhead was Sadie's blue eyes.

Chapter 36

Aboard the *Sea Scout*
North Sea
380 miles southeast of Edinburgh
4 July, 1548 Hours

When Saunders first woke up, he was surprised that he had, indeed, awakened at all. He was lying on his back on something hard. Then the pain settled in. He raised a hand to his head and felt a bandage on his forehead and noticed that someone had placed a folded towel under his head for a pillow. The next thing he noticed was that he seemed to be soaking wet. Thinking at first it was blood he ran his hands along his chest and pulled them up in front of his eyes, which weren't all that sharp yet, and was relieved to see clear moisture and not blood. Water from a leak?

The control room was quiet. It seemed to him the boat was sitting still and listing to starboard, if he got his naval directions right. Carefully, he raised himself to a sitting position and looked around. He started to get up when a pair of hands pushed on his shoulders.

"Don't be hasty, Sergeant," said the doctor. "You might have a slight concussion."

"How long was I out?"

"A few minutes. You have a nasty bump on your head. Just stay put."

"Yes, sir. What's happening? Are they still depth charging us?"

"Yes. They're turning around for another pass."

"Don't they ever run out?"

"I don't know. It's my first time, too."

At this point, the captain noticed Saunders was awake. "You feeling okay, Sergeant?"

"I think so."

"Well, good to have you back. You listen to the Doc, now."

"Yes, sir."

"Splashing sounds, sir!" said Ears.

"Hold tight, everyone," said the captain.

The doctor put one hand on each of Saunders' shoulders and pushed down. "I've got you."

"You're not mad at me any more?"

"No. I understand why you hit him."

"Okay."

Two explosions sounded, but they seemed far away, high above them.

Saunders was curious how they could miss by so far and said as much.

The captain answered the question. "We've lost power to the electric motors and since we don't have any forward movement, we're sinking. We're at three hundred fifty feet. They think we're not that deep. There's a cold water layer between us and them now and it's messing up their sonar."

At hearing the word 'sinking,' Saunders was immediately sorry he'd said anything.

There were two more explosions even farther away.

As the sounds of the explosions faded, Ears put the headset on, holding them an inch away from his ears.

Kelly spoke to the executive officer, "Bill, go aft and see if there's anything we can do to help them get the power going."

"Yes, sir. I'll ring you as soon as I know something."

The captain nodded, then turned his attention to the chief. "Prepare to blow some ballast. We've got to slow our descent."

"Aye, aye, sir." The chief moved over to one of the bulkheads, grabbed a lever, and turned to the captain, waiting.

Kelly was about to give the order when Ears suddenly sat up straight and put the headset right on his ears. "Sir, he's turning to make another pass. Wait, I hear something else. Gunfire! Sir! He's firing his deck guns." Ears was listening intently, eyes closed.

"I have a splash. High speed screw. Another splash! Aerial torpedoes in the water!"

Saunders looked up at the doctor. "What does that mean?"

Out of nervousness and fear, the doctor had to swallow and work up some spit before he could speak. "We might get out of this," he croaked.

Ears pulled the headset away again, in hopeful anticipation of the torpedoes striking the destroyer.

"Torpedoes directly above."

Saunders thought he imagined, or was it? high-pitched sounds traveling overhead.

Suddenly, an explosion. A second later, another.

Ears reported, "I have breaking up sounds."

Cheers went up in the control room.

Then Ears shouted, "Hold on! Bloody hell, he's right on top of us! His momentum carried him right over our position."

The captain grabbed the phone and when someone answered, said in a voice that Saunders was amazed was so calm, "We have three thousand tons headed our way. You have two minutes to get that power restored."

Chapter 37

Miller climbed aboard the Horten, joining his copilot Butler, and the navigator and bombardier, Mike Hoffman, and settled into the pilot's seat.

"Well, boys, you ready for a fun ride today?"

Both men replied that they were.

When the crew had met Lawson and were given their initial briefing on their upcoming mission to bomb Hitler's headquarters in Poland, they'd been skeptical, thinking their commander and the unknown OSS officer were yanking them around, but when it finally sank in, they grew excited. They fully understood what the flight meant, and the irony of bombing the dictator's headquarters with his own airplane wasn't lost on them. The public relations aspect of bombing Hitler's hide out would be an enormous boost to morale, both for servicemen and civilians.

They were all business in the cockpit and the three men

started on the preflight checklist.

Fifteen minutes later, the Horten shot skyward, leaving a trail of flame and smoke behind.

Not long after, they were over the Atlantic Ocean, climbing rapidly toward their target altitude: 40,000 feet. They had turned on the oxygen at ten thousand feet as well as the heat. Miller had been astonished to discover that the Horten brothers had found a way to heat the cockpit. He knew the bomber boys in the B-17s, as well as himself, had suffered frostbite at 25,000 feet altitude, where the outside air temperature was minus thirty degrees Fahrenheit. It was expected that at 40,000, the temperature would fall to more than double that, about minus seventy.

Miller was anxious to see what the Horten's reaction to the ultra high altitude would be. He fully expected her to be faster, due to, if to nothing else, the thinner atmosphere. His primary worry, though, was how the engines would behave. In the deep dark place of his mind where, since the war started, he'd learned to keep all his fears, was the thought that the engines would starve and flame out, turning the Horten into the highest ever flying brick.

"Passing thirty thousand," said Butler.

Miller checked the instrument panel and was satisfied with what he saw.

A few moments passed and the copilot said, "Thirty-nine thousand."

Miller responded by pushing the wheel forward to reduce the flight angle and prepare to level off.

"Forty thousand."

"Leveling off," replied Miller. Scanning the instruments, he saw they were flying level on a heading of two-seventy, due west. The engines seemed to be doing fine in the thin air. The airspeed dial showed six hundred miles an hour and seemed to be increasing. As he watched, the needle spun steadily farther and farther clockwise. After a few minutes, Miller let out a whoop that startled his crew. "Six–twenty, boys!"

With the cockpit located so close to the nose and having a bubble canopy, the visibility was even better than from his beloved P-51. Off to the north, Ireland rose like a green gem from the Atlantic's blue waters. Beyond that, nothing but blue water as far as you could see.

Miller was beside himself with excitement. The Horten had performed flawlessly with the engines' temperature maintaining normal range all the way. On a whim, he had taken her through some evasive maneuvers testing her reactions to the stress of sharper turns and was satisfied with the smoothness of her reactions, even though she was slower to respond than at lower altitudes, again due to the thinner air rushing over the control surfaces.

"Okay, Butler, ready to take over?"

"I'm ready," replied the copilot. Miller liked to alternate landings with his copilot to make sure the man would have the necessary experience.

As they flew home, Miller took the opportunity to talk to his crew about the upcoming bombing raid on Wolf's Lair. Even though they'd met Lawson and gone over it several times, Miller's process before action was to cover all eventualities with his crew, or as he had done before the Horten, his squadron.

Soon they arrived over Hampstead's airspace. Within minutes, Butler brought the aircraft around, lined her up on the runway, and performed a perfect landing.

Once the plane was parked in front of her hanger and the crew were out on the tarmac, Miller said, "Well done, boys. Be back in two hours. We're going up for some practice bomb runs."

Chapter 38

Aboard the *Sea Scout*
North Sea
380 miles southeast of Edinburgh
4 July, 1550 Hours, Paris time

Saunders struggled to get up, having to fight the doctor, who kept telling him to stay put. Finally, Saunders gripped the man's bicep and squeezed, not too hard, but enough to get the doctor to stop pushing him.

"Look, Doc, I have to get to my men. I have to be there with them. In case, you know." Saunders's gaze seemed to bore into the doctor's, who suddenly understood. He nodded.

"Here, let me help you."

Saunders managed to stand up. "Thank you," he said, though gritted teeth. His head pounded.

"Ready to walk?"

"Aye."

Carefully, the doctor began guiding Saunders toward the passageway.

Suddenly, the boat moved. Slowly, at first, then she picked up speed.

The captain reacted quickly, "Hard to port, down plane ten degrees." He wanted to gain precious seconds by going deeper.

The *Sea Scout* responded normally and the captain kept that course for thirty seconds, then asked, "Ears, where is he?"

The sonar man had turned on his active sonar and was watching the return dial carefully. "Fifty yards astern and passing two hundred feet. Sir, we are clear of the debris field."

Cheers went up.

"Rudder amidships! Blow ballast. Bow plane up ten degrees."

Saunders felt the boat change position and relief flooded through him. Maybe he'd get to see Sadie after all.

Dr. Morgan said, "Okay, Sergeant, let's get you to sickbay."

Saunders nodded and was immediately sorry. Maybe it *was* a concussion. "Okay."

By the time they'd made it to sickbay, word was out as to what happened to the destroyer and men were slapping each other on the back up and down the passageway. The doctor got Saunders situated on a bunk and gave him the once over, checking pulse and respiration, then he clicked on a penlight and shone it into Saunders' eyes one at a time.

"Well, the good news is your pupils are responding properly. Are you feeling nauseous?"

"No, sir."

"You're positive? It's important."

"I'm sure. No nausea. Just a pounding headache."

"If I turn my back on you to get an aspirin, you'll still be lying there when I turn back?"

Saunders grinned, or at least thought he did. "Aye, doc."

The doctor stepped away quickly and got the aspirin and some water from a built-in sink. He handed both to Saunders who took the little white pill and swallowed some water with it.

A knock on the door was followed by Barltrop entering the sickbay, concern on his face.

"Sarge, you okay?"

Saunders was surprised to see Barltrop. "How'd you know I was in here?"

"We're confined inside a metal tube under the ocean. News

travels fast."

"Hm, yes. How are the men?"

"Fine. Looking forward to jumping out of a perfectly good airplane again after this."

"Aye, me too."

The doctor heard this and said, "I wouldn't like to see you jumping out of anything for the next week to ten days."

"I'll be fine, doc," protested Saunders.

"You will be if you pay attention to what I said."

Saunders sighed, then rolled his eyes for Barltrop's benefit, who chuckled.

The doctor caught sight of Saunders play and said to Barltrop, "You're second in command?"

"Yes, sir."

"You have to keep your sergeant honest and make sure he follows my instructions. Can you do that, or will I have to send a letter along to your commanding officer?"

Saunders answered for Barltrop, "No need for the letter, doc, I'll be good. For a week to ten days, as you said."

The doctor stared at Saunders for a moment. "The medical corps is a close community, Sergeant. I know people virtually everywhere. Believe me when I say this: I will find out if you get rambunctious. By the way, you will stay here and rest for the remainder of the voyage home. I'll have a corpsman check in on you." Then he smiled and left the sickbay.

"Bloody hell," muttered Saunders.

"I'll keep you company," offered Barltrop, with a wicked grin.

"Oh, truly bloody hell," repeated Saunders.

Chapter 39

Port of Edinburgh, Scotland
5 July, 2025 Hours

As the *Sea Scout* smoothly approached her berth at the dock, sailors poured out onto the deck, like ants from an anthill, to get her tied up and secured. The setting sun threw long shadows across the port and sunlight glistened and sparkled off the water.

A canvas covered Royal Military Police truck trundled down the pier and stopped next to the *Sea Scout's* berth. A hand, reaching out from inside the canvas, unlatched the tailgate, which clanged open. A half-dozen men jumped out. They were wearing the famous Red Cap berets and red arm bands with white MP letters.

The Royal Military Police had a long and storied history dating back to 1813 when the Duke of York proposed a Staff Corps of Cavalry to be attached to units. Members of these new units were authorized to hang looters and other offenders. Wearing their own uniforms at first, they tied red scarves around their right shoulder, leading the way to the red arm bands and the red caps.

These were tough men, who'd seen it all, and they looked it. The man in charge, a six-four sergeant major with a ragged knife-fight scar down his right cheek earned in his youth, gave the word and they double-timed to the spot where the gangway would soon be positioned. There they stood at the ready with their holstered Webley Mk VI .455 caliber revolvers hanging heavy at their side.

When Saunders made it to the deck, albeit a little slower than usual, he spotted the Red Caps right away and was pleased, and perhaps a tad bit surprised that they were there at all. The radio conversation earlier must have done the trick, although he hadn't been sure at the time. First, after the *Sea Scout's* radio man made contact in the middle of the night and verified the transmission with the code word of the day, Saunders had to convince the radio operator at the naval base to get his boss, a lieutenant, on the horn. Next, he explained the situation carefully to the officer, who was dubious and made Saunders repeat some things, but at last, finally agreed to make the phone call to the Royal Military Police Provost office in Edinburgh.

Saunders raised a hand and the alert sergeant major saw it, giving the commando a nod in return.

The dock hands finished maneuvering the gangplank into place and the Red Caps marched across. When they reached Saunders, the sergeant major asked as a matter of confirmation, "Saunders?"

"Aye, that's me."

"Williamson."

The men shook hands.

The sergeant major eyed Saunders for a moment. What he saw there, the stout determination, the combat veteran's hardness, satisfied him. A man like himself. A serious man.

"Your prisoner coming up soon?"

"Aye. I've got some of my men bringing him now."

"What's the story?"

Saunders gave the man a brief overview of how things had gone.

Williamson nodded here and there, and when Saunders finished, said, "Sounds like a normal outing for you chaps." He gave Saunders a smile, which reached all the way to his eyes.

"That would be correct."

A commotion behind Saunders caught Williamson's attention. Three men had climbed up onto the deck, two commandos and the prisoner. Barltrop and Redington were tying the man's hands behind him. They'd had to free them to get him to the top. Finished with the task, the two men each grabbed an elbow and marched the prisoner over to where the two sergeants stood.

Saunders moved in front of the man. He hadn't bothered trying to talk with the prisoner during the rest of the voyage. Let the intelligence men take care of it. Besides, Saunders needed to rest. Doctor's orders.

Saunders suddenly grabbed the man by the shirt, yanking the collar open. Then he slid his other hand inside the shirt and removed the identification tags for Joe Burnett. Holding them up, he asked, "These belong to a real person, right? What happened to him?"

"Yes. He's dead. Everything I told you about me, where I'm from and so on, is accurate."

"How'd he die?"

"Captured after parachuting from his B-17 over Germany. Then the Gestapo got hold of him and extracted his information. He died at their hands."

The big commando frowned and shook his head at the news, then asked, "What's your real name?"

The German hesitated, then realized nothing would be gained by refusing to answer. "Reinhard Vogel."

"You know, Vogel, if we were on the battlefield, I'd kill you without a second thought."

Vogel nodded. "And I, you, Sergeant." A moment of silence passed between the two men, then the prisoner asked, "And now?"

"I have no desire to kill you. There's no need. Your war is over." Saunders smiled grimly. "Well, almost. You're going to go with these nice men. They're taking you to meet someone who will have many questions for you. Day after day after day. I'd suggest you answer them. Then your war will truly be over."

Saunders expected the prisoner to snap off some retort or yell some more Nazi bullshit, but instead, a sad expression crossed the man's bruised face. He said simply, "The war was over on June 6th."

"What was that shite about us being weak and inferior?"

"Anger. Fear. One last shot at my enemy."

"Didn't work out so well, did it?"

"No. No, it didn't."

Saunders nodded, then turned away to say to Williamson, "Thanks for being here on time. I appreciate it."

"You're welcome." The sergeant major turned to leave, then stopped and faced Saunders again. "Where you headed?"

"Barton Stacey."

"Hanging around with the Americans?"

Saunders shrugged. "They're not so bad." His red moustache twitched as he grinned.

"So you say."

With that, the sergeant major waved a hand at his men and they surrounded the prisoner. In no time at all, they had him loaded into the truck.

As the police vehicle drove away, Saunders turned to Barltrop and said, "Let's get the men up here so we can get off this boat."

"You'll have no complaint from me, Sarge. You're going turn in those ID tags, aren't you?"

"Aye. At least then his family will know the truth."

"You're a good man, Sarge."

Saunders glanced at his second in command. "Don't be spreading any rumors, Steve."

"Wouldn't think of it."

Barltrop left to corral the men.

Saunders spotted the captain and the doctor headed his way. He strode their way and stopped a few feet away, and saluted, which they returned.

"Captain, thanks for your hospitality."

"Our pleasure, Sergeant. Hope you heal up soon." The captain put his hand on the doctor's shoulder and said, "It's best that you do what the good doctor told you." Then he leaned forward conspiratorially, "He knows people everywhere."

Saunders laughed. "So I hear. Don't worry, I'll be good."

The doctor offered his hand and Saunders shook it with a

smile, then shook the captain's.

"Your crew is quite impressive, sir. Extraordinary calm in the face of battle."

"Thank you. They are excellent sailors. A captain couldn't ask for more. Although, of course, being the captain, I always do. I have to say you and your men are fine soldiers. What you accomplished was amazing. I saw that the prisoner got picked up by the Royal Military Police. I hope they learn some things of value from him."

"I do, too. The truth is, I'm going to call in a favor from a friend who used to be in MI-5. See if he can make something happen."

The captain looked surprised. "You know someone who was in MI-5?"

"Yes, sir. Hard to believe, I know, but we crossed paths recently. He works directly for the Prime Minister."

"Bloody hell. You have friends in high places."

"Doesn't keep me out of trouble, though, sir."

"No, it sure doesn't." The captain glanced around at his men working on deck. "Time for me to get back to it."

"Yes, sir." Saunders saluted and the two officers moved away.

Saunders looked out across the deck to the darkening North Sea. He put his hands on his hips and just stood there. It had been a rough mission. Successful, if you counted the positives: five U-boats destroyed, a training facility for German saboteurs discovered and also destroyed, a captive saboteur. On the negative were the loss of two fine men, Padgett and Merriweather.

He sighed deeply at the thought of writing the letters to their families. While in most units, the commanding officer did that, Saunders preferred to do it and no officer had ever said no. He doubted stern, crabby Colonel Jenkins would object.

Turning his head to his left, his gaze followed the contours of the sub's conning tower all the way to the top, then along the mast to the Union Jack waving in the gentle breeze. His nation had suffered brutally at the hands of the Germans, and her servicemen to the Germans and the Japanese.

A sudden welling of pride rose in his chest and he gave in to impulse and snapped to attention, then saluted his nation's flag. He slowly lowered his hand and his gaze. To his surprise, every sailor on deck was facing him, their hands raised in salute to him. He returned the salute solemnly and the sailors returned to their tasks.

He and his squad still had a long trip home. He figured he would be able to arrange a flight back some time the next morning. Right now, though, he had but two goals: get his men to the nearest pub, and to plan his trip to see Sadie at long last.

Chapter 40

As usual, Dunn and his men were not going to land in a plane, choosing instead to jump out of it. Well, maybe not exactly their own choice. But they knew it was the only way in to their eventual target, which was a mere thirty-five miles from downtown Paris. Also as usual, they would be surrounded by the enemy.

This jump, however, was going to be rough, as if they all weren't. Due to the proximity of the enemy, Dunn and his squad would be performing a Very Low-Level Static Line Jump. This type of jump had two advantages: it quite simply got them out of the sky where they were easy pickin's for the Germans and it reduced the distance between the men when they hit the earth. The plan was to bring the ship in over the target at 750 feet. This was not the record low, which was 245 feet, and the extra five hundred feet would, in theory, improve the odds of a successful landing by the squad. The disadvantages were found when Dunn had read the analysis reports gathered from hundreds upon hundreds of jumps. Dunn was especially interested in one statistic that showed the percentage of static line parachute canopies that opened, which was 99.98%. He realized that was a good number, that is, unless you were one of the .02% failures. The other, and equally important, item was the time a soldier would have to open the reserve parachute if he was indeed among the .02%: 6.4 seconds. That was where Dunn expected serious injuries, and possibly and while praying against it, fatalities, his included.

The men had done a couple of practice jumps during the past few days over the English countryside north of Andover. Everyone survived and no one was injured, which Dunn took as a miracle. Maybe, he thought, just maybe.

Dunn was standing next to the jumpmaster. The door was open and Dunn could see stars against the black backdrop of night. He couldn't see it from his side of the aircraft, but the half-full moon was out, which would provide ample light for him and his men. Hopefully, they'd get to the ground before the moon helped the Nazis shoot them out of the sky.

The red light suddenly blinked out to be replaced by a green one. The jumpmaster tapped Dunn on the shoulder. The Ranger took a quick step to the door and jumped. The slipstream carried him past the tail of the plane. When he hit the end of his tether line, the parachute released and he could hear the flapping of the canopy. A satisfying moment later, he felt another jerk as the canopy fully deployed and bit the night's cool air. Dunn glanced up quickly to ensure the canopy was okay all around, which it was. Then he looked below and saw the French countryside rushing upward at a rather alarming rate. He found his target field just ahead, a pasture, or what he thought may have once been a pasture, and prepared for his landing. Seconds later, his boots crashed into the hard ground and he performed a perfect tuck-and-roll. He got to his feet and scanned the sky quickly counting open canopies. To his immense relief, there were nine, all fully deployed, lines untangled, and descending at the correct speed.

He unhooked his parachute harness and got it off quickly, then began the task of rolling the mass of cords and canopy into a smaller ball-shaped package. The rendezvous point was a grove of trees about fifty yards directly south. Dunn waited until all nine of his men landed and got back to their feet. Satisfied that they had all alighted safely, he turned and took off toward the trees at the double-time, knowing his men would follow momentarily.

Reaching the grove, Dunn powered his way in through the dark underbrush, looking for a hiding place for the chutes. Moonlight filtered through and he found a fallen tree. He made his way to where its roots were sticking up out of the ground, and began digging in the softer earth. By the time his men joined him, he'd scooped out a depression large enough for all ten parachutes. The men tossed their packages in, then they all set about covering them up with the loose dirt. Once done with the dirt, they sprinkled dead leaves around haphazardly completing the illusion that nature, rather than man, had been at work.

According to mission planning, the coordination with the local French Resistance group was prearranged and they were to meet their contact, known only as Georges, at a farm house near a T-intersection about two miles south. Since standing still was not an option, in case the Germans saw or heard the C-47 and sent out a patrol, Dunn got his men together and they began to make their way toward the meeting point.

A half-hour later, they were lined up in the ditch on the north-west side of the east-west road, the part forming the top of the tee. From their point of view, the tee was upside down. The farm house sat on the southeast corner of the intersection. It was dark. Foreboding trees surrounded it on all sides. An overgrown driveway curved toward it from the north-south road. South of the house were the remains of a barn that appeared to have imploded due to extreme old age.

"Damn, you think they could've picked a more forlorn place?"

Dunn grinned to himself at Cross's remark because he'd been thinking along the same lines.

"No, I expect not."

Both men were kneeling, their Thompson .45 caliber machineguns cradled in their arms.

Dunn was about to send two men to scout out the area around the house, and especially behind it, when the sound of a large vehicle's engine reached him. It was coming from the east and he turned his head that way. There was nothing in sight on the narrow black ribbon leading east. Knowing that machine sounds carried miles at night, Dunn waited impatiently for the vehicle to reveal itself. When it finally did a couple of minutes later, Dunn muttered under his breath. "Damn." To Cross, he said, "German truck coming."

Cross replied evenly, "Of course there is."

Chapter 41

Sergeant Barltrop turned on a light in the small room where Saunders was sleeping on the lone bunk. From a safe distance of a few feet, Barltrop called Saunders' name a few times, each a bit louder then the one previous.

Saunders took a deep breath and whispered, "What is it, Steve?"

"There's a phone call for you."

"What's the time?"

"Five of five."

"Who is it?"

Barltrop hesitated too long.

Saunders sat upright and kicked his feet off the bunk. "Who is it, Steve?" A low growl.

"It's Mr. Hughes, Malcolm." Barltrop almost never used Saunders' first name.

Suddenly fully awake and alert, Saunders jumped up and ran

out the door, down the length of the barracks, passing his still-sleeping men, to the office at the front.

He closed the door behind himself and grabbed the phone so hard his knuckles turned white. "'ello, Mr. Hughes. Is everything all right?"

"Malcolm . . ." a weak voice started.

"Mr. Hughes, please. Is Sadie all right?"

"No, Mac. No, she's been hurt. Real bad, son. Buzz bomb. London. You best come. Hurry."

Chapter 42

"I see it," continued Cross.

As the truck grew closer, hitting the five hundred yard mark, Dunn began calculating its risk to the mission's success. At the low end was the truck driving on by and out of sight. At the other end, being forced into a firefight with the truck's occupants could attract the attention of other German units and the mission could be blown. Whether the truck was there because of their suspected presence or on some other task, Dunn couldn't say. He gauged the truck's speed to be about thirty miles an hour, and figured it would be on them in less than a minute.

Another sound pierced the night and Dunn groaned. Coming from the south was a black van, traveling fast. Dunn knew the two vehicles would reach the intersection at almost the exact same time.

"That's got to be Georges," whispered Cross.

Dunn decided. His men weren't in the best place to conduct

an ambush on the truck if it stopped in the intersection to intercept the van. They would be at a sharp angle to it, and the canvas-topped truck would provide cover for its men once they jumped out.

He tapped Cross on the shoulder and said, "Follow me."

Cross nodded and passed the word quickly, then took off after his sergeant.

They advanced east, running bent over. Dunn stopped when they reached the place he thought was best for the ambush. Everyone squatted down, weapons ready, and waited.

It was a short wait. Someone in the truck had spotted the van barreling down the road toward them. The German truck braked to a halt in the middle of the intersection where Dunn had figured it would. From his vantage point, Dunn could only make out two soldiers near the tailgate on the truck's left side, but he had to assume the truck was full of soldiers. The passenger door opened and a soldier stepped out, then walked around the front of the truck. Squeaking brakes told Dunn the van had come to a stop on the other side.

Dunn was cursing the bad luck of not being able to get across the road. At least then he could see what was happening. He was surprised that none of the soldiers had climbed down out of the truck. Then he heard snippets of a two-man conversation that he couldn't understand, but thought was in German.

Suddenly, laughter burst out from the two men, and shortly after, the soldier came back around the front of the truck, still laughing and shaking his head. He opened the door, jumped up on the running board, and climbed back into the cab. An appreciative laugh came from within the truck. The soldier had obviously passed on the joke. The truck started moving and was soon completely out of sight.

Dunn watched the van go up the driveway to a spot near the house and stop. The man got out and, even from a distance, Dunn could tell he was huge. He had to be close to six-four and three hundred pounds, with broad, powerful shoulders.

The man walked across the yard toward the T-intersection. When he reached the edge of the yard, he stopped and looked around. Seeing no one, he cupped his hands around his mouth and called out, "*Bonjour*? Dunn?" He thumped his chest with a big meaty hand. "*C'est moi, Georges.*"

Dunn rose and waved. The two men were less than ten yards apart. Dunn kept his attention, not on Georges, but the house behind him. Dunn had not forgotten the treachery of Luc, the French Resistance fighter turned Gestapo agent that had cost him the life of Timothy Oldham and blown a mission, also getting Dunn shot, then captured. If not for the kindness and courage of the French doctor treating Dunn's head injury, Dunn would have faced torture and eventual death at the hands of another brutal, sadistic Gestapo agent in Calais. Luc's demise at the hands of Madeline, the French Resistance leader, had brought Dunn considerable satisfaction, but did nothing for the sorrow Dunn felt when he wrote to twenty-year-old Timothy's parents back in rural Kentucky telling them about their son's death.

Dunn ducked back down, turned to Cross, and gave him quick instructions. Cross ran down the ditch to the west and grabbed his men. They rose as one and ran across the road to the south, then down into the ditch on the west side of the road. They brought their weapons up, aimed at the house.

Georges, for his part, seemed unconcerned with this apparent aggressive mistrust. He simply raised his hands and stood perfectly still.

Dunn and the remainder of the squad climbed up to the road surface and marched toward the Frenchman, weapons aimed at the lone man. Dunn positioned Schneider next to himself.

Dunn stopped a few feet away and eyed the man. "Dunn here."

Schneider spoke to Georges in French, translating for Dunn.

The American sergeant and French Resistance leader exchanged code words to each man's satisfaction.

Dunn said, "You can lower your hands, Georges."

"Ah, thank you." The Frenchman lowered his hands and then grabbed Dunn's right hand, his steak-sized ones dwarfing the ranger's. Georges shook vigorously. "I am pleased to finally meet an American soldier! You don't know what it means to us that you are here. We have suffered so much for so long. Thank you."

Dunn smiled and worked his hand free, then patted the big man on the shoulder. "You're welcome, Georges."

Georges turned and, with a flourish of a sweeping hand, said,

"Shall we?"

As they walked toward the house, Dunn asked, "We thought for sure you'd run into trouble with the Germans, but then we heard you and the German laughing. What was that all about?"

Georges chuckled, a deep rumble. "I showed them my papers, which say I'm a baker, which I am. The Germans *love* bakers. Then I just happened to mention that I was heading home where my wife would be expecting me to service her, and as I was just leaving my mistress, I said I didn't know if I would be up for it."

Schneider laughed out loud before translating back to Dunn.

Dunn and his men laughed, too.

Making their way to the porch, Dunn told Cross to post a couple of sentries outside, out of sight. Georges unlocked the door, stepped through, holding the door open, and the men entered. The Frenchman led the way through the living room and into the kitchen, where he opened another door and started down the stairs to the cellar. He flipped on a light switch and a dim bulb brightened.

The men trooped down the stairs and gathered in the surprisingly large area. The floor was dirt and shelves lined two walls where a farm wife may have once stored home canned vegetables and fruit preserves in glass jars.

In the center of the room was a table. Georges opened his jacket and then unbuttoned his shirt. He removed a map and laid it on the table. When Dunn leaned over to examine the map after Georges had unfolded it, he noticed it was a tourist map. *Well, you use what you can get.* He knew that both the Germans and the Allies used the same type of maps.

Georges looked at Dunn for a moment, then asked, "You are really here to kill Rommel?"

"We are."

Georges glanced around the room at the grim-faced men. They appeared to be so calm, stoic even, and he knew what it meant to be called a Ranger. It had been, after all, Rangers, who had helped secure Omaha Beach by scaling the cliffs overlooking the killing zone.

Looking back at Dunn, he nodded. "I believe you." He pointed at the map. "Here is the Château La Roche Guyon, Rommel's headquarters. You see it is on the north bank of the

Seine, at the top of the meandering loop. The castle is essentially impenetrable. Rommel's forces in the village number about fifteen hundred, while there are only five hundred villagers.

"Rommel is a most unusual occupier. You will not see a single Nazi flag draped anywhere. He doesn't impose any curfews. He even strolls about the village without much protection, sometimes none at all. Yet, there are always Nazi soldiers around." Georges shook his head. "I am unable to see how you could possibly get to him in the village."

"Fifteen hundred, huh?" Dunn eyed the village, the wandering Seine River, the roads, the bridges. Rommel had selected his headquarters extremely well. It was positioned only sixty miles from the front and roughly equidistant to various points along the line.

Dunn stood perfectly still for what seemed a long time to Georges. The American was apparently just staring at the map. But Dunn was already in the planning stage and his mind was moving fast. His focus traveled west from the village across the river, following the main west-bound road. The one that led to the front. The one Rommel would surely travel when visiting his various commands.

Finally, Dunn raised his head and said to the group, "Here's what we're going to do." He looked at Jones, the Chicago sniper. Slung over his shoulder was his M1903 A1 Springfield.

Jones simply nodded.

Dunn laid out his plan.

Chapter 43

Northern Hospital at World's End Lane
Winchmore Hills, Enfield, far north outskirts of
London
11 July, 0640 Hours, London time

As an emergency bed service hospital, Northern Hospital was filled to capacity. All hospitals in central London had been evacuated and left standing empty long ago, due to the German V-1 buzz bomb attacks. Built in 1883, the hospital was actually made up of several two-story brick buildings spread across an expansive property. The hospital had quite a good reputation going all the way back to its beginning when, in 1893, the mortality rate for the dreaded scarlet fever was only 2.5 percent compared to 6.3 percent in other hospitals.

Saunders sat hulking in a chair next to Sadie's bed, his hand holding hers, his head hanging, tears streaming down his cheeks. She was in a ward with nearly thirty other patients. Her head was swathed in a bandage covering everything above the ears and eyes. A cast ran the length of her right leg, ankle to hip. Her eyes were closed and unmoving under the bruised lids. A two-inch line of stitches ran from the right side of her swollen lips toward her right ear.

Saunders had talked to her father on arrival, and he'd told him what the doctors had said. With all of her injuries, including a concussion, especially the concussion, which had put her into a coma, her odds were fifty-fifty for survival. The next day or so would decide her fate.

Saunders called Colonel Jenkins and told him he needed to get to the hospital north of London and why. The usually brusque colonel gave permission to leave immediately. Within minutes, Saunders was dressed and running, and Barltrop had a tough time keeping up with his sergeant. While Saunders ran around the front of an Austin Eight right-hand drive staff car to get in the driver's side, Barltrop took the short cut by climbing in the passenger side. He immediately yanked the key out of the ignition switch.

Saunders jumped into the driver's seat and shouted at Barltrop, "Give me the bloody fookin' key!" He lunged toward Barltrop, who retreated against the passenger door holding the key out the window.

"No, Sarge. Let me drive you. You're in no condition to drive. You won't get there safe. Let me drive."

Saunders' face turned as red as his hair and his eyes seemed to bug out. He grabbed Barltrop's shirt and shouted, "Give . . . me . . . the . . . KEY!"

Barltrop didn't resist by trying to remove Saunders' hand, but instead kept his left hand out the window. "No, Sarge. You can beat me to a pulp, but you're not driving."

This remark seemed to nonplus Saunders and he let go of his second-in-command's shirt.

"That makes no sense. If I knock you out, I'll get the key."

"Maybe. I'm willing to take the risk."

Without a word, Saunders got out of the car and ran around to the passenger side. Barltrop scooted over just before Saunders got back in the car. He started the engine, put it in first gear and tromped the gas pedal.

It wasn't until thirty minutes later, when they were nearly half way there, that Saunders finally spoke.

"I'm mad as hell at you, Steve."

Barltrop kept his eyes on the road and shrugged. "I don't care, Malcolm. I'm just doing my job: keeping you alive."

Saunders grunted, then said, "Piss off."

Barltrop said, "You're my friend, Malcolm. You'd do the same thing for me. But I'd tell you to piss off, too."

Saunders grunted again and was still.

The sounds of approaching footsteps caused Saunders to raise his head and look around. Coming toward him were Mr. Hughes and his wife. At the far end of the ward, standing outside and looking forlornly in, were Sadie's three little brothers. An older woman, who Saunders recognized as their aunt, had her arms around them.

Saunders stood to greet the Hughes. He hadn't talked to the Missus yet and she threw herself against him in a hug. "Oh, Mac, what are we going to do?"

Saunders hugged her tightly and said, "We're going to sit here and pray and wait, Mrs. Hughes."

She released her mother-bear grip on Saunders and stepped back. Seeing the wet streaks on his face, she opened her purse, then dabbed his cheeks and eyes with a handkerchief.

When she was done, Saunders stepped back and said, "Thank you, Mrs. Hughes."

"When are you going to call me Margaret?"

"Maybe some day, Mrs. Hughes."

Mrs. Hughes patted Saunders' bicep gently. "Well, when you're ready."

Saunders started to say something, but stopped and looked at the floor.

"What is it, Mac?"

Saunders raised his head enough to look at Mrs. Hughes. "Why was she in London?" he asked plaintively.

Sadie's parents exchanged a look, which when Saunders saw

it, his heart nearly stopped beating.

"She wanted to buy a new dress. Wouldn't settle for anything local. You know Sadie."

"Because I was coming to visit."

"It's not your fault, Mac," said Mrs. Hughes as she moved closer to touch Saunders' shoulder.

Saunders shook his head, then grabbed it with both hands and began sobbing in grief, rocking back and forth. The Hughes wrapped their arms around him.

"My fault. My fault . . . "

"No. No," whispered Mrs. Hughes.

Time passed slowly. Saunders stopped rocking and lowered his hands. He let Mrs. Hughes guide him out of the ward room and into a small waiting area with wood-slatted chairs. She pushed him gently into one of the chairs. Sadie's little brothers followed like a gaggle of baby geese and stopped in front of Saunders, looking up at the huge red-headed man. At first, Saunders didn't notice them, and Mrs. Hughes tried to shoo the boys away, but then Saunders' eyes grew alert. He looked around the room, clearly seeing it for the first time. Then he spied the three brothers staring at him, all with blue eyes identical to Sadie's.

The boys looked frightened to death. They knew something bad had happened by the way their parents had been behaving. They'd only been told their only sister had been hurt and that doctors were helping her. They also knew they'd never seen the strong, hearty, and funny British soldier look like this. It was Saunders' reaction that scared them the most.

When Saunders opened his arms to them they all clambered up onto his lap and hugged him. He bowed his head, touching theirs, murmured comforting words, then said a prayer.

Chapter 44

Château de La Roche-Guyon
16 July, 2100 Hours, Five days later

The Château de La Roche-Guyon dominated the northern bank of the Seine river, which wound its way toward the Normandy coast. The castle itself sat atop a chalk-cliff one hundred fifty feet above the river level. Built in the twelfth century, it was a simple design above ground, but buried beneath were tunnels upon tunnels boring through the hillside connecting the living quarters. This was home to the de La Roche family until the mid-thirteenth century, when a more modern and fortified manor house was built at the base of the cliff. A few more centuries passed, and a formal garden was created, measuring a hundred fifty by two hundred yards. Just in front of the house, was a fifty yard square open space surrounded by a low stone wall. Adjacent to the far wall was an east-west road.

Max Mayerhofer, the lead engineer for the Pulse project, sat at a table for eight in the Grand Salon, completely and totally awestruck by his surroundings. General Rommel's headquarters was extraordinarily opulent. Paintings that were at least two hundred years old adorned the massive walls that rose to the twenty-foot ceiling. Across the wide expanse of the round table was Alfred Jodl, the Armed Forces High Command Chief of the Operations Staff. To his right, was Rommel himself. The rest of the seats were filled with various high-level staff officers for each commander. Rommel, playing the host, had made the introductions as the men arrived, but Mayerhofer could only remember Jodl's name. Rommel had merely explained that Mayerhofer was a scientist with no further elaboration.

Mayerhofer had been flown in on an Fi 156 Storch, a two-seat reconnaissance aircraft, from the same airfield where the Pulse Weapon had departed for its test. He'd been grumpy about leaving his Citroën in the hands of Pachter and Rademacher, but had been given no choice.

Based on the dinner conversation, Mayerhofer determined that this group was explicitly trusted by Rommel, although he realized his own presence likely altered the topics discussed. About the time the wait staff, who were dressed in white coats and black slacks, and wearing their military insignias, were finishing serving dessert, Rommel tapped a spoon gently against a wine goblet. Conversation died out immediately.

Rommel paused until the waiters left the room. "Gentlemen, *Herr* Doctor Mayerhofer is the leader of a special project, approved by the *Führer*, that may well turn the war to our favor."

Murmurs of surprise went around the table. Jodl gave one of his staff a look saying, *Rommel has gone crazy like the Führer*.

Virtually everyone at the table knew that the war was over. Winning was not possible. The only hope was to hold out and survive. With the Red Army rumbling toward Germany from the east and the other Allies from the west, it was just a matter of time. The generally held thought was that the war would end by Christmas. Everyone at the table, except Mayerhofer, also knew that if Hitler had let the generals lead instead of sticking his nose into every possible military decision, the war would be in a totally different state. The loss of a complete army at Stalingrad, due to the *Führer's* insane insistence on standing to the last man, was a fatal blow to the eastern front. If commanders on the ground had been allowed to pull off a fighting retreat, the

German army would have been able to regroup, and reestablish a solid defensive line farther west. That would have led to a stalemate at worst, and Germany would still have the buffer zone of an impenetrable defense along the Polish-Russian border. This would have allowed the Germans to pour huge numbers of men and materiel into western Europe. But now, the *Wehrmacht* had been forced to trade space for time, able only to slow the onslaught and make it costly for the Allies on both fronts. For Rommel to suggest that the war could be saved and won seemed a fool's errand.

Rommel sensed the mood of the men at the table. "I realize this seems too good to be true, so I suggest we give *Herr* Mayerhofer time to set up a movie projector. Then he will introduce what we're about to see." Rommel turned to Mayerhofer and said, "If you please."

"Yes, General." The scientist spent five minutes setting up a projector and carefully placing a portable screen against one of the walls.

He faced the important men at the table. At first, he was surprised at his lack of nervousness, then he realized he had been presented to the *Führer* and not only survived, but had received accolades.

He began to speak, using layman's terms where possible, and precise analogies, explaining what the Pulse weapon was and could do. After a couple of minutes, he noticed a visible shift in the men's demeanor. They were alert, attentive, and each man had unconsciously leaned forward in his chair. He wrapped up his ten minute speech and said, "Please allow me to show you the weapon in action."

He stepped quickly to the projector as Rommel himself got up and turned off the lights. The three minute long film played, the only sound that of the projector. When it finished, and the freed tail end of the film flapped against the projector's frame, Mayerhofer turned it off. Rommel turned on the lights.

Jodl was first to speak. "General Rommel, *Herr* Mayerhofer, I must say this gives me hope."

Rommel nodded and rose. "I suggest we take an after-dinner brandy to the war room where we can determine the best places for deployment of the weapon."

There was agreement amongst the men and they delayed rising until the wait staff came in and poured French brandy into snifters for everyone.

Once in the war room, two floors below, in a sub-basement safe from Allied bombers, the men gathered around a map table measuring two meters by three. The room was brightly lit by a dozen lights hanging a meter or so above the men's heads. Mayerhofer, feeling uncertain about where he should be, hung back. Then Rommel grasped him by the elbow and pulled him to the table next to himself. "You deserve a place here. To see where your work will do its best for the Fatherland. I believe you'll earn yourself a place in German history."

"Thank you, General," Mayerhofer replied. He felt a surge of pride. In himself, his work, his country. Yes, he would become famous. Maybe not until after the war, but certainly soon after. Perhaps a monument in his hometown of Berlin, dedicated by the *Führer* himself!

Chapter 45

5 miles southwest of Château de La Roche-Guyon
On the *Route de Caen*
17 July, 1005 Hours

Dunn and his squad were in a small house that sat abutting the main road west from La Roche-Guyon. It was a winding road, rising from the river valley of the Seine, and the trees of the forest it ran through for a little more than a mile were quite close to the roadway. They'd been in the house since early morning, waiting and watching for Rommel.

The squad was spread out around the house, some resting, some keeping watch. Dunn was taking his turn at the front window, peering through a small opening between the drapes.

The sound of a powerful engine caught his attention and, shortly after, Rommel passed by in his big, heavy Mercedes staff car, whose convertible top was down. He was sitting in the passenger seat, the front right, and accompanied by his driver and another man, dressed in a civilian suit, who sat in the back seat behind the driver. His head was turned toward Rommel and Dunn couldn't see his face. Rommel was looking back over his left shoulder, engaged in conversation, and Dunn thought Rommel's expression, which he could clearly see from ten yards distance, was friendly.

As the car disappeared from view, Dunn turned to Georges and asked, "He always uses this road?"

"Yes, without fail. From this one road he can reach all the other roads leading to his various commanders' headquarters. He tends to keep to the same schedule. As I mentioned last night, he doesn't worry about his safety here." Georges smiled, or perhaps it was an evil grin. "Perhaps it will be his undoing, no?"

"Yes, we hope so. We need a location where the road has a bend in it and where we can set up our shooter at a higher point than the road, facing down the road."

Georges looked at the ceiling, thinking. He snapped his fingers and smiled. "I know such a place. It is a mere kilometer farther west. Would you like me to show you?"

"I would." Dunn walked into the small kitchen where Jones was sprawled, fast asleep. He kicked one of the sniper's boots.

Jones sat bolt upright and his right hand slid down to his 1911 Colt .45. When he saw it was Dunn who'd kicked him, he jumped to his feet. "Something interesting, Sarge?"

"Rommel just passed by going west. Georges is going to show us a likely spot for your sniper's nest."

"That's swell! Let's go."

Dunn smiled to himself at Jones' excitement.

"Grab your weapon."

"Yes, Sarge."

Jones carefully picked up the sniping weapon, examined it closely, then shouldered the sling. Next, he picked up his all-purpose shooter's bag that was filled with everything he would need from ammo and the sight, to the bag filled with fine sand for a steady form-fitting platform. It also had his good luck piece: one of his late uncle's identification tags.

Dunn woke up Cross and, between the two of them, they got everyone else who'd sacked out on their feet and gathering gear. Once all were ready, they slipped out of the house through the back door. The yard was surrounded by trees and the baker's van was pulled in close to the stoop. Getting all the men inside the van proved to be a challenge again, just as it had earlier, but in the end they made it and Georges closed the doors behind them. The inside of the van would have been spacious if not for the ten men crammed inside. The lingering aroma of baked goods made a few stomachs grumble. Dunn squeezed his way toward the front of the truck, pulling Schneider, his interpreter, behind him. The passenger cab was separated from the back of the van by floor-to-ceiling metal that had a small window in the center.

Georges climbed into the driver's seat, started the van, and pulled away from the house. He guided the van along the dirt driveway and stopped just short of the road on which Rommel had just roared by. He turned off the engine and cranked down his window, then put his head out the window making Dunn think of a dog lapping at the wind, but Dunn knew the baker-fighter was listening for vehicles. Dunn strained to listen, but nothing was there. Apparently, Georges thought so, too, for he restarted the motor, then pulled out onto the road heading in the same direction as Rommel.

After only a couple of minutes driving, Georges slowed the van to a crawl as they crested a hill. The road then curved left and ran straight south for thirty yards, then curved right and started downhill, running toward the west. Just before going downhill and without stopping, he said, "To your left is a good spot for your sniper. It has a perfect view right down on the road."

Dunn examined the area just off the left side of the road. The ground rose steeply about fifteen or twenty feet and was topped by a ring of small boulders, about three feet in diameter. Trees surrounded the firing spot and would throw valuable shade, helping to prevent any sunlight reflecting off the front glass of the Springfield's telescopic sight.

"Let us out here."

"Of course." Georges pulled onto the grass shoulder and stopped a few yards down the hill, where he turned off the motor. He got out, went to the side of the long, middle-hinged hood and opened one side. Motor trouble, you see. Behind him, Dunn and Jones let themselves out and looked around carefully. Seeing nothing alarming, they ran across the road and quickly found their way to the top of the small hill.

The boulders were set in a rough semicircle near the edge of the hill. It seemed as if given one little shove they would all tumble down to the road. There was a flat area at the top covered with knee-high grass and wildflowers.

Jones set his bag down near the middle boulder and walked back and forth along the stone ring. Their tops were about two and a half to three feet above the ground. He knelt, opened his bag and withdrew the sight, which he attached with a few deft twists and clicks. He removed the lens covers and put them back in the bag.

Dunn stood beside his sniper and looked down at the road from the perch. "What do you think?"

Jones raised the Springfield to his shoulder and peered through the Unertl sight. The road appeared, huge and black, and clear.

"It'll do nicely."

"Good. What range are you planning on?"

Jones didn't answer right away. He looked up at the trees above him, gauging the wind. It appeared to him the wind was about five miles an hour and a typical summer southern breeze just like back home. Sighting again through the scope, he paid close attention to the grasses along the side of the road at his target range. Wind speed down there seemed to be about the same. Being consistent at both ends was a huge plus and so was not having thirty-mile-an-hour gusts.

"You see the point down there where the road is going downhill, then flattens out? It's three hundred yards."

Dunn looked and said, "I see it."

"Okay, so I'm aiming for a spot about ten yards farther down road. From here, the car will appear to be level and I should have a clear shot over the top of the windshield instead of through it."

Dunn examined the area at the spot Jones had pointed out, paying close attention to the foliage along the side of the road. From here it looked perfect for his other purpose.

"Sit tight. Get your stuff set up."

"Will do, Sarge."

"I'm going back down to get the men set up. Their position will be a hundred yards this side of your target point on the south side of the road. You form the end of the ell and I'll be your spotter and an extra shooter, if needed."

Jones took a few moments to just stare down the hill, picturing the layout. Then he nodded. "Perfect, Sarge."

Dunn chuckled. "Glad you approve."

Jones seemed surprised by Dunn's comment.

"I'm sorry, Sarge."

"I'm just kidding." Dunn patted him on the shoulder and left.

Jones made sure his weapon was on safe and leaned it against the stone to his right, being careful so that only the wood stock was touching the rock. Then he set about fine-tuning his sniper's nest.

When Dunn got to the van, he gave his orders briskly. As his men ran to their positions along the side of the road, he pulled Georges and Schneider aside.

"Is there a place nearby and east of here where you can wait in hiding?"

Georges nodded effusively. "Yes. A side road is just back over the hill."

"We'll need you to come pick us up after the shooting is over."

"I can do that."

Dunn offered his hand and the two men shook vigorously, and the big baker clapped Dunn on the shoulder with his other hand. Georges repeated this with Schneider, then closed his hood, got in the van and started the motor. He pulled away and drove down the road slowly, turned into a farmer's access road and did a quick turn around. As he passed by Dunn and Schneider, he waved and the van disappeared over the hill, and soon the sound of its motor faded.

Dunn and Schneider ran back up the road, Schneider breaking away to find his position. It took a moment to find the others as they had already gotten themselves camouflaged with bits of shrubbery and tree limbs. Wickham helped Schneider get vegetation properly attached to his uniform and in the net around his helmet.

Dunn made the rugged climb back up to join Jones. He found the shooter set up with his rifle's forestock resting on the small sack of sand. His shooter's bag was to his right and on top of it rested four extra clips, twenty more rounds. His canteen was propped against the bag with the lid unscrewed and hanging from its bathroom-stopper-like chain. The sniper's nest was in total shade.

Dunn knelt beside Jones, on the shooter's left.

"Have everything you need?" Dunn asked.

"Yes."

"Good."

Dunn raised and focused his binoculars quickly, scanning the side of the road, checking for any giveaway signs of his squad. He was pleased when he couldn't find a single man. He zoomed out and followed the two-lane road as it went straight west then up a long hill about a mile away and disappeared. The entire length of the road was lined with shrubs, wildflowers, and trees. Dunn nodded in appreciation. Georges had selected the exact right place for an ambush.

It was time for a soldier's patience to take over as they waited.

Chapter 46

Pamela parked her bicycle next to City Hall's stone building. She was wearing her nurse's uniform and had decided to stop at the city hall on her way to work at Camp Barton Stacey hospital.

It was time to get the marriage license. She shook her head in wonder, and smiled to herself as she ran up the stairs into the building.

She found the city clerk's window and was relieved to see it was open. She'd hoped it would be right after lunchtime. As she stepped up to the window, a pleasant looking woman in her forties rose from her seat behind a massive wooden desk and met her at the window.

"Hello, may I help you?"

Pamela smiled and said, "Yes, I'd like to apply for a marriage license."

"Certainly." The woman leaned forward and looked out into the hallway. Seeing no one there but Pamela, she asked,

"Where's the lucky man?"

"Oh, he's away right now. He's an American soldier."

If this bothered the woman, she hid it well, but did say, "We need to have him here with you."

Pamela lost her smile and bit her lip. "Um, but he's *away*, don't you see? I thought I could make the application so when he gets back," Pamela's voice broke, and she fought back tears. "When he gets back, everything will be ready."

The woman shook her head. "I'm supposed to have him here to sign the papers." She paused, thinking. After a little bit, she asked, "Do you have anything written from his commander? You know, something granting permission to marry?"

Pamela's face brightened. Maybe there was hope. "Yes, I do." She opened her purse and rummaged inside, then pulled a paper out, unfolded it and handed it over. It was signed 'Mark Kenton, Colonel, Commanding.' Dunn had given it to her before he'd left on his mission.

The woman read it through once, then said, " Oh, yes, this will do nicely."

"So I can do it today?"

"Yes, dear, you can. Let me get you the papers to fill out."

Fifteen minutes later, Pamela was back on her bicycle pedaling furiously and happily toward the hospital.

Chapter 47

5 1/2 miles west of Château de La Roche-Guyon
On the *Route de Caen*
17 July, 1815 Hours

It had been a long afternoon. The temperature had risen steadily to around seventy degrees, and the southerly breeze had risen to about fifteen miles per hour, which Jones had checked hourly. This would make the shot slightly more difficult, but not impossible. The summer sun was sinking in the southwest sky, moving toward a spot that would be directly in his eyes in about thirty or forty minutes. Not the best. He was starting to get concerned about that when Dunn stirred.

Dunn had remained in place, keeping his eye on the road with a fierce intensity that Jones admired. Conversation had been limited. Both men knew too much was as stake for chit-chat.

"Car coming. Cresting the other hill."

"Roger," said Jones.

"I see three people."

"Roger," repeated Jones.

He took a view through the sight and the detail of the road seemingly came within inches. He raised his head to get a view of the road in its entirety. Hypersensitivity took hold and he heard the car's engine and the whine of its tires on the macadam. There it was, the big black Mercedes with the top still down. He could make out two dots behind the windshield and one more in the back seat, behind the driver. Jones estimated the speed at about sixty miles an hour.

He lowered his head and sighted. He found the vehicle. The barrel dropped slightly. He took a deep breath and let it out slowly. Just before he slipped into the shooter's zone and the world ceased to exist anywhere except in the telescope, his ears registered another engine somewhere above. He ignored it. Then silence. His heart slowed. The car was one hundred yards from his preselected firing point on the road.

He placed his finger on the trigger. Perfect. The car would reach the firing point between heartbeats. The pad on his finger flattened as he began to gently pull the trigger.

The staccato sounds of large machineguns broke his spell. Bullets smacked into the roadway, then streaked into the left side of the car, striking Mayerhofer and the driver. The big Mercedes swerved left, then right. As it slid and bounced off the road toward the ditch, Rommel ejected from the car, landing in the middle of the road, sliding and rolling, still at sixty miles an hour, leaving behind scraps of clothing, skin and blood.

Jones took his finger off the trigger and raised his head.

A British Spitfire roared overhead at only fifty feet altitude. Jones caught a glimpse of a grim-faced pilot. The plane climbed in a sweeping, graceful curve and was out of sight in seconds.

"Fuck!" was all Jones could think of saying.

Dunn put a hand on his shoulder and said, "Let's get down there. Grab your gear and catch up."

"Yes, Sarge."

Dunn dashed down the hill to the road, while Cross and the others hotfooted it toward the car. Dunn ran past Rommel's crumpled body and didn't bother checking for life. No one could survive slamming into the pavement like the general had.

Cross reached the car and found the driver and passenger amazingly still in their places, but dead. Their blood was everywhere. Lying on the backseat's floor was a briefcase. Cross leaned over Mayerhofer's still form and grabbed it.

When Dunn arrived, the men were milling about, but Dunn saw the briefcase in Cross's hand.

"That belong to the passenger?"

"I think so. Was on the floor in the back seat."

"Anything else there?"

Jones arrived just then, and before Cross could answer, the sound of a motor came to them from the east.

"Off the road!" hollered Dunn.

The men ran across the road to the other side and made their way to the tree line.

To their relief, it was a baker's van. Georges.

The van stopped right in front of them, and Dunn got his men on the run and into the van in seconds.

"Thanks, Georges!"

Instead of answering, Georges stomped on the gas pedal and the van tore out, heading west. Before long, they were cresting the far hill.

Dunn hadn't bothered asking anything until now.

"I take it the krauts are on their way?"

"Not yet, but they will be. I could hear the guns firing clearly and I'm sure everyone could hear the airplane. It was flying extremely low near the river. We best be far away. Did you get Rommel?"

"The Spitfire got him. That was him lying in the middle of the road."

"I saw. Didn't know it was him. What a horrible mess. But no sympathy for him, even if he did treat the townsfolk with kindness. He's still the enemy."

"Where are we headed?"

"A little village called Tilly. About fifteen kilometers south. My brother-in-law, Rousel has a safe place at his bakery."

"Your brother-in-law is a baker, too?"

"Yes, it was through him I met my wife, Julia."

"That's swell. Is she a baby sister?"

"Oh, yes, he did not like Georges at first. But over time, he came to trust me. It only took ten years." Georges laughed and Dunn joined him.

Georges stopped talking long enough to slow down and take a left turn to head south. "Are you married, Sergeant?"

"Not yet. Engaged to a British girl. Pamela."

"Congratulations!"

"Thanks." Dunn glanced toward the back of the van where Jones was sitting, next to the doors. His head was down, his expression seemed dark, morose. Dunn excused himself and maneuvered past the other seated men, then squatted in front of Jones.

Jones looked up at his sergeant.

"Disappointed, huh?"

Jones nodded glumly. "Fucking limeys. Ruined a perfect shot."

"Maybe so, but somewhere, there's a pilot who knows he shot up a staff car. Imagine what will happen when reports of Rommel's death start coming in."

"Exactly, the guy'll be famous. He'll have girls swarming over him."

Dunn's eyes flamed and Jones swore later that they had become a darker brown, black even. "Famous? You want to be famous for doing your job? What do you think we're doing here? Auditioning? You best get it through that thick skull of yours that we survive only by our experience, training and our smarts. Getting famous is not what we do. Is that clear, soldier?"

Jones tried to shrink away from Dunn's rare outburst of anger, but had unmoving sheet metal behind him.

"I asked you a question."

"Yes, Sarge. It's clear."

"As for girls, maybe if you'd clean up once in a while, you'd have a chance. Introduce yourself to a razor."

Jones stared at Dunn for a moment, unsure whether to be mad or just laugh at that one. Finally, he did laugh.

Dunn chuckled with him and patted him on the shoulder, then said, "You just do your job. Let the higher-ups worry about the public relations work."

Jones smiled. "Okay, Sarge, whatever you say."

"Yes, that's correct. You just remember that and we'll get along famously." Dunn snickered at his own pun and Jones groaned.

Dunn made his way over to Cross and said, "Let's get that briefcase open and give it to Schneider."

Cross nodded and lifted the case onto his lap. When he tried to open the clasps they wouldn't budge. He pulled his knife from its scabbard, placed the point under one of the brass clasps, and gave it a quick twist. The lock popped open. He repeated that on the second lock and put his knife away, then lifted the lid. The inside was brimming with papers. Cross handed the case over to Schneider.

Schneider pulled a stack of papers out and started reading.

A truckload of German soldiers arrived at the scene of the attack on Rommel. The sergeant in command recognized the staff car in the ditch. He jumped from the truck cab and ran to the general's side. Kneeling, he felt quickly for a pulse and was shocked to find one. Shouting commands to his men, he then oversaw the careful and gentle handling of the general as they loaded him into the back of the truck and drove away at high speed.

While he waited, Dunn glanced around the inside of the van and noticed, for the first time, a couple of metal tubes hanging on the opposite side, above Hanson's head. He stared for a moment, then laughed to himself. Georges had a pair of Panzerfausts in his van. Shaking his head, he thought he would have to ask the baker how he'd acquired the anti-tank weapons.

When Schneider finished with the papers, he said to Dunn, "These are scientific papers, physics to be precise, and from what I can tell they are discussing the inner workings of a new weapon. Let me look for more information."

Dunn nodded his approval.

Digging into the case, Schneider found a stack with schematic drawings of a long cylindrical object. He held them up for Dunn and Cross to see, and said, "It's four meters long."

The object was a bomb.

Chapter 48

In route - 2 miles north of Tilly, France
17 July, 1830 Hours

Cross snatched the drawing from Schneider's hand and stared at it. "I thought we just took care of their atomic bombs." He angrily waved the drawing at Dunn, who then grabbed it and stared at the bomb himself.

The men all crowded around, trying to see the drawing, too.

"This isn't an atomic bomb," Dunn said finally. "I don't know what it is, but it's a completely different design. See, there's a wing on top, like they're trying to give it more control. An atomic bomb only needs to be in the ballpark, this one has the look of something that's supposed to be right on target."

While Dunn had been talking, Schneider had continued rummaging through the briefcase. Not known for cursing, no matter the circumstances, everyone in the back of the van was surprised to hear him say, "Holy Mother of God!"

The men turned to see what would cause this outburst.

Schneider's face was white and in his hands was a large stack of glossy black and white pictures, which he held out to Dunn.

Dunn flipped through the stack of about thirty pictures in complete silence. When he was done, his face, too, was white. He handed them over to Cross and the men pushed in to see. A couple of men coughed, in that funny way you do when you're trying to keep from launching your last meal all over everywhere.

"Whatever that bomb does, it's all bad for us. Schneider, read faster. We have to know where that monster is being built. Understand?"

Schneider was already leafing through the rest of the papers as fast as possible. "Yes," he replied without looking up. Before he found anything useful, Georges slowed the van and turned left, then left again immediately after. He stopped the truck, leaving it running, and got out.

Dunn peered through the windshield as Georges opened two garage doors in a large stone building. Once open, the entrance looked just wide enough for the van to slip through. Georges got back in and carefully guided the van into the building, then shut off the motor.

Cross got the men out and Dunn stayed with Schneider who was apparently so engrossed in his reading that he'd not even noticed where they were. Dunn had no interest in interrupting the translator, and sat patiently with him. He tried making sense of the words himself, but he just couldn't do it. For the first time, he wished he'd taken German classes in high school or college.

Cross rejoined Dunn and Schneider, sitting across from them.

The rest of the men made themselves comfortable in the large garage-like room, which was big enough for three vans. Along the wall opposite the doors, which Georges had quickly closed, was a row of six brick and stone ovens, with cast iron doors two feet wide. The room was cool, so obviously the ovens were off. To the right was another door that appeared to lead out to the front of the bakery, where the customers would be.

Georges made his way to the back of the van and peered in at the three soldiers, who were in turn focused intently on the papers from the briefcase. Georges put a hand on the top edge of the opening to support his weight as he leaned in.

"Any luck with all that?"

"Maybe," mumbled Schneider. "I find several references to a manufacturing site at or near a place called Château d'Alpes-le-Vieil." Schneider finally tore his eyes from the papers and asked Georges, "Do you know where that is?"

Georges looked at the ceiling, thinking, then replied, "Yes, I know the place. It's maybe two hundred and fifty kilometers south and a little east of here. It is an old château, some would call it a castle. I believe it has a moat."

"And a drawbridge?" asked Dunn, only half kidding.

"No, I think no. Just a simple bridge."

Dunn opened his map of France, a larger one for this trip, and examined it briefly. After converting Georges' number to miles, one hundred fifty-five, Dunn found the area where the castle would be. Then he checked the latitude and longitude coordinates.

Looking at Schneider, he said, "Remember that order about staying away from a certain place or be killed?"

Schneider blinked in surprise. "Yeah, I do."

"The castle is right in there."

"I'd say we found the testing site."

"Yep. Does that say when they're starting production? Or have they already?"

"Just a second, Sarge." Schneider read a few more pages quickly. "Okay, the dead guy we took this from is Max Mayerhofer. He's the project lead. The name of the project is *Puls*, or pulse, which as far as I can tell without any training in physics is the type of weapon it is building, the one in the drawing. What it does is emit massive amounts of focused electromagnetic energy that will shut down all electrical components. The deaths are an unintended side effect.

"The next two guys are Fritz Rademacher, a mechanical engineer, and Johann Pachter, an electrical engineer. And get this, here's a letter from Albert Speers, the Minister of Armaments. It also says he's in charge of the *Geheimwaffe Projekts Abteilung*, Secret Weapons Projects Division." He handed the letter over to Dunn who saw Speer's signature on the bottom. Dunn handed the letter over to Cross.

"And here's one I don't think I need to explain." Schneider gave Dunn another letter, which was brief, one paragraph. At the bottom was Speer's signature again, but the one that caught Dunn's attention was the scrawled *A. Hitler.*

"Approval at the highest level. This is a desperate measure." Dunn gave this one to Cross, too.

"Yes," said Cross.

"Uh oh," said Schneider in a tone of voice that caught everyone's attention.

"What is it?" asked Dunn.

"It's a deployment order."

"When?"

Schneider held the paper in one hand and ran a fingertip down the page. "Oh my." He looked up, his face pale. "Today's the seventeenth, right?"

"Yes," said Cross.

"They're dropping the first of these weapons near Caen on the nineteenth at seven in the morning!"

Cross and Dunn exchanged a look. Unspoken understanding passed between the two intelligent, quick-thinking men of action.

Dunn turned to Georges, who was still hanging onto the top of the van with one hand. "How long to get to this château?"

The baker did a mental calculation, then said, "Four to six hours, depending on how many back roads we have to take. You plan to attack the château?"

"Can you get us a radio?"

"Of course, we are the Resistance, after all!"

"Great. To answer your question, yes. We may have to find a way to storm the castle."

Chapter 49

75 yards south of Château d'Ainay-le-Vieil
Village of Ainay-le-Vieil, 156 miles due south of
Paris
18 July, 0215 Hours, 28 hours 45 minutes to
detonation at Caen

Dunn and Cross lay in deep grass in a grove of trees just south of the castle. In the very dim light of a sliver crescent moon, the Castle d'Ainay-le-Vieil was a foreboding monstrosity. From their position they had a clear view of the bridge that traversed the water-filled, thirty-foot-wide moat. Connected to the bridge was a paved road that passed within yards of Dunn's and Cross's position, then turned left toward a main road. At the other end of the bridge, the gate to the castle was housed between twin towers that rose forty feet. A half dozen dark, vertical lines were bow-and-arrow slits from the middle ages. High atop the wall that ran west from the gate towers were square windows. None were present any lower. During earlier scouting trips, the Rangers had learned the castle was a odd nine-sided structure. It was roughly the shape of a capital D when viewed from the north, with the straight edge along the east side, and the round part on the west side.

They had seen no traffic, motorized or foot, in the hour they had been watching the castle and its surroundings. There were no lights on anywhere, which was to be expected in war torn France, although neither man could fathom why the Eighth Air Force would want to pulverize d'Ainay-le-Vieil as it seemed to be, literally, a sleepy village. Perhaps this was why the Germans had chosen it.

The tree branches above their heads rustled in the breeze, still from the south, but now at a higher speed than earlier in the day, as if signaling the onset of bad weather.

Dunn didn't want to say it, but did anyway, "I see no way in to this thing, other than the gate."

"What we need is a spy on the inside to let us in through the secret passageway."

"Gee, I wish I'd thought of that."

"That's what you have me around for."

"Uh huh, right."

"This place makes the Project Dante lab look easy," said Cross.

Dunn stared at the gate and the bridge. Cross was right, though. They'd gained entry to the lab through an iron door less than half the size of the gate. Maybe they could breach the gate with explosives, and in the confusion, make their way into the manufacturing facility. It wasn't clear at all where the facility could be unless, as the Germans had been prone to doing, they'd put it underground. Which was just another reason neither the British or American bombers could cause enough destruction here.

A new sound, from behind, reached the soldiers' ears and they immediately raised their Thompsons and aimed in the direction of the noise.

"Dunny!" came a whisper. "Dunny!"

Dunn lowered his weapon, as did Cross. It was Jack Hanson, the only person in the world who could get away with calling Dunn 'Dunny' for reasons even Dunn didn't understand. Maybe it was just the little guy's toughness. Even in a whisper, his high-pitched voice carried quite a distance.

Hanson crawled closer and stopped next to Dunn.

"What is it, Jack?"

"Bob needs to see you. He said it was important."

"Okay," replied Dunn immediately.

As he started to rise, a squeaking noise suddenly came from the gate. It was rising. After it stopped moving, a dark, two-tone sporty car came roaring across the bridge. As it passed by the Rangers, the passenger, who was on the car's right side, and therefore, nearest the Americans, lit a cigarette. His face glowed red when he took a drag, and while Dunn didn't know who the man was, he memorized the features. The car then turned left, and was soon out of sight. Dunn was certain there were only two men in the car.

"I'd give a plug nickel to know where that car is going," said Cross.

"Yep, well I don't believe in coincidences."

The three men left and made their way back to the house where Georges had earlier taken them for hiding. The one hundred fifty mile trip from Tilly had indeed taken nearly six hours as they'd had to skirt farther west to avoid any close proximity to Paris, which was teeming with Germans. He'd shown them around the house, making sure to pull all the shades, and gave Dunn and Cross the lay of the land, what little he knew of it. Then he left to go get the local Resistance leader. Dunn and Cross had left on their foray near the castle before Georges returned.

Dunn found Schneider poring over yet more of the papers from the briefcase, sitting cross-legged on the floor and using a hooded flashlight. The windows had curtains drawn over them, but Schneider wasn't taking any chances.

Dunn knelt beside his translator and asked, "What'd you find, Bob?"

Schneider set down the paper he was reading and plucked another from one of the piles of paper surrounding himself. It was creased from being folded into a tiny size.

"The manufacturing facility isn't in the castle."

"Where is it?"

"It's elsewhere, Sarge."

"Why'd you just now find out?"

If Schneider was upset by Dunn's question, he showed no sign of it. "I was curious why none of the papers stated exactly where the factory was, so I started tearing things apart. This paper was folded up and slipped between the lining and the outside of the briefcase. It gives the location and says that all shipments for the project are to go to it. Have been going to it. It's where they built the one we saw the test results from." Schneider grimaced at the memory of the pictures. If only he could forget.

While Dunn was unhappy that they'd spent so much time watching the wrong target, he understood that if it weren't for Schneider's perseverance, they'd *still* be watching the wrong target.

"Nice job of sticking with it, Bob. Where's Georges?"

"Out back, getting some shut eye in the back of the truck. The other two French guys are patrolling the perimeter with Morris and Fairbanks."

"Go get him up and bring him here."

"Yes, Sarge."

A few minutes later, Schneider returned with a sleepy-eyed Georges. Dunn handed over a metal cup of coffee, which the Frenchman took gratefully.

"Georges, we need to know where this place is." Dunn handed over the paper to Schneider who read the address.

"I'm sorry, but I don't know this area that well. We should get Bertrom in here. He can answer all of your questions. He's outside."

Dunn nodded to Cross, who left to go find him.

Once outside, Cross cautiously called out Bertrom's name and soon a thin man appeared out of nowhere. He was carrying a British Sten.

"*Oui?*"

Cross merely pointed and said, "Georges."

Bertrom nodded and swept his hand as an invitation for Cross to lead the way.

Shortly thereafter, they joined Dunn, Schneider and Georges.

Georges made the introductions and the men shook hands. He then asked Bertrom where the location Schneider had uncovered could be found.

Schneider translated quickly as Bertrom spoke.

"That's between the towns of Le Vernet and Las Landes. About seven kilometers southeast of us. They make machine parts for the German Tiger tank."

Cross whistled appreciatively. Everyone was afraid of the Tiger, including other tanks.

"Do you have anyone on the inside?"

Bertrom shook his head sadly. "We did. He was caught and executed. Many of the workers are French. They have to work there to provide for their families."

"You'll get no judgmental comments from me."

Bertrom tipped his head.

"How many guards?" asked Dunn.

"Usually two or three walking constantly in circles around the fence, separated by a few minutes. One always has a dog."

"What about large groups of soldiers?"

"They do have trucks coming and going all the time, but we've never seen a large number of soldiers."

Dunn nodded, then absentmindedly took out a pack of cigarettes and offered them to the men around him. Georges and Bertrom immediately took the terrific American cigarette. Cross and Schneider passed. Georges pulled out a silver lighter and fired it, then held it out for Dunn who grasped George's hand to steady it, and lit the tip of his cigarette. Bertrom did the same. Georges lit his own. The three puffed silently for a few moments and a blue cloud formed over their heads.

"I need to know what your group's capabilities are and what resources you have that we can use to destroy the factory."

Before answering, Bertrom asked Georges, "Is it safe to tell him about us?"

Georges nodded. "It's safe. He is who he says he is. We verified identity when he arrived."

"Okay." Bertrom looked at Dunn and said, "No offense, Sergeant."

"None taken, Bertrom."

Bertrom smiled. "Very well. I have myself and a dozen patriots. We have three farm trucks. We are armed with the Stens," he lifted his own weapon to show, "and a variety of handguns, Lugers, Berettas, anything we can find.

"We have several dozen German grenades." Bertrom puffed out his chest and said, "We also have fifty pounds of British plastic explosives, and two hundred pounds of German dynamite."

"Wow, okay. That's an excellent armory."

Bertrom grinned wide when Schneider translated Dunn's compliment.

Dunn waved at the floor, and asked, "Shall we sit?"

After everyone sat down on the wooden floor, Dunn said, "Tell me about the factory building."

"It was originally used to build farm equipment, mostly tractors."

"No, I mean, what's it made of?"

"Ah, I see. It's a metal support structure with wood siding and roofing."

"How big?"

"Fifty by one hundred meters."

"What's the floor made of?"

"It is wood planking over packed dirt."

Dunn thought for a moment, calculating. His cigarette burned a quarter inch. Everyone waited, although Georges and Bertrom, not being accustomed to Dunn's way of working things out, exchanged glances.

Dunn came out of his trance and looked at Bertrom. "How much gasoline can you get your hands on?"

Chapter 50

Pamela and her mother rose from their chairs as a colonel strode toward them wearing a big smile.

"Colonel Kenton?"

"At your service."

"Hi, I'm Pamela. Let me introduce my mum. Mum, Colonel Kenton."

"Very pleased to meet you both, Pamela, Mrs. Hardwicke."

"And I, you, sir. We spoke briefly on the phone recently," said Mrs. Hardwicke.

Kenton blushed. Dunn had asked him to call Pamela if anything happened, which he did, reluctantly. He'd felt guilty ever since telling Pamela her boyfriend's airplane had been shot down. Even though it looked like everyone on board had safely parachuted, they were in German occupied eastern France. How Dunn and his squad would get home was unknown, and he was overjoyed when Dunn had remarkably returned within a few days.

Pamela noticed Kenton's discomfort and said quickly, "Colonel, please don't worry about that phone call. It was better for me to know. That way we could pray."

"Thank you for that. I have been worrying. I know it was difficult."

"You're welcome. Let's sit, shall we?" said Pamela.

Kenton sat down across the table from the two women. He looked from one to the other a few times, thinking how remarkably closely they resembled each other.

"Thank you for coming to meet with us, Colonel." Pamela bit her lip.

Kenton noticed it and assumed, rightly, as he would find out later from Dunn, that she was nervous.

"You're welcome. What can I do to help you?'

The waiter interrupted to take their orders for dinner.

When she left, Pamela answered, "I know you can't tell me anything about where Tom is, or when he'll be back . . ."

Kenton nodded, but smiled to soften it.

" . . . but, well I was wondering how a military wedding would be conducted. I know most American-British weddings are just held at city hall, with, you know, family only, but we, um, my mum and me, want to have it at our church. But we didn't know how hard it would be to have all of his men present."

Kenton smiled broadly. He was so attached to Dunn that this would be like his own son's wedding, whenever that would occur. His son had recently been appointed to West Point and would start school in the coming fall.

"I can have someone help you with the military aspects of it. I'll have a Lieutenant Adams give you a call. Have you gotten your marriage license yet?"

"I just did yesterday."

"No problems?"

"Only at first, because Tom wasn't with me, but because I had your permission letter, the lady went ahead. She was quite sweet."

"Well, I'm glad that worked out. I assume you've already set a date in the near future?"

Pamela's expression was nonplussed. "But I thought you had to interview me first. Then it would still be sixty days after that."

Kenton grinned. "Look, Pamela, as far as I'm concerned, there's no need for an interview. I thought Tom would have told you."

Pamela shook her head.

"If you like, we'll just count tonight."

This pleased Pamela and after adding sixty days to today's date, said, "A late September wedding, then."

Kenton suddenly looked mischievous, reminding Pamela of an older Dunn. "Did you check the date on the 'permission' letter?"

"Oh, no, I don't think so. It's here in my purse." She fumbled through her purse and when she got the letter out and read the date, her expression was even more confused. "But it's dated May fifteenth! How can that be? He didn't ask me until June nineteenth . . ."

Kenton merely smiled.

Pamela's eyebrows shot up and her hand flew to her mouth, covering a silent 'oh.' She jumped to her feet and ran around the table, leaning over to hug Kenton. Pulling back she said, "I don't know how to thank you."

"You can invite me to the wedding."

Pamela gave the colonel a radiant smile. "You are first on the list!" Then her expression turned mischievous. "Please don't tell Tom we talked."

Kenton said, "You're going to tease him aren't you?"

"Oh, yes. Time for payback for him forgetting to tell me about the interview."

Chapter 51

Heavy woods, 50 yards north of the Pulse Weapon
Factory
4 miles southeast of Ainay-le-Vieil
19 July, 0507 Hours, 1 hour 53 minutes to detonation
at Caen

The road from Ainay-le-Vieil ran northwest-southeast past the facility, but Georges had veered left onto another smaller road a half-mile northwest of the factory and ended up behind the woods that bordered the building on two sides. Bertrom followed in a truck bearing his fighters, and a third one, carrying explosives and gasoline cans, was last in the convoy.

Leaving the men behind, Dunn and Cross crept through those woods from the north, which would bring them out at the north corner of the building. Knowing there was a dog and his handler somewhere around the perimeter made them ultra cautious. The good news was the wind, which had picked up some more, was still from the south and wouldn't carry their scent to the dog. It might even reduce the likelihood that the dog would hear their footfalls. Earlier, it had started to look more and more like rain, then on the drive to the target it had started to drizzle. Now it was raining harder, and water dripped off the leaves as well as the helmets and ponchos Dunn and Cross wore.

Eventually, they made their way to edge of the woods and, standing behind a couple of trees that were only a few feet apart, eyed the building. The structure looked enormous with its nearly three story height. From their vantage point, they could see down the length of two walls, one that was perpendicular with the road, and one that was parallel to it. The long side, running to their left was as described by Bertrom, at least one hundred yards, while the shorter side to their right was fifty yards long. Even in the gloom of an overcast morning, to their left they could clearly make out a back entrance and three loading docks, about ten yards apart. The building appeared to be painted a dull gray, like a battleship, thought Dunn.

The fence they would have to breech was about thirty feet from the building. The distance between the fence and the building was covered with concrete pavement. Dunn lifted his binoculars and studied the entrance. It seemed to be a standard metal door found in thousands of manufacturing buildings, and had one small horizontal window centered at eye level. Next he examined the nearest dock door. It was made up of two metal doors about seven feet tall, each about three or four feet in width.

Movement to their right caught Cross's attention and he nudged Dunn, who lowered his binoculars. Coming around the far corner nearest the road was the guard with a dog, fittingly, a German Shepherd. Dunn checked his watch: 05:11. Both Rangers stood perfectly still. A minute later, the guard and dog were on their way to the south end having given no indication of detecting Dunn and Cross. Waiting patiently, Dunn saw another guard, no dog. He checked his watch again: 05:13. He expected the guard with the dog to return in two minutes, which he did.

As soon as the pair were out of sight again, Dunn tapped Cross on the shoulder and pointed back through the woods. Cross nodded and the men started back. They approached the far side of the woods cautiously; they had posted a perimeter around the trucks at a distance of fifty yards along the road.

Stepping carefully out in the open near the trucks, Dunn held up a hand, waving the perimeter back in. Wickham and Hanson jogged toward him from the north and Ward and Fairbanks from the south. Dunn rapped on the van and Bertrom's truck, then gathered the men in a semicircle around himself.

The Frenchmen had been awestruck when they met Dunn and his men. These were the first Americans they'd ever seen, let alone met. They admired the uniforms and helmets, their expressions wistful; they wore dark clothing, some threadbare, and had no helmets, wearing instead black watch caps. They carried Stens, although not the silenced version.

The Resistance fighters ranged in age from around seventeen to the mid-forties, and size varied widely, too, with the tallest being about Dunn's six-two and one Hanson's height of five-seven. Their eyes were bright, intelligent and all wore the same determined expression, which Dunn was relieved to see.

Earlier, outside the safe house in d'Ainay-le-Vieil, Dunn had been surprised to find such a large group in Vichy controlled France and asked Bertrom about it.

"It is far more difficult to accomplish much in so called 'free' Vichy, France because not only are the Germans on the lookout for us, but our own police," he took a moment to spit his displeasure, "also chase us and cause us trouble." He grinned. "But we persevere!" Bertrom had wholeheartedly agreed that his men would be under Dunn's 'command.' His men had all raised their fists in agreement.

Dunn had elected to go over the plans twice back at the house where Schneider could take his time in translating, ensuring that the precise details were abundantly clear to the fighters. Now, just minutes away from the assault, he went over them one more time.

It was known that the guards stayed in the facility to eat and sleep, keeping only a couple of men on rotating duty at night. The location of the guards inside the facility was known as well: on the north end, at the front facing the road. It was expected that there would be about a dozen Germans in various states of alertness. This exhausted the knowledge of the interior. Without a complete floor plan, initial going would have to be slow, cautious, until all threats were identified and eliminated.

"Questions, anyone?" asked Dunn.

No one raised a hand, and a few of the men shook their heads. "Okay, then. Let's head out."

Cross took point and he was followed by Dunn and the rest of the Ranger outfit, then came the French fighters. The troop wound its way through the woods and when they hit the tree line, Dunn's squad went left, spreading out parallel with the fence, while the French went to the right.

The tree line was about five yards from the fence, which was eight feet tall and topped with barbed wire. Jones and Ward were tasked with cutting the fence, and Bertrom had provided two pairs of wire cutters.

A minute passed and the guard with the dog came around the corner first. Dunn wasn't sure whether he was glad the dog was passing now, or if it would have been better later. No matter, he had no say. Everyone had been warned to stand perfectly still, and soon the dog and guard were out of sight.

Jones and Ward set to work immediately, knowing they only had two minutes. Dunn started timing them. They were done in sixty seconds and peeled the fence back, then charged through to the corner where the next guard was expected in less than thirty seconds.

Standing with their backs to the building, both men flipped their Thompsons' safety switch to off. Jones was closer to the corner, so he knelt. Ward took a step farther from the building to be clear of Jones.

The guard noticed the motion. Surprised to see American soldiers here, of all places, but reacting quickly, he brought up his Mauser.

Jones and Ward fired first, striking the German in the torso. He went down with a clatter as his weapon bounced off the pavement.

Soon, the German Shepherd came into view at a full run, his leash flapping in the air behind him. His master was not far behind.

Everyone saw each other at the same time. The Shepherd gracefully and powerfully changed directions, charging right at the Rangers

The Rangers opened fire. The man and dog fell dead.

Dunn got his squad, and the Frenchmen, through the fence

headed for the back entrance.

Dunn and Cross arrived and took a quick look at the back door. Cross tried the door knob, but it was locked.

Then Jones and Ward joined them.

"Everyone stand aside," said Dunn. When the men had moved out of danger, he raised his Thompson and, from a distance of a couple of feet, fired a long burst at the doorknob. The metal disintegrated, leaving a smoking hole. Dunn raised his right foot and kicked the door where the knob had been. The door flew open. Cross and the rest of the Rangers burst through the door.

They fanned out in what turned out to be a ten-foot-wide hallway that ran all the way to the far side of the building. To the right were offices and on the left was the manufacturing area.

Several Rangers ran the length of the hallway, opening and closing office doors, finding no one.

Cross stood ready at the closest door leading into the manufacturing side. Dunn nodded and Cross pushed it open a few inches. He peered through and in his limited field of view saw all manner of equipment, lathes, presses, welder's tools, and sheets of metal that were probably aluminum. But no people.

Shoving the door farther open, he leaned into the room. A flurry of shots rang out.

Cross collapsed.

Chapter 52

Château d'Ainay-le-Vieil
Near the Village of Ainay-le-Vieil
19 July, 0535 Hours, 1 hour 25 minutes to detonation
at Caen

Johann Pachter dropped the telephone receiver and scrambled up the long staircase. He didn't bother knocking on the door and burst into Fritz Rademacher's room. Grabbing the sleeping form by the shoulder, he shook hard.

Rademacher awoke to the sight of a wild-eyed Pachter leaning over him. "What?"

"Max is dead!"

Rademacher pushed Pachter's hand away and sat up, leaning against the heavy headboard. "Calm down, Johann. What are you saying?"

"Max is dead! He got killed while on that damn tour with Rommel."

"How?"

"An enemy airplane attacked the car. It killed Max and the

driver, but Rommel survived somehow. What are we going to do, Fritz?" The last was said plaintively.

"Where's Max's briefcase?"

"They didn't find it."

"Did they search his room? No, wait! Max would never have left it alone. It had to be in the car. Are they sure it wasn't in the car?"

"Yes, they searched everywhere."

Rademacher's face registered shock, but he was thinking fast. "It doesn't matter. He only carried copies of things that are stored in the office."

Max was dead, there was nothing to do about that. However, the mission could still go ahead without him, thought Rademacher. *It's time for me to take the lead. Make a name for myself.*

Rademacher jumped out of bed, pushing Pachter out of his way, then he grabbed some clothes from the closet. Dressing quickly, he said, "Do you still have a copy of Speer's order to deploy the weapon today at Caen?"

"Yes. In my room."

"Go get dressed and bring the order. I'll call the sergeant of the guard and tell him to get some men ready to follow us to the airfield. We'll stop at the factory for the original order, just in case. It should be in the office."

Pachter looked dumbfounded and didn't move.

"What are you waiting for?"

"We're going ahead with the deployment without Max?"

"You're damn right we are. We have everything we need and we know everything Max knows, so yes, we're going ahead with the deployment as well as the continued production of the weapon."

"I don't know."

Rademacher walked over to Pachter and stood toe-to-toe. "Don't chicken out on me. We're doing this." He grabbed Pachter's pajama top with his left hand, sidestepped, put his right hand on the still-shocked man's back and pulled-pushed him toward the door.

"Go, Johann. It will be all right. Trust me."

Pachter left.

Rademacher put on his shoes and ran out the door.

Once downstairs, he snatched up the still-dangling telephone receiver, pressed down on the disconnect button and dialed a short number. The call was answered immediately and he gave brief instructions.

Five minutes later, the two engineers were in the burgundy and black Citroën roaring across the moat's bridge, Pachter driving. A truckload of soldiers was right on their tail.

Chapter 53

Taking fire inside the Pulse Weapon facility
4 miles southeast of Ainay-le-Vieil
19 July, 0537 Hours, Paris time, 1 hour 23 minutes
to detonation at Caen

Dunn grabbed Cross before he could hit the floor and dragged him away from the door, shouting the whole time, "Lay down fire in there. Breech the damn doors."

The Rangers and Frenchmen did just that, cracking the doors slightly and pouring lead through, hoping to make the Germans keep their heads down.

Cross lay on his back, his eyes out of focus.

Dunn worked fast, pulling up the poncho, then tearing open Cross's jacket and shirt. Blood was pouring from a wound that was about one inch in from Cross's left side. Dunn wiped away blood quickly to get a better picture. Then he rolled his friend over and saw the raw exit wound.

"Good news, buddy. It went through and I think the only thing it hurt is your pride. Nothing important."

Dunn started to open the sulphur packet to douse the wound to help stave off infection, but a now alert Cross grabbed Dunn's wrist with surprising strength. "Give me that," he said. "I can manage. You get in there. So much for surprise, huh?"

Dunn didn't argue and handed over the packet and the gauze. He patted his friend's shoulder. "I'll be back for you."

"You better. I'm not driving home."

Dunn looked up just in time to see the Rangers and Frenchmen rush through a pair of doors, firing madly.

He jumped to his feet and, after taking a quick look through the door, burst through, firing at two German helmets poking up from behind some kind of large metal press. Both dropped.

The sound was incredible.

Machineguns firing non-stop echoed.

Whining ricochets.

Screams as men were hit.

A blast shook the room, then another. Hand grenades.

Even in all the din around him, Dunn was able to think clearly. Based on the muzzle flashes he saw coming from the Germans, they'd stumbled into a platoon. That would make the initial odds roughly three to two in the Germans' favor. Not the best odds for the attacker. The Germans had clearly reacted quickly to the sounds of gunfire outside, but why they were there in triple the expected number was unknown. Perhaps it was due to the upcoming deployment or simply the planned production.

The distance between the two forces was just thirty yards, as the Germans had retreated to be able to get behind some of the heavier, more protective equipment. They would be on the forty yard line on an American football field, with the attackers on their own ten yard line. The Germans had set up a line running the length of building from front to back. Dunn instinctively knew that this was a mistake. Something nagged him and, as he tried to work out the solution, from his right and above came the unmistakable sharp crack of a high-powered rifle. Glancing up quickly, Dunn could make out the barrel of Jones' Springfield sticking out over the wooden edge of an observation walkway. This was good news. The Germans, like all soldiers, hated snipers and feared them above most anything else in battle.

Dunn saw the Germans ducking. He knew Jones would fire

only a few rounds, then he'd duck and run to another point on the walkway and fire a few more rounds. He'd found the perfect sniper's nest. One that was fifty yards wide.

Dunn's solution presented itself and it was tied to the fundamental difference between the goals for a defender and the attacker. By the very nature of the conflict, wherever it was, many times the defender was required to care about what they defended, while the attacker would be quite happy to accomplish the destruction of that same thing. This was the German weakness and Dunn planned to fully exploit it.

Dunn searched for Wickham and found him on the far left of the line. Dunn ducked and ran. As he passed Schneider, he told him to join him. When Dunn reached Wickham, he tapped him on the right shoulder. The Texan ducked and looked at Dunn, who pointed down. There, at Wickham's feet, was one of the satchel charges they'd put together. It contained plastic explosive and had a glass champagne bottle filled with gasoline tied to it. A miniature poor-man's napalm bomb. It was rigged with a pull cord that would give the handler ten seconds before igniting.

Schneider had a satchel over his shoulder.

"I need this to the left of their line, against the wall." Dunn pointed.

Wickham simply nodded.

To Schneider, Dunn said, "Yours has to go off on the far right wall. Dunn checked his watch, "In exactly three minutes."

Dunn held up a finger to both men, the sign to wait. Then he whistled sharply. His men all ducked down behind cover and looked his way. Dunn raised Wickham's satchel just high enough for his men to see and held up three fingers. All the men nodded. Dunn gave a simple set of hand signals to direct fire, then he whistled again and the men began firing again. Above them, Jones' Springfield was working overtime.

"Schneider, you'll have to warn the French as you pass, but make it quick. Get going."

"Okay Sarge."

Schneider took off. Dunn watched him tap a few Frenchmen as he went by to alert them of the plan. When Schneider made it to the far wall, staying down, he turned to face his sergeant.

Dunn checked his watch. Two minutes to go. He counted

down thirty seconds and raised his hand, then dropped it like a race starter. At the same time, he said to Wickham, "Go!"

Dunn raised his weapon and began firing along the left side of the German's line. The Rangers, following Dunn's hand signals, shifted their fire either to the far left or far right of the Germans' line to pin those men down so Wickham and Schneider could make it to their target.

The Germans replied in kind, focusing their attention and weapons fire on those Rangers shooting at them.

Bertrom directed his fighters' fire into the middle of the German line to help keep them too busy to notice the activities against their flanks. Return fire dropped two of Bertrom's men, dead.

Jones dropped to a knee and slammed in a new magazine. He was now back at a point about midway across the walkway. He raised his head to peek over. At twenty feet above the floor, he had a perfect view of the entire battle. At first, it looked like all of the Germans were on the line firing, but then he spotted movement about ten yards farther away. Two soldiers were carrying long tubes and making their way back to the line. Even at a distance of fifty yards, Jones knew what those things were with the brutish ugly bulge on the front end. Panzerfausts, carrying almost two pounds of explosives each.

Jones raised his rifle.

A loud clang sounded and Jones fell back, dropping his weapon, helmet flying off.

Schneider reached his detonation point first. An empty, rolling cart had been on his way, so he had thrown the satchel on it and rolled it onward. He placed the cart and the satchel against the wall. Checking his watch, he waited three seconds, then yanked out the handle. Turning on his heels, he ran for his life back to the line.

Fifty yards away, Wickham was almost to his release point when a bullet tore through his right calf, knocking him down. He scrambled to his feet in spite of the burning pain, and hobbled forward a few more feet, then dropped to his knees. A machine table was a few feet from the wall. That would have to do. He jerked the handle.

Jones' bell had been rung. Hard. He grabbed his helmet. A

deep, shiny gouge ran along the left side. He put it back on and picked up his rifle. He checked it closely, finding no scrapes. The scope still seemed to be properly tightened, but he could only hope it was still sighted in. Raising his head again, he peered over the wall. He quickly found the two soldiers with the anti-tank weapons and raised his rifle. Abandoning hope of saving everything, the Panzerfaust men had raised their weapons, aiming for the center of the Rangers. They were trying to take out the more experienced American soldiers instead of the French fighters.

Dunn checked his watch. Eight seconds.

Schneider dove for cover behind a machine next to a French fighter. Motioning with his hands, he got the man to duck.

Jones lined up the crosshairs on the chest of the left-hand soldier. He fired. A puff of pink plumed out and the soldier collapsed.

Wickham half ran, half fell toward safety. Dunn saw he wasn't going to make it and sprinted out to grab him by the jacket. Dragging him behind a machine, Dunn fell on top of him, covering him with his own body.

Jones worked the bolt and put the crosshairs on the remaining Panzerfaust shooter, who was looking at right back Jones.

The German shifted his aim.

Jones fired.

So did the soldier.

The satchel explosions were enormous in the enclosed space. Even though each wall blew open, creating an opening wide enough to walk through, enough of the pressure waves had bounced off and tore ten yards into the German line, instantly killing ten men on each side.

The Panzerfaust round flew right below the walkway and struck the wall leading to the hallway and exploded.

The walkway under Jones shook as if in an earthquake, but stayed up. Once it stopped shaking, he raised his head and looked over the edge.

Dunn raised his head and peered over the machine.

German soldiers were holding their heads with both hands, trying to get to their feet.

Jones chambered a round and sighted on one soldier. His

finger slipped inside the trigger guard. He began to squeeze. Then the soldier raised his hands, palms forward.

Eight German soldiers, all that remained, were now standing with their hands raised.

Dunn stood up and hollered, *"Kommin sie her!"*

The confused Germans looked at Dunn and slowly started walking toward him.

Suddenly, Bertrom and his French Fighters opened fire. The German soldiers went down.

A shocked Dunn looked down the firing line at Bertrom, then his anger boiled up and he ran toward him. The French leader simply stared back, waiting. Schneider saw what was about to happen and ran over. Dunn grabbed Bertrom's shirt and yanked him close, shouting, "What the hell did you do that for?"

Dunn was certain that having to wait for Schneider's translation took some of the sting out of the question, but figured Bertrom understood perfectly his tone.

Bertrom gently grasped Dunn's fist and pushed. Dunn let go, breathing hard.

"We don't take German prisoners. I saved you a lot of trouble. What were you going to do with them? Eh? You're in Vichy, France. You're almost four hundred kilometers from your own front line."

"You can't just kill men who were surrendering."

"Yes, we can. You don't know what it's like being under the Germans' thumb for four years. Even here, in the so-called 'Free Zone.'"

"It makes you no better than they are."

Schneider hesitated at Dunn's words.

"Translate word for word, Bob."

Schneider did.

"Then so be it," replied the Resistance leader with a shrug.

Dunn realized that continuing the argument was senseless. The men were dead and nothing would change that.

"We have work to do. I suggest we get on with it. We need a couple of your men to stand guard at the front of the building."

"Oui."

Bertrom snapped off a command and two men peeled out of the group, heading for the front of the building through the hole in the wall.

"Gather the rest of your men here."

"*Oui*." Bertrom gave the order to his men and the Rangers and French fighters rallied around their leaders, including Cross and Wickham. Cross had somehow managed to get a bandage on the front and back by himself and seemed to be holding up. Wickham was able to limp along, now that his leg had been bandaged by the new kid, Lindstrom. The bullet had missed the bones by less than an eighth of an inch, punching through the meat of his calf.

"All right, men, get those explosives set and the gasoline spread. Be careful not to splash any on yourself." He turned to Hanson and Morris. "You two focus on the offices. We are not leaving those bastards anything to build back up from."

Next, Dunn spoke to Jones, who, slightly worse for wear after the near miss, had joined the group late.

"Find a way to the roof. Take out anything coming this way."

"Roger, Sarge."

Jones took off in search of a path to the roof. On his way, he stopped to grab an object, which he slung over his shoulder.

Every man, American and French, knew what do. Within a few minutes, the men were at work laying the explosives and spreading gasoline throughout the facility.

Meanwhile, Dunn had his own responsibility. He worked his way around the manufacturing area, searching. He'd made it nearly to the far side when he found a large room. It was as if someone had simply dropped a big box into a corner of the building. He went though the double doors and quickly scanned the room. Across the way, he spotted an odd-looking cart on fat rubber tires. It was heavy duty steel and clearly built for something big. He ran over to it and the realization of what he was looking at hit him. Hard.

It was the empty support rack for the bomb.

Chapter 54

Sadie's parents' house
Cheshunt, 15 miles north of London
19 July, 0445 Hours, London time

The living room was dim, lit only by the dying fireplace. An exhausted Saunders sat on the sofa, his head down, eyes closed. Sadie's parents had gone to bed long ago, citing fatigue from the long day. Sadie's brothers had to be dragged away from Saunders, but finally went to bed, too. Saunders had chosen to stay awake all night with Sadie, checking on her obsessively throughout the night, but finally dropped off around three.

Saunders stirred awake but kept his eyes closed. The past week was worse than any week he'd ever experienced in combat. Perhaps he'd grown used to the pain and suffering he'd seen on the battlefield. Yes, he was certain he had. He thought about all the close calls he'd survived, from the snap of a German bullet next to his ear to the incessant shelling in Africa and Italy, to the near crashes from tangled, almost useless parachute lines, to believing he would die three hundred feet below the surface of the North Sea.

He'd watched his men get wounded or killed. He'd written the letters home, all saying much the same thing: your son died a hero serving his country and protecting his mates. After suffering through the last seven days, he came to understand that the words were just words. Nothing could assuage the pain felt by the families. The loss of a loved one was the worst thing possible, he now understood. Watching Sadie's parents suffer through the fear was terrible to see.

He and they had spent time with Sadie covering the days in shifts, talking to her, touching her, combing her hair, washing her face with cool washcloths. She appeared to be wasting away right in front of their eyes. The doctors always said the same thing, day after day: only time will tell.

With Sadie's head in his lap, he absentmindedly caressed her hair. Now he knew what he'd almost lost. He understood fully what loving someone truly meant.

She'd awakened while Saunders was on "duty" at noon the previous day. He had dozed off himself, but felt her stir and his eyes flew open.

Sadie's blue eyes were staring at him, drinking in his face.

Saunders eyes watered, tears flowed down his cheeks. He leaned over and kissed her gently, then pulled back. It took a moment for his throat to open enough to speak.

"Oh, Sadie. My girl. Welcome back."

"Hi Mac." She looked around the hospital room and realization settled on her face. "What happened to me?"

"You don't remember?"

"No."

"You were in London. Wanted to go shopping. A doodlebug exploded nearby."

"I was in London?"

Saunders nodded.

"Why don't I remember?"

"You have a severe concussion. Sometimes that can wipe out memories, sometimes a whole day or more."

Sadie blinked, trying to comprehend what Saunders just said.

"You were with Alexandria, but she'd gone on to another store while you were picking out a dress. She's okay."

"Oh, good."

"How do you feel?"

"I don't know. My head hurts."

"I'm sure it does."

"What else happened to me? What else is messed up?"

"That can wait."

"Oh no you don't! You tell me now."

Saunders smiled, glad to see her innate fire surfacing. "Your thigh bone and lower leg are both broken." He took her hand and placed it on the cast. "You'll be in this for a while."

"No horseback riding, I take it?"

Saunders laughed. She loved horses, maybe more than she did him. "No."

Saunders stood up, kissed her again, and said, "I'm going to go get the doctor, and call your mum."

Sadie nodded, grimacing. Then she smiled and Saunders heart melted away.

The embers of the fire were turning black. Sadie opened her eyes and looked up at Saunders. Lifting a hand, she stroked his cheek and his eyes opened. He bent over and she raised her head. They kissed.

Chapter 55

The Pulse Weapon Factory
4 miles southeast of Ainay-le-Vieil
19 July, 0550 Hours, Paris time, 1 hour 10 minutes
to detonation at Caen

Dunn rushed to rejoin his men, reaching Schneider first.

Just as the men were finishing the demolition preparation, one of the Resistance fighters guarding the front of the building raced back in. He found Bertrom and started talking rapidly, gesturing toward the road. Bertrom nodded and pointed at the front of the building. The man bolted back through the hole in the wall.

Bertrom found Dunn with Schneider and said, "A German truck is coming from the north, probably from the castle. A civilian car is leading."

Jones heard the vehicles long before he saw them. He'd found the roof's indoor access ladder and scrambled up and situated himself along the front. The wall running around the edge of the roof was about two feet tall and six inches wide. He'd selected the midpoint so he could maneuver north or south as needed.

With the new sounds, he ducked and ran to the northwest corner. Kneeling, he raised the Springfield and took a look through the sight at the road coming from the north. At the far end of his field of vision, about a mile away, a burgundy and black car, and a German truck crested a small rise in the road. The roadway dipped into a low spot and wouldn't crest again until the vehicles were about half a mile away.

The sniper quickly checked the trees nearest the building, then those at three hundred yards. The wind was southerly, which put it going slightly left to right from Jones' perspective, and he estimated it at twenty miles an hour. It was still raining, and that would require a slightly higher aim. Put together, the wind and rain would make it a tough shot.

He took the object he'd picked up along the way, did with it what needed to be done and settled into his firing position.

He focused on his breathing as he slid the crosshairs onto his target point on the road. He waited patiently and time did its usual slowdown. Sound ceased to exist except for his own respiration. His world was solely what was visible in the sight.

Dunn issued orders. First, to Georges and the other drivers to get their trucks out on the road and drive south a few miles. Then to his own men and Bertrom. Everyone was assigned a place across the road, ensuring they were at least one hundred yards away. Dunn helped a weakened Cross, and Lindstrom gave a shoulder for Wickham to lean on. While all the men exited the building as fast as possible and headed across the road, Dunn checked his watch: three minutes until the satchel bombs would go off. Once in place himself, he turned and scanned the roof. He found Jones' low profile silhouette. He hoped his sniper remembered the timer settings.

The French and Americans formed a firing line about fifty yards wide. The ambush would be the only thing that would keep the Germans out of the building and from finding some of the explosives and possibly disarming them.

Jones was so in the mental firing zone, he had no idea his own men were across the road. With his other eye he saw the car crest the hill. The car should arrive in the rifle sight in less than a minute. The truck would be perhaps ten seconds later.

Dunn and his men could clearly hear the whine of the big truck's tires, and the higher pitch of the sports car engine. All took up a kneeling firing position.

Jones closed his non-shooting eye. His breathing was perfect, as was his heartbeat. He slid his forefinger's pad onto the trigger and pulled gently.

The left bumper of the car entered the sight.

A hood slid by, foreshortened due to the magnification.

Chrome around the bottom of the windshield crossed the horizontal crosshair.

The steering wheel appeared.

Jones completed the pull.

The rifle kicked.

The bullet sped away at 2,800 feet per second, 1,900 miles an hour.

Johann Pachter would never know what it was that killed him instantly. Jones' .30-06 round entered right between the eyes. Pachter slumped over onto the steering wheel. A shocked and frightened Rademacher stared at the bloody mess. With a sick feeling, he realized no one was driving the car. Just as he frantically tried to grab the steering wheel, Pachter's body slipped off the wheel, turning it just enough.

The car careened off the road. The tires slid across the wet grass and dirt, then caught and the car began to roll. Rademacher flew out through the side window and saw the tree coming that would kill him.

Jones calmly worked the bolt action, then lined up on the truck driver, the only person in the cab. Another gentle pull.

The dead driver's hands fell off the steering wheel, and he slumped over onto his right side. His right foot, shifted forward by the position change, pushed down on the gas pedal. The truck immediately accelerated. At first, it maintained a straight and true course, then slowly the camber on the road forced it left.

Jones saw what was going to happen, as did everyone else

watching from the safety of the other side of the road. The truck was on a curving line that would end at the corner of the building over which Jones had just fired.

Dunn shouted, "Fire!" hoping they could blow out the tires and stop the truck.

Seeing it was too late to get off the roof, Jones dove for cover as far from the wall as possible.

One tire blew, but the behemoth charged on.

German soldiers started jumping from the tailgate. They landed hard and rolled and flopped, breaking everything breakable. None moved.

The truck roared through and demolished a twenty-foot section of the fence, wire trailing behind and underneath it. When the truck hit the corner of the building, it sounded like a five-hundred-pound bomb going off, but there was no explosion, no fire. The truck crushed the wall and buried itself ten feet inside the building. Remarkably, the rest of the wall above it remained intact.

Jones' sense of time told him it was now or never. He unconsciously slung his rifle while running to the corner, and grabbed the rope he'd tied off earlier and threw it over the side. He slid and fell the twenty feet to the canvas top of the truck. Still holding onto the rope, he swung himself over the side of truck and hit the ground softly.

Jones ran. He heard the men on the other side shouting.

Just when he thought he might make it, the world shook and flamed and then he was on the ground, but he had no recollection of being knocked off his feet.

He got to his feet unsteadily and looked over his shoulder. The Pulse Bomb factory was an inferno. Fire rose a hundred feet in the air. Smoke was rising and blending into the gray clouds above.

Instinctively, he took a step backwards, but hit something solid with his heel and did a not-so-graceful back flip, rolling over something hard and hot and full of sharp edges that jabbed into his back, then landed face down.

Just at that moment, Dunn and Schneider ran up.

"Are you all right, David?" asked a worried Dunn as he knelt beside his sniper.

Jones got to his feet. About to make a typical smartass retort, he looked down. He'd fallen over the truck's engine block, which had buried itself six inches deep into the ground. He suddenly realized it had landed mere inches from his noggin and sat down abruptly.

"We thought you were a goner," said Schneider.

From his surprisingly comfortable spot on the ground, Jones said, "So did I."

He lifted a hand, which Schneider took, pulling the sniper to his feet. Schneider held on for a moment until he was sure Jones was steady enough to walk.

"Okay?"

"Yeah."

Dunn patted Jones' shoulder. "Glad you're okay. I see you saved your rifle."

Jones noticed the rifle still slung over his shoulder. How it had stayed with him was beyond him. "So I see," was all he could say.

The trio walked back to the men who had gathered together across the road far from the inferno. In the distance, to the south, Dunn saw the shapes of three vehicles coming their way. Georges and friends.

A few minutes later, the trucks pulled off the road near the men and an awestruck Georges stepped out, staring at the complete destruction of the Pulse Bomb factory.

"I've never seen anything quite like that."

Schneider translated for Dunn.

"It seems to follow us around," said Dunn dryly.

"Now we get you home?" asked the baker.

"Ah. Nope. Bit of a problem.

Cross heard this and said, "What now, Sarge?"

"The bomb wasn't there. I found the empty rack for it. We've got to find out where it went." To Schneider, he continued, "Anything in that briefcase tell us where they would have taken it?"

Schneider look skyward, thinking, recalling what he'd read. After a moment he said, "Nothing comes to mind."

"Well, they need a plane," said Dunn. He waved a hand and called out, "Bertrom!"

The Frenchman trotted over. *"Oui?"* From his open expression, it was clear he'd put the argument with Dunn behind him.

"Where's the nearest airfield?"

Schneider translated, got Bertrom's reply and said, "There's one about five miles from here. He said it was small, but there is activity there. A few planes."

"Any bombers?"

"Yes. Just one."

That was enough for Dunn. One bomber, not a whole squadron. Has to be it.

"Get the men loaded up. We're leaving!"

Chapter 56

German airfield
Near Ainay-le-Vieil
19 July, 0610 Hours, 50 minutes to detonation at
Caen

Dunn knelt close to the outer edge of a wooded area. The rain had stopped a while back and the sky was brightening in promise of clearing soon. He raised his field glasses and examined the airfield. Even at this distance, he could clearly make out what was happening. A twin-engine German bomber was parked near the airfield's lone hanger. A small, one floor building was about ten yards south of the hanger. The road to the airfield came from the south and ended at the back side of the building. Knowing they were over two hundred miles from the front lines, Dunn doubted the place had been used very much until it was needed for the bomber.

Men were working on the aircraft, some under the fuselage's belly and some under the left wing, perhaps doing something to the engine. A truck was parked nearby and a perimeter of soldiers surrounded the aircraft. Dunn estimated there were a dozen.

Close to the hanger was a fuel truck.

Dunn's men were dispersed along the tree line, as were Bertrom's men. The Ranger was debating the folly of a frontal assault, which would certainly be ugly due to the naked landscape surrounding the airfield. Dunn lowered his binoculars and scanned the distance between his men and the plane. No cover anywhere. No approach at all. They couldn't just drive up, even in the vans. By the time they scrambled out, the Germans would react. On the other hand, the Germans had no cover either. There had to be a solution, he just didn't see it yet.

In any case, the immediacy of finding one grew when the truck drove away. What had been hidden behind lay exposed: a rubber-tired rack, identical to the empty one at the factory, this time with the bomb on it. Even though he'd expected it to be at the airfield, converting that to reality was jarring.

"Cross, what do you make the distance?"

Cross, sitting cross-legged right beside his sergeant, eyed the space carefully. "Four to five hundred yards."

"I think so, too." Dunn turned his head to look down the line. He found Jones, the fifth man to the right. To Cross he said, "Pass the word for our sniper to come here."

A few moments later, Jones arrived and knelt beside Dunn.

"How much ammo do you have left?"

"Lots. A hundred rounds." Jones was already checking out the airfield as he talked. Taking in the layout and noting where each enemy soldier was took only a few seconds for his ultra-sharp eyes. "I start by taking out those closest to the hanger. As the others react, I shoot them while they're trying to figure out what the hell is happening. By the time they guess where I *might* be, they'll start running toward the hanger."

"What do you think the distance is?" asked Cross.

"It's four-fifty to the airplane."

"You sure about this?" asked Dunn.

"I can fire five rounds in twenty seconds. That'll be five kills or wounded out of the dozen out there."

While Jones was talking, several men rolled the bomb underneath the plane and began loading it.

Dunn was listening to Jones intently, working out a picture in his head of the events that would unfold. Then the solution hit him. He mentally ran through it quickly again, then turned to Cross and told him. When he was finished, he asked, "What do you think?"

"It'll work."

The door to the building opened and five men marched out, heading toward the aircraft.

The three Rangers saw them at the same time. Dunn raised his binoculars and Jones lifted his rifle and peered through the scope.

"Jones? See the two in the lead?"

The men were wearing officer's hats.

"Yes."

"Those are the pilots. You are not letting them get aboard that aircraft. They're your new first and second targets."

"Got it, Sarge."

Ten minutes later, after leaving Lindstrom with Jones as a spotter and defender, Dunn and his men were back in the van, with Georges driving. Bertrom and his men followed in the other van. On passing the end of the airfield's landing strip, Georges increased his speed on the paved, one-lane road.

Jones was already lined up on the first flight officer when the vans neared the small building. The German soldiers had grown alert and focused on the vehicles.

Lindstrom said quietly, "Got two looking like they're gonna go check out the trucks."

Jones opened his other eye. The two Germans just south of his target were starting to display antsy body language. Shifting his aim, he targeted the nearest of the two.

The vans drove behind the building.

Jones fired. The first man dropped. Working the bolt, Jones aimed and took out the second man, then shifted back to the officers. Firing quickly, he dispatched the pilot, then the copilot. He began acquiring new targets.

The moment Georges's van was behind the building, he stopped, while Bertrom drove on past to get to the far side of the hanger.

Dunn's men poured out, Wickham coming last, hobbling along on his gimpy leg.

German soldiers and ground crewmen were running at full speed toward the hanger. Jones had knocked out his five men, who were sprawled on the grass, lifeless lumps. He picked off a man who was outrunning his comrades, and the men right behind him peeled off to their left. No one made any attempt to return fire. They knew they were being sniped, and that the shooter would be far out of their weapons' effective range.

Bertrom's men jumped out before the van came to a complete halt and ran toward the hanger's back door.

Dunn led his men around the south side of the building. When they passed the last corner, they fanned out, and began firing. Seconds later, the sounds of Stens firing from inside the hanger joined in. The Germans were caught in no-man's land and, between the Stens, Thompsons and the distant Springfield, men began dropping everywhere. Two threw themselves to the ground and started firing, but they were immediately targeted. Bullets tore into them from all directions.

"Cease fire!" Dunn shouted over the din. A few lone rounds snapped off, then stopped.

"Anyone still moving?" asked Jones.

"No. They're all down," replied Lindstrom, his voice tinged with awe. Even though he'd just come fresh from the factory firefight, it was the first time he'd ever been a spectator to a slaughter. He'd known he'd joined something special from the start, but now the reality of what the highly trained, cohesive, and deadly squad could do set in. He hoped he could live up to them.

As Dunn and his men made their way to the bomber, they checked the Germans. All were goners. Dunn noticed the French fighters were stripping the dead German soldiers of their weapons and taking everything worth having from their pockets. *That's one way to replenish supplies*, he thought.

"One last thing to do here, gentlemen," said Dunn.

"Well, we're fresh out of plastic explosives," said Cross.

"We'll have to try something else," replied Dunn evenly. To Ward, he said, "Go check that fuel truck. See if there's anything in it."

"Right, Sarge," replied Ward as he ran off.

Georges, and Bertrom and his men joined the group around Dunn. They all seemed to be accounted for, no wounded, and in very high spirits. It had been a been an extraordinary day for them.

"What can we do to help?" asked Georges through Schneider.

"Last thing to do is to destroy this aircraft and the bomb on it." Dunn pointed at the gas truck and Georges and Bertrom nodded their understanding.

Although he didn't show it, Dunn was worried. He'd seen the effects of this bomb. Would blowing up the plane set off the pulse weapon? If it did, he didn't know what its deadly range was.

"Schneider, did you come across anything about the effective range on this weapon?"

Schneider thought briefly and replied, "Yes, about one point five kilometers."

"Oh shit."

"Well, another thing I read was a bit odd. It was set to explode at an altitude of seven hundred and fifty meters."

Dunn raised his eyebrows at this. That might be good news, he realized. The weapon's range must be reduced the closer it got to earth. Therefore, since sitting in the bomb bay put it about five feet off the ground, it might be severely reduced.

"Georges, do you have any rope in that van of yours?"

"*Oui!*"

The fuel truck started up and Ward drove it over near the plane. Dunn motioned for him to pull it up right next to the plane's left side.

From his sniper's nest, Jones watched all this and decided it was time to head to the rendezvous point with Lindstrom as Dunn had ordered.

Dunn outlined his plan to the men, making sure everyone who had a task understood it, then gave the go ahead.

Hanson asked Schneider what the German word was for fuel, then he climbed up on the left wing and looked around until he found it. Lifting the access plate, he unscrewed the cap. The aviation fuel's sharp smell assaulted his nose.

Georges drove his van from behind the building to a spot near the aircraft. He got out and went in the back. After rummaging around briefly, he climbed out. Then he started uncoiling a fifty-foot length of rope, feeding it to Ward, who in turn shoved it into the truck's main fuel storage tank.

Bertrom had taken his men to their van and driven away.

Cross, Wickham, Fairbanks, and Morris hurriedly climbed into the back of Georges's van.

Once the rope had been shoved in as far as possible, Ward began pulling it back out by dragging the sopping wet fuse toward the airplane, leaving a long length inside the fuel tank. He climbed up onto the wing and handed off a four-foot-long dry section to Hanson, who then stuck it into the plane's fuel tank. Hanson wrapped the fuel cap's chain around the rope to secure it. Finished with his task, he and Ward hopped down then ran to the van where they jumped in.

Dunn told Georges and Schneider to get in the van and for Georges to start it.

The Ranger waited until they'd done that, more than a little relieved the van *had* started.

Now the tricky part. He found the point of the rope that was roughly equidistant from the aircraft and the truck, and laid it on top of an empty Thompson clip, which in turn rested on the ground. Then he used his Zippo lighter to set fire to the underside of the rope. It ignited immediately thanks to the thorough soaking of the fibers. Dunn waited just long enough to make sure the flame was following the jerry-rigged fuse, then bolted toward the truck, diving in head first and yelling, "Go!"

Georges didn't wait for the translation and floored the gas pedal. The van flew across the airfield to the road.

With his men's help, Dunn got to an upright position and closed the doors he had flown through. He was uncertain how long the rope would take to burn, but prayed it was long enough for them to get out of range.

The van sped along the road and when it got to an intersection, Georges slowed just enough to navigate the turn to the right. When they arrived on the other side of the woods, Bertrom's van was already there and Jones and Lindstrom were standing next to it. Dunn shoved open the doors and called to his men, who ran full speed to the van and climbed in.

Dunn pulled up his mental map and guessed they were about a half-mile from the bomb, with about a quarter-mile of trees between. Not knowing if they were safe, Dunn told Georges to drive farther south.

The two vans sped away.

Behind them, the flame on the rope leading to the fuel truck won the race. The hungry flame leapt the last foot into the vapor surrounding the opening.

The resulting blue fireball finished the job and the truck exploded. *Its* fireball engulfed the aircraft, then the plane's fuel ignited, creating a secondary fireball.

Inside the bomb, the detonator went off and its energy shot forward. But because the bomb's propeller wasn't turning, the armatures were stationary and there was no magnetic field to create the killing pulse. All the detonator did was speed up the destruction of the last Pulse Weapon as the entire weapon incinerated.

Even through the van's rumbling road sounds, everyone heard the double whumps of explosions behind them. Dunn pushed open one of the back doors and the fireball and smoke rising over the trees told him what he needed to know. But he had to verify, so he told Georges to turn around and go back.

Standing outside the van, Dunn eyed the destruction. He could feel the heat emanating from the smoking, charred and twisted wreckage from a distance of fifty feet. He raised his binoculars and focused on what had been the bomb bay. Nothing remained. Of that he was certain.

Back in the van, he made his way up behind the baker and said, "Thanks for everything, Georges."

"But of course."

"We do need a little more help. Time to get back to England."

"But of course."

Chapter 57

After driving thirty minutes from the airfield, Georges had pulled into the barn of a large farm. The wounded were tended to again, and plans were finalized. Dunn's men, all exhausted, had slept soundly for most of the day with the Resistance fighters standing guard. A meal of bread and cheese appeared around supper time and the men ate quickly. When dusk began to settle in, Dunn's men said their farewells to the French fighters and climbed back into the baker's van.

After driving over three hours, they had skirted to the south of Poitiers, heading for a spot on the beach a few miles north of La Tranche-sur-Mer to meet their submarine. Georges had only been able to average forty-five miles an hour due to the darkness and having to use many back roads to avoid as many checkpoints as possible. Fortunately, the two they'd been unable to miss were manned by pairs of bored Germans who couldn't care less about a baker rushing to see his ill mother.

Cross was sitting next to Dunn and woke up suddenly with a start. He got his bearings and adjusted himself to get more comfortable. "My ass is killing me."

"You sure it's not your face?" asked Dunn, deep concern on his face.

Cross frowned. "What's wrong with my face?"

"It's killing *me*, Mister Cross."

Cross laughed. "Walked into that one."

"Too easy."

"Why you picking on a wounded man?"

"You're the only one awake."

"Lesson learned." Cross settled back and closed his eyes.

"Dave?"

"What?"

"I'd like you to be my best man. Will you do it?"

Cross opened one eye. "Took you long enough to ask."

"Been busy. The war, you know."

"Ayup, I'll do it."

"Thanks."

"Welcome." Cross closed his eye and was fast asleep in seconds.

1 mile northwest of La Tranche-sur-Mer
19 July, 2350 Hours

The road turned bumpy and the truck groaned and creaked as it slowly moved forward. Dunn stuck his foot out and tapped Schneider's boot. The translator's eyes opened slowly, then found Dunn. "Yes, Sarge?"

"Ask Georges how much farther."

Schneider did that and when he got the answer, said, "Just a few minutes."

Georges pointed out the windshield. Dunn could barely make out a ribbon that was less dark against a vast darkness. He hoped that was the road.

"We go through a forest, then we find the beach."

When Dunn peered more closely, he imagined he could see

the tops of trees swaying in the wind.

Dunn gave Cross a nudge, then said to the group at large, "Up and at 'em, boys."

He was met with a variety of moans, groans and curses, but everyone was awake and stretching as much as possible in the cramped truck.

"Listen up, men." Once Dunn had everyone's attention, he continued, "The pick up window is between midnight and oh four hundred hours. It's now ten 'til midnight. Once we get to the beach, we'll set up a standard perimeter and then give the signal. Wickham and Cross with me. Any questions?"

No one said anything.

The truck stopped just short of the beach. Georges turned off the motor, got out and opened the back doors. The men got out and did some more stretching. Jones, Ward, and Hanson fanned out heading north along the beach, while Morris, Fairbanks, and Lindstrom went east, following the road. Dunn took the southern part of the beach with the injured Cross and Wickham, and Schneider and Georges.

Cross sidled up next to Dunn and said quietly, "I told you so."

A puzzled Dunn replied, "What?"

"I told you not to say anything about luck and you jinxed us." Cross pointed at his bloody shirt. "See?"

"I thought you said you didn't believe in that stuff."

"Well, I was right, though."

"What about that stuff about me being damn good at this?"

"You are, Tom. Shit happens. This time me and Wickham got the shit. Don't worry about it, okay?"

"Okay. You win. I won't mention 'luck' again."

"Oh, not again!" Then Cross laughed.

Dunn joined him.

Dunn glanced up. The cloud cover had completely broken. There was no moon tonight, but he could see what must be a million stars, which shed considerable light on the beach. The sound of the surf was all he could hear and he could smell the salty sea water. He looked over at Cross. His friend had a wistful expression on his face. No doubt thinking of his fisherman father back home in Maine.

Dunn thought about his own dad. They'd always had a close

relationship, even in the turmoil of the teen years. Looking back, Dunn recognized that his dad had shown remarkable restraint, giving Dunn the chance to work things out, to make his own mistakes and to learn from them. Right after getting his license at the age of sixteen, while out driving on a Saturday afternoon with Paul, his best friend, Dunn had fooled around on a gravel road. Giving the car too much gas on a curve, the rear end slid out to the right and caught the ditch. The rest of the car followed, bouncing through the ditch and into a cornfield. Although unhurt, the boys had been forced to run to the nearest farmhouse and ask for help. The farmer had towed them out of the corn with an Allis-Chalmers tractor with wide-track front wheels. He'd turned down their offer to pay, but urged them to be more careful in the future.

That evening, Dunn had been sitting on the porch sweating it out, having said nothing to his dad. His dad opened the screen door, whose spring squealed its protest, then sat down next to Dunn. He held something in his right hand, but kept it out of Dunn's eyesight.

"Beautiful evening, isn't it?"

"Yes."

"Makes a person glad to be alive to see this sunset, don't you think?"

"Yes."

Mr. Dunn looked at his son and noticed the tense expression on his face. Turning away for a moment to smile, he looked back at Dunn.

"Enjoy your ride this afternoon?"

Dunn hesitated. "It was okay."

"Well, I'm glad. Driving is such a fun thing to do. Of course, it carries a lot of responsibility, too. Don't you agree?"

"Yes."

Silence descended on the two, father and son, and lasted for several minutes. Dunn stared at the sunset, thinking hard. Eventually, he made a decision and turned to face his dad.

"I wrecked the car today, dad."

Mr. Dunn looked surprised. "Did you? You're not hurt, are you?" Concern filled his tone.

"No. We're okay, Paul and me." Then Dunn told the story.

"I see. Well, these things happen. Did you learn from this?"

"I did, dad."

"And you're both unhurt?" Mr. Dunn asked again.

"We're not hurt."

Mr. Dunn put a hand on Dunn's shoulder. "I'm very relieved you're not hurt. I also know it was hard to tell me what happened."

Dunn could only nod.

"Since you were honest with me, even if a little late in the day, you're only grounded from driving for two weeks." Mr. Dunn stared into Dunn's eyes. "Seem fair to you?"

"Yes, dad."

"All right, then."

Mr. Dunn rose and went back in the house. He strode down a long hallway, passed through the kitchen and then stepped out onto the back porch. There, he removed the lid from the corrugated metal trash can, opened his hand and let something fall in.

The piece of cornstalk sank into the can.

Mr. Dunn had removed it from under the bumper where he'd found it lodged as he walked past the car.

Dunn smiled at the memory. His dad hadn't told him the story until after high school graduation.

Now, he naturally thought of Pamela and suddenly wondered what kind of dad he would be.

"Sarge?"

Startled back to the present, Dunn said, "What?"

"It's midnight," said Cross.

"Oh, uh." Dunn lifted his left hand and rotated his wrist until there was enough residual light on the watch face. "Yes, thanks, Dave."

Dunn was embarrassed that he'd let his mind wander and worried that he was losing his edge. He realized he'd need to think about that later. Back to business. He raised a flashlight, pointed it out to sea and blinked it on and off three times quickly, paused, then did two more.

Within seconds, the reply came and Dunn felt enormous relief. Even when he'd set up the pick up point with Colonel Kenton on the radio back at Georges's brother-in-law's bakery, he had been uncertain. But now, it was time to go home. He estimated that the British submarine was about five hundred yards off shore. Hopefully they'd be quick and the rubber boats would be here soon.

Five minutes passed. A sound, distant and faint reached Dunn's ears. A mechanical thrumming. At first, he thought he was hearing the sub's diesel and that the sub was maneuvering to maintain position. Then, as it grew louder, he realized it was coming from his left, the south. His head swiveled in that direction, searching.

"Dave?"

"I hear it."

Suddenly, a German patrol boat appeared, slicing through the water, the slap of water against the hull sounding like a rifle shot.

Chapter 58

Dunn turned around and took off at a full run. He cleared the beach, opened the back door of the van, and jumped inside. He quickly unhooked the long tubes from the wall. By the time he got back to the beach, the boat had almost drawn even with his position. It seemed to be staying on the same course as before, which put it about twenty-five yards off shore.

Dunn handed the extra Panzerfaust to Cross.

"Hold this."

Cross took the weapon.

Dunn knelt, and said to Cross, "Get clear,"

Cross moved away.

The Panzerfaust's sight was a crude, folding leaf type, but Dunn lined up the shot the best he could, leading the boat by a few yards. He squeezed the trigger. The blunt-nosed explosive round streaked from the tube. Dunn and Cross watched it fly toward the boat.

With dismay, they watched it soar right over the boat's bow. A searchlight blinked on and the beam swung toward them. With no time nor desire to run, Dunn and Cross held their ground. Cross handed over the last weapon.

"Perhaps a slight correction, eh?" asked Cross.

"Perhaps."

The beam found them.

"Uh oh," said Cross.

"Shit," said Dunn.

A machinegun began to fire. Sand kicked up around them.

Dunn fired. Once again the two rangers watched and hoped. Dunn had adjusted his aim.

The explosion blew the craft in half, flinging German sailors into the air. A fireball shot into the sky illuminating the water and the beach.

Dunn jumped to his feet, hands in the air. "Yeah!"

Cross pounded Dunn on the back, then grimaced in pain as his wound reminded him it was there.

"Way to go, Sarge!"

Schneider and Georges ran over and congratulated Dunn.

Dunn grinned and said to Georges, "Sure glad you had those in your truck."

"That is a good way to return German property to them, no?"

"Yes, it is."

Dunn glanced down at his feet. He noticed pock marks from the machinegun's bullets just inches from his left foot. He looked over his shoulder and followed the indentations with his gaze. They went as far as ten yards. He gauged the angle and realized he'd almost been hit. Yet another close call.

Cross looked at his sergeant with a concerned expression. "You all right, Sarge?"

"I'm okay."

Cross took a closer look. He'd watched what Dunn had done, and now did the same thing himself, coming to the same conclusion Dunn must have.

Putting a hand on Dunn's shoulder, he said, "You're okay. Close, but they missed. Maybe there is luck." Cross smiled.

Dunn chuckled, then said, "Yeah. Maybe there is. I'll be all right. Not the first close one, you know."

"That's for sure. I think I've lost track. Must have given up somewhere in Africa."

For no reason, this made Dunn laugh again.

Dunn's men, disciplined men, had all stayed at their assigned spot, even though they, too, wanted to go pat Dunn on the back.

Ten minutes passed.

A single dot flashed not ten yards from shore.

Dunn dragged his flashlight out of his pocket and replied. Dunn gave a short whistle and his men ran toward him.

The Rangers walked to the water's edge and could finally see the black rubber boats. If they looked real hard, they could make out shapes above the boat. The boats beached.

A British voice called out, "Nice shooting. Now get your arses in these here boats."

Chapter 59

In flight aboard the Horten 18
5 miles west of target
20 July, 1810 Hours

The air at twenty thousand feet was clear and smooth, and the Horten 18 screamed toward her target, Wolf's Lair, near Ketrzn, Poland. Carrying eight one-thousand-pound bombs, she was loaded nearly to the maximum. They'd reached cruising altitude quickly, then settled in for the one and a half hour flight. Mike Hoffman, the navigator and bombardier had studied the aerial reconnaissance photos endlessly over the past week in preparation for the attack on Hitler's Eastern Headquarters. Their flight path had taken them directly over Germany, and as expected, they'd met no flak or Luftwaffe aircraft. The Horten's composite wood and resin skin was working. They were virtually invisible to radar.

Prior to leaving Hampstead, Miller arranged for his crew and the Northrop engineers to write pithy remarks on the bombs with chalk, a common practice amongst bomber crews. Miller's own addition had been 'Thanks for the airplane. Hope this sends you to hell where you belong.' Now they were about to deliver the weapons.

"Airspeed two-forty, Mike," said Miller.

"Roger. I'm ready for the aircraft."

"Roger. Handing off the aircraft in three, two, one."

"I have the aircraft."

Now everything was in the hands of the Norden bombsight and Hoffman.

Hoffman bent over to peer through the bombsight viewfinder. He could clearly see the heavy woods below. He knew he'd get one chance at putting the pickles in the barrel. If he missed his release point they would have to circle back for another try. During practice bombing runs, he'd been within fifty yards of the target center ninety percent of the time. A superior grade by all measurements.

He was looking for the rail line that would lead right to the Wolf's Lair. Suddenly, there it was! A straight line through the woods. He rotated a dial on the side of the bombsight and the crosshairs slid to the right and lined up on the rail line. The plane began to drift slightly to the right as she had come onto the rail line at a very slight angle. Rotating the dial again corrected the plane's aspect. At the top of the view finder, which represented the front of the aircraft, he saw where the tracks abruptly ended.

He zoomed in slightly. A few buildings appeared, as did a thin ribbon of dirt, which was the road leading into the formerly top secret location. The pips appeared in the viewfinder.

Hoffman pressed a button to his right, never taking his eyes from the bombsight viewfinder.

"Bomb bay doors opening," said the bombardier.

A whirring sound came clearly into the cockpit, lasting ten seconds.

"Doors open."

The pips moved closer and closer to each other.

They suddenly lined up perfectly.

Pressing another button, Hoffman said, "Bombs away."

Hoffman could see the bombs clearly as they fell, but eventually they disappeared from sight. In soundless explosions, the bombs hit the target. Hoffman could see the pressure waves smashing their way through some buildings and the dense forest.

"Direct hit!"

Miller and Andy Butler, the copilot, both cheered.

"The plane is yours, Captain."

"I have the plane. Well done, boys. Let's head home. We'll be there in time for a late dinner." Miller banked the Horten and Butler pushed the throttles to the maximum.

The Horten screamed her pleasure at being turned loose.

Chapter 60

The submarine ride home had been uneventful and the doctor on board had treated both Cross's and Wickham's injuries, pronouncing them to be all right and that they would heal just fine. After disembarking at Portsmouth at 1730 hours, the squad had needed only to take a truck the thirty miles home.

Dunn had given his men strict orders to take it easy the rest of the night, and when Cross had insisted on joining Dunn at the debriefing session, Dunn had put his foot down and said 'no.' When Dunn left the barracks, every man was sound asleep.

Having done away with the niceties, the colonel and the sergeant got right into the debrief session. The late Mayerhofer's briefcase, a little worse for wear due to the lengthy travels across France and around the west coast of Europe, lay open on Kenton's desk. It still contained all of the papers Schneider had read and translated for Dunn along the way.

Dunn removed the stack of photographs and spread them out

on Kenton's desk without a word.

Kenton stared at them, a horrified expression on his face. "I've never seen anything like this."

"Me neither, sir," replied Dunn.

Lieutenant Adams' expression mirrored Kenton's.

Kenton sifted through the papers in the briefcase. He found a schematic drawing of the Pulse Weapon and pulled it out. Being written in German, he had no idea what the drawing said, but it was a cutaway view of the interior of the bomb. He studied it for a minute, then said, "I wonder if our scientists could work from what's in here."

"If they're anything like Dr. Herbert, I'd say yes," said Dunn. Herbert was the German physicist who was in charge of Project Dante, the Nazi atomic bomb program. Dunn had liked the little scientist, who had decided there was no way on earth he would give the madman Hitler a weapon like the atomic bomb. Herbert had been shipped to America a few weeks ago to join the atomic bomb program there.

Kenton put the schematic back in the briefcase, then scooped up the pictures and slipped them back in, too. Closing the lid, he said, "We'll log this in and send it up the chain. We might hear about it again. Better us than them to have it." Kenton sat back. "That's another job well done."

"Thank you, sir."

"You continue to impress me with your skills and effectiveness. You make great decisions and they lead to successful outcomes. Ordinarily, I would put your name in for a battlefield commission—" Kenton held up his hand as a stop sign when Dunn opened his mouth to object. "But for two reasons I won't. First, if I do, the army will reassign you elsewhere as a platoon leader, which would be a grave mistake as far as I'm concerned. I can't afford to lose you. Your squad is just too damn good as they are. And second, I know you'd fight it because *you* wouldn't want to leave your men."

"I'd say you hit it right on the head, sir."

"Don't forget I said *I* can't afford to lose you. You're staying here. I am, however, promoting you to sergeant first class. You're a five-striper, effective today. A nice little bump in pay."

"That is something I can accept."

"You've earned it. Congratulations."

Kenton glanced at Adams, and a smile tugged at the colonel's lips, and Adams grinned. "There is one more thing."

Dunn had spotted the exchange and thought, *this is not good.*

"We've come up with a name for your squad for the press."

"Oh no, sir. Please. I thought you'd decided against it."

"Sorry, but we need this."

Dunn suddenly grinned, and an ornery, boyish look came over his face. "Did you decide on Dunn's Dummies, then, sir?"

Kenton shook his head. "Oh, ah, son of a . . . no . . . Lieutenant Adams, would you care to take the honors?"

Adams, still grinning, said, "You are now officially known as 'Dunn's Daring' and the brass love it."

Dunn laughed. It started out slow, but it took over and he laughed uncontrollably for a long while. Finally, he managed to slow it down, wiping his eyes with his sleeve. "Oh wow. Really?" Forgetting himself, he asked, "What idiot thought that one up?"

Adams drew himself up and replied tersely, "This idiot, Sergeant."

"Oh, oops. Sorry, sir. I meant no disrespect."

Adams nodded, but Dunn could tell he was upset by the remark. "I am sorry, sir. It's fine. Please accept my apology."

"Apology accepted."

Kenton had kept a straight face the entire time, but now he grinned. "You have the joy of telling your men."

"Oh, ah, wouldn't it be better coming from you sir, or maybe the lieutenant?"

"No, they should hear it from their sergeant. Don't you agree, Mr. Adams?"

Adams picked up the ball. "Absolutely, Colonel. Things like this must come from the men's sergeant. After all, sergeants are the heart of the army, right, sir?"

Dunn held his hands up in surrender. "Oh, for crying out loud. Okay, fine! I'll tell the men."

"Good man," said Kenton.

"Will there be anything else, sir?" asked Dunn.

Kenton hesitated. He'd debated telling Dunn about his meeting with Pamela. She had asked him not to, so she could surprise him, but he also felt an obligation to his man. In the end he said, "Not right now. You may tell the men to take a few days off." Kenton then opened a desk drawer and removed a file a half-inch thick. He laid it on the desk.

Dunn had a sinking feeling as he leaned over to read the title. Sure enough:

Dunn's Daring.

"Some upcoming mission possibilities for you, Sergeant. We'll discuss soon."

"Very good, sir."

Chapter 61

Dunn's barracks - Camp Barton Stacey
2 miles northeast of Andover, England
22 July, 1544 Hours

As Dunn readied himself to call on Pamela, his mind wandered. When were the Germans going to stop trying to build and deploy super weapons? Surely Speer was running out of scientists and material, or both. Maybe it was the maniac Hitler who insisted on putting so much effort into these programs. Was there anything left in that crazy head? Dunn hoped not. With two out of the last four missions involving a strategic bomb and a battlefield weapon, Dunn sorely wanted an end to it. He much preferred missions like the one to La Haye. Breaking in and grabbing important papers, which had gone on to aid the Americans immediately. By knowing the German disposition of troops, the Americans had been able to punch through and had advanced another fifty miles inland across Cotentin Peninsula. Now they were south of Caen and pushing to meet Montgomery.

Just as he was combing his hair, he heard pounding footsteps, then Cross, Jones, and Schneider came barreling into his room. Or actually, Cross and Schneider were side by side and got jammed up trying to go through the door together. Dunn saw them in the mirror and chuckled. Then he said, "Nyuk, nyuk, nyuk, the Three Stooges have arrived."

The two men laughed at themselves. Cross swept an arm for Schneider, who went in first. The men surrounded Dunn, who held up his comb. "Stay back. I have a comb and I know how to use it."

The men laughed.

"What's so important you had to run here to tell me?"

Cross was first. "Did you hear the news?"

Dunn shrugged.

"They tried to assassinate Hitler Thursday."

"Who did?"

"Some German Army officers. Some colonel planted a bomb at a place called Wolf's Lair. Big headquarters in Poland, I guess. It failed, though. Hitler's still alive."

"There was an attempted takeover in Berlin and that failed, too," added Schneider.

"So we're stuck with Hitler. I wonder if we're better off?" asked Dunn, as he pocketed his comb. He moved to weave his way between the men to leave.

"Couldn't say, Sarge," said Cross, then he cringed.

"Your side bothering you?" asked a concerned Dunn.

"Just a little. Nothing to worry about."

"You make sure you follow the doctor's orders with that. Hear me?"

"Yes, Sarge."

"Okay, now let me out of here."

The Hardwicke Farm
1610 Hours

Dunn stood in the Hardwicke's barnyard just taking in the sights. It was a clear day, bright sunlight shone, warming his back. Behind him, the jeep's engine ticked as it bled off its own heat.

Different bird songs reached his ears, although he had no idea what they were. Back home in Iowa, the only two he recognized were robins and cardinals, but there didn't seem to be any around here. It was funny, the things you missed.

Dunn rotated to his left. The barnyard sloped downwards toward the west and about fifty yards away was a barbed-wire fence around a pasture. Another smaller building was to his left, a work shed, full of farm tools and left-over parts. Farther west, going back up a hill, a small herd of cattle grazed.

Suddenly, Pamela's two dogs, a black and white Border Collie, and a black Labrador charged Dunn, barking happily. When they reached him, he held out his hands at waist height, palms down, and then lowered them, a Pamela trick. The dogs stared at his hands then looked at his face, their tails wagging furiously. Dunn tried again, and in desperation added, "Sit."

The dogs promptly sat on their haunches and licked their lips. Dunn bent down to pet them, rubbing behind their ears. He was amazed at how relaxing that was. The war seemed so far away from the farm. If only the memories would fade.

He turned his head toward the barn and his mind's eye saw his best friend's brother, Allen, falling, screaming from the second floor of the barn. They had been moving hay bales and Dunn had been the closest to him when Allen lost his balance and started falling. Dunn had grabbed his shirt, but it ripped, leaving the seventeen-year-old Dunn holding a scrap of white cloth. Dunn had blamed himself for Allen's death and it was only a few weeks ago that he'd been able to come to grips with the guilt and forgive himself.

Since that terrifying day in his youth, he'd killed, seen his own men killed and nearly been killed himself. On one level, he knew he would manage to make it through the emotional barrage war forced onto men, and on another he wondered what his post-war self would be like, should he be spared and survive. Would he be a callous, cold man? Could he ever return to his old self?

"Tom?" came Pamela's soft voice behind him.

Dunn stood and turned around quickly.

Pamela ran to him and they hugged and kissed. The dogs began running around and barking. The Collie seemed disappointed when Dunn's hat made no move to fall off, which would have provided a fine, new chew toy.

Dunn gently pushed Pamela away. "Let me look at you." While it had only been three weeks since they'd last had dinner at the Star & Garter, it seemed ten times that to Dunn.

Pamela smiled her smile at him and Dunn had a sudden insight into his fears of a few minutes ago. A peculiar calm settled over him, and he knew, *knew*, that with Pamela by his side, he *would* be okay. He would be able to find his real self again, the one that was buried away so he could function as a soldier.

He pulled her close and hugged her tight, running his hand through her gorgeous long blond hair. After a moment, Pamela whispered, "Are you all right, honey?"

Dunn pulled back and gazed into her startlingly blue eyes. Eyes that had nursed him back from his bullet wound. Eyes he'd fallen in love with. Eyes that were now searching his face.

"Yes. I'm all right."

She raised a hand and laid it on Dunn's cheek. He closed his eyes and tilted his head into the touch.

"I have some news, Tom."

Dunn opened his eyes and said with a smile, "You're expecting?"

Pamela gave him what she thought was a stern look. "Don't be cheeky, mister. No. I met with Colonel Kenton."

This perked Dunn right up. "What'd he say? Wait a minute, when did you see him? He didn't mention it last night."

"Oh, um, it was last Tuesday. Mum and I met him at the Star and Garter. And guess what?" Her face grew somber.

"What?"

"He said the regulations have changed and now it's a three month waiting period."

Dunn's face said what he thought of that. "You're joking!"

Pamela grinned.

Dunn shook his head, then looked to the heavens. "Oh, Lord, give me strength with this woman."

A satisfied Pamela said, "Just having you on. But that's what you get for not telling me he wasn't going to interview me!"

"Oh. Didn't I?"

"No, you big lunk, you didn't. He waived the sixty day rule.

We can get married as soon as we want. Isn't it wonderful?"

Dunn smiled. "Yes, it is wonderful. Do *we* have a date in mind, dear?"

"Yes, *we* have a date in mind." She raised her right hand at face level and gave the wrist-wrist-elbow-elbow royal wave.

Dunn laughed.

Dunn grabbed her by the other elbow and said, "Let's take a walk. You can tell me what I'll be doing at my own wedding." Then he took hold of her slim, cool hand and they interlocked fingers.

They started off toward the west side of the barn. Beyond that was a path through the woods. The dogs followed.

"There you go again, being cheeky."

"Yep. Guilty. Better get used to it."

"Hmmpf. Okay, I talked with the vicar of our church, and he said we could pick any date after the twenty-fourth of this month."

"Why after that?"

"Oh, the roof has been leaking. They're patching it and won't be done until then."

"Did you mention that we might have to change dates at the last minute?"

"Yes, I remembered. He understood, you being a soldier and all. And since mum and dad, and me, too, are members, there's no fee. He did, of course, mention that a small contribution would be appreciated. Especially for the ladies guild who would be providing the flowers."

As they passed the barn, they heard the scream of a falcon somewhere in the sky above them.

"You can wear your uniform, your best of course."

"Sure, okay. What about your wedding dress?"

Pamela gave Dunn a wry smile. "Well, that's going to be a surprise. The hardest part will probably be the wedding cake, the material shortages, sugar, you know."

"Hm, yes."

"But we'll make do."

Dunn laughed. "I love 'do.'"

"Ha ha. You better love 'I do.'"

Dunn chuckled. "Oh, I will. So what's the date?"

"I'm thinking next Saturday, the twenty-ninth."

"Really? That doesn't leave much time for getting things together."

"I've been working on this already," replied Pamela with a smug expression. "Mum's been helping, too, and dad got himself roped into helping, too. It's all set."

Dunn's mouth dropped open. "You mean everything's already ready?" He laughed at his word choice.

"Yes."

Dunn nodded, thinking that the Hardwicke women were really the ones in charge. He smiled.

"What are you smiling at?"

"Just picturing your dad decorating the church or something like that."

Pamela giggled a little girl's giggle.

Dunn laughed again, thinking, not for the first time, that he was a lucky man.

"Have I told you lately that you are a spectacular woman?"

"You've *never* told me I'm a spectacular woman!"

"Ah, well, there you go, then."

"Have you heard from your parents? What do they think of us getting married? Are they mad they can't be here?"

Dunn held up a hand at the flurry of questions. "Whoa, lady! Yes. They are fine with the wedding and no, they aren't mad. I sent them some photos of you. Gertrude thinks you should be a movie star, but then she's only eighteen."

"Ha ha."

"Mom and dad think you're beautiful and if I think you're the girl for me, then you are. They all send their love and hope to meet you soon."

"Me too." Pamela leaned into Dunn and he wrapped an arm around her.

They walked a little farther into the woods, then Pamela suddenly stopped. She turned toward Dunn and raised her face, expecting a kiss. Dunn was happy to oblige her.

Pamela pulled back at last, then said in a rather urgent, husky voice, "Take me home, Tom."

Not being dumber than a mule, Dunn knew what that meant and he spun her around and they ran back to the jeep.

Chapter 62

Miller sat comfortably in the pilot's seat, his hands adjusting the wheel every so often to maintain a straight line through the partially cloudy sky. He was losing altitude for his landing back at Hampstead. Next to him in the copilot's seat was Fred Laughlin, the cockpit and instrument equipment designer from Northrop. Behind them in the navigator's spot was the mechanical engineer for propulsion, Greg Gillespie. Earlier, Miller had taken up the aeronautical engineer, designer, and team lead, Gary Babcock for a "fun" ride in the Horten.

Miller had flown far enough west for the men to experience the perfectly clear airspace over the Atlantic. As they had flown, Miller checked their faces periodically; all looked like schoolboys on the perfect vacation, a feeling Miller enjoyed often.

Miller guided the big plane down smoothly and performed a perfect landing. He throttled back the engines and the plane rode out on her stored energy, momentum, to the end of the runway. He turned the wheel and steered toward the hanger.

The crew chief and his men were ready and waiting, and got the wheels chocked as soon as Miller shut down the six Junkers engines. The crew chief placed the rolling ladder on the port side, next to the trailing edge of the wing. He ran up the stairs and stepped out onto the wing, being careful where he walked. Reaching the cockpit, he waited until Miller had unlocked the bubble canopy, then pulled it toward the tail, much like a Mustang's canopy.

Miller climbed up and out of the plane, shook hands with the chief, then made his way down the ladder, where he waited for his passengers.

As each man reached the ground, Miller shook hands with him.

Both were bubbling over with excitement.

Laughlin pounded Miller on the back. "What a joy!"

Miller grinned. "She is that, sir."

"I appreciate you taking us up before we leave. Of course, we might be back in soon with a new sister bird."

The men started walking side-by-side toward the Horten's hanger with Miller taking up the center position.

"You've worked out where you're going to put the manufacturing facility?"

"Yes, we have a place that's turning out B-24s in Missouri. We're going to retool one of the lines for the Horten."

Miller stopped suddenly and bent over to pick up something on the tarmac. It was a green screw about a quarter of an inch long. He examined it briefly in the palm of his hand, then deftly pocketed it. He noticed that the two engineers were staring at him. "Wouldn't do to have this suck up into one of the jet engines," he explained.

"Yes, we know. We just don't know how you saw it!"

Miller grinned. "I am a pilot, you know. Better than perfect vision is helpful to stay alive up there."

"Point taken."

Once in the hanger's office, Babcock and Howard Lawson met them.

Lawson held out his hand to Miller, who shook it gladly.

"You know, Mr. Lawson, I believe I owe you an apology for being upset at you for this assignment. I'm sorry."

"No need," said the man from the Office of Strategic Services.

"Yes, there is. This experience has been one huge adventure, and I wouldn't trade it for anything." He paused to look out the window as the Horten was being towed toward the hanger. "Truth is, sir, I'm going to miss her. She's quite the lady."

"Apology accepted, Captain. You've done an incredible job with her, I must say. And your crewmates. By the way, where are they?"

"I gave them a two-day pass to London. They've earned it."

"So have you."

Miller shrugged as if to say 'aw shucks.'

"No, really. You should take some time off yourself."

Miller shook his head. "Nah. Couldn't do that. I have to get back to the three-fifty-seventh."

"Then I wish you the best of luck."

"You too, sir." Miller noticed that Babcock was holding something in his hand. One of the many original big blue binders the Horten brothers had used to store anything and everything about the Horten. Babcock held it out and flipped it open to the title page:

Horten XVIII

Spezifikation

Volumen 1.

Babcock held out a pen. "Could we have your autograph, Captain?"

Miller smiled, thinking about the pilot who'd given him his first plane ride at an Indiana county fair all those years ago. The yellow biplane was vivid in his memory as was the feeling he'd first experienced that day. Falling in love with flying.

Miller took the pen, glancing at the three men waiting for his signature. They had wide eyes and big grins like boys standing in front of their favorite baseball player.

"Sure, kid."

✪ ✪ ✪

As Miller turned to leave, Lawson sidled up to him and they walked along together.

The pilot looked at the OSS man expectantly.

"Nice job on your attack on the Wolf's Lair. I wanted to pass on some intel before I left."

"Go ahead."

"There was an assassination attempt, a bomb, at the Wolf's Lair the same day you were there, but hours earlier. Following the bombing, there was a coup attempt in Berlin. It all failed completely and Hitler survived and remains in power. At least your mission showed him that we know where he is."

"Good. I hope the bastard has to start looking over his shoulder for us."

"I'm sure he is, Captain. See you."

Lawson peeled off and headed toward the barracks.

Miller looked around for his crew chief and found him busy putting away tools.

"Hi, Sarge."

The chief turned and said, "Captain."

"Any chance you could get *Sweet Mabel* ready for me?"

The chief smiled, a rarity. "Already done, sir." When Miller showed surprise, the chief said, "I figured you'd be busting seams to get back to the three-fifty-seventh."

"I am."

"Well, let's get you aboard. I had your gear packed and stowed, so you're all set."

"You're the best, Chief."

A grin. "Don't you forget it, sir."

✪ ✪ ✪

Twenty minutes later, he was airborne, the Merlin singing. He settled comfortably into his seat, the joystick between his knees. The blue sky beckoned. *What a beautiful place this is to fly*, thought Norman Miller, the boy from Indiana.

Chapter 63

The John Russell Fox Pub
Andover, England
28 July, 2240 Hours

Once word of the wedding's date and time came out, Cross had worked fast to get a bachelor's party set up. The owner of the pub, which was just a few blocks down the street from the Star & Garter, had been pleased at the prospect of a closed party of eighteen American and British soldiers. A guaranteed money maker. As long as they didn't get into a brawl and break up the place. When he'd mentioned this to Cross, the Ranger had laughed and said it wouldn't happen as these were a different breed of soldiers, Rangers and Commandos. The owner had raised an eyebrow, but had taken Cross at his word, and the huge down payment.

The main room had been arranged so that the tables formed a square with the men seated along the outside. Space had been left between two tables for the publican and his two waitresses to get into the center to make it easier to replenish the mugs with British dark ale.

The party was into its second hour, so the men were moving along with their drinks. Dunn was in the seat of honor, and Cross, as best man was to his left and Saunders to his right. The rest of the men were intermingled rather than clumped together by nationality. When Dunn saw how the men had naturally seated themselves, he'd felt a charge of pride.

There were plenty of stories and jokes being told and the room was filled with laughter and cigar smoke.

Cross stood up and said, "Your attention, please."

The room became quiet.

"A few toasts: first, to the men of Dunn's squad. For jobs well done. Also to Jonesy, for making impossible shots when we most needed them."

Jones' face blushed at the attention.

"Hear, hear," replied the men as they clinked their mugs together.

"Next, to our British friends. Thanks for being here to celebrate a new beginning."

"Hear, hear," replied the men again as they touched mugs.

"Last, to my friend, Tom. We've known each other a long time and I'm still in awe of what you can do. But tomorrow, on your wedding day to the beautiful Pamela, you do something that strikes fear in the heart of men everywhere. May you be blessed with many children."

More cheers and clinking sounds.

Cross touched Dunn's mug with his own and said quietly, "I really do wish you happiness."

Dunn nodded, a lump forming in his throat. After a moment he was able to say, "Thanks, Dave. I appreciate it."

Cross sat down and the room grew louder again.

Saunders leaned over and said to Dunn, "Don't want to steal your thunder, but Sadie and me are gettin' married, too."

Dunn turned to Saunders with a wide grin, holding out his hand. The men shook.

"Congratulations."

"Thanks. We had a rough go of it, though, for a while. She got hurt terrible bad in London. Damn buzz bomb." Saunders related the story of spending as much time as possible with her in the hospital. "I finally understood what she meant to me, and what Pamela means to you."

"How is she doing now?"

"Healing every day. I hated to leave her, but had to get back to work. Glad I did. Wouldn't miss this for the world, you old bugger!"

Saunders stood up, holding his mug high. He whistled and the room grew silent. "A toast."

The men joined Saunders by standing. "To the best damn American soldier I ever met. Happiness to you!"

"Cheers!" said everyone.

Dunn lifted his mug and clanked Saunders' and then Cross's, then pulled a long draw and swallowed.

Saunders, still standing, said, "A toast to Pamela Hardwicke, the most beautiful British lass I know who's marrying a yank! Although, what she sees in him, I don't know!" Saunders punched Dunn in the shoulder with a wide grin, his red handlebar moustache twitching happily.

"Cheers!"

More swallows.

The waitresses made rounds to refill the mugs.

Dunn was expecting Saunders to sit, but Saunders remained standing.

"Who wants to hear a yank tell a true story of his childhood?"

"Oh, shit," muttered Dunn.

A roomful of 'Yes!' and 'Yeah!' met his question.

"Who wants to hear a yank tell a true, yet funny story of his childhood?"

Cheers around the room.

Dunn started sweating.

"Who wants to hear a yank tell a true, yet funny, and outrageous story of his childhood?"

Cheers and the added sounds of hands slapping the table tops.

Saunders held up his hand and the room grew silent. In the back, the owner was amazed by the silence.

Saunders turned to Dunn. "The floor is yours, Sergeant Dunn! You know what your orders are?"

Dunn got to his feet and surveyed the room. He rotated slightly and drew his hand back and slugged Saunders in the bicep.

"Yes, I know my orders, Sergeant. You may sit."

Saunders sat down, refusing to rub his arm.

Dunn held up his hand, palm out toward the men. "I swear my story is true, yet funny, and outrageous.

"This is the story of the most ferocious beast found in the wild woods of eastern Iowa. I was fourteen at the time, which makes this story of survival all the more amazing. It was Thanksgiving Day. To you Brits, remember, we were being thankful for no longer being Brits!"

NOT TRUE!

"Boo! Boo!" from the Brits, shaking their fists.

"Yeah!" from the Americans, raising their fists.

"We were at my aunt and uncle's farmhouse. It was an unusually warm Thanksgiving Day, in the forties, and there was no snow on the ground yet. My companions were all my cousins, Dennis Elbur, and Terry and Tim Selwot, on my mother's side."

The men were unconsciously leaning forward. The owner and the two waitresses had stopped what they were doing to listen.

"We were all carrying the mighty and dangerous .22 caliber squirrel rifles we had all gotten on our eighth birthdays. A family tradition, you see?"

Nods all around.

"We left the house around mid-morning, knowing we'd find our targets by lunch time. We were going hunting for squirrels and rabbits, also found in the wild woods of eastern Iowa. At the time," Dunn paused, then in nearly a whisper continued, "we didn't know we would come face-to-face with the," another pause to do a little shiver, "most ferocious beast in eastern Iowa.

"We entered the dangerous woods south of the house. We were walking in line abreast." Dunn paused and saw nods. These men knew line abreast.

"Not fifty yards in, Dennis whispers, 'I see a rabbit.'"

"'Take the shot, Dennis!' I whispered back.

"So Dennis flips off the safety, raises the deadly .22 and lines up the shot. He fires! The weapon roars. He says, 'Got him!' which he had.

"We run up to the dead rabbit. Dennis had shot him clean through the heart. A perfect shot. Dennis picks up his rabbit with pride.

"We walk farther into the woods and Terry and Tim all score

rabbits in less than an hour. Only I have nothing. I'm becoming worried. Would I get one today? Or go home in shame and embarrassment."

"No!" says the room.

"'No,' is right! For only a few minutes later, I spy a squirrel on a tree branch fifty yards away."

"Wow!" says the room.

"I say, 'I have a squirrel.' Dennis says, 'Take the shot!'

"I flip off the safety and lift my dangerous .22 and line up the shot. I fire! The weapon roars. The squirrel flies off the tree and lands on the ground. We run up to the dead squirrel.

"'Oooh,' says Dennis, Terry and Tim.' 'Oooh,' says I. We look at the squirrel. His scalp is torn back and is just lying there like a dead fish. 'Oooh,' we all say again."

"Oooh!" says the room.

"I pick up my prize with the scalp torn back and hold it up. Dennis looks at my prize with the scalp torn back. He looks at his prize dead rabbit. 'I have an idea,' he says."

"What was it?" asked squeaky-voiced Hanson.

Dunn turned his eyes to Hanson and said, "Patience, Corporal."

The room roars with laughter.

"We work on Dennis's idea, right there and then. We walk back to the farm house. We check the time: I had a watch. A birthday gift from my aunt. It was almost noon. We had accomplished our mission. We had scored three rabbits and a squirrel. And even though they wouldn't be our meal for Thanksgiving, that's when we celebrate not being Brits anymore," Dunn repeated with a grin.

"Boo! Boo!" say the Brits, shaking their fists.

"Yeah!" say the Americans, raising their fists.

"We knew we would have them for meals sometime, so we were proud to have provided for our families. But we were most proud of our newest catch. The most ferocious beast in eastern Iowa."

Dunn examined the faces of everyone in the room. They were all in. He refrained from smiling.

"When we step up on the porch, we can see our family gathered in the living room. They were laughing at something. I look at Dennis and Dennis looks at me. We hold our newest and most ferocious beast up to the window and tap.

"Our families turn to look out the window at four boys standing in front of the window with wide grins on their faces. Then they see the most ferocious beast in Dennis's hand."

"God almighty, Dunny! What is it?" asked an exasperated Hanson.

"Are you sure you're ready for this, men?"

A chorus of 'Yes!' from the room.

"It was a Sqwabbitt. A terrible beast to behold with the face and ears of a rabbit and the tail of a squirrel!"

"Ah shit!" says the room. Then laughter bursts out. Followed by applause. The owner and waitresses join in.

Dunn beamed at pulling off the story, then sat down.

Saunders got up and held up his hands. The room grew silent. "Gentlemen," a nod to the waitresses, "and ladies. Stand up if the good sergeant accomplished his mission."

Everyone stood and cheered.

Saunders pulled something from his pocket and said to Dunn, "Please rise, Sergeant Dunn."

Dunn stood, looking warily at Saunders' hand.

"For your true, yet funny, and outrageous story of your childhood, I, with pride, award you the Order of Bullshit Medal." Saunders leaned over and pinned the object onto Dunn's uniform. Dunn looked down. It was a miniature metal cow pie with a B stamped in it.

"I accept your award of the Order of Bullshit Medal, Sergeant Saunders."

The room cheered again.

The owner and waitresses brought more ale.

Cross looked around the room, then at his friend and sergeant thinking, *perfect. Just a perfect bachelor's party.*

Dunn held up his hand for silence. He lifted his mug and said, "A toast. To you. My men and Sergeant Saunders' men. Friends. Allies. We make our living working behind German lines. A toast to you. And to those who didn't come back with us: Timothy Oldham, Casey Padgett, Wesley Merriweather."

Mugs were raised and clinked.

But no cheers or laughter from the room.

Chapter 64

White-haired Vicar Reginald Smythe smiled broadly at the congregation. "Ladies and gentlemen, I am pleased to announce Sergeant and Mrs. Thomas Dunn!"

Applause, cheers and whistles pierced the church's atmosphere.

Pamela's father, a tenant farmer, had done what all smart farmers did, he joined the church his landlord belonged to when he'd first started renting years ago. Pamela and Percy had been baptized here by the vicar and he had conducted the funeral for Percy when his body had come home from Dunkirk.

St. Peter's Church was a Church of England parish. It had been built in 1866 and its single spire rose sixty feet toward the heavens. According to church rules, Mrs. Hardwicke had arranged with Smythe to have the required readings of the banns, a spoken announcement of the intended marriage, on three previous Sundays. This was to allow anyone to "object" to the marriage. For no reason she could identify, Pamela had been nervous each and every time the banns were read, and felt enormous relief when the third one came and went safely.

Dunn and Pamela exchanged a look and then grinned out at their friends and Pamela's family. Her arm was in the crook of his right elbow. Her wedding dress had been her mother's twenty-six years ago and needed only slight alteration to fit perfectly. When Dunn had watched her walk down the aisle with her father, his mouth had dropped open just like when he first saw her in a robin-egg blue dress on their first date. Dunn wore his uniform with the Eisenhower short jacket and highly shined shoes instead of the usual boots.

The congregation rose and, still making plenty of noise, made their way outside to receive the newlyweds. Smythe walked around the couple and followed the crowd.

Dunn and Pamela waited until everyone was outside, then Pamela made a move to go, but Dunn stopped her. Leaning over, he pulled her close and she slid her arms around his neck. He kissed her deeply.

Separating at last, Dunn said, "Shall we?"

"We shall."

Bright sunshine greeted them, along with the crowd.

A lump formed in Dunn's throat. His men, and Saunders' too, were lined up on both sides of the sidewalk. American and British soldiers faced each other. Each held a sword aloft, forming a steel archway. Where they'd gotten them was beyond him.

Dunn turned to Pamela, whose eyes were glistening. "How'd you do it?" he asked.

She simply nodded toward the end of the steel archway where Colonel Kenton stood in the middle of the sidewalk facing them with a wide grin, his back to the iron gate leading to the road.

Dunn and Pamela walked down the stairs and through the archway. As they passed each pair of men, words of congratulations were said.

Upon passing Hanson, the little guy hollered, "Way to go, Dunny!"

Dunn shook his head and laughed.

Dave Cross was last in line on the right.

The moment Pamela passed by, he lowered his sword and swatted her behind.

She gave a little shriek and glared at Cross who was grinning.

Cheers went up.

Pamela gave up and smiled.

Cross said, "Welcome to the family, Mrs. Dunn."

The newlyweds came face to face with Kenton. Out of habit, Dunn started to raise his hand in salute, but Kenton was quicker and grabbed it and shook.

"Congratulations."

"Thank you, sir. Thanks for waiving the sixty-day rule."

"Anything for you. Best wishes to the bride, Pamela."

"Thank you for everything, Colonel," replied the new Mrs. Dunn.

"It was my pleasure." Kenton reached into his pocket and removed something shiny. He held it up for Dunn.

Dunn saw it was a key. He took it with a smile.

"My jeep's over there."

Dunn could only nod.

Kenton stepped aside, and Dunn and Pamela made their way through the rest of the people, then turned back to face them all. The Hardwickes walked up and gave their daughter hugs and kisses. Mrs. Hardwicke hugged Dunn and kissed him on the cheek. Mr. Hardwicke shook Dunn's hand.

Dunn looked over his father-in-law's shoulder and saw Saunders coming his way.

"Congratulations, mate."

"Thanks, Malcolm."

"And to you, Mrs. Dunn."

"Thank you."

"I hear you're getting married, too," said Pamela.

"'Tis true. I'm sorry Sadie couldn't be here to share your joy. She's in a cast up to her hip for a while yet."

"Give her our best, then." Pamela stepped close and kissed Saunders on the cheek.

"Will do."

The two tough soldiers, Ranger and Commando shared a

look, then shook hands. Saunders stepped away.

Pamela leaned over and kissed Dunn on the cheek, then gave him a radiant smile.

"Take me home, Tom."

Chapter 65

The *Reich* Hospital, Berlin
30 July, 1145 Hours

"What of the man who was with me in the car? Mayerhofer?"

"General, I'm sorry, but Dr. Mayerhofer was killed by the Spitfire's bullets," replied Speer, with a frown.

"I see. A loss for Germany. His briefcase?"

Speer shook his head. "Not to be found. We've looked everywhere. Are you certain he had it in the car with him?"

"Yes. He never once let it out of his sight. Even when using the facilities. Incredibly paranoid about it, he was."

Rommel turned his head carefully and looked out the window. The hospital room was dark, the sky outside covered with menacing black clouds. A gloomy day with gloomy news, he thought. Concussion, cracked skull. Instead of honor for a wound earned in combat, he had been strafed by an allied fighter, an ignominious end to a career. The doctors had already told him that although he would eventually recover, he would not be able to return to duty any time soon.

RONN MUNSTERMAN

With a hopeful expression on his face, which was barely visible under the bandages, Rommel looked at Speer. "Well, at least we can still proceed with the Pulse weapon."

Speer shook his head again. "No. We don't know how, but the Allies found the factory and blew it up. It's a total loss; nothing was left standing. On top of that they killed the only other men who could have continued the project. No papers survived the blast and no papers were found where the men were quartered. Then they attacked and destroyed the aircraft along with the last Pulse weapon at the airfield less than an hour before it was to take off to drop the bomb on the Allies at Caen."

"My god, Speer, first we lose the atomic bomb *and* the Horten brothers' jet bomber, and now we have lost the best battlefield weapon ever conceived, even more so than my tanks. It would have changed the face of battle forever.

"You do realize the war is lost, don't you? That this weapon was our only chance at stopping the Allies' advance? Once they break out completely from the bocage country with its hedgerows, they'll rout us all the way back to the Siegfried Line."

"Don't say that, General!" Speer looked over his shoulder at the door to see if anyone overheard Rommel's fatalistic comments.

"Spare me your indignation, Albert."

Speer's face darkened and he started to reply, but Rommel weakly held up a hand to forestall him.

"The next thing the Allies are going to do is invade southern France. They will attempt to encircle us and force the surrender of or annihilate whatever forces are left. The war is lost. Now Germany will suffer horribly.

"A pity young Stauffenberg failed. We could have asked for and received a merciful surrender," mused Rommel.

"What is wrong with you, Erwin? You can't talk like that! People will think you were involved."

Rommel shrugged sadly. "Involved, not involved, it doesn't matter. Only what Hitler thinks matters and his inner circle influences that. Those crazies: Göring, Göbbels, Bormann. They'll come for me some day. You'll see. My advice to you is make sure you're always aware of everything. I'm old. I'm tired.

I have nothing left to give."

"Except your life."

"My life has always been forfeit. For Germany. For my family."

Speer could think of nothing to say to that. The great General Rommel had been right about so many things. But now . . . all Speer was thinking about was how he was going to tell the *Führer* that his *Geheimwaffe Projekts Abteilung*, his Secret Weapons Projects Division, had run out of ideas and time. The war could only be fought conventionally from this point forward. Which *did* mean it was lost.

Epilogue

The honeymoon trip to Hayling Island had been a last minute decision by Dunn and Pamela. When Dunn had asked Kenton for a few days leave the colonel had said to take a week. Dunn hadn't argued.

On their arrival Saturday night, after making the thirty-five mile trip, they'd checked into their beachfront bungalow.

"Hello?" said Dunn as he looked around the small office, waiting for someone to help him.

"'ello, yourself," came a voice from a back room. It was soon followed by a rotund man somewhere in his fifties. He wore a white shirt and black slacks held up by red suspenders. He was totally bald, but wore a warm smile.

"Welcome. Sergeant Dunn, I presume?"

"Correct."

"Let's get you checked in. I'm Mitchell." He paused, then

explained, "Last name."

"Pleased to meet you, sir."

"You, too."

Dunn signed in, feeling both a thrill and an awkwardness as he put down *Sgt. and Mrs. Tom Dunn.*

Mitchell told him the price, which Dunn already knew from making the phone call for the reservation. Dunn paid and the man gave him some change. He counted the number of schilling coins and realized he needed more. "May I have some more schillings for these?" He handed over some pound notes.

Mitchell nodded and handed over a pile of coins.

Pamela had told Dunn to be sure to get plenty of coins, but laughed and refused to tell him what they were for when he'd asked.

Once in the bungalow, Dunn put the suitcase on a desk near the bathroom and turned to Pamela. He held out a palm full of coins. She smiled and said, "Follow me."

She went out the back door and turned right. She stood next to a meter of some sort, unlike anything Dunn had seen before. But then on closer inspection, he discovered it was an electric meter. The little usage wheels were not moving. Then he noticed a slot built into the top. He looked at the coins in his hands, then back at the slot. A perfect fit. He looked up at Pamela who was giggling silently. Her laughter then suddenly erupted, followed shortly by some very unladylike snorting.

"You've got to be kidding!"

As soon as Pamela could, she said, "Nope. Coin-fed electric meters."

Dunn shook his head and began feeding the meter. It sprang to life and began humming. The little wheels started rotating.

Dunn took Pamela in his arms and they kissed. He released his wife and grasped her hand, pulling her back inside. He went to the window and closed the curtains. He bent to turn off the lamp that was now burning brightly next to the bed and said dryly, "Maybe we should have paid the meter later."

With a graceful move, Pamela leapt onto the bed and said, "Whatever do you mean, Sergeant Dunn?"

They fell into a routine each day. Waking when they felt like it. Make love. Have breakfast. Swim in the beautiful sea. Lunch. Make love. Swim. Dinner. Make love. Long walks on the beach.

Hand in hand they walked at the farthest point possible from the resort buildings. The sun was setting over Portsmouth.

"Sergeant Dunn! Sergeant Dunn!"

Dunn and Pamela stopped and looked over their shoulders to see Mitchell running their way. Or perhaps it was more like fast shuffling. He made it to them and bent over gasping, his face beet red. He held up a hand for them to wait a minute. Gaining his breath, he stood up and said, "Sergeant, you have a urgent phone call. He said to tell you it was Colonel Kenton calling. Phone's behind the desk waiting for you."

Dunn said, "Thank you, Mr. Mitchell. Uh, Pamela, would *you* mind walking our host back?"

Pamela had already put an arm around the resort owner. "Not at all."

Dunn took off running, his heart in his throat. Had something happened to one of the men?

He picked up the phone. "Dunn here."

"Tom. I am so sorry to call you on your honeymoon. If there was any other way, I would have taken it."

"Of course, Colonel. I understand. Are the men all right?"

"Yes, yes, they're fine. It's something else. We have new intelligence. Finch and Lawson are here. I need you and your men, and Saunders', too."

"We'll be on our way tonight."

"No, stay tonight, then come at first light."

"As you wish, sir."

"And Tom?"

"Sir?"

"Please give my apologies to Pamela."

"Will do, sir."

Dunn went to the door and looked out. Pamela walked with the owner, talking animatedly, but with concern on her face and a comforting hand on the man's shoulder. *Once a nurse, always a nurse*, he thought. She glanced his way and waved. The way her face lit up at the sight of him made him suddenly realize how happy and lucky he was.

All he had to do was survive the war.

Author's Notes

During the writing of this book, I was able to "travel" to many places once again with Google Earth, and do some very intriguing internet research. As always, I try to be as factual as I can be within the world of Sgt. Dunn. Weaving fiction with fact (and sometimes stretching the truth a little, I am a writer after all) is truly a lot of fun for me. The more I write about World War II, the more I read about it, too. My bookshelf has grown and my good friend Steve Barltrop (yes, Sgt. Saunders' second in command) loans me books all the time on WWII. A person could spend a lifetime researching that era.

Here's a reminder that you should read these notes after you've finished the book because there are some spoilers.

The weapon. Most of us have seen movies where an electromagnetic pulse shuts down the world. When researching this possibility (and by the way, as an opposite to the way *Operation Devil's Fire* came to me, this idea came out of nowhere while on a walk), I found several very long scientific papers explaining how an EMP actually works and is constructed. The physical description of the weapon's inner workings was gleaned from these readings. The flux compression generator is real, not to be confused with Doc Brown's flux capacitor in the *Back to the Future* movies! As for the damage inflicted, it's true an EMP will shut down electrical-based machines. The damage to humans is a stretching of the truth.

Hitler really did have all kinds of ideas for superweapons, including the V1 buzz bombs and the V2 rockets, which were devastating to London, the atomic bomb which literally never got off the ground, and many others which were bizarre and unrealistic like a giant cannon to fire on London from the continent.

You may be familiar with the strafing attack on General Rommel, which did occur on 17 September 1944, as depicted (minus Dunn and squad, and Mayerhofer). There are conflicting reports as to who the pilot was but if you Google it, you'll find a couple. There really was a British Commando squad on their way to capture or kill Rommel around that time, but they arrived a day too late, as the general had been summoned to Berlin the day prior. Since their mission was blown, they spent three weeks making their way back to the British lines, creating havoc along the way, just like Dunn and his men did after attacking the German Division HQ in La Haye.

Rommel's headquarters is as described. Here's a link: http://en.wikipedia.org/wiki/La_Roche-Guyon

Captain Miller's bombing run on Hitler's Wolf's Lair was too much fun to pass up. The Norden bombsight works roughly the way I described, but I had to simplify it because even I got confused. Alas, Miller must get back to flying escort and conducting ground attacks, so the Horten 18 is done making appearances. By the way, I entertained the idea of renaming the airplane, but in the end, just stayed with her original, and only assigned a U.S. tail number and gave her a new paint job.

There really was an *HMS Sea Scout* and Captain Kelly was the actual captain. I hope I got things more or less accurate in the sub.

The castle where the Pulse Weapon engineers were living is as described, check it out: http://en.wikipedia.org/wiki/Ch%C3%A2teau_d'Ainay-le-Vieil

In 1942, the Germans did land men in the United States to conduct sabotage, and the story about the four men told by Colonel Kalb to his recruits is true.

A Harvard University secret lab created napalm in 1943 and it was first used in Europe.

The church where Dunn and Pamela get married is real and located in Stonebridge, south of Andover. The resort on Hayling Island is made up, but the coin-operated electric meters are real! Thanks to Steve Barltrop for that nugget of information.

For those of you who enjoyed the Alan Finch and Neil Marston characters in the first book, I hope you'll forgive me for not including them in this book; never fear, though, they *will* return in the next Sgt. Dunn novel.

A little story about the Panzerfausts used by Dunn at the end. I nearly got it all wrong and only because I double-check things did I learn that the weapon was disposable, not reloadable! Caught it and fixed it, whew.

On the other hand, writers don't catch every wrong detail themselves, but are saved by their FIRST READERS. Steve Barltrop made notes on little colorful post-it stickeys and would peel them off and hand them to me with an explanation. One was about Captain Miller taking the Horten to 40,000 feet for the first time. In the book, you see that the aircraft hit 620 miles an hour. I originally had it at 660 miles an hour. Steve pointed out to me that at that altitude, the plane would have broken the sound barrier! Well, we couldn't take that away from Chuck Yeager, now could we? The funny part (to me at least) was that I had selected 660 simply because it was ten percent more than 600. What are the odds that would happen, huh?

I would love to hear from you. Please email me at sgtdunnnovel@yahoo.com.

RM
Iowa
October 2013

www.ronnmunsterman.com

Follow me on
http://ronnonwriting.blogspot.com/

and

https://twitter.com/RonnMunsterman
@ronnmunsterman

About The Author

Ronn Munsterman is an Information Technology professional of twenty years. He loves baseball, and as a native of Kansas City, Missouri, has followed the Royals since their beginning in 1969. Other interests include reading, some selective television watching, movies, listening to music, playing and coaching chess, and photography. Visit his website for a list of his favorites. www.ronnmunsterman.com

He also writes short stories, two of which have been published, and they are available for free download on his website. His lifelong interest in World War II history led to the writing of the Sgt. Dunn Novels: *Operation Devil's Fire* and *Behind German Lines*.

Ronn does volunteer chess coaching each school year for elementary- through high school-aged students, and also provides private lessons for chess students. He authored a book on teaching chess: *Chess Handbook for Parents and Coaches*, available on Amazon.com.

He lives in Iowa with his wife, and enjoys spending time with the family.

Ronn is currently busy at work on the third Sgt. Dunn novel.

Made in the USA
San Bernardino, CA
16 October 2018